Legacy of Silence

Legacy of Silence

by
Irene Pastor

CREATIVE ARTS BOOK COMPANY
Berkeley • California

For information contact:
Creative Arts Book Company
833 Bancroft Way
Berkeley, California 94710

ISBN 0-88739-290-3
Library of Congress Catalog Number 99-63872

Printed in the United States of America

To my sister,
whose love and support
sustained me through my childhood

Legacy of Silence

Rebecca

Last night my sister called from Alabama to chat. I was only half listening, because my sister has this habit of talking a mile a minute about a zillion things and saying nothing, when suddenly she let slip something that stunned me. She had met the rabbi in her community, a widower, and they had gone out on a date. To say that I was astonished is an understatement. Going out to dinner with a rabbi may seem perfectly commonplace, but for my sister it is an achievement of colossal proportions. From the time she was a little girl and started to reason, she devoted all her energy and skills to obliterating all traces of our Jewish origin. And for the last twenty years, since she became a widow, she banished all thoughts of men from her heart. She boasts that she much prefers the company of cats to that of people, and lives as a recluse in her rapidly decaying Victorian house, tending to her forty-two cats, and on Sunday mornings, going to Mass.

None of the choices she made in her life surprise me. I can look in the mirror with my eyes half-closed and see myself living her life. That scares me. But last night, with a few words, my sister shattered the image I've held of her for the last thirty years. I was dumbfounded. Was everything about to change?

Now don't get me wrong, I was delighted, too. When we were younger, I had often wished she would break out from her fortress. But years went by and she never did. I stopped hoping long ago. Brick by brick she built her walls and stayed inside. I couldn't blame her—too much had happened to our family when we were little. We are children of Holocaust survivors, born in Poland during the Second World War. My sister was born at the beginning of the war and I at the end. Our parents, their families, and all our ancestors are Jewish. That we came out of the war alive is in itself amazing, but it

1

is not part of my story—although I sometimes wonder whether the most important events in our lives happened before we were born, the many pogroms, the brutal killings and rapes, the constant flights and endless wanderings, the Holocaust, the long tragic history of the Polish Jews. Has all that left its imprint on us? Is our past written with indelible ink in our genes, in our hearts, and our minds?

My daughter Carin asked me why do I want to recount those old tales. I need to. How else will I understand who we are? I am hoping to unravel our past to make sense of the present, seeking through memory to shed light on our lives. I have asked my sister to write down what she remembers and she has reluctantly agreed.

I will try to begin at the beginning. Can I remember Poland? I am not sure. I have vague recollections of my grandmother's round face, her arms protecting and hiding me after I wet the puffy red eiderdown comforter that covered Mother's bed. I loved that quilt, I loved sitting on it, sinking, watching it puff up around me when I moved, playing on Mother's warm bed. I must have been a little over a year old at the time. I remember, a little later, sitting on the balcony of our apartment in Krakow, being jollied into eating spoonfuls of hot soup and being told stories about all the people strolling in the park below. Who was feeding me? When I asked Mother a few years after my daughter was born, she didn't know, but she thought it could have been one of my uncles. I remember running out the front door when I heard the click of my father's key, down the steps, flying into the air the last few steps and falling with a big thud on the landing, scaring my father half to death. I remember playing in the park, licking a lollipop shaped like a rooster, the head green, the middle yellow and the tail red. When I mentioned these lollipops to Mother, thirty years later, she looked at me in bewilderment and said she couldn't remember any such thing. A decade later, I visited Krakow and found the same tricolored rooster lollipops in every candy shop.

Mother could not confirm these memories of mine, but she contributed her own. She told me that when I was a few months old we went to Zakopane, in the mountains, and she left me in the pram, in the snow. It was a sunny day, and a neighbor had promised to put me back in the chalet in a short while. Somehow, there was a misunderstanding, and when my mother returned, several hours later, I was still outside screaming. Feeling scared and terribly guilty, Mother checked me over carefully to make sure nothing was wrong. Suddenly, she noticed I was cross-eyed. She became hysterical. She didn't know what to do. She put me in a dark room. She put cold compresses on my forehead and eyes. Nothing helped. When I was nine, Mother tearfully told this tale to the Venezuelan surgeon who straightened my eyes. He tried to convince her that I must have been cross-eyed from birth. The specialists we had seen in Germany and Denmark had been of the same opinion. But Mother always believed I wore glasses because of her carelessness, and she could never forgive herself for ruining my looks and my future marriage prospects.

My sister insists she cannot remember anything from before she was five. I find that surprising, because I have so many vivid pictures in my mind from that time. I can almost remember the way things smelled. We lived in Berlin then, and my father worked for the Polish Embassy. No one was aware that we were Jewish. My sister and I were christened Catholics. The house we lived in was in the American sector, and was very large. We had a German governess and maids who took care of us. We saw very little of our parents. In fact, I cannot remember my mother caring for us until we arrived in Venezuela two years later. Photographs from that time show her always dressed in a suit or evening gown looking at the camera unsmilingly. On my dining room wall, there is a picture of my mother and father dancing at some gala, she is wearing a long, sleek black dress with thick gold embroidery going down the side, all the way to the floor, and slit to mid-thigh. She looks elegant and aloof, almost somber. My father is dressed in black also, his eyes are closed and he has a strange self-satisfied smile on his face, as if he had just managed to outwit somebody.

I remember my father more clearly from those times, perhaps because he used to explode in anger at the slightest provocation, yell and scream at us without mercy. We did everything to stay out of his way. But also from this time comes one of the few memories of my father that I cherish. That Christmas, Santa Claus came to our house, and my sister and I stared at him in awe. But as we looked closer, my sister whispered to me "Santa is wearing Papa's gray pants, the ones with the gravy spot." I looked with disbelief, but my sister showed me the same gravy spot my father had raged about the night before. It took us only a couple of minutes to put two and two together. We both got an attack of the giggles, and couldn't stop. When we finally calmed down, we told Father what we had observed, and the conclusions we had reached. At first, he was a little miffed because his effort had been for naught, but he soon recovered and saw the humor in the situation. "You are two smart little girls" Father blurted out, laughing. "The apple doesn't fall far from the tree." Any disappointment we felt at discovering that this was not Santa Claus was outweighed by the exultation we enjoyed for being so clever and getting approval from Father.

The only people I remember clearly from our years in Berlin are the German governess Gretchen, who was young and pretty and had the thickest blond braids I have ever seen, and the chauffeur Otto. Otto let me sit in his lap and blow the horn as often as I wanted on our daily rides to pick up my sister from school. Sitting in the car on Otto's lap was the high point of my day. Otto would drive like a maniac when I was his only passenger, and laugh whenever I honked at another car or startled an absentminded pedestrian crossing the street. We would park right in front of the school, and soon, my sister would come out the front door, bouncing down the steps. She would run across the yard and climb into the rear seat while I also scrambled to the back so I could snuggle with her. I was completely happy then. The interminable lonely hours of the morning had finally come to an end, and I had the whole afternoon in front of me to be with my sister, the person I loved most in the whole world.

I remember waking up in the morning, watching my sister from under my warm covers as she got ready for school. She would pull up her dark woolen tights over her legs, jumping from one foot to the other without once losing her balance, wiggle into her navy dress, struggle for a few seconds to squeeze into her brown leather shoes, and then sit on my bed to braid her hair. I held one strand while she worked on the others and tied her ribbon. Then she would get my slippers and we ran down to the dining room, I still wearing my pajamas. My sister wolfed down her breakfast, licked the milk off her lips, and ran out the front door, where Otto could be heard warming up the car. I sat at the table and stared with dread at the soft boiled egg in front of me. Mother believed that only three-minute boiled eggs were healthy, and had given the maid strict orders to make sure I didn't leave the table unless I finished my egg. No matter how much I cried, I had to swallow every spoonful of watery yolk. To this day I hate soft-boiled eggs.

One day, one of the maids discovered my sister and I had lice. Our beautiful long hair was cut off, the remaining short locks were repeatedly rinsed with kerosene, and our heads were wrapped in towels doused in some stinky substance, which we wore for several days. Gretchen was forced to cut off her thick braids. Mattresses, bedclothes, towels and clothing were washed in boiling water and then left on the balcony to freeze for several days. The whole household was in turmoil, as if we were in a state of siege. Everybody was inspected painstakingly to determine the source of this plague and to discover who was to blame. Shortly afterward, Gretchen was fired. Years later, when I was in my thirties and living in Berkeley, I mentioned this incident to Mother. She looked at me in astonishment. She couldn't remember anything about the lice, but she remembered quite clearly that Gretchen was fired because she had gotten pregnant by Otto.

There was an enormous garden surrounding our house in Berlin, and I remember tagging after my father when he went out to water the tulip borders. He brought home a brood of tiny white and yellow chicks and built a wire fence enclosure for them. I would spend hours outside the fence watching them while my sister was away in school. When Father came home in the evenings, we would go together inside the enclosure and he would let me hold them. I was always eager for my time with the chicks, and I learned to read the clock just to be ready. One morning, we found all the chicks dead. Perhaps it got too cold for them. We never knew. Father promised to get more chicks, but he never did.

We moved to Copenhagen in 1948, when my sister was eight and I was four. I think my father was now employed by the Polish Consulate. We spent several months there, including the month of December and it was in Copenhagen that I experienced the most magical Christmas of my life. On Christmas Eve, we were invited to the house of neighbors who had the most wondrous Christmas tree I had ever seen. It stretched all the way to the high ceiling, and smelled like a pine forest. It was decorated with white candles, which the host lit one by one, as we watched. Large red apples and candies wrapped in colorful, shiny paper hung from its branches. And toward the wall, right next to the tree, stood the most extraordinary doll house in the whole world. Every room in it was lit. It was so big that I had to stand on a chair to look into the upper floors. Inside were rooms filled with miniature furniture, a dining room set, a bedroom set, rugs, blankets, pillows, a white toilet and washstand with towels in the bathroom, plates, pots and pans in the kitchen, all tiny and so perfectly crafted that they seemed more beautiful than anything in the real world. We were told emphatically not to touch anything, to keep our hands clasped tightly behind our backs. This only increased the feeling of enchantment and magic. My sister and I stood transfixed in front of this doll house the whole evening.

It was also in Denmark that we learned to ride a bicycle. I remember starting out on a scooter that looked like a skating board with handle bars, but soon my father got me a big bike like my sister's. When I first sat on it in the living room, I cried because my legs were too short to reach the pedals. Father fastened two thick pieces of wood to the pedals, so I could reach them. That worked very well. The first day, he ran behind me and held the bike steady. Soon, I could ride by myself. Once, after following my sister in the park for quite a stretch, we stopped by a pond to chase the ducks. But when we were ready to go back I couldn't get on the bike by myself. My sister tried to help, but she wasn't big enough. I started crying. Finally a passerby took pity on us. He steadied the bike while I got on, and we were able ride back to where Father was waiting impatiently. That is the last time I remember Father playing with us.

Train tracks ran behind our house in Copenhagen and trains would roar by several times every night. I was always terrified and would try to slip into my sister's bed. Most of the time she would let me. My parents slept at the other end of a long hallway, but we were forbidden to go into their room. The consequences of doing so were scarier than enduring the train roar. Once the door of our room was closed, exactly at 8:00 P.M., we were not allowed to open it again until the next morning at seven. No exceptions to this rule existed. We could not use going to the bathroom as an excuse because both my sister and I had chamber pots under our beds. A large round clock hung right over our door so there was no mistake about the time.

One night, after we had gone to our room and the lights had been turned off, while my sister and I were still giggling and whispering, the door opened and Father burst in. He turned the lights on and ordered us to get dressed in our coats and hats and not to waste any time. As soon as he left and our eyes got accustomed to the brightness, we looked at the clock. It was a few minutes after eight-thirty. I still needed help tying my shoes and buttoning my coat but because we knew from my father's tone that we were to hurry, my sister only had time to do her own. When we were dressed, we rushed downstairs, my untied shoes making such a racket on the wooden steps, that Father turned around to shush and scold us. My parents were standing by the front door, surrounded by suitcases, while a taxi cab waited at the curb. We all trooped down the steps and got into the taxi. The driver crammed the luggage wherever he could, and soon we were at the port. We drove out on a long pier and got onto a ferryboat. I fell asleep but awoke while it was still dark. When I looked out the porthole I saw the most beautiful semicircle of neon lights on the shore reflected in the still, dark waters of the bay. We were in Sweden.

A few hours later, we boarded the ship that would take us to South America, a small cargo ship with only a dozen other passengers. There was nothing to do aboard. The only interesting event I can remember is seeing a black man for the first time in my life. A black man had walked by our house in Copenhagen one morning and all the maids had rushed to the window to look, but nobody lifted me up until it was too late. I only saw his hat and coat from the back as he walked away. I cried for hours afterward and had the governess bring out every one of my fairy tale books that showed pictures of black people. All of them had long droopy mustaches, appeared in colorful turbans, harem pants, and sabers with handles studded with large gems. The black man on the ship was quite unlike the pictures I had seen in my books. He was the cook, and since we were the only children on board he seemed quite partial to us. He always saved the largest oranges for us and once offered me a fruit I had never seen before, a banana. I tried it, but found it too cloying and offered it to my sister, who finished it and politely said it was very good.

Both our parents were seasick most of the time, and kept to their cabin, but my sister and I were free to roam wherever we wanted. We spent a lot of time in the kitchen with our new friend the cook. He managed to dig up some comic books in Spanish and introduced us to Mickey Mouse and Donald Duck. I was enthralled by these stories. Up until that time I had only known fairy tales about princesses, witches and kings in faraway lands. The cook also taught us our first few sentences in Spanish, which was to become our language for the next decade.

Although I can't remember who told me, Father or Uncle Bronek, years later I heard a story of why we left Europe so hurriedly. While we were still in Denmark, Father had put in a request with the Polish Foreign Ministry to serve in the United States. As soon as it was reviewed by the authorities, an order for his recall was issued. Luckily, Father had a friend back in Poland in the higher echelons of the ministry, who called him the night before and let him know what was happening. Father knew well the dangers of a recall. He had no illusions about the Polish regime, and feared he would not receive a fair hearing. Poland had become a Communist country, and every agency of the government was subject to Soviet-style purges. He made up his mind to leave for the New World, under cover of darkness and with only the clothes we had on our backs, on the first ship out of the country. That is how we ended up in South America.

At first, I believed this story implicitly, but now I have doubts. It is true that we had left in the middle of the night, with just the clothes on our backs. But when we landed in Venezuela, Father's family knew we were coming and had made room for us in their small apartment. And when we started our new life there, we had lots of things that we had brought over from Denmark. My sister and I had our bicycles and one doll each. My parents had their photo albums, some linens and tablecloths my grandmother had embroidered with her own hands, a set of silver cutlery, dishes, and later, even a piano arrived from Europe. A whole crate of items arrived in Venezuela after we had been there for a while. There must have been some planning before our departure.

Susanna

This morning my baby sister called me and suggested that I write my childhood memories. She is writing what she can remember, and Carin, her young daughter, thinks it would be interesting if we alternated chapters, one from her point of view, and another, of roughly the same events, as seen through my eyes.

Of course, I refused. As I told her many times, why open Pandora's box? Why relive all the old resentments, and even worse, tell the whole damn world about our horrid childhood? My little sister has some cockamamie idea that it would be therapeutic. She thinks it will exorcise our demons and we will learn something from our past that will help us live our lives more fully. What nonsense! Let sleeping dogs lie, I say. All that stuff happened long ago to the parents and has nothing to do with me. I am satisfied with the way my life turned out. I don't mind living alone with my cats, in fact, I love it. I can think of worse fates. My cats are better company than most people. Besides, there aren't forty-two cats, as my little sister said. There are only eighteen now; the others died when an epidemic of feline leukemia swept through my home.

But then, I started thinking about how wretchedly the lives of the so-called second generation turned out. Not my life. As I said before, I am quite satisfied with my life as it is, no matter what my baby sister believes. I don't see why she thinks I live the life of a recluse. Does she think I am a recluse just because I don't have a man in my life? I need one like a hole in the head! Men are more trouble than they are worth. You can't trust them. Always trying to control what you do, what you say, where you go, and who you see. I don't want to be looking for one either, going to singles bars, and church socials. God forbid, I might get unlucky and find one.

And you won't find me primping and preening for hours in front of the mirror, putting on make-up, fussing with my hair. I won't do that for anyone. I am not going to go on some stupid fad diet, either. I won't stop eating all the things I like, just to look like one of those anorexic models, straight out of a concentration camp. No way. I'll leave all those pleasures to my baby sister, who can't live without everybody's love and approval. So, how am I a recluse? Just because I don't have a job? Who wants the drudgery of work, slaving every day from morning 'til night, doing the same old thing five days a week, having to kowtow and please somebody who thinks he's a big shot? No, thank you, I have only myself to please, and I like it that way. I would have been a dimwit if I didn't quit working as soon as I got hold of some money! Or am I a recluse because I don't rush madly from one country to another and call it a vacation? I hate traveling, I like the comfort of my own home, I like to sleep in my own bed and use my own loo. I feel safe on my own turf. When I'm away from home for more than a few hours I'm miserable. I don't have to visit Italy every year, hike the Himalayas, ski in Switzerland. So there, little sister, you can do all that if it makes you feel happy and fulfilled, just don't judge me. And don't you go trying to change me either.

I started thinking of the second generation in my family, the ones you could call children of Holocaust survivors. I must concur with my baby sister, what a mess they are! Starting with my own sweet Rebecca. I bet she didn't expect I would start off my list with her. After she got divorced, she joined several singles groups and must have dated a hundred different guys. The 'boyfriend du jour' she called it. No way would you catch me falling into that trap. When it comes to work, okay, so she did get a master's degree, but did she ever use it? No. All those years slaving until the wee hours of the night to get that degree, a totally useless degree, even she herself admits that much, to end up working in a language she knew almost from the time she was in diapers? Does that make sense? She certainly could have saved herself all that effort, not to mention money. Speaking of money, when she started teaching Spanish, she was earning only four dollars an hour. Can you believe it? I pay my maid twice that. No wonder her husband asked her to quit. The baby-sitter and gas money came to more than she earned. And now, after working so many years, she still has to go to whatever god-forsaken place they send her, drive miles and miles, sleep in crummy hotels, and eat in roadside diners, just to survive decently. And she has the gall to be surprised that I don't want to live like that? She accuses me of having withdrawn from society, of being afraid of human contact, of being disinterested in life. For God' sake, I have better things to do with my time.

I also started thinking about my two cousins, Andrea and Sonia, who were born in Poland just after the war. The ones I never met because I had already made my escape to the States by the time they arrived in Venezuela. From what I heard from the family they certainly had their share of troubles. Divorce, suicide attempts, mental illness, money problems, children out of wedlock. The younger one, Sonia, got pregnant with twins and was stood up at the altar in her wedding dress. After that, she sat on her bed for several years in her parents' apartment, listening to the radio and smoking, and never went out, not even to buy groceries for herself and her children. Even now, she doesn't bother to get out of her pajamas for days on end. Is that normal? You tell me! Her seventy six year-old widowed mother does the daily shopping, cooks for her and her teenage sons, does all the cleaning, and then she gets yelled at like a slave. The older sister, Andrea, moved back to Israel in her late teens and married a guy who ended up going to jail, where he died under very suspicious circumstances. True, she had left him by then and taken her kids back to Caracas, just to be crammed in that same tiny apartment with her mother, her sister, and her twin nephews. No wonder she fled to Canada as soon as she made enough money. Exactly like me, when I escaped from my obnoxious family and came to the States. Okay, I admit, I have to admire that. She showed a lot of gumption.

But I am getting sidetracked. Back to what made me change my mind about writing. My little sister and I have talked over the phone for years and we haven't been able to define what made our childhood so appalling. When we try to tell our friends, our complaints seem petty. Everything that happened seems so ordinary. The atmosphere of terror and impending doom that prevailed in our home gets toned down, muted, in retrospect. I have to agree it is quite a challenge to try to recount the horror of it all and finally delve into what made us who we are today.

Maybe, after all, my little sister has a valid point. She thinks we shouldn't expunge our past. Or bury it, like I did. Maybe she is right, maybe we can use it for something. Even dung can be made into fertilizer. Maybe, finally, for a change, it will do us some good. Maybe, after all, the lives of second generation Holocaust survivors, are not broken beyond repair. What I am trying to say with all this hemming and hawing is that I've changed my mind. I am willing to give it a shot. So, little sister, I am going to dive into the sewer of our childhood, after all. Since I can't type worth a damn, I hope that you can decipher my awful handwriting. Here goes my first contribution.

This is a daunting project indeed. I have spent most of my adult life emulating a fastidious feline burying feces. I've trained myself not to think about my childhood, especially the parts that cause so much pain. When I told Rebecca that I was trying to remember something good about our childhood to include in my story, she responded, rather derisively, that it was going to be less than one line long. That is, if I was lucky and managed to scare up something.

So now, without further procrastination, it is time to dig into the kitty litter. The first thing I remember is sunshine. Sunshine, and babushka-clad ladies smiling and talking in sweet, melodious tones. I was a talkative, friendly toddler who liked strangers. On the other hand, hindsight is always twenty-twenty. The fact is that I have grown into a talkative old lady who likes to chat with strangers. That is all I remember about Poland. Even though my grandma lived with us all during my first five years of life, and I was told a million times about how I was run over by a car at the age of three, I do not remember my grandmother's face or the accident. But I still bear a scar behind my left ear.

For the life of me, I cannot remember my sister's birth. And I was well over four years old at the time. I cannot remember anything about her infancy either. So much for sibling rivalry! It was as if I had never been there at that time. I wonder. Perhaps I wasn't there, after all. Perhaps Mother sent me off with the broad-faced, heavy-set babushka-head with the missing teeth. At least, she never yelled at me and always spoke in a very low, sing-song voice. To this day I think of round-faced, roly-poly women as good-hearted. After all, whoever heard of a fat witch?

I cannot remember my mother's face when I was a child. I've seen photographs of her, but I cannot reconcile the serene, unsmiling young woman in the photos, who had the face of the Virgin

Mary in an early medieval Italian painting, with the hysterical, irrational woman I remember. To me she looked ugly. There was no resemblance whatsoever to the beautiful young woman with the calm countenance in the pictures. She was always frowning. Her thin hair was short and scraggly, exposing a bald spot at the crown. Her voice was peevish, resentful, and self-pitying. Always lamenting some potential unpleasantness and seeing slights and insults everywhere. And she smelled bad. Perhaps because she smoked, or it could have been her teeth. They were bad as a result of the privations she suffered during the war. She made no bones about my being a burden to her. It seems that I was as glad to get away from her as she was to get rid of me.

Ouch!, you cannot play in the kitty-litter without the smell rubbing off on you. Now I sound peevish and self-pitying. Mother did have it rough. There was a brutal war going on. Life was really hard and frightening during those years. The parents, who were passing off as Catholics, were in mortal terror of being found out and shot. Father had gone through law school sitting on the left side of the classroom, like all Jews, and now that he worked as an attorney, he was afraid that his colleagues might remember and inform the authorities. Watching from the sidelines and cheering as their family, their friends and the whole Jewish community was carted off to the ovens must have been sheer agony, beyond description. Mother should never have had children, but there was no birth control. I am sure she didn't want to have us then, or perhaps ever. Who in their right mind would want to have children in Poland during the war? And that is not even taking into account that we were Jewish! We must have been the result of unwanted pregnancies. Mother must have felt miserable and terrified giving birth to two children in the midst of the war. At least, that could be an explanation for her appalling attitude toward us. Or, perhaps she just plain didn't like us.

I am determined to remember something nice about each stage of my childhood. Mainly to spite Rebecca, who challenged me to remember the good times. I think I've got it. Furthermore, I've got some snapshots to prove it. I remember the sunshine The photos show Rebecca and me climbing a huge bronze statue of a soldier wearing a Kaiser Wilhelm spiked helmet. It was near the Brandenburg Gate in Germany. It must have been winter. We were wearing coats with fur-lined hoods. There is an earlier picture, taken in 1945 in Zakopane, which is a nice resort in the mountains. It is winter, there was snow on the ground, but it must have been warm. Mother is wearing one of her little suits. She liked short, tight tailored suits. She has tied her sparse hair in a bandanna. I think she must have been self-conscious about her thinning hair even then. I am sitting on a rail, holding an apple, squinting my eyes shut against the bright sun. My little sister, still a pudgy baby, has her eyes closed as well, behind her tiny round spectacles. She was wearing glasses before the age of two. I cannot remember any events connected with that picture.

I recently read an article that states: "Over time, psychologists say, people refashion their memories so drastically that most of us routinely remember things that never happened—while forgetting things that actually did." Well, I used to make up a lovely family, with sweet-tempered, attentive parents who cherished us. I used to make up a big comfortable house, with nice furniture, and lots of books and toys. I tried to ignore our unpleasant reality, even if it meant losing all my childhood memories in the process. Every time I try to dig up the past a very unpleasant odor arises from the kitty-litter. But let's not waste any more time and plod on.

Some time later, we moved to Germany. In Berlin, we lived in a sumptuous modern house. I remember that it had an enormous formal parlor with indirect lighting. The light bulbs were hidden behind the plaster crown molding that skirted the entire ceiling of the room. A magnificent, carpeted, very wide staircase at the end of the room led to large, airy, sunny bedrooms. I think that there were French windows that were always filled with light. Father wore a uniform with lots of medals. He was some kind of attachè or diplomat at the Russian Consulate. I don't know to whom the house had belonged previously, but he must have been very rich and an art lover. Father looted the lovely house systematically. It was completely furnished with the belongings of the former owners. Once he showed me a huge postage stamp album, filled with beautiful stamps. I think that he sold it; such things can be very valuable. I remember a gorgeous turquoise Persian carpet. It wound up in our apartment in Venezuela. It probably had a bad stain or a burn somewhere, so that Father could not sell it. We never got to keep anything that was not somehow damaged or imperfect. I think that the German house was the foundation of my father's fortune. He had money when we arrived in Venezuela a few years later.

I remember that Father considered himself a big shot and had a staff. There was a pretty young blond woman to look after us. She used to take us to a park near a beer-garden where she flirted with all the young men, whom she attracted like flies. We were definitely in her way, and she took care of us grudgingly. There is one phrase in German that I remember today as vividly as when we lived there, perhaps because she repeated it so often to us: "I know what you want, you brat, and you can't have it." Every morning she would braid my hair and pull it hard. I think she got a lot of pleasure out of doing that. I didn't shed any tears when she got the sack.

There was also a cook and a chauffeur. Once the chauffeur was driving us somewhere when I noticed flames under the hood of the car, through holes under the dashboard. I spoke up, but Father dismissed me in his usual sarcastic, belittling tone. Fortunately, I had alerted the chauffeur, who by then had begun to feel the heat of the fire. He stopped the car. We all trooped out, I holding Rebecca. I remember thinking that Father was a bad-tempered blowhard and a bully, who thought he was always right, but was wrong more often than not. From then on, I never believed anything he said without a little worm of doubt in my mind.

Another time, Father was driving, and insisted on stopping to gawk at an accident victim. Even though Mother begged him not to, he had to have his way. An old man had been run over by a car. I don't know why I didn't turn my face away, but I managed to cover Rebecca's eyes. To this day, I remember the rivulets of blood. The old man's bald head looked unnaturally bluish in the bright, merciless sunlight. The mangled bicycle was shimmering in the heat and already buzzing with flies. Father wasn't satisfied until he got to talk to some of the bystanders and was able to extract from them what happened.

One time Mother dressed us in our Sunday best and took us to some function at the Russian Consulate. She promptly removed herself from the scene. We were in a large room, with a polished parquet floor. Some small girls, in colorful costumes were rehearsing a folk dance. We were totally ignored and bored to death. After a while, all the children left. A young woman took us with her to collect her little girl. We walked a very short distance to a shabby building. When she opened the door to her apartment I was nauseated by the overpowering stench. The place was the filthiest place I had ever seen in my life, and it was frigidly cold. She dragged the little girl out from under some dirty covers and made room on the food encrusted table by sweeping leftovers to the floor with her sleeve. She sat the sleepy child on the table, and put some dirty clothes on her, without bothering to wash or comb her. Then we all returned to the lovely room with the parquet floor. Some more little girls appeared with their mothers and started rehearsing folk songs. The little girl in the dirty clothes, with the smudged face, had a lovely, clear soprano voice. We weren't allowed to participate in the singing, since we didn't know the words of the songs they were rehearsing. We sat in our chairs, bored stiff again. Eventually, all the children and their mothers left. We were alone. I have no idea what time it was, but we were hungry. My baby sister was crying because she was so hungry. We fell asleep in some large armchairs. It was well after dark when Mother came back for us.

We had one good woolen dress each. Mine was blue, my sister's green. One day, while I was seated by the window, reading a book, Rebecca was playing on the living room carpet, dressing and undressing her doll. After a while she went up the stairs and I heard her rummaging through some drawers. Then, there was silence. Since she hadn't come down by the time I finished reading the chapter, I followed her upstairs. I found her holding Mother's best scissors, surrounded by pieces of her green dress.

"Ela, look, I am making new clothes for my dolly," she told me, brightly.

We were in big trouble. Mother got so angry that she spanked us, not waiting for Father to come home. "I'll never ever buy you a good dress again," she shrieked. When Father arrived, she turned us over to him for further punishment. He took us into his study, closed the door, took off his belt, told us to scream as hard as we could, while he hit the leather sofa over and over. A few minutes later, we all walked out of the room. Father sent us to bed without dinner.

That night I woke up to hear my little sister sobbing. "Stop crying, baby," I whispered. "You'll get my blue woolen dress as soon as I outgrow it." But by the time we got to Venezuela we stopped wearing wool.

Mother kept a small piece of green fabric to remind us how bad we had been. The last time I saw it I was already starting high school.

We were rarely beaten. At least not regularly, or on purpose. All the abuse was verbal; the worst we got was an outpouring of rage and invectives. Father did not live in a state of uncontrollable rage. He would never have survived childhood, never mind World War II and the German occupation, if that were the case. When the situation called for it, Father could be quite deferential and obsequious. Had he been a true ogre all the time, my little sister, who was very intelligent even at the tender age of three, would never have placed herself within throwing range and the next two incidents would have never happened.

It was winter, Rebecca was wearing a rabbit fur coat with matching baby bonnet (there is a picture of it, the one with the bronze statue). Father was in the backyard using a garden hose, and somehow the heavy brass coupling swung around and hit her in the head, knocking her to the ground. I am sure that it was an accident. The little fur baby bonnet saved her from serious harm. But for the life of me I cannot picture the flying sardine can as an accident. Sardine cans cannot levitate by themselves, and attack baby girls in bunny rabbit white bonnets. I don't know why Father threw the sardine can, or even that he threw it at her, but it hit her just above the eye, between the eyebrow and the bridge of the nose. Did you ever wonder how, and where, you got that scar, Rebecca? There was so much blood that the little rabbit bonnet was ruined. She never wore it again. You wonder, little sister, how come you never heard that story? Because Father denied that it ever happened. But I have tried hard to forget these incidents. I wouldn't need much encouragement to believe that it didn't happen. Hell, my whole childhood didn't happen. But once you start digging deep in the kitty litter, uncovering feces, the stink refuses to stay buried and wafts to the surface. I think it was then that Rebecca learned to stay out of Father's range. Actually, we both learned to avoid our parents as much as possible.

Yesterday, March 9 (March 8 was Father's birthday), my little sister called again. She had received my initial efforts at writing and was very encouraging in her praise. Basking in the sun of her approval, I've decided to continue to dig up what I had so very carefully buried for the last fifty years.

I'll fast forward to Denmark, our next destination on our exodus from our native land. Even though it was always winter in Denmark, I loved it. Copenhagen was beautiful at night, it was always night in Copenhagen, even at 2 P.M. It was the first time I had seen big, gorgeously colored neon lights. They were everywhere. The name of a nearby hotel had a flashing crown, in red and gold. The Danish flag was outlined on the roof of another building. And there was Tivoli. When we first came to Copenhagen we resided downtown in a hotel near Tivoli and we used to walk by, admiring the lights. We never got to ride any of the merry-go-rounds, or other attractions at the world-famous amusement park. But it was almost enough to watch the gorgeous, brightly painted, hand-made horses, and listen to the happy music of the calliope.

We didn't expect our parents to spend money on us. Even then we knew better than that. I think they were beginning to hoard money for their eventual emigration. Denmark was only a way-station to our final destination. They could not have stayed even if they had really wanted to. I think we only had temporary visas. Father was no longer a big shot. When we rented a place to live, it was very different from the German mansion. It was clean and well lit, but it was only the upper flat in someone else's house. It was so near the railroad tracks that a solid board fence had been built to prevent children, pets, and drunks from coming in contact with the trains. I imagine that the socially conscientious Danes had laws and regulations about such things. At night the trains not only shook us in our beds, but also lit up our walls as brightly as the noon sun. I am referring to the sun in Alabama, there was no sun at noon, or at any other time in Denmark. Nevertheless, it was a friendly, clean, wholesome place, which treated us well. The house had a modest yard with a fountain filled with hideous, mottled carp, silver with a few orange splotches (my sister believes that these fish are prized by the Japanese). There was a marvelous white Angora cat who performed a much needed public service by inviting the ugly carp to lunch. There was also an elderly gentleman who doted on the carp (maybe they were valuable after all), and tried to discourage the cat's meal dates with the fish.

I started school in Copenhagen. I think that I wound up in the first grade, but was boosted up to second when my teacher found out that I could read fluently. My sister and I got bicycles that we rode in a nearby park. We also started our habit of roaming the streets that year. I remember a kindly, white-haired lady following us home one day, and insisting on talking with our mother. Mother was not home, as usual. The maid served tea and little cakes to the nice lady. Eventually, she left without ever talking to mother. I think she must have been connected with some social services agency, because from then on we were forbidden to leave the house after dark by ourselves.

I was happy in Denmark. I liked the school, I loved my class-mates. I would have been even happier had I been allowed to play with other children, but you cannot wish for everything. My little sister remembers the Christmas tree and the doll house. But I'll let Rebecca wax poetic on its splendors, since it seems to be the one thing she remembers from Denmark. Thinking back, I wonder why the Danish children were not allowed to play with us. Did their parents think that we were dirty and carried plague? Or was it simply that they disapproved of our parents and the way they neglected us? But by then we were beginning to thrive on neglect. We were a little older, more independent, and learned that avoid-ing our parents solved most of our problems.

Rebecca

We endured two weeks of high seas and winter storms and finally we arrived in Venezuela. The relentless, humid heat was the first thing we noticed. Just a few seconds after setting foot on the pier we were sweating and wiping our faces. All colors seemed much more vivid, the sky was brilliant blue, there were a few white puffy clouds, the brick red earth dramatically set off the green trees, heavy with masses of drooping white and pink flowers. Just a couple of blocks behind the port, an enormous, dark green mountain rose from the edge of the sea all the way to the clouds. The port was crowded and noisy. Cars were honking. Taxi drivers were yelling fares and destinations. Peddlers were hawking their wares. The heat, the bright colors, the pungent smell, the din, all have mingled in my mind, and now, whenever I feel hot air on my cheeks, or hear dissonant clatter, or smell the scent of overripe fruit and rotting flowers, I relive the moment of our arrival in Venezuela.

After waiting interminably to finish all the bureaucratic formalities, we finally managed to get all our belongings into a cab and started the long ride up the mountain toward the capital. We passed tiny huts constructed of cardboard and tin. Whole hillsides of muddy red dirt were studded with one-room shacks without windows and only gaping holes for doors. Women carrying babies and large buckets of water walked up the narrow dirt paths, children in rags played in the mud. In horror and disbelief, my parents stared out the window of the cab. Years later my father told me that right then and there he knew he had made a terrible mistake by coming to this country. But we continued the slow trip up the winding road with hundreds of sharp turns. Crosses and shrines, decorated with flowers and religious pictures, marked the road where cars had crashed or tumbled off into the deep ravines, killing their occupants. Finally, the density of the huts started increasing at an alarming rate and we were in the capital.

We were going to be staying with my father's sister until we found our own place and, finally, I was going to meet my two cousins, Adam and Danny. Their apartment was in an old building in the center of the city, next to a quiet plaza called *La Candelaria*. My uncle, aunt, grandfather and my two cousins occupied a small two-bedroom apartment. Our arrival must have really crowded their living space. The building was very noisy, kids played in the hallways and the stairs, their mothers talked loudly while hanging up the wash on the roof. Dogs barked and street vendors announced their presence by yelling the names of exotic fruit. The apartment was too small for such a large number of people, especially since four of us were kids. My cousin Danny, who must have been around three, was in the habit of running around naked, screeching at a very high pitch. My father wanted my aunt to stop him, but she said that she had tried over and over again and had been unable to get him to quit. Shortly after that, my father grabbed him by the hair and beat the daylights out of him. The apartment was much quieter after this. My father got a reputation among the kids for having a heavy hand and being a stern disciplinarian who had to be immediately obeyed.

Some days my grandfather, my sister, our cousins and I went to the tree-lined plaza across the street. While we jumped rope and chased pigeons, grandfather slept on a stone bench in the shade. My sister and I were well behaved, but my little cousin Danny was a handful. He ran among the flower beds, threw stones, and once came back with a baby rattle, which he claimed he found on the path. We had to watch him constantly. At first, we had trouble communicating with him, we spoke only German, he spoke Spanish. But soon we discovered that when he ran into the street a slap on the behind worked wonders. Perhaps, after all, we did learn a thing or two from Father.

After a few months, we moved to a large house in a quiet neighborhood called *Las Fuentes*. Every night, a stream of visitors came to our house, oddly-dressed foreigners with bad breath and furtive manners. My sister and I were told to come out and say hello. We had to endure the obligatory kisses and compliments, and listen to the never-ending whispering about who died, who disappeared, and who might know somebody who might know somebody else who had survived the camps. We hated the pale pasty faces, the tremulous voices full of grief, the stories told and retold, reciting one horror after another. We hated seeing all those numbers engraved on the yellowish skin of their arms. I especially hated all the stories about children who were taken away from their mothers, screaming, crammed into cattle cars heading toward the East, or worse yet, dragged shrieking from their hiding places and shot in front of the eyes of their parents. As soon as it was proper, we would slip out and make our way up the stairs to our bedroom, slip under the freshly starched sheets, and turn on the radio to listen to our favorite program, "Tamacún, the Wandering Avenger."

My parents despised Venezuela—the poverty, the unmerciful heat, the torrential rains that flooded the city every few weeks, the red earth so different from the black Polish soil. And the cockroaches, tarantulas, snakes, the dark-skinned emaciated people shouting and begging in the streets, trying to sell newspapers or flowers, or asking for money to take care of your car, which actually meant that if you didn't pay them your car would be vandalized. At home, our parents had screaming fights that lasted for hours, my father venting his rage and roaring curses and insults like a madman and my mother sobbing and threatening suicide. My sister and I would hide in the farthest corner of the garage, crouched behind the rear wheel of the car, holding each other, making ourselves invisible until the storm passed. Then we would sneak very quietly up the steps to our room and wouldn't come out until the next morning. We missed quite a few dinners this way, but that was better than having to face our parents during one of their frequent fights. Later, when we knew Father's anger was spent, we sometimes would sneak back down into the kitchen for a glass of milk and a cookie.

When I look at the few photographs we have saved from that time, I see two unsmiling round-faced girls, at first with long braids and later in punch-bowl haircuts, their fists balled, looking at the camera with distrust and animosity. We wore the wrong clothes, dresses that were made from sturdy practical fabrics in dark colors so they wouldn't show dirt, always too large or too long. We wore shorts that at that time were never seen on any girl over the age of three. We wore leather boots that needed to be laced up, while all the other little girls wore black or white patent doll shoes. Although we spoke Spanish to everyone in school, we were called "the German girls" because we spoke German between ourselves when we didn't want anybody else to know what we were talking about. The irony of this did not strike me until years later. But, of course, at the time we didn't know we were Jewish.

My sister believes Mother tried to enroll us in a Catholic school run by nuns and that we were rejected. I do not know if this is true, all I can remember is being sent to public school. The school was about two miles from our house. We had to walk six long blocks to a bus stop, ride about fifteen minutes in a public bus, crowded with laborers on their way to work, cross a street jammed with trucks and buses honking like mad, and then we were at the school. Normally, my sister would hold my hand through most of the walk and in the bus. This was comforting and reassuring. As long as I was with her I never worried. But there were times when I had to go alone and, although I knew the way, I always felt scared. I can't remember who, but someone taught me to stand really close to any white, conservatively dressed, woman while waiting at the bus stop, so no one would know I was a five-year old traveling alone. It always worked, I was never stopped or asked any questions.

My sister knew I was her responsibility and took her role seriously. She was in charge. She made all the decisions. My parents were not to be bothered, ever. We knew that any problems we had would incur our father's wrath and our mother's recriminations and we learned to manage quite well by ourselves. My sister taught me never to admit to anything, never to show fear, to always pretend that everything was fine, and appear absolutely sure of myself. We always peeked out carefully from the second story windows before we opened the front door, in case some kids were lurking outside waiting to beat us up. We learned to fight when we knew we could win, and run when we thought we could not. At first, I often slipped up and showed fear and even cried. My sister never did.

We never knew sibling rivalry, we never felt the need to compete for our parents' attention or love. They were too busy and too involved in their own affairs to show us love or attention. They made sure we were alive, well fed, clothed, and had a roof over our heads. My mother had a phrase she used frequently when somebody complained to her about hardship, "You have eggs, ham, butter, and a key to the front door of an apartment. What else do you want?" Father got so tired of hearing her repeat this litany that he responded with a vulgar version of the same phrase which left no doubt where you could stick the eggs, the butter and the key. But food and shelter were the things that mattered during the war, when survival was at stake, and for my parents, these were the things that mattered now, in this strange country. Father was also trying to accumulate money to move to our eventual final destination, since he already knew he didn't want to stay in Venezuela forever.

Mother was obsessed with father's sexual escapades, which were frequent and well-known to everyone who knew our family. As soon as Father walked out the door she would look at her watch and before half an hour had passed she would call the store, or my aunt's house to make sure he was there. Father had a steady stream of mistresses, interspersed with occasional one-night stands. Mother lived in constant terror, just like during the war, but this time she was not terrified of being discovered and killed by the Germans, this time she was afraid of being left alone in a unfamiliar country with two children to support, unable to make a living, and far away from her remaining family and the place where she had grown up.

It was at this time that several things happened that could be considered clues to the extraordinary road my sister was going to follow. First, she shed her Polish name. She no longer allowed anybody to call her Stela. She simply would not answer. She started giving her name as Susanna, a name as far removed from our Jewish roots as possible. I was only five, but even then I realized this was an important battle for my sister and that she was determined to win. She got that look in her face that I knew so well, the look that spelled trouble. Her jaw clenched, her full lips were pressed into a thin line, her green eyes glared and took on a tinge of yellow, her hands balled into fists. I kept my gaze on her, couldn't take my eyes away. She was magnificent. I was impressed by her daring and awed by her tenacity, especially since she prevailed in the end. I became convinced that my sister was unstoppable, that she was capable of accomplishing anything she wanted. Grandfather had a hard time remembering my sister's new name, of course. He kept on calling her Ela, or even Elusia, the name I called her when I was a baby because I couldn't say Stela. He was the only one allowed to call her that. She also refused to speak Polish, claiming she couldn't understand a word my parents said, and never answered when she was addressed in that language. When she didn't know I was around, she would answer Grandfather in Polish, since it was all he spoke. Eventually, she willed herself to forget the language, even though all our cousins and I, all younger than she, speak Polish fluently to this day.

The other event that influenced my sister's life was fortuitous. An American lady who lived a few houses down the road from us became our friend. Her name was Margaret Mead, but she was not the famous anthropologist. I don't know who came up with the idea, but she taught Susanna to speak English. They met for one hour every day and a couple of hours on Saturday. Soon Susanna was reading books in English. At first, Mrs. Mead lent my sister her books, but before long, Susanna was buying her own. An American bookstore at the east end of the city stocked all kinds of children's classics. We would take the bus and spend the whole afternoon browsing among all these treasures. We would pool our money and my sister would make a difficult decision, which of the many books we coveted should she buy? By combining our allowances we had enough money to buy a new book every week. Then she would recount the whole book to me with a wealth of detail. This is how I became familiar with such American classics as the Nancy Drew mysteries, the Hardy Boys, Little Women, Tom Sawyer, Gone with the Wind, and many others. Every night, after we turned off the lights, my sister would start retelling me what she had read during the day. I would wait all day for this moment. I didn't mind going to bed and turning off the lights, because I knew that I would soon be magically transported into another world where things were perfect and my imagination could run unchecked. I guess my sister must have dreamed of inhabiting this foreign world, too, because a few years later, while attending high school, she caused such an enormous upheaval and commotion, that my parents had to send her away to a boarding school in a different country. But that was much later, and I don't want to get ahead of my story.

We were on our own most of the time. Father, who was managing a clothing store he later purchased, was gone from early morning until late at night. Mother was at the store in the afternoons to help out and to make sure that he was not having sex with the salesgirls in the storeroom. Mother rode the bus to the store around lunchtime, carrying a casserole and several other shopping bags with pots containing food for lunch and dinner. My parents disliked the fare served in nearby restaurants. They never got used to local foods, always suspecting they were dirty and unsanitary and likely to cause all kinds of tropical diseases. Around ten at night, after we were in bed and had turned off the lights, our parents would return home together. We never had to give an accounting of where we had been or what we had done while they were away.

On Sundays, we piled into the car and drove to the coast, about ten miles away. The new freeway hadn't been built yet, and the road was narrow and full of hairpin turns. More often than not, a car would break down or crash descending a steep slope or overheat on the way up, and we would be trapped in nightmarish traffic jams. Then, the parents would scream and fight about Father's newest paramour. Mother sobbed and threatened to jump out of the car and throw herself into a deep ravine. Father would cuss at her, call her a filthy slut, a good-for-nothing turd, even slap her, forgetting he was at the wheel. Many a time he lost control of the car and we ended up scraping the mountain side or slamming into the rear of a stopped car. I would sit very still in the back seat, close my eyes and tell myself long involved stories, like serials, that would continue from Sunday to Sunday. Sometimes I managed to get so involved that I didn't realize we had arrived at the beach.

The beach was marvelous. A long strip of golden sand shaped into a slight semicircle, bordered by tall, swaying palm trees and sea grape berries on one side and clear blue, shimmering water on the other. My sister and I would immediately wriggle out of our sweaty clothes, get into our bathing suits and run on the burning sand to the shore. The water was inviting and warm. We jumped waves and pretended to swim, while our parents sat under an umbrella and dozed until the early afternoon. Then Mother would call us for a picnic lunch. She spread out a towel and set out several dishes—cold chicken, cheese, hard-boiled eggs, pickled cucumbers, bread, butter, and fruit. I liked the pickled cucumbers best and would always try to get as many as I could. We were allowed one more dip in the sea after lunch, just to wash off the sand, and then it was time to put our clothes back on. This was the part I hated most, I could never get the sand out from in between my toes and my panties, and afterward, when I sat in the car I could feel my skin chafing and burning. Susanna would always get her face sunburned, as she had very fair skin. In the car, Mother would scold us for playing too long in the water, and for getting sunburned. We kept the windows of the car down, and in the back the breeze would blow our hair every which way. I would close my eyes and continue my serial story wherever I had left off in the morning. Both Susanna and I loved going to the beach and hated coming back to the city.

My parents didn't celebrate birthdays, holidays, or other special occasions. When Carnival came around, in February, all the kids dressed up in costumes to go to parties and to walk or ride in day-long parades. My sister and I were left out because we didn't have costumes. When my sister's English teacher, Mrs. Mead, became aware of our situation, she did something about it. She looked through her closet for colorful skirts, blouses and aprons and made us two wigs out of orange yarn, then placed large bows in them. In a couple of hours, my sister and I were ready to join the fun. Each of us had a Raggedy Ann costume. The fact that we had no idea who Raggedy Ann was didn't detract one bit from the happiness we felt.

The next time Mrs. Mead got involved in our life was on one of those days when it rained cats and dogs. I was in first grade, my sister was in third grade. We had gone to school together by bus that morning. By mid-morning the city streets started flooding. Soon parents were trickling in to pick up their children and in less than half an hour I was the only child left. The teacher took me to the principal's office, where I was told to call my parents. I knew that my mother couldn't do much because she didn't drive, and my father would not be able to leave the store unattended. But I had no other option, I had to call, so I swallowed hard and called my father at the store, knowing quite well that I was breaking the rules. We were never supposed to call there, but I explained that my sister's class had been let out quite a while ago, and I was the only kid left at school. I needed somebody to pick me up. Father told me to tell the principal that I was to meet him at the back entrance of the school, where he would be waiting for me, but in reality to go across the street to the bus stop and take the bus home, as usual. So I walked to the rear of the building and, as soon as I was out of sight, I doubled back, crossed the street and waited for a bus. After an endless wait, a bus finally arrived and I got on. Unfortunately, it stopped a couple of blocks down the street because the water had risen too high. Everybody was told to get off the bus. I didn't know what to do. I decided that walking home would be the least of all evils. I knew the way well, I had walked home with my sister on many occasions, but I was terrified by the rushing water and started whimpering. I tried hard to keep my books dry. I lifted the hem of my dress so it wouldn't get muddy. Suddenly my glasses fell off and disappeared in the muddy torrent. They were expensive. My parents would be angry. Now I really had a good reason to cry. I started bawling loudly. The water got deeper and deeper. It rushed by me ever faster. I was having trouble standing up. Suddenly, somebody grabbed me and lifted me onto the bed of a parked truck. With a small group of wet and shivering people I waited for the water to recede. When it was finally safe to leave the truck a man took me to a nearby police station. I tried calling home and the store over and over, to let my sister or my parents know where I was, but most phones in the city were down because of the flood, and I didn't dare to keep asking to use the station's only phone. Everybody there seemed very unconcerned by my fate, and that only increased my fear. I was sure that I would never be found.

My sister later told me that when she got home and realized I wasn't there she ran back to the bus stop to wait for me, but no buses were getting through. She waited more than an hour, then went back to the house, but it was still empty. And the phones weren't working. She started to panic. Finally, she thought of going to Mrs. Mead's, who took charge of the situation like a drill sergeant. She got into her car with my sister and drove to her husband's office to enlist his help. Between the two of them, they managed to locate me early that evening, at the police station near the school. My hair was plastered to my head, my dress and shoes were mud-caked, my glasses and books were lost. During those long hours at the station I had become terrified that this disaster was too big even for my sister, but I could see I was wrong. I flew into her arms and wouldn't let anybody pry me loose. I was so exhilarated I didn't stop chattering until we got home.

The Meads took me home, cleaned me up, fed me, and put me to bed. My sister told me that Mrs. Mead waited for my parents and that when they arrived, around ten, all hell broke loose. Mrs. Mead became enraged. She threatened to call the authorities. My Father told her in no uncertain terms to mind her own business and in what part of her anatomy she could lodge her complaints. Fortunately for my parents, Mrs. Mead did not speak Spanish well enough to deal with the Venezuelan bureaucracy. My sister's English classes, of course, were canceled. We were told to never even traverse the sidewalk in front of Mrs. Mead's house. We were ordered to cross the street.

After a week, Susanna began missing her classes so much that she started a campaign to be allowed to continue taking her English lessons. Our parents wouldn't hear of it. My sister threw raging tantrums. She screamed and sobbed, her face got almost purple. She stomped with her feet, flailed her arms, her rage increased until she could hardly breathe, then she threw up. After that, she got the hiccups for the remainder of the day. I couldn't stand watching her. Finally, my parents relented and she started going to Mrs. Mead's home again, but relations remained frigid between my parents and the Meads. We were told to never ever broach the subject of this incident again.

A couple of months before I turned six, my mother decided I should take piano lessons. She dredged up from God knows where this Austrian piano teacher and had him come to our house once a week. He was short and fleshy, sixtyish, always hot and sweaty in an old rumpled suit, constantly blowing his nose and dabbing at his watery eyes with a dirty handkerchief. As soon as my mother would leave the room he would take out his member and lift my left hand, cover it with his right hand, and move it up and down his purple pecker until it would squirt. Meanwhile, I had to keep playing scales with my free right hand so as not to arouse suspicions. He told me to keep quiet about this, to never tell anybody. This was to be our secret. I felt ashamed and dirty, and afraid that we would be found out. The hour-long class seemed to take forever, I would look at my watch every few seconds and the hands seemed to be stuck. I would fantasize he was struck by a bolt of lightning and collapsed, writhing in agony, his face contorted and as purple as his penis, his eyes popping out of their sockets, dead at my feet, right under the piano bench. Then I would wait for a few minutes to make sure he was really dead, before calling for help. I hated this repulsive old man and the piano lessons with all my heart. For the first time in my life I knew what hate felt like.

"You are a lazy girl," Mother said, when I tried to tell her what was happening. "You'll make anything up just to get out of having your piano lessons. Don't think you can fool me with you whining and whimpering. You know very well we are spending a lot of our hard-earned money to give you this opportunity. I wish my parents had done the same for me."

Several times I managed to prevail upon Mother to stay in the living room during the whole lesson, but of course, the professor didn't do anything inappropriate then. "I knew it," Mother hissed. "There is nothing going on. He is such a nice gentleman. I should have never listened to your nonsense."

I was trapped, unable to stop this nightmare. I endured this torture for several years, never progressed at the piano, and dreamed of the day that I would be free. I think I must have willed my hands to never grow, so that I could use my tiny hands, always three notes short of an octave, as an excuse to quit the piano. Finally, at the age of ten, I was able to rebel and quit. My parents were upset by my lack of appreciation of the finer arts, especially since one of my third cousins, who was a year younger than I, was already giving concerts. I was reminded of this fact again and again. But I felt free, as if I had been reborn. My hands never grew, even after I quit, and remain disproportionately small to this day.

Years later, in my thirties, I mentioned this to Mother and she reminded me that the professor came highly recommended to her and was well regarded in the community. She told me I must be mistaken, that I must have misinterpreted what went on at the time because I was so young, or that I remembered wrong because so much time had elapsed. I felt an enormous surge of rage that left me speechless for the rest of our visit. I couldn't bear to look at her, sitting primly in her living room, sipping tea and nibbling daintily at a piece of chocolate-covered marzipan she got from the fancy box I had brought over. I gathered my things, got my daughter out of the swimming pool, helped her get dressed, and left as soon as I could. Now that I myself was a mother I looked at my innocent and beautiful child, and finally felt all the rage I had never been able to feel before, uncomplicated by feelings of shame and guilt. I am not sure what I hated more, that dirty old lecher from my childhood, or my mother's unwillingness to believe me, even now, thirty years later.

On her tenth birthday, my sister found an abandoned, starving, black cocker spaniel puppy and brought him home. She could never resist any creature in distress, be it animal or child. My parents wouldn't hear of keeping the poor dog. It was just another mouth to feed, a nuisance. As always, our wishes were not considered. But Susanna, my very resourceful sister, knew what to do to get her way. She went on a hunger strike. She wouldn't eat, she said, until my parents agreed to keep the dog, at least temporarily, until we could find him another home. She threw screaming and foot-stomping tantrums when our parents tried to force her to eat, usurping my father's prerogative of being the only one to holler at meal times. This battle raged for several days, both parties were adamant, and would not relent. My sister was very clever, she had an instinct for these things. This was a brilliant move on her part. Nothing upset my mother more than somebody who refused to eat. This threatened the very core of her being. Mother made Father's life impossible, whining and worrying about Susanna's hunger strike. Eventually, Susanna won. The dog stayed outside, in the fenced patio. He was not allowed into the house, and we were totally responsible for his upkeep and care. We went out of our way to make sure the dog didn't bother anybody and took pains so that it wouldn't howl or bark. At night, if it wasn't raining, we took turns sleeping on a mat in the patio, so the dog wouldn't whimper. We were trying to train him to become invisible. Unfortunately, we found the poor dog dead a few weeks later, after he ate some rat poison that some neighbor threw over the fence into our yard. To this day, my sister believes this was no stranger, she suspects our parents.

I broke my arm three times the year I was six. I don't know whether this was a last ditch attempt to try to gain my parents' attention or just a growth spurt and not enough calcium. The third time I remember most clearly, because it happened a couple of days before my seventh birthday. My sister and I had been roller-skating on a hilly street where Mother had forbidden us to go, and I fell and hurt my wrist. Soon it became swollen. The pain was awful. We went home and wrapped it in a wet towel, but it continued to swell and the pain became worse. Of course, we didn't tell the parents to avoid being scolded. My mother always reacted with such hysterics when we were sick or hurt that we preferred to keep quiet. After two days of slinking around, trying hard not to use my arm or let anything touch it, we decided that we had to confess.

"Why now? Why us?" Mother screeched, "Why did you do this to me now when you know perfectly well I am so busy. Why did this tragedy have to happen to me, haven't I suffered enough already, dear God?"

In the end, we had to take a bus to the emergency room of a nearby hospital. After sitting in the waiting room for over two hours, a young doctor took an X-ray and then reset my wrist, which hurt more than anything I had ever experienced. I didn't cry. I didn't want to be reminded by Mother that I had only myself to blame. The doctor mixed some white sticky stuff in a bucket and wrapped my arm all the way from my thumb to my elbow. We waited until this bandage hardened and then were told we could leave. In the bus on the way home, my mother continued her recriminations, which we were taking quite stoically, until she reminded me that the next day was my birthday.

"Now, look what you've done, you see what happens when you don't do what I tell you. We had to spend the whole afternoon at this horrible, filthy emergency room, and now there is no time to get you a present or a birthday cake for tomorrow."

All the tears I had managed to keep back with such effort burst forth. I started wailing, and kept it up all through the bus ride and the six-block walk home. When we got in the house my sister promised to give me her best scissors, the ones I had been coveting for several months, to cut out my paper dolls. And the next day, she made a whole chocolate pudding from a box, just for the two of us. The cast on my arm made me an instant celebrity in my class. It turned out to be a good birthday, after all.

Mother's attitude toward illness kept us from falling sick. Staying home from school and succumbing to my mother's ministrations was punishment beyond endurance. She would delve into the manner in which we may have acquired this illness at length, And then she would apportion blame.

"Why did you go play in the rain? Why didn't you wear a sweater? Why did you run, jump, climb a tree? Don't you know you could hurt yourself? And then who would take care of you? Why do you torture me this way? Do you want me to die from all this heartache?" Mother would keep us in bed, make the room dark by lowering the blinds and not allow us to read or play. We had to take all kinds of disgusting teas and potions, she would demand news of our bowel movements, and make sure we thoroughly hated every second of the entire sickness experience. We would never dream of staying home from school and malingering, and would only admit to being ill when we were near death.

When I turned seven, all my classmates and my best friend and neighbor Rosita, started preparing for their First Communion. Everybody was learning prayers and planning the ceremony. They talked about lacy long white dresses, fancy shoes, flowers, candied almonds, and presents. My family was making no such plans for me. I was not surprised, since I knew my parents didn't believe in making a fuss over holidays and such, but I really wanted some sort of celebration even if it was small. I kept insisting, I kept asking about making preparations. I must have really pestered my parents, because my mother got angry at me.

"You can't have a First Communion" she told me impatiently. "You are Jewish, and you should never ever, under any circumstances, reveal this to anybody."

Jewish? I had never heard that word without the adjectives *cochino, marrano*, both of which mean pig in Spanish. I was stunned. How could it be that one day I was Catholic like everybody else, and the next day, suddenly, I was Jewish? Could Mother be saying this just to get out of having to prepare for my First Communion? No, I discarded that idea when I took a look at her face. I never again mentioned my First Communion.

Much later, in college, I learned that the word marrano refers to the Jews who stayed in Spain, converted to Catholicism, but secretly kept practicing their religion of belief. As a kid, I only knew being Jewish was somehow related to who we were, that it was humiliating and shameful, and I had to make sure that nobody ever found out our dirty little secret.

This sense of shame and secrecy about who we were and where we came from kept cropping up all through my childhood. Knowing that we couldn't say anything about who we were must have kindled the idea within us that somehow it was sinister and evil. We didn't join the Jewish community in Caracas, we didn't go to the Jewish school, we didn't live in the Jewish neighborhood. I don't know why, but my best guess is that my parents were still traumatized by the fear they experienced during the war, that they kept on pretending to be Catholic much after it stopped being necessary in order to survive.

My sister to this day won't tell anybody that she is Polish and Jewish. Not only has she kept it a secret from her neighbors and acquaintances, but she has never told her husband or her children. When my two nieces were in their late teens, they read my father's memoirs that had just been published in an English translation. The book tells how he had survived the war as a Jew in Poland, by passing as a Pole and a Catholic. When my nieces asked my sister about this, she had her answer ready. She told them he was actually not her father, her father had been a Catholic Pole who died early in the war, in the Warsaw resistance movement. Mother, she told them, remarried very soon after to the man who was the Jewish grandfather they knew all their lives.

Both my nieces believed this story for several years, until we were leafing through a photo album in my house and saw pictures of Father, holding my sister, who was just a tiny baby. Since I knew nothing of my sister's tale, I assured them that the Jewish grandfather they had known all their lives was Susanna's birth father. My nieces seemed neither shocked nor upset. They seemed to gain new understanding of what the family had gone through, especially their mother. They decided never to confront her with this knowledge, and if it ever came up they would insist that she, herself, had told them on some occasion, quite a while ago.

Many years later, I asked my sister when she found out this shameful secret of ours, that is, that we were Jewish. She told me she had suspected for quite a while that something was fishy. We had been going to Mass with the neighbors, but my parents never went. Religion was not mentioned in our house. My sister says she remembers Grandfather praying and using some sort of shawl and saying words in a weird language, but then, that was not a surprise to me, since Catholic prayers were said in Latin, which was also a weird language.

It had never occurred to me that there could be different religions. As far as I knew, everybody in the world was Catholic. When I finally went to live in the United States and began telling my friends, when asked, that I was Jewish, they were always amazed that I didn't know the names of the Jewish Holidays or what their meaning was, or that I had never set foot in a synagogue, or had never attended a Seder. They could not believe such ignorance was actually true. They suspected me of putting them on. I tried to explain to them that most of my life had been spent hiding the fact that we were Jewish, and my parents believed, that the less the children knew the less they could blurt out by mistake. Ignorance at first, and later secrecy, were a way of life for us, even in Venezuela, when it was no longer essential for our survival.

It was a good thing that we did not adhere too closely to any religious teaching, because as far as the Ten Commandments go, I think my sister and I broke all the ones that could be broken without suffering dire consequences. Perhaps the most salient for me was envy. I not only coveted all the toys my best friend Rosita had, her dolls, her doll house, with all the furniture inside it, her tea sets and dishes; I also coveted her clothes, her beautiful lacy dresses, her patent shoes, her bedroom with the white bedspread and embroidered pillows and matching curtains, her stuffed animals piled high on the bed. I coveted her family, I wanted to be part of her household, to be the daughter of her parents. I wanted to participate in the parties, the frequent festive visits from friends and other family members, the easy laughter, the incessant comings and goings and all the preparations that these entailed. I often imagined ways in which I could become an orphan and be found and adopted into her family. My sister also must have wanted a different family, since a few years later she invented a new identity for herself, one she has kept until now.

One year, right before Christmas, Rosita's mother went to visit relatives in Chile and when she returned she brought us each a doll. My doll had a porcelain face and brown hair, the most elegant sheer pink dress, dazzling white socks with lace and black patent shoes. My sister's doll was even more splendid, with blond hair, a little hat that matched her gorgeous blue dress and lacy socks and shoes. Both dolls even had lacy underpants. Rosita's doll looked like a French lady from the Eighteenth Century, with an antique satin dress and her hair piled up on her head, but this time I didn't envy her, I had my own gorgeous doll to admire and play with. My sister and I walked about in a state of rapture for the next few days. But my wish to become part of Rosita's family became more intense.

At Christmastime, all the families in Caracas would put out their nativity scene. My sister and I wanted one badly, but my parents weren't about to spend money on such trifles. We discovered that Sears had small plastic crèche figures that could be bought one piece at a time, and that was what we started doing. But Christmas was approaching fast, and our Nativity scene was a sorry sight. We had managed to buy a little baby Jesus, the crib, the virgin Mary, but we were still missing Joseph, the donkey and all the little sheep, not to mention the manger itself and the three kings. We were getting desperate. Finally my sister approved a plan. Each time we went to buy a figure, we could take something of lesser value, a small sheep, a piggy, or some straw for the manger. We were caught and taken to the manager's office, scolded, told that we would end up in jail for years and not released until we were already old and spent. The crèche was never completed. Our only consolation was that we were allowed to have a tiny plastic Christmas tree with folding branches in our room, which we would put up early in December, decorate carefully and lovingly, and keep until the beginning of spring.

Stealing was not the only commandment we broke. We also lied. We lied whenever we were caught doing something forbidden, hitting another kid, breaking or taking something that wasn't ours. We never admitted where we had been or what we had done, and this became almost a routine. But sometimes we were suspected and blamed for things we didn't do. One day, my mother came back home and discovered that the glass plate that covered the dining room table was broken. She launched into an investigation that lasted for several weeks. We were interrogated for hours, our cousins were brought into this, and the maid, too. I felt especially vulnerable because on rainy days I had allowed my two cousins to play soccer in our dining room. Often, I would even join in. But we never broke the glass plate. Nobody admitted to knowing anything, and much less to having committed this abominable crime. How it happened and who did it remains a mystery still.

Another puzzle cast a shadow over our existence at that time. My aunt lost her ruby and diamond ring, which she took off only to do the dishes. We were questioned again and again. Who had seen it last? Where had it been? Did we perhaps remove it from the bathroom? Or from the shelf above the kitchen sink? Did we take it to play with, perhaps unaware of its worth? Did we see anybody else taking it? My cousins were questioned separately, to see if one of them would break down and confess. Grandfather was interrogated for days on end. And, the poor maid was grilled mercilessly. The ring was never found.

My cousin Adam told me recently how the mystery of the missing ring finally came to be solved a half century later. My aunt, who is now in her eighties and is in a wheelchair, decided to make her way to the upper floor of her house. Thinking she was alone, she used her walker and held on to the banister and with much effort made it to the second floor. She opened the bedroom door and the naked butt of her eighty two year-old husband, moving rhythmically up and down, was right in front of her eyes. Under him, on the bed, was the day nurse, a strapping redhead who had been caring for my aunt during the last few months. My aunt lifted the walker high over her head and brought it down with all her might on my unsuspecting uncle. She whacked his back and his head really hard, opening a large gash on his bald spot. Blood gushed all over the bed. Luckily, there was a nurse at hand, who took immediate action. An ambulance was called. My uncle was rushed to the emergency room of a nearby hospital. His head wound required a large number of stitches.

That evening, when he returned home, my uncle was in a dark

rage. He brazenly told my aunt not only of this affair, but about all the other maids, secretaries, salesgirls, neighbors and employees, who had been his mistresses through the years. Many years ago, he got one of the maids pregnant and sent her back to the provinces to live with her family. Since he was not a heartless man, he wanted to help her financially when the child arrived, but was afraid to make a sizable withdrawal from the bank because he and my aunt had a joint account. As the maid was leaving for the provinces, impulsively, he gave her my aunt's ruby and diamond ring.

We never knew what would incur Father's wrath, what would make him explode like a volcano and his rage to pour out like hot lava, and what he would simply shrug off and consider too trifling to bother about. Once, when we were playing outside, minding our own business, some neighborhood kids decided to gang up on my sister and beat her up. They knew my sister could make short shrift of them individually, so four of them seized the opportunity and attacked her. They were on top of her in a heap, hitting, pulling her hair, while my sister screamed defiantly, "It doesn't hurt at all, it doesn't hurt." I threw myself on top of the heap, hit wildly with my fists, grabbed and pulled whatever came my way, hair, ears, a shirt sleeve, but couldn't get them to let go. I felt a strange pain in my stomach, as if I was the one getting the beating. I panicked, I was afraid they were going to kill my sister. In despair, I grabbed a large stone and started hitting the boys on top. I landed several hefty blows and, after some more shoving and hitting, they finally dispersed. When our mother and father arrived home that evening, a long line of neighborhood parents was at our door. They had come to complain about my outrageous behavior, which had grown to become a rock throwing spree against innocent kids who just happened to be standing nearby. My parents assured the other parents that we would both be punished to the utmost. But they only admonished us to stay away from these kids, to keep out of trouble in the future and not make any waves.

The last thing my family wanted was to call attention to themselves. They had the immigrant's dread of being noticed by the authorities. Their maxim was to lie low and never make any waves. Their fear of officialdom bordered on paranoia and it extended to minor figures, even concierges, security guards, social workers, and teachers. Many a time I heard my father or my uncle say "soon we will buy a new car, but don't tell anybody," or "this summer we'll take a vacation, but keep it a secret." The last time I visited Venezuela, still traveling on a Venezuelan passport, in the seventies, I stood for hours in a long line to get a stamp on my passport showing I didn't owe any back taxes, thus allowing me to leave the country. As I was waiting in line, wishing to be somewhere else and hating every second of this ordeal, I noticed an old couple discreetly signaling to me. They both wore overcoats in spite of the afternoon heat, the woman had a kerchief covering her head, the man wore a hat, and dark glasses. To my astonishment, I recognized my aunt Alina and her husband Bronek. I rushed to greet them with hugs and kisses only to be rebuked by my uncle who whispered, "Please, please, Rebecca, pipe down. Don't tell anybody you saw us here. We are going to Israel for a week, for the first time in our life, and we don't want anybody to find out." I never discovered who and what they were afraid of, here in Venezuela, in the seventies, but I complied with my uncle's wishes and went back to my place in line.

I must admit I have inherited some of that fear of authority, even though I try to extinguish even the slightest manifestation of this trait I find so detestable. I remember walking down a street in Warsaw in the late sixties, with my friend Steven, who speaks perfect Polish and teaches it at an American university, even though he was born and raised in Wyoming and his ancestors came from Great Britain before the revolution, when suddenly we were stopped by a couple of men in military uniform who barked the order "Show your identification." I immediately started rummaging through my backpack to show my passport and visa, but before I could come up with all the documents that proved my right to be where I was, I heard Steven bark back "Who the hell are you? What right do you have to demand to see our documents? I want to see your badges at once! Give me your name, rank, and name of your superior!" I don't know whether it was this response, so utterly American, or Steven's very American looks, or his slightly foreign accent in his otherwise perfect Polish, but the two military men gushed forth with an agitated outpouring of apologies and beseeched us to forget the incident had ever happened. It is this quality I admire so much in my American friends. I call it their 'divine right to be,' to take up whatever space they find themselves in. Maybe it comes from being born and growing up in such a large country, or from never having been invaded by a foreign power. Or maybe it is the result of living for so long in a democracy, where power is vested in the people. Whatever the cause, I certainly would like some of that attitude to rub off on me. I would like to feel some of that sense of innate legitimacy that has been denied for so long to immigrants and Jews. I have always felt I was an outsider wherever I lived, and for that reason had to be twice as careful not to break any rules.

However, when I was a kid and my sister was with me, we delighted in breaking rules, but only as long as we thought we would never be found out. I always felt this sense of excitement when I was with her, and at the same time felt safe, because I knew she would take the blame for whatever happened, if we were ever discovered. My sister always had her own ideas about what she wanted to do and felt unfettered by silly rules, and I always fell in with her plans. We found we could attend any school events we wanted, including day-long trips to all kinds of interesting places, by forging Mother's signature on school notes. She would never allow us to travel anywhere in a school bus. She had warned us repeatedly about the dangers.

"Don't even ask! I am not going to allow any daughters of mine to go by school bus to the provinces. I know those old buses, the brakes will fail and the bus will careen full speed down a steep grade, ending up in a heap at the bottom of a deep ravine after turning over twenty times. Then the gas tank is going to explode and you will all burn to death. Good God, nobody will be able to recognize the charred bodies, so I won't find out that you are both dead until the week after. Who knows, we might even have to delay the burial until then. We might not have the remains to bury."

Her fears may have been justified because school buses in Caracas were notoriously old and decrepit. But we didn't let these warnings deter us. I became an expert forging notes to teachers, not only excusing our absences, but also giving permission for different outings, all signed with my mother's name. I did this quite innocently at first. Whenever a note was required my mother would ask me to write it, since my knowledge of Spanish was so much better than hers. Then she would attach her name to it. Soon we figured we didn't need to bother her with all these trifles, and I would do it all myself. My sister always delegated this job to me because my handwriting was so much more legible and prettier than hers.

I felt lucky that my sister had confidence in me, that she trusted me enough to include me in all her ventures. I loved the feeling that we were a team, that we stood together, belonged to each other, had each other to love and to rely on. The bond created between chil-dren who are neglected is very strong. It was not until many years later that I realized that this was my reality, not hers. I always had my sister there, ready to love and protect me, she was my security blan-ket, my mentor, my teacher, my idol. I worshipped her. I don't think she realizes to this date the enormous power she holds in my heart.

But recently I realized her reality must have been very different from mine. There was nobody around us she could trust or rely on. She didn't have anybody to go to with her own troubles. I often won-dered whether her one-sided attachments as an adult mirror this relationship of our childhood. She finds it easy to love those who need her help and protection. She surrounds herself with beings who are unequipped to deal with life, children, the weak, the helpless, the broken-hearted, and of course, her cats. Her childhood wounds run too deep to allow her to develop love or a friendship of equals. That, she finds much too threatening. She learned her lessons well, she doesn't trust or rely on anybody, she doesn't ask for love and doesn't expect to get it.

Susanna

Finally we were in a place where we could linger a while. Our nomadic existence came to a physical end, but not to a real end. Father's constant talk about moving on poisoned our hopes of ever achieving any stability. Our family did not live in a house, it camped out. We had no permanent furniture. Everything was thrown together, helter-skelter, as if the bags might be packed at a moment's notice and we might have to emigrate again. Father just couldn't settle down, he constantly talked about moving back to Europe, or some other god-forsaken place. My sister and I loved Venezuela. We didn't want to go to Europe, or anywhere else.

At first, we lived with my father's older sister Alina and her family. That is, if you can call it living. Nine of us were crammed into a tiny flat in the poor section of town. As usual, Father made everyone miserable. We were guests of his sister, but that didn't stop him. He bullied and bossed her mild mannered husband Bronek. He beat her children and was disrespectful to his own father, who also lived there, calling him dim witted and dumb. Father believed respect and power were the same thing and that it was acquired by instilling fear in others. He actually once told me that he admired the way the Germans inspired respect in other people. Can you imagine that! Respect, my foot! They inspired mortal fear, and with good reason too.

We did not attend school when we first arrived. Perhaps it was summer vacation. Jammed into that little flat, we could not get away from our obnoxious parents. We were thoroughly cowed and nearly afraid to breathe. Father exploded at every opportunity. It didn't matter that we followed his orders to the letter. He always found something to rage about. Sometimes, Grandfather saved us by taking all the children to the park. It was only a short walk away, which was a godsend, since Grandfather had never learned to drive.

The park had no swings or playground equipment. But that was not important. We were away from the hollering and cursing. There were many large shady trees and a nice fountain. Grandfather would sit on a bench, unbutton the top of his trousers (they were too tight, but no one would move the buttons for him) and hide behind a newspaper that he could not read. No, he was not illiterate, the paper was in Spanish, a language he did not know. He would doze off, concealed by the newspaper. We were on our own. As the eldest, I felt responsible for the other children. It didn't worry me, I was used to looking after my little sister, who was a nice obedient child, always eager to please and do the right thing, not given to straying or engaging in forbidden activities. Danny, my youngest cousin, was a mischief maker. He must have been about two and a half or three, very smart, adventurous and very naughty. His brother, Adam, older than Rebecca, but younger than I, was a huge help. He was used to doing for his bratty brother what I did for my sweet, obedient baby sister. Between us we saw to it that the little ones came to no harm and never disturbed Grandfather. We would have liked to play with the other children who came to the park, but I knew better. It was our duty to make sure that nothing happened to our siblings, even though Grandfather, not us, would be blamed. If something happened, the outings to the park would come to an abrupt end. We would lose the only bright spot in our day.

Grandfather was blamed for many things, some that took place years ago. Whenever my aunt Alina became angry, she would bring up this story from her childhood. Grandfather, together with his wife and their five children, was living in a small village in eastern Poland. One night, he went out with his buddies to have a few drinks in the village tavern, and didn't come back. Grandmother was very worried, she was beside herself. At dawn, she went from house to house, trying to find him. Finally, a neighbor told her that all the able-bodied men who had been drinking in the tavern that night either volunteered or were taken by force and conscripted into the army. My grandfather did not return for eight years. He claimed he wrote several letters, but none reached my grandmother. He fought the Red Army for several years. He was shot in the leg, sent to a hospital, where he languished for almost a year. Then, he was interned in a hard labor camp in Siberia. When he was finally released, he started making his way back home. Russia was in the throes of enormous upheaval. Travel was very difficult at that time. Armed bands of revolutionaries, bandits and displaced soldiers were roving the land. When Grandfather finally arrived in his village, he found that his wife and children had been unable to make it without him, and were no longer there. To keep from starving, the family had split up. Some of the children had been taken in by relatives who lived in other towns. Grandmother was in a hospice, dying of tuberculosis. Her oldest daughter was working nearby and taking care of her. My aunt Alina had moved to Lvov, where she worked as a beautician, and where she later met and married my uncle Bronek. She never quite forgave Grandfather for his desertion. She kept bringing this up whenever she was vexed with him, until the day he died. My father, the youngest of the five, had been taken in by his school teacher. When the school year ended, the priest in the next large town allowed him to live on the church grounds and attend classes in the high school, in exchange for keeping the buildings and the yard clean.

It was here that my father learned the skills that later, when all Polish Jews were being rounded up for extermination, helped him pass off flawlessly as a Catholic. And it was here that Father came years later, to ask the old priest for the christening documents that saved our family. The priest took a large heavy key from the pocket of his cassock, unlocked a drawer, removed a stack of these certificates, which he signed and stamped with the seal of the Catholic Church. He then returned them to the drawer, but did not lock it. He looked at my father sternly and said, "I can not in good conscience disobey the Catholic Church and justify committing such an act." Having said this, he politely asked my father whether he would like some tea, then left the room to look for the housekeeper. A quarter of an hour later, he returned balancing in his hands a large tray with a steaming copper kettle and a couple of tall glasses.

After his stay in the church, Father moved to Krakow, where he entered the Jagellonian University to study law. His older brother, my uncle Stasik, left for Russia to join some distant relatives. Poor Grandfather was never again able to get his whole family together.

The next time Grandfather incurred the wrath of the family

was in France, right after the war. My aunt Alina, her husband Bronek, their three year-old son Adam, and their new-born baby Daniel were living with Grandfather in Paris, as war refugees. The French had extended them a temporary visa for six months while they were waiting to be admitted into some South American country, where they would be allowed to stay permanently. One cold winter day, Grandfather took Adam for a walk down one of the quays on the river Seine. Adam kept running ahead and cavorting on the icy path, when suddenly he slipped and fell into the freezing waters of the river. Grandfather didn't know how to swim and, in a panic, ran to get help. But he didn't speak French. All he could do was to drag people over to the river bank and point. Luckily, an American soldier who had seen the incident from a nearby bridge ran to the spot and jumped in. The water was murky, but he managed to grab Adam by the hair, and in no time had him out. A small crowd formed around them. A couple of people wrapped their coats around Adam and the American soldier. Somebody produced a flask of brandy. Then the whole group accompanied Grandfather, who was carrying Adam, to the apartment. Using broken English, French, and lots of gestures, they all recounted the whole nerve-wracking tale to my aunt. At first aunt Alina burst into tears, but after she ascertained that her father and son were all right, she became livid with anger and didn't stop reproaching and berating Grandfather for weeks. Grandfather was never allowed to go out alone with Adam again.

By the time our family reached Venezuela, my aunt Alina was working as a cosmetician and had clients who came to the apartment to try out and buy lotions and creams. Adam was in school, but Danny was too young to attend even kindergarten. She couldn't have a three-year-old brat running around at all times, so Danny was left in Grandfather's care. Danny took full advantage of grandfather's inattention and did exactly as he pleased. Only his high intelligence and common sense kept him from serious harm. It was 1949, and Grandfather, who was about seventy-five, must have been senile. The adults were extremely disrespectful, even offensive, when they addressed him. But then, they were no different when they addressed each other. Even that little snot Danny was disrespectful to poor old Grandfather. Only Adam worshipped his grandfather. He always treated him with the greatest respect and affection, until the day Grandfather died in 1960.

Within a few months, we had worn out our welcome and moved to our own house, a rented place in a quiet neighborhood far from the center of the city. The parents never bought a home in Venezuela, even though they had plenty of chances. Father was too stingy to spend money on something the family would enjoy. Our rented house was in a newer part of town, near a field where Chinese immigrants were growing vegetables. We lived in an enormous duplex that had a tiny yard. On the other side of the duplex lived the Villareal family, husband, wife, and five children. Three of the boys were older than I, one was younger, and Rosita, the only girl, was five, my little sister's age. These children became our first friends in our new country.

That fall we started school. My little sister wanted to go to the same school with her best friend, Rosita. She attended one of the oldest academies in Caracas, a girls school, run by Carmelite nuns in a convent. One morning, Mother told us to put on our best dresses and we rode the bus to the convent school. We were ushered in and told to sit in the vestibule, a clean, bare little room with a holy water well by the door, a crucifix on the wall, and a beautifully carved wooden bench, where my little sister and I waited while Mother disappeared behind a dark wooden door with the Mother Superior. I liked sitting in that room with my little sister, who was unusually quiet and looking solemn. Shortly, Mother, appearing hot and disheveled, returned from her interview with Mother Superior. We were escorted to the door by one of the nuns. We never got to attend the convent where Rosita went to school. Next week, we started classes at a public school. I liked it, and so did my little sister. Perhaps it was good we didn't end up in the convent school as I had a penchant for asking irritating questions of the old priest who taught religion in our public school.

One day during the hour-long daily religion class, the priest told us to pray extra hard and long to win the spelling bee we had the next day. I put my hand up.

"If I pray extra hard and long, will I win for sure? If I win, does it mean that the other kids didn't pray hard enough? Does God keep score?"

"God doesn't need to keep score. He knows who prayed the hardest. It has to do with devotion, more than with the length of the prayer. He knows who is the most devout and he will reward that child," the priest answered reluctantly.

But I wasn't satisfied with this answer. It didn't make sense "What if we all pray really hard? Who will win and who will lose then? And why do we need to study for the spelling bee if it is in God's hands?"

"God will decide, it is always in His hands. Now stop interrupting and let's get back to our texts." Now he really seemed angry.

I shut up, but I wasn't happy with his answer. I kept thinking about this business of prayer. What if there was a tornado and the people in one house pray really hard so their wishes get granted and the tornado turns in another direction and hits another house, killing all the other people inside? Does that mean the other people didn't pray hard enough? Or perhaps they were not Catholic? But what if they did pray? How does God choose between the prayers? Could it be the length of time, the loudness, the number of people praying? I made a mental note to ask in the next class.

It turned out to be a lousy idea. The old cantankerous priest became incensed. I was told to leave the room and not come back until I could behave myself and not ask any more stupid questions. I came back just a few minutes before the bell rang. From then on I kept my mouth shut and I never again asked any questions. But word spread that I had been kicked out of religion class. Nobody ever got kicked out of religion class. I got a reputation as a troublemaker, even though I never again did anything to annoy any of the teachers. But I did learn to keep my questions and my thoughts to myself. That worked well at school and at home.

Our next-door neighbor Mr. Villareal was also a bully, although he was not as irrational and volcanic as Father. He used to beat the four boys with his belt, but he never touched Rosita, his only daughter. The boys probably deserved it. They were not afraid of their father and were lively and wild, always getting into trouble and finding new ways to annoy everyone.

I worshipped Magali Villareal, his wife, who was the youngest girl in a family from Margarita Island and had married when she was fourteen. She was at least fifteen years her husband's junior. She was beautiful. She was short and slight and had the shiniest black hair I had ever seen, large black eyes, and high cheekbones. She was twenty seven when we met and not yet pregnant with her last child, a girl born two years later. I followed Magali everywhere she went in the house and listened to her talk to me as she sewed.

She hand embroidered the most exquisite dresses for Rosita, and later made the layette for the last baby. Rebecca and Rosita, who were the same age and had similarly sweet temperaments, played together and got along beautifully. Magali never made derogatory remarks about our parents. But she taught us by her kindness and patience, that there were other ways to raise children. She even tried to teach me manners, God bless her! I was a true little savage.

Three years later, we when we moved away to another part of town, it was Magali that I missed the most. It was from her that I had learned how to be a mother. I already knew how not to be one from my own mother.

It was there, in Las Fuentes, where Mother used to leave us alone in the house in the evenings that I learned to always fend for myself. That is the most useful thing I ever learned. I have never faltered. We would return home from school to an empty house. Even the maid was gone (oh yes, Mother always had a maid). We would have been happy to be alone, but unfortunately, the house was full of terrifying strangers. Our thrifty parents rented out rooms to boarders. There were three extra rooms. One was kept locked. The German porcelain and crystal, which the parents imported and sold, was placed there for safekeeping. The other two rooms were rented out to a Polish couple and a Dutchman. I thoroughly disliked the Polish woman, who was rude to us, and threatened us with all kinds of horrors if we told about her forays into the locked porcelain room. As if we would tell our parents anything! They wouldn't believe us anyway, they constantly belittled our opinions. Even when they knew that what we said was true, they would call us liars, because they did not want to take action to correct the situation. We learned to say nothing. Eventually, we paid dearly for our silence. We both have damaged hearts, from rheumatic fever caused by strep throat, because we would not report our sore throats to the enemy. We had to be dying to tell the parents anything. For heavens' sake, my little sister was molested by her piano teacher for several years. When she told Mother, she was not believed. We knew from an early age that asking for help would get us nothing, only scoldings and recriminations. So we learned never to ask. My little sister thinks the parents were too busy and preoccupied with their lives in a new and strange country to concern themselves with our needs. But I think they felt just like that German maid in Berlin who always told us

"I know what you want, you brat, and you can't have it".

I hated the Polish woman who rented a room in our house, but I was absolutely terrified of the poor old Dutchman who never harmed us, never came into our room, hardly ever spoke to us. To this day, I cannot understand why, but I still feel an irrational fear when I think of him. Perhaps it was his appearance. He was tall, stooped, cadaverously thin, pale, and wore a wig. Perhaps he reminded me of the image of a mad-scientist or ax-murderer hidden in my subconscious. There was something that screamed insanity about his stooped, shuffling gait. One night when we were left alone, right after a torrential rain storm, there was a blackout in our neighborhood. My little sister and I were climbing the steep stairs to go to bed, each holding a candle, when we spied a large man in a trench coat and hat standing on our balcony. We were paralyzed with terror. We stood on the stairs for several minutes, which seemed like hours, without moving a single muscle, or making the slightest noise. A sudden gust of gale-like wind blew the trench coat to the floor and the hat off the balcony. It turned out that the Dutchman had come home dripping wet and had hung his long raincoat and hat on a nail on the balcony to dry, before going out again. We were extremely relieved, of course, to find out that our monster was imaginary. But we were still scared enough to go next door to the Villareals to await for power to be restored. To my great relief, the Dutchman did not stay too long. The parents expanded the porcelain business, which they had recently begun, and eventually ended up evicting all the tenants, and the porcelain dwelled in their place. We were not afraid of the porcelain. It was a welcome change.

One of the duties I hated with all my heart was accompanying Father on errands. Mother, who was always afraid he would stop for a visit with whoever was his current mistress, thought that if I went with him Father's indiscretions would be foiled. Well, she couldn't have been more mistaken. Father would tell me he had to deliver something in this or that neighborhood, and make me wait in the car, sometimes for more than an hour. I would be bored out of my mind, sitting in the hot car, sweating, looking out the car window every minute, waiting for him to reappear. I learned to bring along a comic book to keep myself entertained. Father told me that this was our secret. If Mother asked, I was to say that there had been a enormous traffic jam, or road work on the freeway. As if I didn't know what he was up to. Once one of his floozies actually came down to the car to say good-bye to him, and gave me a small half-full bottle of a strong smelling perfume. I tossed it out the car window as soon as we were out of view.

Every so often Mother would have to go to the hospital for a few days because of what everybody called "female trouble." At first, I had no idea what was going on. But once I overheard Mother fighting with Father about some remedies my aunt had suggested for avoiding babies. As I listened more carefully, I finally understood all her hospital trips. She was having abortions. Neither of my parents wanted more children. This was their contraception method, an abortion every few months. When I finally told my little sister she couldn't stand looking at Mother for several days. After that, every time Mother went to the hospital, we would fantasize in our room at night, making up names for the baby that would never come.

Around this time, my baby sister started sleepwalking. I was afraid she would hurt herself. Once she opened the front door and went outside. I didn't know if I should wake her up. I had read in one of my books you weren't supposed to do that. She stood on the sidewalk for several minutes, in her faded pink nightgown that had become too short, looking up at the moon. But before I could intervene, she turned and slowly retraced her steps. She stopped at the top of the stairway and looked down and, for one terrifying moment I thought she was going to come tumbling down, but then she walked back to her bed and let me tuck her in. I trained myself to sleep lightly so that I would wake as soon as she got up. Luckily, no harm came to her and by the time we moved to the East side of the city she had stopped wandering around in her sleep.

I detested the continuous air of misery and catastrophe in our home. The constant expectation of disaster. When Father was a few minutes late coming from the store, Mother started fretting that he had been in a car accident. If we didn't come as soon as she called, she would get hysterical and imagine us lying in a pool of blood in the middle of the street. She always expected and predicted the worst. The few times she was rewarded and something did happen, she almost gloated in her repetitious chorus "I told you so, I told you not to do this, but nobody ever listens to me." Then she would call aunt Alina and retell the story several times from beginning to end repeating "I knew this would happen, but nobody ever listens to me." Every incident was a calamity and she was always the one to suffer more deeply and longer than anybody else. If my little sister skinned her knee, my mother was the one who had to bear the injury. It was something we had done to her, on purpose, in spite of her constant warnings. Things like that happened, she would moan, because we were careless and had no regard or consideration for her feelings, and this after all she had suffered and endured during the war.

Once we dared to asked for roller skates. "How could you even think of asking for something that is an accident waiting to happen, something that might kill you, or at least cripple you, break both your legs, and then you will require care for the rest of your life. Who do you think will take care of you? I will for a while, but what about after I die? This will shorten my life by several years. It will give me a fatal heart attack!" That we already had bicycles and had been riding them everywhere for several years did not matter. Roller-skates were the devil's plan to ruin my mother's life.

Eventually, we did get skates. Our neighbors, the Villareals, who had seen us watching with longing as their kids skated, gave us each a pair for Christmas. The Villareal kids skated to their hearts content, and I never saw their parents have a heart attack over it, even when the kids fell and skinned their knee.

When my little sister was in second grade, she was selected to participate in a school folk dance performance. She was so excited she couldn't talk about anything else. She taught me the words of the songs and all the dance steps, and practiced every day after school in the kitchen, with me as partner. A couple of weeks before the big day, Rebecca brought home a note from the dance teacher informing parents that they were expected to pay for the costume. The cost was small, perhaps the equivalent of ten dollars today. All that was needed was a white cotton blouse, a brightly colored full skirt, and the typical Venezuelan black cloth slippers called *alpargatas*. Rebecca showed the note to Mother, expecting this to be quite all right because the parents could easily afford such an expense.

"Why doesn't the school pay? If they want to have a performance and want you to dance in it, why do we have to pay for the costume?" Mother whined. "I certainly can not go to your father with such a request. He will get angry and scream at all of us and with very good reason. We can't waste hard-earned money on such trivialities. Absolutely not! I don't want to hear one more word about this ridiculous idea. If you want this so badly, you go and ask —no, demand that the school buy the costume."

Rebecca fled to our bedroom and started crying quietly. At school, we were among the families that were considered well-off. We did not qualify for free bus passes or free lunches. There was no chance that the school would provide the money. I had to come up with a plan before the deadline, only ten days away.

We pooled our resources. We reluctantly broke Rebecca's ceramic piggy bank, a Christmas present from her best friend Rosita. We counted and recounted all the coins and added up all the money we had been saving for books, but it wasn't enough. We stopped buying candy bars and comic books. We started walking home after school instead of taking the bus. Five days into the plan, we were still far from our goal. We sold some of our toys to classmates for a few pennies, we even sold our lunch-bags. The deadline was approaching fast and we were still short.

I wracked my brain, but nothing I could think of was feasible. We couldn't ask our aunt or uncle because they would tell the parents. We couldn't borrow from the neighbors; I didn't want them to pity us. We had nothing left that was worth selling and there was no paid work we could do. The situation was serious.

On the day the money was to be collected, we were still a couple of dollars from our goal. I said the best thing would be to tell the teacher about this shortfall. Rebecca believed that pretending she had forgotten the money would be better. It was Friday, she reasoned, and we would have an additional weekend to collect money or think of some other plan. We had tried everything we could think of. I knew she was fooling herself.

My little sister went to school without the money. When the dance teacher came to the classroom during her first class, Rebecca was told to turn the money in before noon, or else she wouldn't be allowed to dance. She ran all the way home, crying. When the maid opened the door, to find Rebecca back so early in the morning and with tears in her eyes, she asked what was the matter. Rebecca blurted out the whole story. The maid went to the kitchen, rummaged in her purse for a couple of minutes, and came up with a couple of crumpled bills that made up the remainder of the money. Rebecca ran all the way back to school, and just beat the deadline. The day of the dance Rebecca was radiant. She looked beautiful in her red skirt and her snow white blouse. Her feet, clad in the black sandals, hardly seemed to touch the ground, she danced like an angel and wore an ecstatic smile through the whole performance. We paid the maid back a little at a time. Mother never bothered to find out where we got the money. She must have assumed the school paid for the clothing after all.

I still get angry when I think of this incident. I can't help it. Rebecca, little goody-two-shoes, thinks Mother was so scared of Father's anger that she couldn't bring herself to see how important certain things were to us, that all she was trying to do was maintain peace at any cost. But I knew better. I never forgave Mother. I knew she didn't care about us. She told us she had a difficult childhood, she had suffered during the war, she had been deprived of a normal life. As if that was justification for her behavior. She couldn't stand the idea that we could have a better life. The truth is that she wanted to deprive us of our happiness, because she had been deprived of hers.

Mother's histrionics and lamentations were just a way to hide her deficiencies and deflect her guilt for being inadequate. She was always in a panic, thinking that somebody would find out she was a lousy mother. That's why she became hysterical if we were injured or sick. She was afraid it would reflect badly on her. When she was busy with her own concerns, when it was not convenient for her to take care of us, she would leave us alone without a second thought. She let us take public buses all over the city, she let us go to school alone when I was only in third grade and my little sister in first grade. In the afternoons and evenings, she left us by ourselves at home and didn't return until after ten. She didn't mind that we were alone until all hours of the night, what dangers we could be exposed to. It was a miracle that nothing awful happened. She didn't even consider that my little sister's piano teacher was molesting her. She didn't bother to find out what was happening. She just dismissed the whole problem because she didn't want to trouble herself with us. That's who she really was, a fake, a phony. Not at all like the facade of a concerned and worried mother she tried to project to the rest of the world, to family and friends.

A lot of the things Mother did drove me crazy. Some I attributed to her being Jewish. Her constant complaining, moaning and groaning, the air of sacrifice and tragedy, the expectancy of calamity. She had the nerve to forbid us to run, to ride roller skates, climb trees. And she would scream and carry on like it was the end of the world if one of us was slightly injured or sick. Go figure. It took me years to understand that there was no contradiction here. Mother's upbringing was such that she believed she had to smother us in order to appear, in front of the family and even perhaps herself, as a caring mother. She had no clue as to any other type of parenting. She never thought of us as real people with our own thoughts and desires. On the rare occasions she remembered she was a mother, she would start frenzied activity to thwart us, restrain us, put limits on us, stop us from doing anything that made her uncomfortable. That was the only behavior she could come up with in her limited repertoire. That, and bemoaning all the sacrifice and suffering she had to endure to bring up two daughters in such adverse conditions, in what she called a dreadful, uncivilized country.

Before I was ten, I lost the last shred of respect for Mother. Even though I was not openly disobedient or disrespectful, I felt only contempt for her. I was too young to feel pity. That would come much later. Children tend to see everything in black and white, and are quick to judge and slow to forgive. My sister thinks Mother was not aware of what she did or failed to do to us, because she lived in unspeakable fear that blinded her to all things that were not related to her great obsession, Father. But I know better. Many a time she called me cold, standoffish, and unloving. True! I gave as good as I got. She must have realized the true outrageousness of her behavior, but could not change it. No more than an alcoholic or a drug addict can kick the habit. When she tried to befriend me, which she did very rarely, she got total rejection. I treated her with the same utter contempt that Father treated her. She recognized the signs all right, but was helpless to deal with the situation. We declared a truce and tiptoed around each other like two enemy nations that must trade with each other for mutual survival. She couldn't resist sniping at me occasionally, though, and always received looks of utter contempt, which made her complain that I was cold, detached, and unloving. Sometimes she made me mad, which she thoroughly enjoyed. It was a victory of sorts. It meant I couldn't ignore her. Then I would throw a tantrum, scream and yell at her like a Banshee, just as Father did. I did learn something from him. That always had the effect I wanted. She would get scared and leave me alone.

We spent our waking hours trying to avoid our parents. When they were home we went out, but as soon as they were gone we would return. Their constant vicious fighting frightened us. We were always at the edge of a great abyss. We never knew when or what would set Father off. Every night, we heard yelling and cursing. Father would threaten to leave us, Mother would grab a knife and threaten suicide. We went to bed not knowing what we would find the next morning. An empty house? Would Father abandon the family? Would he murder Mother before leaving? Or would she commit suicide?

One night, when the yelling and crying was particularly violent, my baby sister asked me what would happen to us if Mother killed herself.

"Don't worry," I said, after thinking for a while, "things wouldn't change much. You and I can manage fine. We already make dinner every night, we put ourselves to bed. We can do the shopping, too, if Father gives us the money."

"But what if Father left us?" I didn't know what to say. I tried to sound reassuring "We still have a lot of porcelain in the other room. That's worth quite a bit. We could sell it."

"But what if we ran out of porcelain? What would we do then?"

"We could sell the furniture, little by little. By the time we sold everything I would be much older and could start earning money." She looked at me doubtfully. She was not convinced. "I could be a mother's helper, I could babysit."

"But who would take care of me?" I heard tears in her voice.

"Don't worry, baby. You'd always come first. You could help me babysit. Okay? Don't worry. Go to sleep."

We covered our ears with pillows to muffle the shouting. My little sister sung herself a lullaby very softly, while I dreamed of escape.

Rebecca

We moved to the east end of the city, a new area of tall modern buildings erected recently where farmland had existed before. Now we were far away from our only friends, the Villareals. Without them, we no longer went to Mass on Sundays, we didn't even bother to find out where the nearest church was. I missed Rosita terribly, she was my best friend. I no longer had anybody to play with. On the first Saturday after we moved, the Villareals promised to bring Rosita in the afternoon to play. I sat on the curb waiting, looking at all the cars that came around the corner. When it got dark I went inside. She never came.

Our apartment was on the second floor of a new building. Upstairs lived Grandfather, Aunt Alina, Uncle Bronek, and my two cousins, Adam and Danny. The apartment was small, a long dark room that served as a living and dining area, two bedrooms with a bathroom in between, a large kitchen and maid's quarters. My sister and I again shared a bedroom.

I can't understand why, but instead of enrolling us in a public school, our parents sent us to a German Lutheran school. The school was very inexpensive and not far away, only a twenty minute walk from where we lived. I was in fourth grade and my sister in sixth, but even though we were in the same classroom, we weren't allowed to sit together. Fourth grade kids sat by the wall next to the door, fifth graders sat in the middle row and the sixth grade sat by the windows. I watched Susanna, longing to be next to her, so we could chat and help each other, but most of the time she kept her eyes focused on the horizon, beyond the window. We didn't make any new friends in that school, we kept to ourselves.

Susanna taught me to do her homework, which I enjoyed doing. At first, she had to give me a few instructions, but after a while I got the hang of it and I would hurry to finish my assignment so that I could start on hers. It was always more interesting. I took extra care with my handwriting so that the letters would came out plump and beautiful and never strayed from the line. I checked and rechecked all the arithmetic so there wouldn't be any mistakes in her math problems. Sometimes she would even allow me to read a chapter or two in her history and geography books, so I could accurately answer the questions at the end. I felt proud and privileged that she had entrusted me with such important duties. Now she could use her free time to daydream and read her beloved books in English. I knew I was earning her good will and affection, and that meant the world to me.

Caracas had one public library, the National Library, but books were not allowed to leave the premises and children were not permitted inside. Fortunately, the American bookstore was only a few blocks away from our apartment. Most afternoons we browsed through the shelves, choosing the book we would buy that week. By now the staff knew us well and would suggest books. When there was a sale they saved the best books for us. My sister could read an entire book in English in a couple of days, without resorting to a dictionary.

One day, when we were at the bookstore, the manager told us about a book lending club. Children could not become members, he said, but he would personally sponsor us to get around this restriction. We could borrow up to ten books every month and pay only ten bolivars. My sister and I were ecstatic, we became the most assiduous readers in the club. Not one month went by that we didn't borrow the ten books allotted. Reading was our escape to interesting and exotic places, our passport to a wider world. Because of what we learned from books, school was easy and we were excellent students. Our parents never once had to go talk to our teachers and never once set foot in our school. This arrangement made everybody happy. Our parents, who were too busy and too tired in the evenings, would have considered it a chore and an imposition. The teachers, who had sixty children in each classroom were grateful for my parents absence. My sister and I wanted to keep our school world separate from the strife of our home life. Years later, when I graduated from high school, I never told our parents, and they never thought to ask.

When we moved to the east side of the city, we started playing

more with Adam and Danny, who lived upstairs in the same apartment building. My cousins were under much stricter supervision
than my sister and I. We were allowed to roam freely at all times of
the day, and even late at night. Nobody was ever home and we did-
n't have to account for our actions. My cousins had to do their
homework right after school, before they could come out to play. My
aunt made sure that this regimen was adhered to, and when she was-
n't home, the maid, Edda, policed my cousins' activities. When my
aunt was helping her husband at the store, they had to report by
phone every hour. If they were found outside playing when they
were supposed to be home studying, my aunt would hit them over
the head with whatever object she had in her hand, a newspaper, a
magazine, or her purse, and berate them loudly in front of everybody. "You dumb oxen, you will never amount to anything, you'll be
shoe maker's apprentices all your lives, and who will take care of
you then? Not I, I'll probably be dead from all the pain you are
inflicting on me now. And, worse yet, you'll never be able to take
care of me, in my old age. Why is God punishing me like this? What
have I done to anger Him? I took care of my own father, and my sick
mother too, who died in my arms."

This difference in the philosophy of child rearing was a bone of
contention between our families, and the cause of much bickering.
My aunt said that my parents were negligent and allowed us too
much freedom, especially considering that we were girls. All that
freedom would end in disaster, or even worse, spoil our marriage
prospects. We would become too willful and independent to entice
a worthy young man to marry us. My parents felt aunt Alina was
overprotective and meddlesome, especially when she dared to criticize them. My sister and I felt proud that we managed so well by
ourselves. We didn't want anybody looking over our shoulders.

My cousins were good at dodging supervision and devised complicated schemes to fool their mother into believing they were home
studying. They would unhook the phone, then call their mother from
the corner grocery store and say the phone wasn't working at home
but they were on their way up to the apartment to do homework.
Then, we had the whole afternoon to play, ride bicycles, roller skate
and invent all kinds of games. We just had to make sure that Danny
and Adam were back in the apartment before their parents returned.

Danny was my favorite playmate. When it rained, we would
spend the whole afternoon in my room playing with dolls. When I

was eight and he was only seven, he enlightened me about where babies come from and how they are made. "The daddy pees baby seeds into the hole in between the legs of the mommy" he told me, with great assurance. "The baby grows inside her until it is a year old, then it comes out from the same place, screaming". "Why screaming?" I asked. "Because he is drowning in pee." Danny had a reputation for having an unbridled imagination. He was always the first to see flying saucers and talk to little green men from Mars. At first, I didn't want to believe him. My father wouldn't do anything like this to my mother. I waited for my sister to come back from school and asked her, in tears, whether this was true. My worst fears were confirmed. Danny's information on sex turned out to be mostly accurate. From the time he was a toddler, he displayed a special awareness of and curiosity about sex. He was the first to figure out what the Hungarian woman who lived in a downstairs apartment with her five-year-old son did for a living. She was disliked by all the neighbors because she never lost an opportunity to say that she was a countess who had lived in luxury in the old country, but lost everything during the war and now had to suffer in these reduced circumstances among the lower classes. Danny noticed her little boy sitting on the door steps until all hours of the night and wheedled out of him the information that his mother received visits every night from different uncles who gave him a penny to stay outside until they left. Danny lost no time enlightening me with a wealth of detail, what the Hungarian woman did with the uncles. He stole a pair of high- heeled shoes from his mother's closet, then swaying his hips from side to side and imitating the woman's high-pitched voice, in heavily accented Spanish, he intoned "Come into my bedroom, dohlink, I'll show you a good time." He took off his shorts, lay down on my bed, spread his legs, and in a falsetto voice shrieked, "Stick it in, dohlink, stick it in, quick. I want it." I didn't understand, but I laughed at his antics, especially the clever way he imitated her voice and accent. Danny ended his performance by repeating one of aunt Alina's favorite maxims: "Every Chihuahua was a great Dane in the old country."

Danny's most uncanny ability was predicting military takeovers. At first, nobody believed him. But again, his information proved to be correct. One evening Danny warned us not to go to school the next day. A military coup was in the making, he said. My aunt scolded him for making up lies to stay home, a ploy he used on a regular basis. But when we woke up the next morning, airplanes were flying over the city, tanks were rumbling down the streets, and all regular TV programs had been canceled to broadcast speeches by the dictator and his generals, who droned on and on about how the situation was under perfect control and all the rebels had been apprehended. Much later, we found out that Danny listened in on phone conversations between the maid and her boyfriend, who was the chauffeur for a five-star general who took part in the uprising.

Adam, who was fearless and full of outrageous ideas, was the leader when we played outdoors. He invented all kinds of activities to keep us entertained. Climbing high fences and trespassing never deterred him. One of our favorite targets was a nearby golf and tennis club. The manicured green lawns, the well-maintained ponds and sand pits, and the clusters of leafy shade trees were a constant temptation, since we lived in apartment buildings and played on asphalt-covered streets. The club was patrolled by two guards on motorcycles, who hunted us down and kicked us out many a time. We tried to evade them as best we could. As soon as we heard the roar of motorcycles we ran away or hid. Once we climbed a tree and sat, without moving, high up on a branch, waiting for the guard below to leave. He had settled for a beer and snooze under our shady tree. Another time, after we learned that American tennis pros were playing exhibition games in the club, Adam had me climb on his shoulders, straddle the fence and drop to the other side. Once Danny had done the same, Adam climbed the fence and the three of us sauntered nonchalantly toward the tennis courts. As we headed toward the seats in the last row, a security guard asked for our membership number. Adam, undaunted, gave the first number that came into his head. Something about our appearance must have alerted the guard, because fifteen minutes later he came back to escort us to the club office. We were told if we ever sneaked in again, we would be arrested and jailed.

We loved bicycle riding. Adam would get bored quickly riding with two younger kids, so he invented ways to make it difficult and dangerous. He came up with the idea of riding blindfolded, just listening for clues from the street and using our instincts. The person who rode the furthest would be the winner and the prize was everyone else's allowance for that week. The stakes were high. Both Danny and I agreed that Adam should go first, to give us a demonstration. But Adam told us this wasn't fair, we should toss a coin. I lost. Adam covered my eyes with a kitchen towel and I started my ride down the street. Through a tiny slit between my cheeks and the blindfold I could see parked cars on my left. With these as my guide I rode to the corner without falling off the bike. Now, it was Adam's turn. When I tied the kitchen towel around his eyes, I made sure he couldn't see. He started riding down the street, going faster and faster as he gained confidence. But he wasn't riding in a straight line. I was about to warn him, but Danny stopped me. Before we knew it, he had crashed full speed into a parked van. He was unhurt except for a bleeding knee, but the bike was a different story. The front wheel looked like a pretzel, the chain was broken, and the pedals were bent. Adam looked toward the corner and realizing he was still fifty feet away, became enraged and beat us. His knee hurt, his bike was broken, and he had lost the prize. That was more than he could endure. Danny cried when a punch connected with his face, and then wailed even harder because he hadn't gotten a turn. I felt bad for both of my cousins and, to restore peace, confessed I had seen from the side of the blindfold, and wasn't entitled to the purse. Adam immediately brightened up. He hated to lose. He ordered Danny to shut up, telling him he was lucky he didn't get to ride, he could have been killed. Now that the three of us were friends again we had to come up with a story to explain the damage to the bike. Adam thought we should say we left it in the driveway, and a car had run over it. But we would be punished for not caring enough for such expensive toys. I elaborated—we could say we propped the bike up against the wall and a gust of wind threw it onto the driveway, and then a car ran over it. Danny came up with the winning idea. We should say that a car careened full speed around the corner and Adam had just enough time to jump off and save himself, but had to leave the bike on the road. My aunt would be so grateful that Adam had survived, that she would not make a fuss over the broken bike.

Whenever Adam was in charge, most of our games ended in disaster, our knees skinned, our bikes dented or bent out of shape, our clothing ripped. When my aunt came home, we were scolded and punished. We devised a system to minimize the consequences of our transgressions. My aunt, while she beat her own kids and took away their privileges, didn't feel comfortable punishing me with more than a reprimand, so I took the blame for all our pranks. I developed a reputation for being a little savage, while Adam kept intact his role of the injured, innocent child who, against his better judgment, was tempted into mischief by his wild cousin.

One of our favorite friends was a classmate, Enrique, who lived in an old house not far from us. My aunt Alina didn't approve of him because his mother was a servant. Class distinctions, which may seem absurd given our situation as penniless immigrants, nevertheless existed. Enrique was shy, polite, and soft-spoken, having been brought up by the three old-fashioned spinsters his mother worked for. Whenever we went to his house to play, I could tell by the frowns and distressed looks exchanged by the three old spinsters that they didn't approve of us, either. They always wanted us to play in the kitchen, listen to the radio, read stories and color pictures, where they could supervise all our activities. We wanted to play outdoors with our bikes, skates, racquets and balls. My cousins and I must have appeared rough, noisy, and much too wild to them. In the summer we got a guest pass to take Enrique to the swimming pool and, after much hand-wringing and precautionary advice, he was allowed to come with us. We knew how to swim, but Enrique did not. We came up with a game we called 'drowning boy rescue'. We threw Enrique into the deep end of the pool and watched him thrash and sputter until he signaled that he wanted to be rescued, then we would jump in and drag him to the shallow end of the pool. The surprising thing was that he seemed to enjoy it as much as we did. At least, he must have enjoyed all the attention he got, because more often than not, he was the one to suggest we play this game.

One summer afternoon when we were bored and trying to find something to do, we went to look at a nearby construction project. We lived about a block from one of the main arteries in the city, the Avenida Francisco de Miranda. In the eight years we lived there I can't remember a time when this street was not under construction. It seemed that every time one project was finished and the street resurfaced, another one would start and the street would be torn up again. That day we noticed that the workers were pouring cement. Adam came up with an idea. We would return at five, after everybody was gone, jump the fence that separated us from the fresh cement, and walk on the wooden planks laid for the workers. We waited impatiently for the clock to strike five, and soon we were walking on the planks. After a while we became bored just walking, and decided that skipping was better, then we started running, and when we tired of this, we decided to fashion blindfolds by wearing our T-shirts over our heads, and we walked blindfolded. Danny was the first one to fall from the plank into the still-wet cement. He sank down to his knees. Adam and I tried to pull him out, but it was very difficult because we were standing on such narrow boards. We each grabbed Danny by one arm and pulled and pulled, so hard I was afraid his arms would pop out of their sockets. Finally, we dislodged him and he sprang out barefoot, flying full speed, leaving his shoes and socks deep in the wet cement. The force of the pull made us lose our balance, and Adam and I fell backward into the cement on the opposite side of the plank. We managed to extricate ourselves and climb up on the plank, but left two large body imprints in the fresh cement. We couldn't stop laughing, but we were also pretty scared by all the mess we had created and decided not to waste any time trying to recover Danny's shoes and socks. We ran back home, taking turns carrying my barefoot little cousin piggyback. Because we knew that nobody was home, we went to my apartment first to clean up. We took off our clothes and threw them into the washing machine and cleaned our shoes the best we could. We had to come up with some story to explain the loss of Danny's shoes and socks. I no longer remember what we concocted, but it must not have been very convincing because my two cousins were grounded for the rest of the summer.

Spending the remainder of the summer at home did not mean that we were idle. We invented games that kept us occupied. We started the time-honored game of trying to set fire to our own farts. We would darken the room by closing drapes, lowering shades and making sure that all lights were off. Then we would lower our pants, light a match, and the fun would start. We had contests to see who could produce the loudest explosion and whose flame lasted longest. Adam dubbed this game *Son et Lumiere*. When that game got old, we decided to form a musical trio of 'fartistes', and with that lofty purpose in mind, we spent hours practicing. Adam was partial to taking over the "drum and vibes" section, my younger cousin Danny was capable of producing the most mellifluous flutey tones, which at times resembled a violin and at times a flute, while I proved to be very versatile and fitted in wherever needed. We became so adept that we entertained and delighted friends with our newly acquired skills, and were asked several times to perform at children's birthday parties and such. Both my cousins are well-known doctors now, and move in the best circles of society. I am quite sure they wouldn't want to be reminded of these pranks. But at the time, we not only enjoyed the well-deserved fame and applause that greeted our little performances, but we had fun shocking our audiences.

While my two cousins and I were thinking of new and interesting ways to get into trouble, my parents were weaving their own dreams of escape. Whenever we sat down to dinner, Father would talk about our wonderful future in a different country, a place where he would be appreciated and highly regarded because of his many university degrees and accomplishments, where he would be an attorney or a judge, not a shop owner selling underwear, where he would live in luxury and enjoy untold riches, where he would own a mansion and not live in a two bedroom apartment, where he would drive a fancy car and not our old clunky Chevy, where he would hire servants to do all the housework, where he would go to the theater and opera and belong to the best clubs and mingle with the best of society.

My sister and I were not fooled. We didn't believe that we could shed our immigrant status, odd manners, foreign customs, unsuitable clothes, our impossible-to-pronounce last name. We didn't think by a stroke of magic, we'd become members of high society and fit in with the local blue-bloods. Father's unrealistic daydreams only strengthened my sister's conviction that if she wanted to escape and change her future, she would have to start by reinventing her past.

We spent the summer of 1955 in Europe, ostensibly on vacation, but Father was looking for the ideal country to settle in. We visited Switzerland, France, and Portugal. In Switzerland, Mother got sick and stayed in bed in various expensive hotels, took mineral baths and other therapeutic treatments, Father chased some of the toothsome widows that frequented these resorts, and my sister and I were left to our own devices. We managed to fight boredom by looking for trouble, we climbed a cherry tree on a farm and ate most of the ripe fruit. The farmer brought us down and escorted us to the hotel, where Father had to pay an inordinate sum of money to compensate him. In town, we came upon a municipal swimming pool that happened to be closed, but that didn't stop us from jumping the fence and trying it out. Again we were escorted to the hotel, this time by a policeman.

We were allowed to visit the sights in Paris on our own. My sister was only fifteen and I was eleven and we didn't speak a word of French, but we walked to the Eiffel Tower and climbed to the top, strolled in the Tuillerie Gardens, rode the Metro, visited Notre Dame and bought the most incredibly delicious ice cream from a hole-in-the-wall shop in one of the islands on the Seine. All this while Mother window-shopped the whole length of the Champs Elyseés and finally ended up buying herself a raincoat and an umbrella at Printemps. Father disappeared to visit a friend from his university days who happened to live near Paris. We were staying at the Ritz, in room 555, and my sister and I would return late at night, tired and hungry, and take turns asking the night concierge for the key, saying very quickly *san-san-san-san-san-san* and burst into giggles when he couldn't understand. Once, when we got back to the hotel, the light in our parents' room was already turned off, so we went to dinner by ourselves. We took the metro to the Boulevard St. Germaine and sat at a little bistro table on the sidewalk, ordered steaks and *pomme-frites* and felt very adult and capable.

A week later, we traveled to Portugal, where we lingered three weeks on the beach in Estoril. My sister was followed by an adoring entourage of young men wherever she went. Father gambled at the Casino and courted some dark-haired divorcee with a daughter my age, while Mother pretended not to notice and went shopping some more.

When we returned home in the fall, Father had dropped the idea of living in the lap of luxury in Europe. Now, at the dinner table, he talked about the advantages of moving to Canada or the United States, or the possibility of going south, to Chile or Uruguay. The next trip in search of utopia was undertaken by Father alone. He went to Uruguay, and came back less than enthusiastic. But before any decision was made, my sister threw a monkey wrench into his plans and created an upheaval of colossal proportions that splintered the family and changed forever the course of her life.

My sister was inventing her new life. She was thirteen years old when she entered high school. A new school meant new friends, which she took as an opportunity to create a new reality out of her fantasies. Nobody knew her in this school. She created a new identity for herself. She couldn't pass for Venezuelan because of her looks. She had golden wavy hair, green eyes, light skin that got pink easily, a small nose, shapely full lips and a round, cherubic face. My mother says that as a baby she looked like an angel. Whenever Mother took my sister out in the stroller in the streets of Krakow, the German soldiers who occupied the city would approach and play with her, give her candy and sweets from their rations. She must have reminded them of the children they had left behind. At first, Mother was taken aback by this show of effusive affection from the Germans, especially since we were Jewish, though of course, nobody else knew. But soon she became accustomed to this attention and started taking my sister out twice a day in order to collect all this food that was so scarce during the war. Later, when we arrived in Venezuela, my sister was the only blond head in a sea of dark-haired children and again she was considered an extraordinary beauty. Her reputation as the prettiest girl in school lasted all the way until she left to go to a boarding school in Canada.

I had dark brown hair, green eyes, thick glasses, a very round face with freckles that my mother spent much time and lemon juice trying to erase, ears that must have stuck out since my mother used to tape them back every night (without any eventual result) and a sweet smile. Whenever we were brought out to greet my parents' friends, they were struck by my sister's beauty, and then they would add lamely that I must be the smart one who played the piano. We were considered big for our age, in fact, in school we had to line up by size to enter the classroom starting by the smallest, and I was always the last one in line.

My sister felt that if she couldn't pass for Venezuelan because of her golden hair, green eyes and fair skin, she could nevertheless stop being a Polish immigrant, and that is what she did. Everybody in this school believed her to be the daughter of an American oil executive living in Caracas. Foreigners were generally disliked in Venezuela, but there was a hierarchy, and at that time, Americans were considered a higher social class than Poles. My sister had been preparing for this moment with great care. She had learned English from Mrs. Mead and from the many books she read, she had copied the clothes and shoes American girls wore from fashion magazines, and she had created a new history, a new past, a new family for herself. She had rehearsed in her mind many times how wonderful her life would be, if she could only shed her real past, her origins, and her own family, like a snake shedding its old skin to emerge fresh and more beautiful than ever.

At the time, I didn't understand the depth of my sister's despair at being foreign, always looking in from the outside, always singled out as the one who didn't belong, the object of ridicule and contempt. We were openly avoided by our Venezuelan classmates and their parents, and felt humiliated by this immutable rejection. We were reminded time and again that we were dirt-poor immigrants, who didn't belong in this country, who weren't asked to play with the Venezuelan children, who were never invited into their homes, their birthday parties, their other celebrations. When kindness was shown, it was out of pity, and my sister detected that immediately and rejected it.

Susanna never got praise or encouragement at home. That was one thing Father was incapable of. Mother's praise was worthless, even if it had occurred to her to dispense it, because her opinions never counted in our family. I was much luckier. My sister cared for me, she praised me when I deserved it and scolded me, even spanked me, when I misbehaved. She never got that. No wonder she was dreaming of escape.

I had finished sixth grade and, following the Venezuelan school system, I was about to begin my first year of high school at the Liceo Andres Bello, the same school my sister had been attending for the last two years. Before the first day of class, Susanna took me aside and told me that everybody in this school believed her to be American, the daughter of an oil executive stationed in Caracas. In fact, she was called *La Americanita* by all her classmates and friends. I was to confirm and corroborate her story, or else I wouldn't see another dawn. I knew her well enough to see that she meant every word of it. Even though I was eleven now and bigger than she, she was still capable of beating the daylights out of me. Even worse, she could use the silent treatment, and cut me out from her life and there was nothing I feared and hated more.

"Rebecca, you must give me your word that you won't tell anybody I am Polish, or else you are dead meat," my sister said.

"Sure, whatever you say. I give you my word," I replied.

"No, that's not enough. There is no 'whatever you say' about it. No mistakes. Remember, I am American. Promise me you won't tell anybody I am Polish. Not now. Not ever. No matter who asks you and what they ask you. No matter what happens. Okay?"

"Well, what am I supposed to say? Everybody knows I am Polish. How am I going to explain that?" I was starting to get upset.

"You figure out something to say. But if I ever find you told somebody I'll never talk to you again. I mean it, I am dead serious."

She informed me that she had told her classmates that she was born and raised in the south of the United States and her father was an oil executive assigned to Venezuela. I wasn't sure how I was going to fit into the scheme, but I decided the less said the better. Things went well for a while, I was busy with my new classes, my new friends, and all the excitement of a new school. But after a couple of months, a girl who had been in my class in grade school and was a foreigner as well, became suspicious. Under the guise of needing to review some old math assignments, she asked me for my home phone number and called Mother. Of course, Mother wasn't in on our secret, and when asked about our birthplace didn't have any qualms confirming that we were indeed Polish, every member of our family had been born in Poland, and nobody had ever set foot in the United States.

The next day, word spread all over school that the blond American cutie in the third year of high school was actually a Polack. By ten that morning, my sister had gathered all her books and taken the bus home.

Gossip spread like wildfire and before noon, the whole school knew what had happened. When I arrived home at about five, the door of our room was locked from the inside. I knocked several times and called, but there was no answer. Finally, after I had been trying for over an hour, Susanna told me to get lost and not bother her again, and I sat at the dining room table, unable to do my homework because I was so worried about what was going to happen next. My parents arrived as usual, around ten. Susanna wouldn't come out to talk to them. They screamed at her and threatened her with all kinds of outlandish punishment, but she didn't relent. That night I slept on the sofa. The next morning, when I heard Susanna go to the bathroom, I raced into the bedroom to get clean underwear. She returned as I was getting dressed and kicked me out. I went to school alone.

Susanna never again set foot in our high school. Our parents yelled and screamed and raged. One evening Father came into the bedroom to make Susanna see reason. She wouldn't talk to him. He started screaming, berating her, calling her names.

"What do you think you are, a princess? You stupid cow, you piece of shit, you turd. You are going to do exactly as I say or you'll be sorry you were ever born!" Father roared.

She still didn't answer. Father got angrier and angrier. He started slapping her, and as always, she screeched "It doesn't hurt, not one bit, it doesn't hurt at all." The more she said it didn't hurt, the more enraged Father became. Finally he slapped her so hard that she stumbled and fell against the bed. Her face was purple and her nose started bleeding.

I felt sick with pain, I couldn't stand it any longer, I howled. I rushed at Father and rammed him against the wall with my head. It took him completely by surprise. He stopped dead in his tracks, looked at both of us, turned around, and walked slowly toward the door, where Mother stood whimpering.

"You better do something to control these vicious savages you gave birth to," he said icily as he passed her.

During the next few weeks, Susanna threw tantrums that were more violent and longer lasting than ever before. I was afraid she would collapse and die from all the sobbing and screaming. Her face would turn red, and then purple. She would flail her arms, stomp her feet, and scream until her voice became so hoarse it disappeared. Father tried everything. He threatened to get rid of her beloved collection of English books. She responded with her usual answer to all his threats "I don't care, you do what you want."

Next day, when I came back from school all her books were gone. She wasn't allowed to go out, or talk to anybody, not even to me. It made no difference to her. After a few weeks, Father tried to bribe her, promising she could have whatever she wanted if she just went back to school. Her answer was still a resounding "No." Most of the time, I was forbidden to enter our bedroom. The first few days, Susanna locked herself in and wouldn't let anybody come in. But after a week Father had the locks changed and she became a prisoner. The door was kept locked nearly all the time, with a chamber pot under her bed in case she needed to go to the bathroom while our parents were away. Father had taken our books, the radio, everything but the beds and the dresser. I had to do my homework on the dining room table and sleep on the sofa. My clothes were stored in a dresser drawer that had been placed under the dining room table, and my books and school supplies were in a cardboard box, also under the table. Father said my sister couldn't come out until she changed her mind about going to school. Susanna made it plenty clear that she'd rather die than change her mind.

My sister spent the remainder of the school year at home, sitting on her bed, watching the walls. We didn't have a TV, and the radio and all her books were gone. Late in the afternoon, when I returned from school, I would sneak her an American magazine, a book or a piece of chocolate, by leaning out and stretching my arm as far as it would go from the balcony and she stretching hers from the bedroom window, even though this was strictly forbidden. We also talked. I asked her what she did all day.

"I am thinking," she said.

"What about, Susie?"

"About my life, my future. About who, what, and where I am going to be."

"Are you going to run away when they let you out?" I asked.

"I already have, in my mind. Wild horses won't keep me here, you can be sure of that."

A couple of months later, when my parents finally realized that no earthly force could make my sister go back to school, Father asked her to help out at the store.

"Susanna, now that all you do is sit all day long on your ass, you might as well come with me to the store and help the salesgirls put merchandise back on the shelves, before you become a lazy good-for-nothing cow."

Susanna turned purple with rage. "I am never, ever going to help you in your stupid, godforsaken store. I hate that store! I am not going to let you ruin my life! It's your fault that I sit here on my ass doing nothing. I am not going to be one of your salesgirls and let you scream at me and insult me all day long. In fact, I don't care if I ever see you again!" she yelled at the top of her voice and burst into tears.

Father stormed out of the room in a frenzy of loud curses, went into the kitchen, and started yelling at Mother. "You stupid whore, go into the bedroom and make that daughter of yours behave."

Mother tried her best but came away empty-handed. No amount of cajoling worked. My sister had made up her mind and didn't budge.

Unnerved by Susanna's brazen disregard of all authority, I watched this clash with a mixture of anguish, fear, and guilt. I was afraid, as the battle intensified, that Susanna would end up hurting herself more than anybody else. At the same time, I felt a perverse pleasure at the outrageousness of her conduct. She broke all the rules and no one could make her change her behavior. Now that she was finally allowed to come out of her room, she still remained seated on her bed, staring at the walls.

In the spring I was allowed to move back into our bedroom. Our parents had given up, and made other arrangements for Susanna's education. Just like in the romantic novels of the last century, my parents scoured the list of their most distant relatives, and found some long-lost third cousins living in Canada. My sister would be sent away to a boarding school in Toronto in the fall.

I was left to pick up the pieces. I had a lot of explaining to do at school. I came up with some lame story about my family, how we were actually Polish, but my sister had been born in the United States during a trip my mother took while she was pregnant and ill. She gave birth in an American hospital, only to come down with a serious case of amnesia before returning to Poland. This story took a lot of imagination and finesse on my part, and a very thick skin not to be upset by the looks of disbelief of my classmates.

That summer we went to Canada, to accompany my sister, who had been enrolled in boarding school. Father, prudently, decided to stay in Caracas. He couldn't leave the store for such a long time, he said, especially since the year before he had gone to Europe and Uruguay. I suspected he wanted to be as far as possible from my sister in case she refused to attend boarding school. This was also to be another exploratory trip, to see whether Canada had all the requisites to be our next utopian land. Mother and I were designated as judges of the suitability of this new country. The traveling party consisted of my mother, my sister and I, my uncle Bronek, and Adam and Danny. For the first part of the summer we went to a resort by a beautiful lake, in the Laurentian mountains, where we spent six peaceful, fun-filled weeks. There was nobody to rage and holler at us. We felt carefree and relaxed and did what we wanted. These were the most marvelous six weeks of my childhood.

My sister spent her days lying by the lake, day-dreaming and acquiring a suntan. My two cousins and I continued our tradition of playing games. We took long rides on horseback and pretended to be Canadian Mounties or a regiment of the Cavalry, or we took a boat out on the lake and played pirates. Adam always led. He was the captain, the chieftain, the Arab sheik. Danny and I were his soldiers, his troops, his crew. We would row out to a small island on the lake, tie the boat to a tree-stump on the shore and pick blueberries until we were satiated. I loved finding the plump dark blueberries, plucking them from the bushes, and popping them into my mouth. The sudden burst of sweet and tart flavors was something I had never experienced.

We swam, water-skied, went on long bicycle rides, played table tennis, and at night took part in all kinds of cook-outs, campfire songs, amateur theater performances, and dances. My uncle, who was even more of a womanizer than my father, met a very tall and buxom lady and spent most of his time wooing her. Seeing my short uncle dancing close to her, while she nestled her ample bosom against his bald head was quite a sight. Mother was the only one who didn't seem happy, perhaps she was worried about what Father might be doing while she was so far away.

Unfortunately, all too soon it was time to travel to Toronto to leave my sister at the boarding school. Adam was also going to stay in Canada, in a Scottish boarding school for boys where they wore kilts on Sundays and holidays. Danny and I couldn't resist inventing silly jokes about what he would wear under the skirt, and how he would walk and sit after a year of parading around in it. We still had about a week remaining before classes started, so we decided to go to Niagara Falls. This was a thoroughly enjoyable trip for all of us and I realized how much easier and more pleasant life could be when we were far away from Father.

When we returned to Caracas, I found myself alone for the first time in my life. I missed my sister terribly. Her departure left a hole in my life the size of an ocean. Now I was alone in the apartment after school. The whole apartment seemed eerily quiet. I couldn't settle down to do my homework. I would go into our room and look at my sister's empty bed. There was no screaming, no tantrums, no tears. No locked doors, no wild schemes to escape, no need to sneak around, to keep secrets. The days seemed long and unexciting. I was lonely and my life was sad and boring.

I needed to get more involved in school, make new friends. I resolved to go to the club more often. I started swimming competitively, playing tennis and table tennis in tournaments, staying at the club until almost midnight. Nobody seemed to find it strange that a girl barely twelve was allowed to stay out so late, or at least, nobody told me I couldn't do it. I spent as little time as possible at home. There was nothing for me there, it was just a place to shower and change clothes and, late at night, to sleep.

After my sister left, Father decided that having only one driver at home was counterproductive. Mother was too afraid to drive, although Father had been teaching her for the last ten years. On Sundays, when they went out for a driving lesson, he would shout at her ceaselessly.

"Don't change lanes now, you idiot! Look in the rear-view mirror, you dunce, you have to know what's behind you. Look ahead, stupid, you are going to crash into the fence. Don't hit the brakes, you useless cow, somebody is going to run into you. Faster, you cretin, you are slowing down the whole city."

Mother always came home sobbing. Finally, Father told her she was too stupid to learn and if I could make arrangements for a fake driver's license he would let me have the car, even though I was six years under the driving age. I made inquiries among the older kids in my high school and was able to locate a provincial driver licensing office, where for a certain sum of money and with the help of a dishonest clerk, anybody could get a license. Soon I had a driver's license that listed my age as eighteen, and I had the car. Every morning I would take my father to work, and then the car was mine. I became a celebrity in school, instantly popular with my classmates. Once in a while, several of us would cut classes, pile into my car, and drive down to the beach. At night, around ten, I was expected to pick up my parents from the store. But more often than not, they would ride home with my Uncle Bronek, whose store was half a block away on the same street.

Besides driving the car, I obtained other privileges without having any confrontations. My sister had fought all the battles for me, she was the one that always struggled with our parents. I remember the screams, the tantrums, the scoldings, the tears. She remembers them as well. In fact, she has trouble remembering little else from our childhood. My parents, after a prolonged conflict that lasted a couple of years, finally allowed Susanna to wear high heels and make-up. As soon as the dust settled, I followed suit, and nobody seemed to mind. My sister had to open new trails in the jungle with a machete, while I just sauntered easily behind her, enjoying all the same advantages. Now that I was the only one left living at home, my parents treated me as an adult. They never interfered with anything I did. Most of the time they didn't even bother to find out where I was and what I was up to. I had total freedom.

School had always been my refuge from home. I liked it, not because of the quality of the teaching, which was abysmal, but because I enjoyed the feeling of being competent and successful. School was where I found the validation I craved. Most of my teachers were uninspiring, but two I remember as outstanding and I owe my love of art and literature to them. The passion they felt for their subjects was contagious. I could hardly wait to read a book or gaze at a painting they praised. Academically, I was far above my classmates, and I loved the approval I got from my professors. But I had to be careful about the feelings aroused in my classmates. To be an excellent student was considered treason to the student body and a sellout to the establishment. I didn't feel secure enough or popular enough to deal with this kind of label. I developed an attitude of studied nonchalance and outward indifference toward my schoolwork, although I never missed an assignment and always got the best grades.

My social life was a different matter. I never belonged to any of the social cliques in school. I was most often by myself, or with one girlfriend who was as much a misfit as I. I professed not to care about all the dances and parties I was missing. I pretended dancing was beneath me, that I despised parties and popular music, that I hated dressing up and putting on make-up. But in my heart, I loved dancing. I used to watch all the other girls dance and I would practice alone at night, in front of the mirror. I yearned to be invited to these parties and dance with a live partner all the steps, turns and twirls I practiced every night in my bedroom holding on to the doorknob. I dreamed of being popular and beautiful, of having fashionable and expensive clothes, of being surrounded by admiring friends, classmates and, of course, lots of boys. Being excluded from all the things I really wanted, I learned to project an image of self-sufficiency. I developed a false persona. It was easier to pretend that the grapes were green, than to try to penetrate this society which appeared unassailable.

Being a foreigner was another problem I had to contend with at school. Venezuelans disliked foreigners. They couldn't tell by my accent or my looks, luckily, I managed to blend in. But as soon as they saw my last name, they knew I was not one of them. My father had changed our German last name to a Polish one, because in wartime Poland a German name meant you were a Jew. Unfortunately, our new name consisted of most of the last letters of the alphabet. Spanish-speaking people found it impossible to pronounce. This was enough to create a stumbling block between my schoolmates and me. This discrimination against foreigners took many forms, some quite obvious and direct, others more subtle.

One incident that caused me a lot of anguish and pain happened in the fifth grade. I was elected class president, but before my term started, a committee of several students and teachers asked me to resign, saying that the school should not be represented by a foreigner. I was dumbfounded, and very hurt. I had been duly elected and felt that, at the very least, I should have been told this before I became a candidate. Besides, I really didn't feel I was a foreigner, I had arrived in the country before I was five and started first grade right there in Caracas. But I didn't remonstrate, and quietly let the vice-president take over the position. I pretended everything was fine, but inside I was crushed. Once again, I appeared to the world composed and smiling, while I felt mistreated and frustrated. The injustice of it rankled. That was my first and last attempt to participate in school government. From then on, I became a private person, an island of one. But I couldn't help but dream of living in a place where I would be appreciated and liked, where I would dare to openly show myself and be seen for who I was, where I would be free to become the person I wanted to be.

Susanna

Rebecca asked me, quite recently, when did I know I was Jewish. Well, it was not an epiphany, that's for sure. I realized gradually. First, I observed poor old Grandfather at prayer. When we first arrived in Caracas, we lived in the cramped quarters where Grandfather made his home. In that hot, stuffy, little place he would envelop himself in a voluminous, black and white, fringed shawl, face the wall (later I learned he was facing east) and chant and sway. I had no idea this had anything to do with being Jewish, but I knew that he was praying. It was not until we moved away from *Las Fuentes* and saw more Jewish people that a germ of dread started gnawing at me. I had heard about Jews. I could accept that Grandfather was a Hebrew (calling him a Jew in Venezuela, would have been offensive). But, dear Lord, I did not know it was contagious. I was a Catholic, and I enjoyed following all the rituals. Eventually, I understood that our parents were Jews, and so were we. It seemed to be a nationality, like Pole or American, and not merely a religion. It was one more thing to detest about my life. How unlucky can a little girl be? It was one more obstacle in my fervent desire to belong, to be like everybody else, to be Venezuelan.

We had so many strikes against us already. Venezuelans are xenophobic. In that, they do not differ from any other nation, but at that time I thought it was a peculiar Venezuelan trait. I knew that the word *musiu*, which is what they called all foreigners, was an insult. Oddly, as a people of mixed race, the Venezuelans constantly yearned to become whiter, prizing a white complexion above everything else. They were constantly bemoaning that we allowed the sun to darken our white skin. Old women would stop us when we played on the beach and beseech us to get out of the sun or, at least, wear a large hat. Once we started speaking the language we began to fit in. Especially my baby sister, who had arrived before ever going to school, had the light complexion so valued by Venezuelans and was not marred by being a blonde. Of course, the cumbersome foreign name, totally unpronounceable in Spanish, gave us away. But that was not such a huge obstacle. Hopefully, it would become obliterated by marriage. When we thought of ourselves as Catholics, we had a hope of being assimilated, of finally belonging somewhere. But as Jews, this was a pipe dream. Venezuelans did not marry Jews.

I felt harassed in school because I was the only blonde. My classmates called me "the albino musiu" or "the washed-out freak." That is, when they weren't busy calling me a dirty Pole. When I finally realized that no matter how piously Catholic I became I would still be Jewish, I gave up my most cherished dream. I knew that I could never be assimilated into Venezuelan society. A Rabbi in Toronto, who is a Holocaust survivor, preaches that the Holocaust was God's punishment for the sin of assimilation. Well, maybe I couldn't help being Jewish, as I couldn't help being short, but dear God! I was never ever going to be like my parents.

My parents were always distrustful and suspicious. I can understand quite well that after spending the war in Poland pretending to be Catholic Poles, seeing with their own eyes what was happening to all the Jews around them, they had every right to be fearful and suspicious. I can understand why they believed that everyone was out to get them. Everyone really was out to get them, Poles, Germans, and Russians, and sometimes even other Jews. I can understand that after all they suffered they had earned the right to be paranoid. Goodness knows, they would have to be crazy to be trusting. Nevertheless, I hated this trait with all my being. In fact, it drove me nuts. I felt I had to fight with all my might to avoid being like my parents. The fact that they were often proven right only strengthened my resolve to become the exact opposite.

Mother believed that the maids were always trying to steal from her. She inspected the maid's bags as she was heading for the door. Several of them were let go because Mother couldn't find a dress or a blouse which later appeared at the cleaners. Once Mother started shouting at a maid because she arrived wearing one of Mother's dresses. The maid burst into tears.

"Señora, I swear on my mother's grave that you yourself gave me this dress last week. Don't you remember? You also gave me the white shoes and the señor's shirt for my father."

Of course, at that point Mother remembered that, indeed, she had. But the maid continued crying and sobbing through the whole morning and could get hardly any work done.

Mother was convinced that all merchants were trying to rob her. Grocers increased their prices and padded their bills as soon as they saw her traipsing toward their shop. She believed that all scales were rigged so that every cut of meat was twice as heavy in the butcher shop as it was once we got home. Mother swore that the fruit she unpacked at home was not the perfect fruit she had chosen at the store. Somewhere along the way a substitution had occurred, even though she always watched the grocer like a hawk. Once she went as far as taking back a head of lettuce because she had found a slug when she cut it in half. She accused the green grocer of giving her that lettuce knowing that a slug was hiding inside it and, when he tried to protest, she told him that he was a cheat and a liar and she would never again set foot in his shop. This was an idle threat, since there was no other shop nearby and Mother didn't drive. When we went to the fabric store, after the clerk measured the cloth, Mother always insisted on measuring once more herself. She was sure the salesgirl had shorted her. Salesclerks are taught to slip their thumbs on the inside of the yardstick, she said, so that at least an inch is lost for every yard of fabric they measure out. And, after she noticed that the seamstress' daughters were wearing hair ribbons fashioned from the blue taffeta of one of my dresses, she ordered the seamstress to return the leftover scraps of fabric with every dress she made, "in case we need them to repair a rip in the dress" she told her.

Father was no better. He was convinced that all the sales clerks in his store were busy pilfering the stock and lavishing merchandise on their own friends and family when he wasn't looking, or charging nothing for it. Father took inventory at the end of every day, so that he could reorder next morning whatever had been sold. He also correlated all sales receipts with the items missing to find out if any of his employees were stealing. If he found a discrepancy, he shouted and screamed at the sales girls, calling them thieves and crooks, until they were all in tears. Only then did he feel satisfied and conceded that perhaps a customer had pilfered something when the store had been really busy.

Mechanics existed solely to fix non-existent problems in Father's car, and change perfectly good parts for other used parts, just to extract more of his money. Once he left his car to be serviced and, when we came back the car was still on jacks. The mechanic told us we would have to wait another twenty minutes. He was a little late with the work because the tires were wearing out unevenly and he had decided to rotate them. Father wanted to see for himself. When the mechanic escorted him inside the workshop, Father flew into a rage, yelling at the top of his voice "Do you think I am blind? Or stupid? These are not my tires, mine were practically like new." When the owner of the shop, a Lebanese man, came to see what was the fracas all about, Father told him that the mechanic had stolen his tires and he wanted new ones or else he would call the police. After a lot of haggling they reached an agreement, Father would get four new tires for the price of two. As we were driving back I asked Father whether he was sure that the tires he rejected had not been his. "What does it matter?" he said with a laugh, "I feel good, I have new tires. And that old Lebanese crook ought to feel good too, because he just sold a set of tires."

Dentists and doctors lived to invent maladies just so they could extort more money from my parents. Or even worse, operate on them unnecessarily. The parents felt so strongly about this that they chose an old Polish dentist, who practiced without a valid license and whose knowledge and equipment were antediluvian. He didn't know a thing about anesthesiology or any of the newer procedures. He ended up destroying my father's teeth and Father had to get dentures. Both my baby sister and I hated going to him. I always felt that he leaned on my face when he worked on my teeth, it felt as if he had put his elbow in my mouth. After a dental appointment, my whole face was sore for days.

To avoid being cheated, deceived and swindled, my parents lived in a state of perpetual vigilance. They knew how the people they dealt with would treat them, because if they had been in the same position, they would have cheated, deceived and swindled. In fact, Father boasted that he did just that at the store. One of the few things that really made him happy was to get the better of someone. I remember a story Father told us once when we were gathered at the dinner table. That morning, a large shipment of ties had arrived, just in time for the Christmas season. He separated the ties into three piles, without bothering to look at them. The first bunch he piled on a table on the sidewalk, by the entrance of the store, priced at five bolivars each. A few steps behind he positioned another table, where he placed the second batch, at 10 bolivars. And further in, close to the cashier, he had a rack with the last batch, each on its own hanger, at twenty bolivars. As customers were lured into the store by the low price of the first ties they saw on the table by the entrance, Father would talk them into buying a nicer present for their loved ones. More often than not, they left the store feeling quite satisfied, having paid 20 bolivars for a tie that was no different from the five-bolivar tie by the door. Father called this business savvy. But I considered his behavior, his lack of trust, his constant suspicion, as part and parcel of being Jewish. I wanted more than anything else to avoid living like that. I swore to myself that my life would be different.

At home, all native foods were suspect. The parents accepted oranges, bananas and pineapples, because they had seen them in pictures or heard of them in Poland. But they stopped there. We never saw mangoes, papayas, guavas, or plantain at home. Not surprisingly, my sister and I developed an enormous hunger for Venezuelan food. We would buy it from the grimy street vendors with pushcarts who peddled their tasty morsels from every corner in the city. We bought *chicha,* a sweet white milky drink made from corn. We munched on crispy fried plantain chips. We sucked on *mamones,* a small tart fruit with an enormous pit, or popped tamarinds into our mouth, chewing on the sweet and tart brown fibers. Just thinking about these delicious tidbits makes my mouth water. We feasted on hallacas, a delicious confection of meats and dried fruit wrapped and cooked in banana leaves. We tasted all kinds of forbidden foods. The more exotic, the more we liked it. If the parents ever found out, I am sure they would have a heart attack.

At home, Mother cooked *wienerschnitzel, goulash,* and boiled potatoes. She served stewed fruit compote. She took special pains to find European bakeries and delicatessens, and brought home black breads and German cold cuts and liver spreads. She believed that Father had a weak stomach that caused him to pass an inordinate amount of gas, loudly and explosively. She was convinced that because of this peculiarity he needed to ingest only bland foods, cooked with no seasoning, and had to avoid anything spicy, fresh or raw. She prepared boiled chicken or fish, boiled potatoes and cabbage, boiled vegetables, boiled dumplings and boiled fruit. We drank boiled water, boiled milk and boiled tea. It was no wonder that my sister and I couldn't wait to get out on the street and scarf down all kinds of savory snacks. To this day I won't touch anything boiled. I have an almost allergic reaction to the foods that were served at home. My little sister and I soon discovered what every kid knows, that everything that was good was forbidden and that everything that was forbidden was good.

Mealtimes at home, when we were all together seated at the table, always ended in disaster. The only good thing was that they were so infrequent. The parents would either fight and scream ferociously at each other, or talk doom and gloom at the table. Father would complain about how the world was getting worse and worse. Crime was increasing. Prices were going up. The possibility of another world war was looming. Father had to kill himself working to help the rest of the family, who were all sponging off him, and so on and on. My little sister would sit in her chair very quietly, her eyes half-closed, her mouth shaped into an idle grin, like the Cheshire cat. She was in a trance, not listening to anything, just daydreaming.

Once, when I saw her in one of these trances, I asked her point-blank, "Rebecca, what are you doing?"

"Nothing," she said smiling innocently.

I wasn't about to be put off. "No, really, tell me what you were doing just now."

"Thinking."

"Thinking? What about?"

"Things."

"What things?" This was like pulling teeth.

"I don't want to tell you. You'll make fun of me."

"Don't be silly, of course I won't. Come on, tell me what you were thinking about?"

"Promise you won't laugh?"

"Cross my heart."

"Today I was watching a movie in my head. At other times I tell myself a story or paint a picture."

"What was the movie about? Come on, baby, you can tell me."

"This one was about a happy family living on a farm, with two little girls, and all kinds of animals, puppies, kitties, little chicks, and ducks, and a small brown lamb. One day the two little girls each got a horse for their birthdays. One horse was black and really shiny, the other one was reddish-brown. The little girls were learning to ride their horses very quickly. Soon they could go all the way to the forest. That's when you started asking me questions and I had to stop the movie."

I was glad Rebecca had found a way to remove herself from all the crap the parents dished out. She was barely eight, and had already learned how to escape. I remember when she was younger she would hear Father shouting and Mother sobbing and she would bite her nails to the quick, often drawing blood. Her tiny hands had ten little red stumps. Sometimes, if the yelling went on for a while, she would take of her sandals and start pulling off her toe-nails. I was delighted that she had found another way to deal with her anxiety. Unfortunately, I hadn't learned how to do that. I seethed inwardly as I listened to Father's gripes and criticisms. I knew where this was leading, and I didn't like it one bit. Another move, another country, another language, another beginning, which would solve nothing. I only hoped for escape.

My aunt Alina, Father's older sister, was the only relative in our family worried about my future. And all she worried about was my marriage prospects. She felt that girls should have only one goal in life, and that was to marry well. Every conceivable effort and subterfuge was to be used to achieve this end. She considered me much too wild, too independent and too unladylike to find a suitable husband. She tried to beat some sense into me, since I was the oldest, in the hope that my example would rub off on my little sister. My aunt would look at me with an appraising eye, find fault, and try to correct it.

"Don't slouch, keep your shoulders back. Show off your chest, now that you have one. That's what it is for," she would scold. "And don't stint on the rouge, lipstick, and mascara. Men can swear all they like that they prefer women who don't wear make-up, but don't you believe a word of it! They always make a beeline toward the ones that look like French chorus-line girls." My aunt had studied to be a cosmetologist and had a strong belief in lotions, potions, and creams. "And, above all, remember, young ladies shouldn't fart. At least, not until after they are married."

Aunt Alina communicated her consternation to Mother, who

then started nagging me to behave more charmingly and alluring-
ly. One afternoon, the two of them concocted a plan to show us off
to a couple of "nice Jewish boys." If I remember correctly, their last
name was Silverstein. They were the two youngest sons of a Rabbi
who aunt Alina had known in Lvov. We girls weren't told anything
about their intentions, but I suspected something was afoot
because Mother made me wear a dress when aunt Alina invited us
over for tea and petit-fours. Usually, we went to her apartment in
our tee-shirts and jeans, and all we got was soda water and saltine
crackers.

When we got to her apartment, Aunt Alina pulled me into her
bathroom and darkened my eyebrows and eyelashes with kohl,
instructed me to put lipstick on, and applied rouge to my cheeks.
I looked in the mirror and saw a teenage floozy. Fortunately, my
aunt ran out of time before she started on my baby sister, who was
looking at herself in the mirror making all kinds of funny faces and
sticking her fingers in her nostrils while my aunt worked on me.

The doorbell rang and the two young men walked in. They sat
stiffly on the living-room couch, one next to the other, across from
us. The older one, Samuel, was already balding even though he
was only in his twenties, wore thick glasses that rested on his
fleshy nose, and had flaccid jowls. The younger one was a redhead, a little taller and not as flabby, but I could see that in time he
would grow to resemble his brother. I was wrong about that, I
learned a couple of years later that before he had time to grow into
a replica of his brother, he committed suicide at the end of his
freshman year at MIT, where he had gone to study physics. He had
thick, wet lips and an enormous mouth. He put a whole petit four
in that giant mouth and couldn't close his lips over it. A big slop-
py chunk of cake and frosting dropped on the carpet. While he was
discreetly trying to retrieve it, he sloshed the tea he was balancing
on his lap. A dark stain spread on the front of his pants. Rebecca
couldn't stop staring at it. He followed her gaze and noticed it too,
and went to the bathroom. He must have tried to rinse the stain off,
maybe because these were his best Sunday pants. When he
returned the stain was twice as large. Rebecca glanced at me and
started giggling so hard that our aunt ordered her to the kitchen to
get everybody a soda, although nobody was thirsty or had asked
for one. Besides, it didn't really do any good, because we could
hear her laughing from the living room.

My aunt never tried this ruse again. But she didn't give up either. She kept on trying to find me a desirable husband. Until the time I left, she kept giving me unsolicited advice and mentioning friends who had sons she wanted me to meet. Would-be doctors, dentists, lawyers, and accountants. Hell, I couldn't think of a worse fate!

While my aunt was worrying about my marriage prospects, her husband showed his concern in a different manner. Uncle Bronek never paid any attention to me before I turned thirteen and grew breasts. Then, suddenly, he became very friendly and quite interested in my upbringing. My little sister and I were in the habit of taking long rambling walks all over the city and the surrounding hills. We called it "exploring our planet." Uncle began accompanying us.

"Now that you are a well developed young lady you shouldn't wander around all alone. Anything could happen, especially since you are so blond and pretty, Susanna," he said. "You could be sexually harassed, molested or much worse, you could be raped."

Those thoughts had never occurred to us. Uncle's descriptions of the dangers we exposed ourselves to by walking alone were vivid and complete and left little to the imagination. Soon we felt we needed an army to protect us and we welcomed his presence.

Uncle would wait until we were in some deserted stretch of the trail and invite us to sit down on the grass. There he would regale us with very involved stories about his sexual conquests among high society ladies in Lvov, the city where he grew up.

"I hobnobbed with the rich and famous. All the aristocracy welcomed me because I was such a famous pianist. Everybody wanted me to come play the piano at their *soirees*. I kept company with countesses and duchesses," he boasted. "There was hardly any palace I didn't know. And quite often I knew the bedroom and the boudoir much more intimately than the salon. Every member of the nobility had a *soiree* or a musical event on a different evening of the week, and I was always invited. I was a frequent guest of the likes of the Radziwills, the Potockis and the Lubomirskis."

Uncle especially liked to dwell on the lavish clothes and fine jewelry the ladies wore, down to the silk and lace undergarments and intimate apparel. He would describe how refined were his contacts with the ladies, how adroitly he danced with them, how elegantly he kissed their hands and how very impressed they were with his debonair presence and courtly manners. His portrayals became more and more sexually explicit. One afternoon, while we were seated in a copse in the woods, Uncle told us he knew how to arouse desire and passion among the most beautiful married women in high society. He had discovered the secret of how to make any woman deliriously happy.

"Men! They are all dunces, they know nothing! You have to learn what to say, when to say it, where and how to touch a woman, and always take your time, never rush things," Uncle said. "A soft caress, a sweet word whispered in their ear, blowing hot breath on their skin, that is what does it. None of that crunching, squeezing and rubbing. I know what I am talking about."

"Susanna, I don't think Uncle is telling us the truth," Rebecca told me,once, when we were returning from one of our walks.

"Why not?" I asked, a bit perplexed. "Why would he lie?"

"Well, Aunt Alina doesn't seem to be deliriously happy. Most of the time she nags and gripes." Very observant of my baby sister, but she wasn't old enough to get the point of the stories that Uncle told.

One day, Uncle brought a blanket on one of our walks. He set it down in a tiny meadow surrounded by a thick grove of trees, and we all sat down. He sent my little sister to the park concession, which was a good half-mile away, to get sodas and candy. As soon as my sister was out of sight he lunged toward me, popped my blouse open, unhooked my bra, and started fondling my breasts. At first, I was so taken by surprise that I didn't try to stop him. Without warning he was on top of me and was unzipping his pants. He felt very heavy and sweaty as he was pressing himself on me. I felt uncomfortable and mortified. I didn't like any of this, but I didn't quite know what to do.

"What are you doing?" I managed to say. "Get your hands off me or I'll scream."

"You are so beautiful, Susanna, so fresh, like a budding rose," he panted.

I didn't scream. I didn't want to make a scene and embarrass myself. Now I understood why the old goat had been so attentive and nice to us lately. I kept on squirming and trying to push him off. Finally I squeaked "I have my period. I need to go to the bathroom urgently," and I wiggled out from under him, jumped up and rushed off, buttoning my bra and my blouse.

I met my little sister half way down the path, as she was coming back carrying the sodas and the candy.

"What's wrong, Susanna, what are you doing here? Did I forget to get something?" asked my little sister. "You look all hot and messy."

"There is nothing wrong. I am just very hot and I have my period. I just wanted to feel the breeze and stretch my legs," I lied.

By the time we got back to Uncle, he was sitting on the blanket, his back leaning against a tree, his eyes closed. I could tell that the old lecher was pretending to be asleep. He wasn't fooling me. He was probably wondering whether I had told Rebecca. I hadn't, but I wanted to keep him wondering and worry him a bit, so I started whispering to Rebecca out of his hearing range. I could see I was making him uncomfortable and that felt good. As soon as we finished the sodas, he stood up, folded up the blanket and we started walking back.

That was the last hike we took together. After this, Uncle always was too busy at the store to join us. Good riddance! From then on I made sure Rebecca didn't spend time alone with him. We had enough stumbling blocks to overcome at home, we didn't need to add one more.

Money was a bone of contention in our family. Even though he was making good money, Father was terribly tight-fisted. It wasn't until after Father died that I discovered that he had accumulated a small fortune. I had always thought we were poor. At home, Father would grill Mother daily about every cent she spent. When she couldn't come up with a complete and satisfactory explanation as to where exactly did the money go, he would reduce her to tears. He never allowed her or any of us to buy clothing, furniture, linens, household items or other things he called "luxuries." We were expected to have superior values, we were supposed to despise such ostentatious items and feel contempt for those who indulged in owning such useless, nouveau-riche stuff.

"What, you are out of money already?" he would holler at Mother. "I just gave you fifty bolivars last week. What do you think I am made of, hundred-bolivar bills?"

"But it was the beginning of the month. You know the gas and electricity collector came with the bill. And then the man from the phone company came to collect just last Friday," Mother would start to shake and her voice would start breaking.

She knew quite well this was a lame excuse, but she tried it anyway, since she couldn't come up with anything better. Father had devised a system in which he left several well-marked envelopes to pay for utilities and other bills, each with the correct amount of money. When collectors arrived at our door, usually sometime at the beginning of the month, all Mother had to do was hand them the envelope with the payment. But when Mother was short of money for groceries or some other small unexpected expense, she would take a little from one envelope, and then if that collector came first, she would borrow from another envelope, and so on and on. Soon, all the envelopes were missing a small amount and none matched the actual invoice. Mother would became totally hysterical when she couldn't pay the collector, who was waiting at our front door, his motorcycle double-parked on the street below, the engine still running. If the collector had to come back another time, a small fee would be added to the bill and Mother would have to explain to Father why the collector hadn't been paid the first time he came around. Father would explode in anger. He would holler and berate Mother for half an hour. Mother was so terrified of this moment that she would make up all kinds of lies. She would tell Father that she had been in the shower and didn't hear the bell ringing. Or that she had been on the roof hanging up the wet wash. As if she ever did that. The maid did the wash and hung the clothes on the roof.

Mother tried to keep a expense diary, including food, but poor thing, she didn't have a head for numbers. Her entries were a mess and never tallied with her checkbook. The parents had innumerable fights over the discrepancies in her accounts, and Mother shed countless tears over shortfalls that didn't amount to even one dollar, until finally, after many years and many tears, it occurred to Father to give her a twenty dollar slush fund. That was all Mother needed. She never went above that amount. Now, Father had to find other ways to make her life miserable.

My baby sister and I knew better than to ask Father to spend money on us. We had heard him say thousands of times that money didn't grow on trees and he wasn't a bank, so we avoided the whole lecture by never asking for anything.

Paradoxically, Father was devoted to certain brand names he had heard of as a penniless young man, and didn't mind spending money on these articles. The high point of our trip to Switzerland was that Father bought a pair of Bally shoes. From then on he never said, "I am going to put on my shoes"; it was always "I am going to put on my Ballys." When he bought a shirt for one of the uncles it was always, "I gave him an Arrow." Much later, in California, he felt the need to own a Mercedes, which he kept spotlessly clean in his garage and rarely drove. Whenever he needed a car, he drove my mother's Honda, a car he actually liked.

I thought these loathsome traits came from being foreign and Jewish. I certainly never saw any self-respecting Venezuelans behave this way. Venezuelans were big spenders, eager and ready to have fun. Whenever they had money, they were more than willing to treat everyone. In fact, money was never mentioned, talking about it was considered uncouth. To this day I connect everything Jewish with deprivation, self-denial, sacrifice and suffering. The parents never did anything impulsively, just for fun, especially if it meant spending some of their precious money. From the time we were little, whenever my baby sister and I wanted something the parents didn't consider indispensable, they always brought up the privations they had experienced in their youth and the suffering they endured and saw around them during the war. When I talked about this with Rebecca, she reminded me we had the bicycles. What she doesn't remember is that they were given to us by the neighbors in Copenhagen, whose children had long ago outgrown them.

When my baby sister, who was quite talented, wanted to study painting, she knew better than to ask for money. She found free evening classes at a government sponsored art school. But she still needed money for some meager art supplies and a small amount for bus fare. I guess she must have forgotten about the time she needed to buy clothes for her folk dance performance, because she made the mistake of asking the parents.

"Why in the world do you need to waste money and time on such worthless pursuits? What will you get out of it? My parents never bought me any such things!" Mother whined.

And Father chastised her: "I remember when I was little boy, most Jewish children were happy just to get a hot meal in the evening and have a roof over their head. And in the ghettos in Poland, children had nothing to play with, not even a crayon. And later, in the concentration camps, children worked all day long, from dawn to dusk, in freezing temperatures. They were more than grateful when they got a crust of bread and a little thin soup with a potato peel."

What did that have to do with anything? Go figure! We were not living in the ghetto or in the camps. We were living in a large South American city in a tropical country, where we never lacked food or a roof over our heads.

No matter what we asked for, the answer was always a resounding no, a word I think they enjoyed saying, especially if we asked for something they had never done or never had in their childhoods. There was no laughter in our family, no fun, no joy. Nothing was worthy of celebration, there were no happy occasions. "Don't bother, don't try, it isn't worth the effort, it isn't worth the expense, it's too much trouble." That's all we heard from Mother and Father.

Father belittled our achievements and turned our triumphs into failures. He was quick to blame and unwilling to praise. That's why we never bothered to show him our grades, which were always outstanding. That's why my baby sister never invited him to any of her swim meets. That's why she never told Father about the medals she won playing ping-pong. That's why she never told the parents about her high school graduation. Thank God, I was there for her, at least when she was little. I made sure she got the praise and applause she deserved. Father would never consider any of that important, worthy of praise or celebration. He would find something to pick on, something that displeased him, something to spoil the moment.

I envied the Venezuelan kids with all my heart. Their lives seemed so carefree and easy. So lighthearted, so full of excitement and laughter. There were so many celebrations, holidays, festive occasions. So many reasons to be happy. When I was a kid, being Jewish meant that I always had to be aware of all the tragedies of our past. That I could never forget what had happened to our family in Poland. That I would always look at life through distorted glasses that turned every glimmer of pleasure into misfortune. That I would never be able to laugh freely, enjoy life like all the kids around me. To this day, I get upset when I hear people waxing sentimental about their happy childhoods. What the hell are they talking about? I don't have an inkling. My childhood was something to get over with as quickly as possible. I wanted to start living real life, the way I wanted it.

The supreme irony is that my parents were not really good Jews. They had not chosen to be Jewish, any more than I had. They weren't waiting eagerly for the war to end, for the extermination and persecution of the Jews to end, so that they could go back to their roots and to their religion. They didn't return to their former beliefs and customs like other Jewish families. They did not try to go back to their own traditions, rituals, habits. There were several Jewish societies in Venezuela. There was a Jewish community, a Jewish school, a couple of synagogues, even a Jewish neighborhood. None of that interested my parents.

And when they finally had the chance to shed their accursed past, they did not have the guts to get rid of their detestable baggage. They did not dare to start anew, to forget the horror, the injustice and all their dead relatives and friends. They did not change their name, adopt a new religion, make a new life for themselves and for the next generations. Father came upon a golden opportunity to do this. It was a once-in-a-lifetime stroke of luck. Our next-door neighbor, Villareal, was appointed governor of the state of Miranda, which is a short distance southwest of Caracas. He was terribly impressed with Father's many university degrees, not to mention Father's inflated accounts of what he had done for the Polish government. Although Father's Spanish was less than exemplary, he asked Father to be his assistant. Father pondered this offer. Weeks went by and he couldn't make up his mind. Finally, he decided against taking the job. Father's craving for a position of prestige and recognition succumbed to his fear of making waves, of being known as part of a government that could, God forbid, fall in a couple of years, or a couple of months, for that matter. Father declined the appointment. Then and there, I made the decision that if I ever found myself in a similar situation, I would never be so spineless. For goodness sake, even my most pusillanimous cat shows more nerve than that.

But maybe Father made the right decision, since he seemed unable to learn Venezuelan ways. He could not master the Venezuelan greeting, a very complicated ritual and a must when two men meet and want to express just the right mix of familiarity and esteem. Father was too awkward and stiff. He could never relax enough to extend the right hand and at the exact moment lift the left arm to lightly pat a couple of times the back of his colleague. Without that skill, you might as well forget it, you are sunk

in Latin-American politics. Instead, Father would grab the prof-
fered hand and pump it vigorously up and down several times.
Such a greeting might be appropriate for people of Prussian ancestry, but it was considered outrageously bombastic in the tropics.

I remember seeing old pictures of Father from Poland and
Germany. Standing stiffly at attention in full military regalia, surrounded by portly men in similar outfits, he was greeting minis-
ters and other government officials. He looked like part of the
group, he fit in. But no matter how hard I tried, I couldn't imagine
him as a member of the governor's cabinet in the state of Miranda.
It was even harder to imagine Mother appearing at official func-
tions with the first lady of the state. With her too-short, too-tight
outfits, her disheveled hair that never managed to cover her scalp,
her gold teeth peeking out of her mouth, she would be ludicrous.
Mother would be as out of place as a plump goose among foxes.
But there is no point dwelling on lost opportunities. We never
belonged in the country where we resided. Father declined his
chance for the appointment. He was too faint-hearted. He kept
doing his job as a store manager, an occupation he despised with
his whole heart, an occupation he considered beneath him, an
occupation that turned him into an embittered and resentful old
man.

I promised myself that I was not going to be like my parents. I
wanted to belong somewhere. To put down roots in one place. To
feel at home in a community. I knew even then that if I wanted to
find some shred of happiness, I would have to live far from the
family. As far away as I could go. The family would forever remind
me of who I was and where I came from. And that I could not tolerate.

I knew then what I had to do. I would invent my own life. I
would create a past that wouldn't drag me down and mark me forever as a member of a third-rate, often hated group. I would build
a future for myself. And if I ever had children, I would free them
from this curse, protect them from this dreadful history, shelter
them from the pain and misery. My children would be free to live
normal, happy lives. I began to plot my escape.

Unfortunately, escape meant leaving my beloved Venezuela,
the one place I knew I wanted to fit in. But I knew now, without
the shadow of a doubt, that I was never going to belong in
Venezuela. I certainly did not want to return to Europe, the source

of all the traits I found so repulsive. The only two places left were Canada and the United States. But after spending one long unhappy year in Canada, I rejected that idea. The United States seemed to be my only option. I knew I would move heaven and earth to escape my present situation and reach the United States. For me, there was no other alternative. It was either do or die.

I didn't mind abandoning my friends, if you could call them that. I really didn't have anybody I was close to. I quit high school in the middle of my third year, and I never again wanted to see any of my classmates. At the club, I met a lot of different boys. They all wanted to be my boyfriend. Some even wanted to marry me. But I really didn't like any of them. There had a been a young French boy, Francois, who was a year younger than I. Coincidentally, he was the stepbrother of Rebecca's boyfriend Christian. He carved my name on the bottom of the deepest end of the pool. What a silly, childish thing to do! As if I would be impressed with that kind of infantile behavior. And there had been Robert, one of the U.S. Marines stationed at the embassy in Caracas. He was kind of cute. I liked him quite a bit. Well, at least more than the other jerks I met. But I soon found out all he wanted was to get me drunk on cheap beer and get my clothes off. At first, I was impressed because he was so different from the boys I knew. He was American, he had already finished high school, he was older, he had traveled, he knew different places, and, of course, he spoke English. But after a couple of weeks, I realized that he didn't seem to have any goals beyond drinking himself into a stupor and having sex. If possible both at the same time. I dropped him like a hot coal. In the United States there would be a lot better ones. I didn't have to settle for the first cute American guy who crossed my path.

My baby sister was like my shadow, following me wherever I went. Like a puppy watching its owner, she never took her eyes off me. As much as I loved her, it cramped my style. She knew all the boys who were vying for my attention. She even had favorites she tried to foist on me. So when I met this bunch of American marines from the embassy, I was delighted. Rebecca couldn't communicate with them because they spoke only English. Finally, I had some privacy, a life of my own, not shared with my little sister. Listening to them talk about life in the United States made me even more resolved and eager to move there. That was my destiny. And just in case it wasn't, I was going to make it so.

I left home at fifteen and returned only twice for very short periods in the summers, until I managed to extricate myself for good by marrying the very first man who asked me. Jimmy, my knight in shining armor, would be my ticket out. I would finally belong somewhere. Be part of a community. Live the life that I dreamt of. The life that had eluded me until then. Of course, Jimmy was totally unaware of all this. And that made him even more invaluable.

My only regret was that I had to leave my little sister behind, alone in the enemy's hands. I was afraid for her. I promised myself that I would get her out too, as soon as I could. As soon as I was settled enough and had the ability to do so. I felt I needed to save myself first so that I would have the strength to rescue her, just like in an airplane you have to slip on your own oxygen mask first and then strap it on your child. I wanted to bring Rebecca to the States and have her attend a college near me.

I never fulfilled that promise. That's something I will always regret. A lot of pain and suffering could have been averted if I had done as I said I would. If I had prevented my parents from dragging my baby sister off to Uruguay. By then, she was almost seventeen. I thought she would be able to defend herself from my parents' onslaught. But I was wrong. My parents had the uncanny ability of finding the things you cared most for, taking them away from you, and shattering your life in the process. And all along they would tell you it's for your own good. Liars! Hypocrites! That's what they tried to do to me, and that's what they were aiming to do to my baby sister. My excuse for not interfering, which now sounds kind of paltry seen in the light of what happened later, was that I was too busy with my newborn baby. I told myself I was all alone in Florida, trying to survive on a miserly ninety dollars a month, confronting myriads of problems. Even if I had known what was going on, I don't think I could have helped. I don't think I could have rescued Rebecca from my parents' clutches. But I will forever regret that I didn't even try.

As for me, I was lucky. I could have done a lot worse. I made damn sure never to live close to my parents again. As a matter of fact, I was a bit miffed when they finally decided to settle in the United States. But luckily, California was as far from Alabama, as Alabama was from Venezuela. After I got married, in 1959, I hardly ever saw my parents again. I didn't go much to California, and they didn't insist on visiting me here. They had 8x10 color pictures of their grandchildren gracing their walls, and didn't evince any desire to visit them. And that was fine with me.

I am neither Jewish nor Polish in America. That is one dirty little secret in my life that I have chosen not to reveal. Not to my late husband, or my children. But it carries a price. The punishment for passing as a member of a group of your chosen peers is to have to listen to derogatory remarks and racial slurs about the group to which you secretly belong.

I don't have any idea how many Jewish people live in my community. Few who will own up to it, that's for sure. There are less than one hundred families in North Alabama who practice the Hebrew religion. There is only one rabbi within a hundred miles. Oddly enough, we are acquainted. We belong to some of the same "save-the-environment" groups. We both volunteer to teach English as a second language in the same school and do community work. We like each other, but we are not really friends. I have never been to his house, he has never been to mine. We have had dinner together once. We chatted about this and that, totally inconsequential matters. I cannot help wondering how he would react if he knew that I, too, am Jewish.

I know that I consciously make an effort to do things very differently from the way my parents did them. Remembering how things were at home makes me veer in the opposite direction. My little sister says that all children of immigrants make sure they never resemble their parents. But for me, it's much more intense than that. To resemble my parents in any way, shape or form, would be punishment beyond endurance. Rebecca tells me that whenever she and Ricardo, the man she married and later divorced, had an argument, he would bring in the heavy artillery. He would shout, "You are just like your father!" and she would be devastated. Well, I have the same reaction, but a thousand times more so.

I refuse to cook the way my mother cooked and eat the foods they ate. I can't stand stews loaded with lard, chicken soup with yellow fat blobs floating on the surface and tasteless large dumplings that taste and look as if they were made out of cement. And I hate compote. There ought to be a law against boiled fruit. I refuse to dress the way Mother did, in her short tailored suits, too-tight button-popping see-through blouses. Tottering in her two-sizes-too-small high-heeled pointy shoes. I refuse to wear pounds of caked make-up, thick runny mascara, dark-red lipstick that cakes in the wrinkles around the lips. I refuse to furnish my house the way Mother's was. Every piece upholstered in lustrous gray brocade with large purple cabbage roses. Hideous dark armoires. Chipped porcelain pieces on every surface, all left over from their porcelain import business. I refuse to live in makeshift apartments and have only a tiny balcony as a substitute for a garden. I refuse to live out of suitcases, as if I were camping. I refuse to postpone every human pleasure until doomsday. And, more than anything else in this world, I refuse to bring up my children in the atmosphere of indescribable anguish and appalling neglect that prevailed in my childhood home.

I am very good at lying to myself. When I say that, I can almost see my little sister vigorously nodding her head. It is my most effective analgesic. It takes the pain away, without the need for alcohol or drugs. Who needs the truth if it is going to hurt so much?

"It didn't happen. You only imagined it. You misunderstood. You are too sensitive. Too quick to judge. Too quick to take offense. You have come to the wrong conclusion." These were the words I learned to live by. I tried to convince myself that this is how it was.

It was better than believing that my parents didn't love me. Even worse, no matter how hard I tried, I couldn't bring myself to love them. I was deeply ashamed of myself for not feeling affection for my mother. It's wrong not to love one's own mother. I knew that from books and movies. What kind of a monster am I? I hid all these feelings behind a veneer of politeness, which I could only sustain at a distance. I am certainly glad I lived so far. I can assure you that it was no accident.

Years later, as my father lay dying, it all came to a climax. Father found out he had terminal cancer. He asked me to come. Unfortunately, no one asked my mother how she felt. No one ever bothered to ask Mother how she felt about anything. Her opinions and her wishes never counted.

I was shocked when I found out she didn't want me there. She didn't even try to hide it. If it were not for the fact that Father's death was imminent (he died two days later), I would have caught the first plane home. As it was, Mother finally put into words what I had hidden so painstakingly from myself all those years. She admitted, with relish, and with unsurpassed venom, how much she had always resented me, actually hated me. When she got wind that Father had asked me to help him dissolve morphine pills in a glass of water, she became hysterical and started choking with rage.

"You ungrateful daughter, you selfish blonde slut! Don't you think I've always known I have to watch you? You've always plotted to take him away from me, since you were a mean little brat. I am not going to let you do this to me," Mother screeched. "I don't want you near him! Go home! I don't want to ever see you again. I am sorry I ever gave birth to you, you snake! I knew you were bad news from the very first moment I laid eyes on you."

Since I could no longer lie to myself, I no longer had to feel guilty about severing my relations with her, a guilt that had burdened me for years. I swore never to see her again and I kept that promise. The poor, pitiful shell of a human being, whom I visited in the nursing home several years later, had nothing in common with the mother who rejected me and made me lie to myself for so long. I have forgiven her long ago. Someday soon, I will forgive myself too.

Rebecca

After my sister left, I was desolate. I would stare at her empty bed, grab a book, get under the covers with a flashlight and read until I couldn't keep my eyes open. Soon I was staying in her bed all night. I looked in her closet to see whether, by any chance, she had forgotten her white cashmere sweater. No such luck. But I did find a couple of tee-shirts she wore often, her blue jeans with the black ink spots on the pockets and her old bathing suit. I began wearing her things. Most of the clothes she left were old and worn, but I didn't mind. They were also too tight and short for me, I had outgrown my sister before I turned eleven. I didn't mind that either. I felt strangely reckless in her clothes, willing to do unexpected things. When I looked in the mirror, instead of my usual cautious goody-two-shoes self, I saw a wilder, more intense, daring girl, sexy and alluring.

I wore my sister's jeans and her striped tee-shirt to go to the club in the evenings. I wore her bathing suit, too. I felt I could swim faster when I had it on. It brought me luck. I started noticing boys. Suddenly I wasn't alone all the time. Boys were everywhere, asking me to play tennis, or ping-pong. Even though I was far from being a beauty, I now seemed to be surrounded by boys I found attractive.

A few days after I turned twelve, I met Christian at a tennis tournament in the club. I liked him from the first moment I set eyes on him. He was French, a couple of years older than I, and very cute. I knew I wanted to impress him on the court, to make him notice me. We were playing mixed doubles, on opposite sides. I played harder than ever, taking risks at the net, trying to return impossible shots. It worked. We started dating. Soon we were spending every evening together.

Christian's father owned several nightclubs in Caracas. We

would play tennis in the evening, then shower, grab a snack and go dancing at the Flamingo or at the Rio, where all the waitresses knew Christian and served us whatever drinks we asked for. The band also played our requests. We felt very sophisticated and grown up, ordering drinks at a club, dancing most of the night. When the school year was over, we played tennis and swam in the pool, or sometimes we drove to the beach. We went to the cinema often and saw all the censored movies because I could show my phony driver's license. Nobody seemed to care that I was only twelve and didn't look much older. We went dancing, we kissed, held hands and talked. It was romantic and exciting. I was enthralled. This is what love should be like. Finally, I was dancing as much as I wanted. Christian was an excellent dancer. He knew all the latest songs and would sing them softly in English, which I thought was enormously clever and sexy. Elvis was king in America, and we were dancing rock and roll in the nightclubs of Caracas. I felt happy and sophisticated, no longer an outcast. Finally I was living my life as it was meant to be, as I had imagined it in my daydreams.

But too soon it came to an end. Christian's father had just remarried. His new wife had a fifteen year-old son in a boarding school in France and they decided it would be best to send Christian to a boarding school in Alaska. I saw him only one more time. He came to Berkeley before I got married to try to make me change my mind. Years later, I heard that he had gone to Vietnam as a foreign correspondent. I've heard nothing from him since, but sometimes, when I feel lonely, I wonder what became of him, my first love.

My sister wrote infrequently. She was unhappy in Canada. She detested the rules at the boarding school, she didn't like the cold climate in Toronto, she hated having to go to church on Sundays, and she disliked staying alone in the empty dorm over the weekends. My parents had asked their relatives in Toronto to take my sister on weekends and holidays, but after spending one whole day in their company she rejected the idea. They were Orthodox Jews who tried to force her to participate in their strange rituals and ablutions, she said, and she wanted to be left alone. In one of the few letters addressed to me she wrote she would rather die than sleep one more night at their stuffy, smelly apartment and eat their heavy, tasteless food. She never mentioned meeting anybody or making new friends. Her letters were filled with inanities and purged of any important news because they were meant to be read by our parents. But I knew her well enough to read in between the lines, and I could tell she was miserable and desperate. I felt troubled by the thought that she was having such a bad time. Had she fought so hard to leave behind a life she hated just to end up in a place where she was even more unhappy? That was terribly unfair.

Finally it was summer and my sister returned. I was excited. I couldn't wait, I had so many things to tell her. At last we'd be together again, she fresh from her last year of high school and I nearly halfway through, almost on an equal footing. Now we could tell each other all the things we didn't dare mention in our letters for fear that our parents would read them. We would be like peas in a pod once more. It would all be like before, but better, because we had been apart so long and we missed each other so much. But I was wrong. That year apart had changed us both. We each had followed our own path and had our own experiences, our own interests. There was no going back to the intense closeness I remembered from my childhood.

My sister seemed distant and preoccupied. She didn't participate in our old activities, didn't seek out her old friends. She wasn't interested in going to the club with me, she didn't want to play ping-pong like we used to, or sit on a towel on the highest diving platform and chat, just the two of us, alone on top of the world.

She must have known that what she did in the next few weeks would either make or break her dream of becoming an American. She started looking for ways to leave again, perusing the last pages of American magazines, looking for colleges that seemed suitable. Soon she made up a list of names, and started writing to these colleges. A short time later, she got various packets from several schools and before I realized it, she was gone again, this time to Florida. There were so many things I didn't get to tell her, so many things I hadn't shared with her. I wished with all my heart I could have gone with her.

My sister arrived in Miami and took a long taxi ride from the airport to the college campus of her choice. The cab driver tried to warn her that she didn't want to go there, but she didn't understand what he meant. She arrived at the campus and was ushered into the president's office by a black girl. The receptionist was also black. So was the president. Everybody looked at my shockingly blond, pink, green-eyed sister with agonizing embarrassment. They explained to her that the college was for blacks only. The administration had assumed she knew. But how could she have? The magazine ad had not mentioned race or color. And since photographs had not been required in the application, they could not have known she was white. Everybody was duly apologetic. The administration immediately issued my sister a refund check, wished her well in her search for a more suitable college, and called a cab for her return trip to Miami. My sister took a room in a hotel and started her search anew.

Susanna enrolled in Stetson University, a college in northern Florida. She kept sending me photographs of herself on her way to various collegiate dances, looking ravishing in gauzy strapless dresses with large fancy corsages. In several pictures, a good looking young man with a rather serious and aloof gaze was standing next to her. I would lie down on my bed with the lights off and imagine endless beach parties on golden sand, young people around a campfire singing, and nighttime swimming in the warm waters of the sea. Or I would imagine my sister arriving at a party in a white convertible, wearing a dress made of a light, airy fabric, dancing the night away under the moonlight on a terrace suffused in the aroma of gardenias. That was the mental picture of college life I carried with me a year later when I applied to the university of California at Berkeley.

As they were leaving Europe, in 1949, my parents had applied for permanent visas to reside in the United States. Because only a limited number of Poles were allowed to immigrate every year, the waiting list was very long. My parents' number would not come up until 1965, sixteen years after their application had been approved. They had already waited nine years and they were willing to wait seven more.

But after my sister left, in the summer of 1958, my parents decided to explore California, still looking for their utopian land. My mother's older sister Esther, who had just come from Israel to stay with us, would take care of me. At least that was what my parents thought. But as it turned out, I took care of her.

My aunt Esther must have been in her middle forties. She was small and slim like my mother, but the resemblance ended there. Although born only a year before my mother, she looked ten years older. She wore a special boot on one foot because one leg was a few inches shorter than the other, and she walked with a marked limp. During the war, when the ghetto was being dismantled and Jews were being rounded up and carted off to the camps, my aunt Esther, her husband and her nine year-old daughter Rachelle and two other families hid in the cellar of an empty apartment house. The German soldiers, who were thorough in hunting down Jews, found them with the help of specially trained dogs, and gunned them down right there on the spot. Only my aunt survived the shooting. When the clean-up crew came to dispose of the bodies she was still alive. Part of her leg had been shot off and had to be amputated. She spent the rest of the war in various concentration camps. After the war she was repatriated to Poland. In 1956, when Poland allowed the Jews to leave, she emigrated to Israel to join her brother and his family. There she was shunted from relative to relative, and during those years she spent time in various mental hospitals. Before my aunt's arrival, my parents warned me to never mention that I knew about my cousin's tragic death. My parents had been contributing to my aunt's upkeep in Israel and must have known about her mental problems.

Even before my parents left for California, my aunt started behaving oddly. I ascribed this to her intuitive feeling that she was not truly welcome. Father said that the relatives from Israel had foisted her on our family because they were tired of dealing with her infirmities. Her arrival had been preceded by atrocious fights, Father cussed viciously and blamed Mother and her whole family for all the woes of the world. Mother, as usual, cried and threatened to commit suicide. Soon after she moved in, my aunt started locking herself in her room and not coming out for hours. She even covered the keyhole after accusing my father of spying on her. She also stopped eating anything she didn't prepare herself. She was convinced somebody was trying to poison her. I was the only person in the household exempt from suspicion. She would allow me to bring her a cup of tea, some fruit, or a biscuit. My parents were so busy with the preparations for their long trip that they failed to notice the strangeness of her behavior.

One evening, a few days after my parents' departure, my aunt walked into my bedroom sobbing. She was wielding a large kitchen knife in her right hand. She told me in a hoarse whisper that she needed to save me from my father, who was the devil incarnate and who would destroy me just as he had destroyed my mother. The only way she could rescue me from his evil clutches was by killing me. Then I would go to heaven to join her little daughter, Rachelle, who was shot dead during the war. She was expecting me in heaven, where we would become good friends. Aunt Esther was weeping hard, and repeating between sobs that she needed to kill me because I resembled her dead daughter and she loved me more than anybody else in this world. Then, her mission accomplished, she could kill herself and end this suffering once and for all.

I started crying, partly from fear, partly from empathy. We wept together, in between her repeated avowals of homicidal intentions. Finally she cried herself into exhaustion, and I managed to pry the knife away from her and put her to bed. She told me, sobbing more softly now, that her life was useless, that she didn't do anybody any good by staying alive, that she was a lot of trouble to her family and would be better off dead. I sat with her until she fell asleep.

Once my aunt fell asleep I became frantic. I wondered whether I should try to barricade my bedroom by dragging the dresser and propping it against the door. The key, that same key that had kept my sister locked in our bedroom for weeks, had been lost. But I was afraid my aunt would wake up terrified and harm herself. Finally, after much hesitation, I decided to do nothing. I would leave my door open and read through the rest of the night. To make sure I didn't fall asleep, I made myself a pot of coffee.

The next morning, my aunt locked herself in her room and wouldn't come out or even answer when I knocked. I got really worried. I knew Father wouldn't want me to ask aunt Alina for help. She would blame the whole crisis on my parents for leaving me alone with an unstable relative. It would only serve to fuel their ongoing war about the philosophy of child rearing. As a last resort, I called Vittorio, the manager of my father's stores. He came immediately after I explained what had happened and called for medical assistance. When Vittorio pried aunt Esther's bedroom door open with a crowbar, he found her curled up in her bed in a fetal position. She looked tiny and scared and didn't seem to recognize me. An ambulance arrived and she was taken to a psychiatric ward. I wanted to be with her in the ambulance but I was told I couldn't, so I followed in my car. My aunt was hospitalized for more than two months and underwent electric shock treatment. I visited often, but she was listless and apathetic, and I couldn't get her to respond to me. I sat by her bed, and told her about my schoolwork, my classes, my friends. I wasn't sure she heard. She never reacted in any way.

I really didn't mind being alone. Quite the contrary, I enjoyed the solitude. I no longer had to spend evenings out to avoid listening to my parents constant bickering. I had peace and tranquility. I would come home from school, make myself a sandwich and a salad for dinner, then read a book until bedtime, or go to the club to play tennis. Nighttime was the best time to play, it wasn't too hot or too muggy, and the club had excellent lights. I didn't feel lonely or scared. I knew I could always call my aunt Alina and stay with her if I wanted. I chose not to.

Miraculously, Vittorio had managed to reach my parents in California, but they decided that everything was under control and cutting short their trip would serve no purpose. Vittorio offered to bring his mother from Italy to stay with me for the remainder of the six weeks, but I convinced him this was unnecessary. I was doing just fine. After my parents returned, my aunt was released to them, and they sent her back to the relatives in Israel, where she lives to this day. I wrote to her in Polish, after my mother passed away, but I never received an answer. I know from the other relatives in Israel that she is still alive. She must be nearly ninety now.

Summer came around again and my sister was due to return once more to Caracas. Mother, at Father's insistence, redecorated my sister's bedroom in an effort to lure her to stay. She bought new furniture, new drapes, a new carpet. I was relegated to the maid's bedroom, the same one my aunt Esther had occupied just a few months before.

This was to be the last time my sister and I lived under the same roof for more than just a few days, but at the time I didn't know it. We had trouble communicating, which had never happened before. Susanna didn't seem interested in anything I did, and didn't want to talk about her own life. Whenever I tried to ask her something or engage her in conversation, she would start reading a magazine or leave the room. I felt rejected and completely shut out of her life. She didn't even tell me what she was studying in Florida. She never mentioned she was planning to quit the university.

My sister stayed less than two weeks, just long enough to have a wedding dress made. She was going back to Florida in August, to marry Jimmy, the brooding guy in the photographs she sent us. I suspected she had been sleeping with him, even though she never told me. I noticed she had the cutest little nightie, a periwinkle blue baby doll, frilly and lacy. When we had shared a bedroom, she always slept in a torn, frayed tee-shirt. But I wanted to know for sure.

"Susanna, you did it? Didn't you?" I asked.

"What are you talking about?"

"You know. That. You did it with Jimmy. That's why you have a new baby doll."

"Don't be daft. If I had done it, and do notice the 'if,' I would have done it naked. For heavens sake! I don't need to buy a night-gown to do it."

"But you did it. I know, I can tell."

"You are nuts. Besides, it's none of your damn business, you lit-tle blabbermouth."

"You don't need to lie to me, I won't tell our parents, you know that. It's not such a big deal. I know that girls in the States do it all the time, even before they finish high school. I just want to know how it feels."

"Well, then, learn for yourself. Leave me out. Subject closed."

But I started to look for telltale signs. I noticed that in the morn-ings she locked herself in the bathroom for an inordinately long time and ran the faucet full strength, just like we did when we were kids and were embarrassed by bathroom noises. She emerged looking disheveled and wan, her face blotchy, her eyed red. Most mornings she locked herself in her bedroom and wouldn't come out for break-fast. I would make a pot of coffee and go to her locked bedroom door.

"Coffee is ready!"

"I don't want any," she would reply.

"Come on, Susie, it's your favorite, Venezuelan coffee. I made a whole pot for the two of us."

"Get lost. Go to hell."

I sat in the dining room alone. I remembered yesterday when she was trying on her wedding dress she told the seamstress to make her dress roomier in the waist. That and the lacy, frilly baby doll finally clicked. I put two and two together. So that was it. I was going to become an aunt! That's why Susanna didn't want to talk to me and answer my questions. That was why she was so anxious to go back to Florida and get married. Now that I knew the truth I was dying to talk to somebody, but there was no one around I could confide in. In school, there had been rumors about girls who dropped out in the middle of the year, but none of them were friends of mine. All I could do was sit tight and watch, trying to suppress my growing excitement.

In August we traveled to Florida for my sister's wedding and I finally got to meet Jimmy. Susanna seemed nervous and made sure there was little contact between the two families. This was not as difficult as it may seem, since we didn't speak English beyond a few greetings and pleasantries, and Jimmy's family didn't speak a word of Spanish. We smiled a lot at each other, but we were as compatible as a cat and a fish. Jimmy's sister took me to a bridal shop, where I was outfitted in a light blue bridesmaid dress that made me look old and matronly. She also took me to her beauty parlor to have my hair done into a bouffant helmet just like hers, but mercifully they were too busy to take me in at such short notice.

Before the wedding, Jimmy's cousin Charlie invited me to go to the beach. It was a swell idea but we couldn't communicate, so we just sat on a blanket, stared at each other and smiled. Suddenly, out of the blue, Charlie proposed to me. At first, I wasn't sure I understood correctly, but he took my hand and pretended to put a ring on my fourth finger. He and Jimmy had always done things together, he said, and if my sister was good enough for Jimmy, then I was good enough for him. I was speechless. Finally, when I found my voice, I managed to remind him that I was only fifteen, I had one more year of high school to finish, and then I wanted to go to college. He said that didn't matter. He would wait.

My parents got a good deal on a rented convertible and I drove around by myself, exploring the surrounding area. I don't remember being worried about being barely fifteen and not having an American driver's license, after all, I had my Venezuelan license that said I was eighteen. I found a gym where I could play table-tennis and spent several afternoons playing with a bunch of college guys who couldn't come to grips with the fact that a girl was beating them. That made my day and helped compensate for an otherwise rather desultory trip.

But I was gripped by a strange sense of uneasiness whenever I looked at my sister. Something was wrong in her life, but I couldn't put my finger on it. I tried to talk to her, like we used to when we were kids, no holds barred, but she avoided me. I couldn't rid myself of the feeling that Jimmy wasn't the right man for her. When I looked at the guests at the wedding ceremony, nobody seemed to be particularly happy, not even the groom, and much less the bride. In Venezuela, Susanna had always been surrounded by adoring boys who would have given anything to get a date with her much less become her boyfriend. She was so beautiful and smart that she could have had any man she wanted. Why had she chosen Jimmy? But I understood she had a dream, a fantasy. She must have thought that even if this was not exactly the fulfillment of her fantasy, at least it came closer than anything she had experienced before.

Susanna seemed to alternate between states of garish effusiveness and grim determination. I could feel an undercurrent of anguish in her mood shifts. Most of her sweet smiles and welcoming words were reserved for Jimmy's relatives and friends, while all the snide remarks and offensive comments were directed at us, her family. I resented terribly being lumped together with our parents. Wasn't I her most loyal supporter, her most ardent admirer, her most faithful ally? Why did she suddenly consider me the enemy? She was exceedingly cordial to Jimmy's relatives, all smiles and compliments. Why was she so brusque and harsh with me?

I pondered about what was happening between us. Perhaps Susanna needed to confide in somebody, but felt I wasn't old enough or experienced enough to give her the advice and help she needed. Perhaps she did not want me to lose the illusion that she always had everything under control, that she always knew exactly what she was doing. Whatever the cause, I soon realized Susanna couldn't restrain herself. She raged at us over the tiniest details, over the silliest things.

We were getting ready to meet Jimmy's parents and Susanna came to pick us up at the motel.

"What the hell are you wearing? Do you want to embarrass me to death?" she screamed at Mother. She rummaged through our suitcases, throwing everything on the bed and, when she ran out of space, on the floor, until she found something suitable. Mother had to take off her purple taffeta suit and her patent leather heels, and ended up wearing a navy skirt, a white blouse with a round collar and black loafers. From the neck down she looked like a college girl getting ready for her sorority pledge. I returned my orange and yellow sun dress to the closet and changed into a navy plaid skirt and a white jersey. Then, Susanna noticed Mother was carrying a small gift-wrapped package and all hell broke loose.

"What is that thing in your hand?"she asked, pointedly.

"Just a little something I brought for Jimmy's mother."

"I can see that, I am not blind. What's inside?"

"An antique porcelain figurine, a shepherdess girl with a lamb," Mother answered.

"Are you crazy? You brought one of those ridiculous chipped figurines left over from your business? I'll die if you give this to my mother-in-law," Susanna groaned.

"But it's a perfectly suitable gift. It's a real Meissen figurine. Lots of people all over the world would be grateful to get something like this," Mother said defensively.

"If you dare to inflict this ugly knickknack on Jimmy's family I'll commit suicide," Susanna shouted and started sobbing wildly. Mother reluctantly put the package back in her suitcase.

Susanna threw tantrums, cried, and yelled at us from the time she picked us up at the airport, until the moment we finally departed. After a few days, when I realized that this was more than just bride's nerves, I decided the best course was to try to avoid her completely. I went about my business, ignoring all the danger signs that now had become so obvious. Not soon enough for me, the two weeks in Florida were over and we went back to Caracas.

I wasn't surprised when six months later we got a baby announcement from my sister. My nephew Ricky was born hale and healthy, weighing seven pounds and, judging from the picture, with a wonderful smile and a full head of blond hair. Mother believed until the day she died that Ricky was a miraculously large premature baby and I was not about to enlighten her.

This was my last year of high school. Academically, I was far ahead of everybody; I didn't have to study. I became involved in the school drama department. We staged several plays, all historical and educational, since that was all the drama department in my school allowed. But in spite of these limitations the experience was wonderful. I started dating Juan Carlos, a new classmate who had just arrived from Spain that year and was also involved in several of the theater productions. The first play we did together was about Simon Bolivar, the great South American liberator, and Juan Carlos played the part of Bolivar. He had only a few lines at the beginning of the play, when Bolivar lay on his deathbed exhorting Venezuelans to continue the fight for independence. The rest of the time he had to remain on stage, lying on a stretcher and covered by a Venezuelan flag, while the other characters reacted to this tragic event and grieved his untimely death. In the second act, Bolivar's young wife enters the room, pulls back the sheet, recognizes her husband, and collapses in grief over the deceased. Unfortunately, the day of the opening performance, the stretcher had been placed facing the wrong direction. When Bolivar's wife pulled back the large flag covering the body she uncovered her husband's feet. Without missing a beat, she went on with her lines and collapsed sobbing on top of the great hero's feet. The audience sitting in the orchestra section didn't know anything was wrong, but the people seated in the balconies got a great view of the mishap. At first a titter spread through the theater, soon it became a roar of laughter. Suddenly the flag covering the stretcher started shaking. The corpse was laughing so hard that all the other actors on stage started laughing, too. Soon, even the sobs of the hapless wife turned into enormous whoops of laughter. At the end the audience clapped and cheered enthusiastically for several minutes. The reviews in the school paper were excellent and we won an award from the district.

Juan Carlos was the intellectual type, he liked to read serious books on philosophy, political thought, and history. When we were not rehearsing at school, we would spend evenings in my room, doing homework, talking, reading poetry and, of course, kissing. I wasn't sure how far we could go before it should be considered risky behavior. I didn't want to find myself in the same predicament as my sister, but I was curious about sex. Susanna had once more opened a door for me, she had had sex, and now I felt I could, too. I wondered what I would say to Juan Carlos if he wanted to go all the way. We had plenty of opportunities. My parents were never home before ten or eleven at night, but even if they arrived early they never came to my room, which, because it had been intended for the maid, was behind the kitchen, far from all the other rooms in the apartment. But Juan Carlos didn't try to go beyond kissing and some light groping. I wasn't sure whether I was relieved or disappointed.

"You know, Rebecca, you may not be the most beautiful girl in class, but I believe you are the smartest and most interesting to talk to. You know how to listen and how to think, you have opinions. I never get tired of talking to you," murmured Juan Carlos. I wasn't happy. I didn't care whether he thought I was smart or a good listener—I had no use for those qualities. I wanted my boyfriend to think of me as sexy and alluring. I wanted at least to get the chance to say no. But I was never asked.

I kept going to the club, swimming, playing tennis and table tennis, even taking part in competition. I was eliminated from the National Tennis Championship in the very first game I played, but I won the table tennis tournament for the third year in a row. I really liked winning at sports. This marked me as an oddity among

Venezuelan girls, who at that time were not supposed to sweat, run, jump, dive into a swimming pool, or do anything that could muss their make-up or spoil their hairdos. The implicit goal of every teenage girl was to catch a husband. No effort was spared to reach this end. My classmates talked endlessly about their clothes, their make-up, their seamstresses, their hairdressers and their manicurists. I was a total failure at appearing "chic" and fashionable, so I stopped trying. It was easier to pretend I was not interested than to try again and again and fail.

I joined the lifeguard patrol at the club. No special training was required, it was enough that I was a good swimmer. Once a week, on Sundays, the club lifeguards would volunteer their services at one of the public beaches. We would check the night before which beach we were assigned to, and early next morning we would pile into my car and drive down to the coast. We managed to drag out a few people from rip tides and rough waves, and received several commendations. I remember one morning when Juan Carlos and I rescued a Portuguese man who had lost his footing after a huge wave dragged him away from the shore. Later that afternoon, he approached the lifeguard station, followed by his teary-eyed wife and children and, after thanking us profusely, insisted that we accept money for saving his life. We were too young and trying too hard to appear cool to understand the emotional significance of this inci-dent. Juan Carlos, teasingly, asked the poor man how much his life was worth, and watched with amusement at how distraught he looked. But after having a few laughs at his expense, we refused compensation. We were having loads of fun on the beach, we enjoyed a sense of importance, we did a lot of things together and we all became good friends. Even though occasionally I was still plagued by feelings of being an outsider, I had developed successful ways of coping. My life seemed to be on track.

But Venezuela was besieged by political problems. Daily riots rocked the university, which caused it to close several times for increasingly longer periods. The country was shaken by a grassroots movement to overthrow the dictator. Even my high school had its share of turmoil. Students gathered in the courtyard carrying plac-ards. There were marches, demonstrations, political speeches. Classrooms remained empty day after day. During one of the most turbulent riots, the administration called in the military police, who surrounded the school. A helicopter landed on the roof and disgorged several soldiers. They entered the school but were met by a mob of angry students who cornered them on the third floor. In the ensuing melee, one soldier fell or was pushed over the balcony railing onto the cement courtyard below. His death prompted the authorities to close the high school for several months.

My parents learned about these events from the papers. They felt alarmed and dismayed that the political climate prevailing in the country had spread to the schools and was interfering with my studies. This incident bolstered their desire to send me abroad to a quiet, peaceful campus where the main focus would be on learning. Berkeley was their choice. During their trip to the United States they had visited the University of California campus at Berkeley and loved the stately buildings, the green lawns, the quiet atmosphere. But Father decided this was the right place for me. History would prove him wrong.

I didn't want to leave Caracas, but I had no choice, I had to defer to my parents' wishes. I felt comfortable with my life, things were going well. But a part of me was also curious, wanting to know how life would be in the United States, the place my sister loved so much and fought so hard to reach. I felt I was following in her footsteps again, reaping all the advantages of her hard-won battles. I was seduced by all the fantasies I had about my sister's freshman year at a university in Florida, and to this I added all the images I had gathered from American movies, where perky girls in bikinis spent all their time flirting at beach parties, roasting hot dogs and marshmallows, dancing rock-and-roll, and playing volleyball. I had visions of fancy college dances, the girls dressed in lovely strapless dresses, dancing cheek to cheek with handsome young men in white tuxedos. In my fantasy, I was the most popular girl, the one who was asked to dance every song, the one who never sat a dance out. Perhaps life in the United States would not be so bad after all.

A few months before I was to leave for the States, another branch of our family arrived in Venezuela. My father's older brother Stasik came with his wife Eva and their two daughters, Andrea and Sonia, both younger than I. My uncle and aunt had spent the war in Poland with false identification papers, just like my father. In fact, it was Father who managed to obtain the fictitious certificates of baptism from a friendly priest. Eleven years after the war, when Jews were finally allowed to leave Poland, my uncle and aunt, with their two small daughters took advantage of this opportunity and went to Israel. Unfortunately, life in Israel was still extremely difficult and they did not manage to acclimate. They found conditions were so wretched that they regretted leaving Poland. After two years of indecision, they emigrated again, this time to join us in Caracas. They had suffered through many hard times and were eager to finally settle down.

Unfortunately, the appalling backwardness of their new surroundings blinded them to the more subtle good points of Venezuela. Uncle Stasik had bitter fights with my father and my aunt Alina, his two closest siblings, blaming them for bringing him to this godforsaken piece of hell.

"You have dragged me and my family here, to this tropical pile of garbage, for what?" he would yell at the top of his voice, while his wife and two daughters ran to my bedroom to hide as far away from the quarrel as possible. "So that you could rub my nose in this squalor, in this poverty? We had it much better in Krakow! You never mentioned anything about the unbearable heat. You never said faucets run dry several months a year. And how about the floods? How come it never occurred to you to tell us about all the snakes, the scorpions, and the filthy cockroaches?"

Aunt Alina didn't scare easily. "So you are frightened by a few cockroaches? Big deal! At least we don't have bloodsucking bedbugs and lice, like you did in Poland. Didn't your wife complain to me that she had to boil sheets for several hours, and in winter freeze them on the balcony to get rid of bedbugs? And then, it was all for nothing, because they came back, they lived in the mattress. She told me that herself. I wish I had saved the letters, they were stained with her tears. So go back to your lice and bedbugs, if you don't like it here!"

"Stasik, Stasik, don't be ridiculous, stop whining." It was my father's turn to jump into the fray. "We got you an apartment, we got you a job, as soon as you learn to drive we'll get you a car, you won't have to ride in those awful buses for much longer. Your wife's got a maid. What else do you want? Paradise? Well, this isn't it, and the sooner you realize it, the happier you'll be."

"An apartment! You dare to call this an apartment? The concierge lives in a better place! You call this dark shack with two tiny rooms and a kitchen the size of a thimble an apartment? Even our apartment in Krakow was larger than this. And there were no cockroaches. This is a hell hole!"

I was given the thankless job of helping my uncle Stasik learn Spanish. The problem wasn't that my uncle was a poor student, quite the contrary, he was quick and motivated, but he had a temper just like Father's and I was afraid of him. Since he had just met me only recently and I was already fifteen, he didn't yet dare to shout at me like Father did, but I was afraid that as soon as we got better acquainted he would start berating me. I could sense his barely contained rage waiting to erupt. Whenever Uncle didn't know a word in Spanish or had trouble learning a new structure, he would holler curses.

"This stupid, asinine language! Damnation! Whoever came up with a language with so many irregular verbs? I hate articles! Who needs frigging articles? Polish does fine without articles!" he would yell and storm out of the dining room, where we were having our daily Spanish lesson. "I am quitting!"

His outbursts were not directed at me, but at his wife and two daughters, who sat very quietly in our living room, trying desperately to remain invisible. My two cousins seemed terrified of him, and I could tell by their dejected faces that they were unhappy in their new surroundings. They did not like their new country, the shabby new school where they hadn't made any friends, and they hardly ever went out without their parents. My cousin Danny, who by then had developed a very sharp tongue, remarked that our new cousins always had a look of faint displeasure on their faces, as if somebody had just farted in front of them but they were too polite to say anything.

During my remaining few months in Venezuela, I rarely saw my newly arrived cousins. Sometimes on Sunday, Uncle Stasik would bring them along when he came over for his Spanish lesson, but we hardly ever talked or played together. The cousins spoke only Polish and Hebrew, they had not yet been exposed to Spanish, neither at home nor in school, since Uncle had enrolled them in the Jewish school. I was busy teaching Uncle, while they sat quietly on the sofa and never said a word. Recently, within the last two years, I have struck up a friendship with the older one, Andrea, who now lives in Canada. She called me unexpectedly, out of the blue. I must confess that I hadn't thought of her for years, and for the first few seconds I had trouble placing her. We have been corresponding ever since. She told me in a letter that when she arrived in Venezuela in 1960, she felt forsaken by her cousins and couldn't understand why we didn't befriend her.

Now that most of my father's family lived in Caracas, a strange pattern of hostilities took hold among the older generation. Father and Aunt Alina would pick a fight with their brother Stasik and stop talking to him for weeks, keeping the grudge alive for as long as they could. Then, a few weeks later, allegiances would switch. The sibling who had been left out before would take sides with one of his former antagonists, and they in turn would dig up something else to quarrel about and gang up on the third one. The newly formed warring sides would unabashedly disparage, ridicule, and belittle each other. We kids never knew from one day to the next who was friends with whom, and who was not talking to the others. It was almost as if my father and his two siblings had reverted to their childhood patterns.

Mother, on the other hand, was much more consistent in her animosity. She would never miss an opportunity to criticize both of her sisters-in-law in the privacy of our own home. Of course, if they were present, she was sweeter than molasses.

"Aunt Alina and Aunt Eva are fat, lazy cows. If they only went to work in the store to help out their husbands, like I do every single day, rain or shine, instead of sitting at home on their fat rear ends eating every morsel in sight and pretending to take care of the children, they would surely lose some of that fat and save money too," Mother often said. Mother was proud of her figure, and used every opportunity to point out that the aunts were plump.

Father complained night after night at the dinner table. "The uncles are dreadfully lazy, good-for-nothing freeloaders, all they want is to get handouts from me. They are sucking me dry!"

"I told you so a hundred times," Mother agreed eagerly.

"Of course, I still have to help them. Even though they don't deserve anything. And after all I do for them, the devil take them!, They have the gall to be ungrateful. Can you believe that?" Father asked rhetorically.

Father's sense of obligation toward his family posed a constant threat to Mother's already much eroded position in the family, so she stoked the fire further. "Their wives spend money as if it grew on trees, they have absolutely no control over their absurd whims. Aunt Alina wants to buy a new two-tone Ford, pink and white, just because it looked good with her white poodle, just think of that!"

"I told them thousands of times this has to stop. Things can't go on this way, I won't be here to help them forever. I could get sick or die. And then, what the hell are they going to do? They'll never amount to anything, the lazy bums. They have no initiative, no desire to get ahead. They are lazy nogoodniks."

"And their wives are slothful, inconsiderate and meddlesome. And all they do is eat all day long. That's why they are so fat." Mother added. The aunts' rotund shape was a subject she never tired of.

"The only reason they stick to me is because they think I am making a lot of money, and somehow, some of it, is likely to fall their way. I am not rich by any means, but if I am doing better than some, it's because I am not afraid of hard work, like some other people I could mention," Father belabored the point endlessly, while chewing on a piece of meat.

This litany, with some minor variations, would be repeated every time we sat down to dinner. Father would gripe about everybody and suddenly stretch out his hand and say loudly "meat" or "bread" or "napkin" while Mother passed him whatever he had asked for. Sometimes, when he didn't want to interrupt the flow of his thoughts, he would just stretch out his hand and Mother would try to guess what he required. She would become more and more agitated as she handed him a knife, a fork, the salt shaker, a glass of water, while he kept on talking with his mouth full and shook his head from side to side to convey that she had handed him the wrong thing. His hand remained outstretched until she got it right. Only then could we all relax, at least for the next few minutes.

The uncles and aunts resented these tirades and my aunt Alina, Father's older sister, was the most belligerent of the bunch. She didn't mince words.

"My little brother thinks he is our boss, the way he wants to control our lives. He presumes to tell us what we can and can't do. God damn it! He conveniently forgets that when he was a baby, I was the one who fed him, changed his diapers, wiped his ass, and slapped him when he didn't behave. And now he has the chutzpah to think he is a big shot. Big shot, my foot! He is a bully and a tyrant."

She complained that Father had kept them from buying the new car they wanted, a grand piano for Uncle, a decent house in a nice neighborhood. "He is a penny-pinching bastard, that's what he is. He never gives anything without strings attached. For him, everything carries a price tag. He makes us pay with our blood and sweat for every little thing. One day he'll be sorry, but then it will be too late."

Uncle Bronek would join in: "My brother-in-law has no understanding of the finer things in life. He is a philistine. He knows nothing about music. For him, everything is money, money, money. Well, I can't live like that. I can't live without a grand piano. Why, he tells me it's a luxury! For me, it's a necessity, it's like the blood that flows through my veins."

Then uncle Stasik would join the battle: "I would have never come to this hell had I known what kind of place it was! All I do is work, work, work, from dawn to dusk, and for what? To have the privilege of living in the basement of a dirty apartment building? In a dingy two-bedroom hovel, without a washing machine? For this my brother dragged me here? This place isn't fit for a mangy dog! I should have never listened to him! I should have stayed in Krakow."

This circus didn't affect us kids very much. Adam and Danny and I were so used to this spectacle that we paid no attention to what our elders were doing. But I think it made it harder to develop a relationship with my newly arrived cousins, Andrea and Sonia.

As the summer approached I started preparing to leave for Berkeley. I graduated with little fanfare. Nobody from my family came to the ceremony, but that was okay. I got rid of many of my books, trophies and other childhood belongings. I packed the few things I wanted to take with me.

A couple of weeks before my departure, one of my friends from my senior class called me. Her name was Isabel, and she and her brother had arrived from the provinces to study in the capital for their last year of high school. Isabel wouldn't tell anybody her age, but the whole school knew she was at least twenty since her younger brother, who was in the same class, was already nineteen. Isabel, who was slim and elegant, always wore nylons, medium heel pumps, narrow skirts with a pleat at the back and white satiny or lacy blouses. She dressed as if she was going to a party, or at least a job interview in a fancy boutique. Her shiny black hair cascaded down her shoulders and her make-up was always flawless. She acted aloof and very rarely smiled. She looked out of place in our high school. I felt an immediate affinity for her, perhaps because I knew I didn't fit in either. Although she and I were an unlikely pair, in fact, one could have said we were opposites, we nonetheless became friends.

All kinds of rumors about Isabel were circulating in our school. Some girls in our class believed she had had a baby and had given it up for adoption. That would explain why her brother followed her a few paces behind everywhere she went, her family must have wanted to make sure nothing like this happened ever again. Others said she had been stood up at the altar a couple of times and, because there had been a terrible scandal, she had to leave town to finish her schooling in the capital. I never found any evidence of truth in either rumor in any of our long talks.

We would walk home together after school, her brother always a few steps behind. Of course, we talked about boys. She told me she had been engaged twice, but both times she broke off the engagement. She wanted to wait for Mr. Right, someone more educated, a professional with a future. She fantasized about her wedding day, her gorgeous lacy white dress enveloping her like a white cloud, the embroidered veil so fine it seemed ethereal, white and pale pink roses everywhere, and she, walking down the aisle, admired by all the elegant and distinguished guests, friends and family members. She fantasized about her honeymoon, which would take her and her handsome, rich husband to Monte Carlo, where all the millionaires of the world partied. The details of the honeymoon were very sketchy, although I listened carefully, trying to fathom whether the rumors about her were true, whether something would slip out that would prove she knew more about sex than the rest of the girls in our class. She talked and I listened, since I had very little to contribute in the boyfriend department. My few dates with friends to go dancing or to the movies, holding hands and kissing, and the two or three short-lived crushes I had on some of the high school's most popular boys, were not worth mentioning.

Soon the school year was over, we took our final exams, and we were free. But not Isabel. She had failed biology and had to study all summer to take the make-up exam in August. If she didn't pass, she couldn't graduate.

We saw little of each other that summer. I was busy, getting ready to come to Berkeley, reading a lot and trying to improve my English. Isabel was studying for her biology exam. One morning she called me in tears. Her exam was scheduled for Friday and she knew she would never pass.

"No matter how hard I study, it's no good. I just can't do it! My whole life depends on this stupid exam," she told me.

She asked me to take the exam for her. "Nobody will find out.

Our student identification cards have no photographs, the teachers who give the make-up exams in the summer are not our regular school teachers. It'll be a piece of cake, you'll see. Please, please, please, Rebecca."

I hesitated, stalling for time. "The final was two months ago, I haven't touched a book since then. What if I've forgotten everything? What if I don't pass?"

"Of course you'll pass. Besides, I am more than willing to take that risk. Your chances are infinitely better than mine. Mine are a big, fat zero."

"But what if we are found out? I'll die if we are found out," I said.

"You already have your diploma, you've already been accepted at a university in the States, nothing can happen to you." she persisted. "I'll get in trouble if we are found out, not you. The thing is that if I take the exam, I'll fail for sure. I know that. I have nothing to lose and I am really, really desperate. Please, Rebecca, do it, just this once. I've never asked you for anything before." By now she was crying so hard, I had trouble understanding her words.

I couldn't refuse. On Friday morning I met Isabel at the school where the exams were to take place. Hundreds of students were milling in the hallways, crowding classroom doorways, trying to find their room assignments. Everywhere was chaos and confusion. Finally, we managed to locate the place where the biology exam was to be given.

The exam consisted of two parts, a three-hour multiple-choice written exam, and for those students who passed this first part, an oral laboratory exam. Isabel handed me her student identification card and I went in. I felt very nervous, but after answering the first few questions I settled into a routine, my reflexes took over and I didn't even remember that I was impersonating somebody else. I finished in a couple of hours and I knew I had passed. I went to meet Isabel, who was waiting at a coffee house a block away from the school. I tried to talk her into taking the oral, but she told me she couldn't do it. She was crying and shaking at just the mention of the lab. She confessed to me that all through the year when we worked in the lab she never touched the microscope, not even to adjust it. She had never prepared a slide, she couldn't identify or classify anything, she had just copied all the results and all the drawings from her teammates. I relented.

At one o'clock, I was back at the school for the second part of the test. I walked into the lab, took a seat, looked up, and to my horror saw professor De Armas, my first year high school biology teacher, walking toward me, beaming a hearty greeting. He was delighted to see me after such a long time, but couldn't believe I was taking a make-up exam. After all, I had been one of his best students, someone he could hardly forget. I wanted to die, I wanted the earth to swallow me. I wanted to run out the door and not stop until I got to the end of the planet. But I sat glued to the chair, my eyes filling with tears. He looked at his list and didn't find my name. He asked me for my student card. For one wild moment I considered saying I lost it. But I knew it was no use, I handed it over. We had been found out, our ruse had failed. I was escorted out of the room, led to the administration office, reprimanded officially and forcefully by the school superintendent, and berated by my old teacher, whom I revered. Isabel flunked her biology class and never graduated.

I wanted to forget the whole sorry affair, to stop seeing the look of disappointment in the eyes of one of my favorite teachers. I wanted to get as far away as I could. I no longer had any doubts about going to Berkeley. That would be my salvation. I thought of my imminent departure as a stroke of luck. I couldn't wait to live in the States. I harbored all kinds of fantasies about America, fueled by all I had learned from watching teen movies starring Annette Funicello and Frankie Avalon. None of these prepared me for the reality of Berkeley.

In August, on my way to California, I stopped off in Florida to visit my sister and her new baby. Jimmy had been drafted into the army and sent to Korea a couple of months after their wedding. He hadn't even been there for his son's birth. Susanna was living in a small room with kitchen privileges with Ricky, her six-month-old baby. I sensed immediately that she was not happy to see me.

We had several fights over nothing. One day, when we had gone to the beach, Susanna asked me to take care of Ricky while she napped in the sun. I fed him a jar of peaches, changed his diaper, and took out the trash. When Susanna woke up she was annoyed because I had fed Ricky at the wrong time, but she really exploded when she found out I had accidentally thrown out Ricky's spoon. She made me go back to the trash, fish it out and go to the restroom to wash it. I couldn't understand what the fuss was all about, after all, it was only a dime store spoon.

Susanna seemed troubled and irritable. I attributed her wretched mood to her circumstances. Her husband had been drafted and she had to deal with a small baby all by herself and live on a pittance in a tiny room in somebody else's house. It was not until twenty years later that I learned her husband had enlisted voluntarily.

Susanna

I told my baby sister that I didn't want to keep on writing. I told her there was nothing more to say about my life. It was no longer interesting. Nothing extraordinary happened to me after I finally managed to escape from home. My life became ordinary, mundane.

I moved to Florida. I met a man. I got married. I got pregnant. My baby boy was born. My husband went to Korea. Goodness! What else was there to say? That I changed sixteen diapers a day? That I talked baby talk all day long? There wasn't anything for me to write about.

But my stubborn sister is not satisfied. She wants me to keep telling my story. I refuse to do it. Enough is enough! I've written all I am going to write.

"Come on Susie," my little sister coaxed. "As long as all the blunders were committed by our parents it was easy to write our story. But now, the time has come to face our own mistakes, and write about all the things we did wrong."

"Leave me alone, Rebecca, go pester somebody else for a change," I told her. What a know-it-all. I am not going to do it. Nobody can make me do something I don't want to do.

"And don't you dare to write about it either! You don't know the first thing about my life," I yelled. Can you believe that? The gall of her! She says if I didn't write, she would continue with our story, anyway. She was always a blabbermouth.

"Wait a minute, Susanna. I don't need to ask your permission to write about whatever I want. This is my life too, not just yours. And if you want me to get it right, tell me about it, or better yet, set the record straight and write about it yourself," interposed my obstinate sibling. "And I don't see why you live in mortal fear of my revealing secrets that will bring disgrace and shame on you. I don't know any such secrets."

"And you won't find out any from me! I am just a very private person who doesn't like to wash her dirty underwear in public, Okay? Subject closed." God Almighty! That little brat never gives up.

I've spent my whole damn life working hard to become the person I want to be. Other people may want to be doctors, teachers, artists, poets. Not me. All I ever wanted to be is American. An average American wife and mother. Living a common, ordinary life in the suburbs. Married to an average American guy, not to one of those complicated, neurotic intellectuals my little sister adores. No way. That's not for me. I did everything I could think of to obliterate my accursed Polish and Jewish origins. I lied about my place of birth. About where I grew up. About my family. About my religion. I created my own autobiography. So what? That's my own damn business. Nobody else's. I'll be damned if I am going to apologize. It's not like I was hurting anybody, or taking something away from anybody. I was finally settled. Now I am part of the community where I live. I am well known and well regarded. And that's the way I like it. I am not about to risk exposure, to destroy everything I have worked so hard to build. I'd have to be crazy to risk that, and I can assure you, crazy I am not. All the world knows that nothing is more important in the South than ancestry. Origins. None of that melting pot nonsense. That's okay for New York, or California, but here, in the deep South, it won't fly. Here, to be somebody, you have to belong. To fit in. And I, at last, belonged.

Rebecca thinks I live a farce. Too bad! I don't care what she thinks. I live in a large Victorian house. I had it built just a few years ago exactly to my taste. My house is perched on a big parcel of land, large enough so that I can't see my neighbors, but not too far for children to come steal apples from my orchard on lazy summer afternoons. I like to watch the kids steal my apples. It makes me feel good. It makes me feel that I belong here. It makes me feel settled. I filled my house with antique furniture. So what if it isn't authentic, I couldn't care less. It looks great anyway. My attic is crammed with things I could have collected had my family lived here for many generations. So what if I bought most of my collections recently. That's my own business. I like every item just as much as if I had inherited from my great-great-grandparents. In fact, I like my things even more, because I chose every single item myself. And if that throws somebody's nose out of joint, they can go to hell.

Now my little sister wants me to tell the story of my life. My true story. She thinks I am going to admit that I have told a few fibs here and there. That I have been living a lie. That I am a fake. She wants me to give up all I have worked so hard to accomplish. For heaven's sake, she must be nuts if she thinks I am going to do that. Not for a million dollars! Why would I want to confront my shameful past? Why would I want to inflict pain on myself? For some misplaced idea that the truth is always best? What rubbish!

"Now, look, this whole thing was supposed to bring us closer together, not tear us apart," perseveres my single-minded sister. "Please think about it. Don't say no quite yet. Give it a chance. You are so good at writing, I really love the stuff you have written so far. Promise me, at least, that you'll think about it," implores Rebecca.

"Flattery will get you nowhere, baby sister. I can see right through your clumsy efforts to get me to continue writing my story. I am no fool. But have it your way. Thinking about it doesn't hurt anything. Just don't get your hopes up. And don't blame me later if you are disappointed."

One thing I can say for my little sister, she sure is obstinate. She won't take no for an answer. She always seemed so sweet and compliant when she was a little kid. What happened? I have trouble recognizing the person I detect underneath that candy-coated facade. When she wants something she acquires the determination of a bulldozer. This is not the little sister I knew. Well, all I said was that I'll think about it. I didn't promise anything.

Rebecca

I arrived in Berkeley in the fall of 1960. I was sixteen years old, and thought of myself as an adult. I immediately fell in love with my surroundings, and with being in a foreign city. Berkeley was so different from what I had imagined, and so different from what I knew. Instead of twenty-story high skyscrapers built of concrete and glass, here were dark wooden houses with beams and turrets that looked as if they were out of a fairy tale. To this day when I go for a walk in the Berkeley hills I cannot stop admiring the houses, each different from the next, but somehow harmonizing with the rest. Instead of the four-lane concrete superhighways I was used to, tiny winding streets climbed the green hills, and in between were foot paths I could follow all the way to the top ridge. Instead of the asphalt and concrete jungle where I had grown up, Berkeley felt to me like a cross between a park and a forest. I was exhilarated.

Armed with the catalog and schedule of classes that had been mailed to me in Venezuela, I tackled that strange procedure called registration. My schedule seemed to indicate that foreign students were to register at 1:30 P.M. on Tuesday, September 16, at window four in Sproul Hall, the Administration Building. Of course, I told myself, I know better. I didn't for one minute believe that there was a Sproul Hall, or a window four, or that the 16th would fall on a Tuesday. But I followed the instructions anyway, just to disprove them. On the appointed day, window four flew up at exactly 1:30 and a young woman appeared behind the counter. I gave my name and she extracted from a cabinet a file that contained all the papers I had mailed to the University. Nothing was missing, everything was complete. Registration took less than five minutes. I was amazed. This was a miracle. I had never known or imagined such efficiency was possible.

The next item on my calendar was going to see the foreign student advisor. I made an appointment for the next day. When I arrived at the department and knocked on the door, a harried-looking young man opened it and handed me a screaming baby. He asked me to hold the baby while he warmed a bottle. When he was done, he took the baby back, and started feeding it. Only then did he introduce himself. He was professor Searle, my advisor. He asked what courses I wanted to take. I said I had no idea. He asked me what I liked. I looked through my catalog, and identified about twenty courses I wanted to take while he was changing the baby. I chose courses in history, world literature, geography, government and languages. I flipped through the pages with my right hand. My left hand was as far away from my body as I could manage because I was holding the dirty diaper professor Searle had handed me. He put the baby in the pram, disposed of the diaper in a plastic bag, then smiled and told me to come back any time I had a problem. I left his office with ten courses on my enrollment card. When I tried to enroll, I was told that four courses were the maximum, and one of those had to be English for foreign students. I didn't understand why, until I started attending classes.

The amount of studying I had to do was staggering. As I enrolled in each class I was given a sheet of paper that listed everything to be covered in each class. In one of my courses, I had to read three chapters in the textbook before the first class. My English course alone was ten hours a week, plus as many hours in the language lab as I could manage. This was certainly different from what I was used to in Venezuela, even though I had attended the best high school in the country. I would have to learn new study habits if I wanted to make it. Also, there was the problem of language. I still needed to use a dictionary when reading English. Sometimes I would have to look up the meaning of entire sentences word by word. There were times I missed something the lecturer said. I especially regretted missing all the jokes. The whole class would burst into laughter, while I looked around in wonder and had no idea what was so funny.

I noticed that as soon as my classmates found out I was from a foreign country, which happened every time I opened my mouth, they would flock to me and try to befriend me. This came as a complete surprise. Not only did I not have to hide the fact that I was different, but I could use it as a social asset. I no longer had to try to become inconspicuous. Now all my eccentricities were greeted with interest and delight. Everybody wanted to talk to me, have a cup of coffee with me, invite me to their dorm, to their apartment, to dinner, to parties. Everybody asked questions about my background and told me how lucky I was to have had so many diverse experiences. Everybody seemed interested in me and vied for my attention. I had to pinch myself to make sure this was no dream. I felt giddy with excitement.

I found a tiny half-furnished apartment about six blocks from campus. I called to order phone service. The man from the phone company told me he would be there the next morning. I asked if he was coming to have me fill out an application. No, he was coming to install the phone. I thought he was kidding. It takes six years on the average to get a phone in Venezuela and about ten years to have your name included in the phone book, unless you pay hefty bribes. A few minutes after nine the next morning, the phone company serviceman arrived and I had a phone.

When I went to Woolworth's I thought had landed in paradise. Here was everything I needed, forks, knifes, spoons, plates, pots and pans, towels, sheets, pillows, blankets. And everything was inexpensive. I bought two large bags of stuff which I arranged in closets and cupboards. I emptied my suitcases and filled the drawers. I placed the books I had bought the day before in the bookcase. I felt as if I was playing house. Soon everything was done. I looked over my domain with great pleasure. Then, I wondered what to do next. I reread the catalog, which mentioned a student center called the International House and found it on the campus map. On the way, I again stopped to admire the gardens bursting with flowers, the green lawns, the beautiful shade trees. I felt I was walking through a park.

There were students from all over the world at the International House, and thank goodness, a lot of them were Spanish speaking. It was such a relief for me to stop speaking English that I stayed until midnight. There was a lounge with sofas and overstuffed armchairs, a coffee house, a music room, a small library, even ping-pong tables. I met many students from Latin America and Spain, most of whom seemed fascinating. One of my new friends, Ricardo, offered to walk me back to my apartment. When he asked to see me again the next evening I gladly agreed. I felt on top of the world.

Soon Ricardo and I started seeing each other every evening. He lived at the International House and was extremely popular, everybody stopped to greet him and talk to him. He introduced me to his friends. I thought I would never be able to remember all of the people I met in such a short time.

One evening we went out for pizza with a couple who were friends of Ricardo. When I found out they were living together without the benefit of marriage, I was in shock. I couldn't stop looking at the young woman, wondering if something would show in her manner or speech that would give her away as a loose, amoral person. I had grown up in a Latin country and considered this a sin of the greatest magnitude. But I was also morbidly interested. I wanted to befriend her, to find out how she felt about what she was doing, how her family viewed her behavior, how she got into this kind of a bind, what led her into such an unfortunate situation. She seemed perfectly poised and serene, unaware of my scrutiny. Much too soon the evening ended, we all said our good-byes, and I never got the chance to find out more about her enthralling life.

Ricardo had been at the University for four years, this was his senior year. I was an entering freshman. He was very handsome, I felt like an ugly duckling. He spoke English well, and I was just learning the language. He had a car, knew the ropes, and offered to show me around. I was especially impressed when he told me he worked as a dishwasher at the International House to help pay for his education. Any person who has lived in Latin America knows that this is a low-class job, to be performed only under dire circumstances. But Ricardo liked his job and felt proud that he did it well and efficiently. I felt very lucky. In less than two weeks, I was in love.

Getting good grades proved harder than I had ever expected. Everybody in the freshman class had been the best student in his or her high school. When I realized that I had to study if I wanted to succeed, things started improving. Soon I had caught up with all my classes and became an expert in how to ace tests. I was invited to some high achievement society called something like Tower and Flame. I attended one meeting, but didn't see the point of getting together with other students just because they had good grades. I had better things to do with my time.

Every evening I saw Ricardo. We talked for hours. When it was still warm, we walked on campus and sat on the wide, green lawn. The fog would envelop us late in the evening and provide a feeling of privacy. If it rained, we sat in a coffee house, nursing the same cup of coffee until after midnight. We also liked going to the only drive-in soda fountain in town, Mel's, where Ricardo always ordered a milkshake, and I a cup of black coffee. Invariably, to our amusement, the waitress would bring me the milkshake and Ricardo the coffee. We decided that I had a milkshake face and he had a coffee face. We spent hours sitting in the car, talking. One night Ricardo told me he would marry me. He didn't ask me, he just made the announcement. I said okay.

Ricardo took me to the mountains to ski at Christmas time. Even though I had seen pictures of myself in Krakow and Berlin walking on snow covered streets, I didn't remember snow. We stayed at the University dorms, helped with chores in the morning and evening and skied all day long. The ski lift was a long, steep rope tow that cost a dollar. I loved skiing, a sport that still brings me enormous joy and fulfillment. Skiing is much more to me than an enjoyable activity in a beautiful mountain setting. It is a symbol of rebellion against my serious upbringing, exactly the kind of activity my parents would have ridiculed because it was impractical, non-productive and expensive. In my early twenties, I spent a whole winter skiing everyday in the Alps. Afterward, Father asked, frowning "So tell me, what exactly did you do? You rode a lift to the top of a mountain, slid down, and kept on doing the same thing all day long? What for? What did you accomplish?"

"Absolutely nothing," I answered. "It was just great fun. Something I dreamt of doing since I was little."

Some weekends we explored California in Ricardo's old beat-up Oldsmobile. I wanted to see Yosemite. When we were kids, Susanna had gotten me a used Viewmaster set with two disks, one of Yosemite and one of Sun Valley. I watched these pictures over and over. I have loved both places ever since. I was awed by Yosemite's mountains, the forests, the waterfalls. I learned to love hiking and backpacking. We visited the Gold Country, historical ghost towns, Indian reservations. We went canoeing down the Russian River, rafting down the Stanislaus, floating down the American river in an inner tube, water skiing in the Delta. I was enjoying things I had only read about in books or seen in movies. All my life, I felt, I had only been making ready for this, my real life.

My only disappointment was with the Northern California beaches. It took me years to learn to see the beauty of gray, foggy, rocky beaches. I was used to sunny Caribbean beaches, a turquoise sea fringed with golden sand and palm trees swaying in warm breezes. Why did my friends gush with praise when talking about these gray strips of gravel, where the wind blew with gale force and you could never take off your jacket? I suspected they were putting me on.

Soon my freshman year was over. Ricardo was going to spend the summer in Venezuela, where his parents resided. I was going to join my parents, who had moved to Uruguay after I left home. They had waited for me to finish my second semester and then sent me a ticket to join them. I was going just for the summer, a couple of months at most. I didn't really want to be separated from Ricardo, even for the summer, but I felt I had no choice. I figured time apart from each other would only make our love stronger.

When I arrived in Montevideo it was June and the middle of winter. The city was somber and uninviting. The skies were gray, almost black. Icy rain fell continuously, a strong wind blew from the river La Plata, thoroughly freezing the streets and sidewalks in the city. The few people who braved the weather would run from their cars to wherever they were going, holding on to lampposts and ducking into doorways, trying to avoid getting soaked or being blown away.

While they looked for a suitable house, my parents lived in a small apartment in an old building in the center of the city. I didn't have a room of my own and slept on a folding couch in the living room. Father and Mother bickered and fought viciously from morning till night. Neither of them had any reason to leave the apartment, since they were not working.

Father had sold the stores and apartment buildings he had acquired in Venezuela. He felt as if he had finally retired and deserved to enjoy his free time. He was exploring new professional opportunities. This was his last chance to live his long-deferred dream of revalidating his law degree, of having a prestigious position in his profession, a beautiful house in an expensive neighborhood and live a storybook life with his wife and children. But his dream was full of flaws. My sister was married and living in Florida, and in just a few weeks, I would return to Berkeley, to continue my studies and to be with Ricardo.

My parents had other plans. Father must have understood he couldn't realize his dream with his wife alone, he needed at least one daughter to fulfill his dream. I was to stay in Uruguay for good, he informed me. No matter how many times I insisted that I didn't want to stay and be part of this chimera, he didn't listen.

I had been ambushed.

"Damnation! I already lost one daughter to the United States and I am not going to lose another," Father shouted.

"Father, I want to go back to Berkeley. That's where my school is, and that's where the man I want to marry lives."

"Hell, no! You are a mere child, much too young to know what you want, much less what you need, or what's good for you! You are going to start the university again here, in Montevideo, where we'll live. And this godforsaken man you claim to love will just have to wait for you until you finish!" he roared.

This argument was repeated every couple of days. Suddenly, after I had spent so many years feeling free and deciding exactly what I wanted, my parents expected me to become their full-time daughter. Now, when they finally had the time to take on the role of parents, they wanted a daughter by their side. No matter how much I protested and fought, I had to obey. I was seventeen with no income of my own. I felt imprisoned, trapped.

My parents were fighting more often and viciously than usual. Father must have harbored doubts about whether this country was the paradise he had been seeking for so long. He was afraid of making another mistake. He felt his dream slipping away, and as usual, he reacted with barely contained fury. He would explode in a frenzy of rage at the smallest setback and shriek angrily at whoever was present, more often than not at my mother and me. I had nowhere to hide. I could not lock myself away in my own room and wait for calm to be restored. I was right in the middle of every battle, an unwilling audience of their quarrels.

I took to leaving the apartment as soon as my parents got up. I would get dressed, put my coat and boots on and walk the streets in Montevideo. It was much too cold, wet, and windy to do this for more than a few minutes at a time, so I would slip into coffee shops or bookstores, or a movie house, and would not return until late at night, when my parents had already retired. I had to make sure that I didn't stay too long in one place because men would try to attach themselves to me. Sometimes they followed me. I always tried to appear purposeful and busy, to keep moving, feigning hurry, as if I were going somewhere important or were on my way to meet somebody. I never knew that one single day could have so many long hours, that I could go to so many coffee shops and drink so many cups of coffee, read so many newspapers and books, and still it would be much too early to return to the apartment.

I made inquiries about attending the university, but it was the middle of the school year, which runs from February to November. I would have to wait until the beginning of next year. I had no friends, nobody to talk to, nothing to do during the day except walk from one coffee shop to the next, from bookstore to bookstore and from cinema to cinema. I don't know how many movies I saw three, four, or even five times.

I felt alternatively doomed and angry. Two months went by, and things only worsened. I could not stand being in the apartment, I could not listen to my parents' vicious fights, I could not deal with my father's seething rage and my mother's tearful, passive acquiescence. It was torture. I became obsessed with leaving. Soon I started thinking that if I couldn't leave the normal way, I would leave feet first.

Once this thought took hold I could see only how liberating it would be, how it would solve all my problems, in one fell swoop. I would no longer be in the vortex of this disastrous family turmoil. I wouldn't have to satisfy my parents' hunger for a dutiful daughter. I would never feel guilty again because I was unable to muster the love they needed, and because I was unwilling to please them, to sacrifice years of my life for their sake. I would no longer have to try to understand and appease my father's rage and frustration, to make up for the years of suffering and hard times they had endured, or feel sorry for my mother's plight. I would never again have to feel that they relied on me to fulfill their dreams. I could make the pain stop. I could be free.

I started thinking of how and when I would do it. I bought sleeping pills, lots of them, in several different pharmacies. In Uruguay there was no need for a prescription for most drugs. Soon I had what I considered enough. Now I only had to choose the right time, that is, if I wanted to do it. Knowing that I had this way out made me feel better for a few days, more in control of my own life. I had almost given up on the notion. Then, my parents had a monstrous fight, an explosion of cataclysmic proportions.

My parents had been looking for a house for several weeks, and they had finally found one that they considered appropriate. The house was in Punta del Este, a fashionable neighborhood outside of Montevideo. They were under a lot of pressure to make a decision. This would be the first house they had ever bought, and it was quite expensive. Perhaps the strain of making this difficult decision precipitated this colossal fight. The selling agent had introduced my parents to the people who lived next door, a warm and easygoing family who invited us over for coffee and cake. Later that evening, Mother mentioned to Father that it would be marvelous to have them as neighbors. This innocuous comment set Father off.

"I despise the people who live in this godforsaken, uncivilized, barbaric country. They are ignorant idiots without any redeeming qualities. No exceptions. Your liking for them only proves that you are also a stupid idiot, a gullible cow, worse than any of them," he hollered. "I detest the easygoing attitude they hide behind to mask their laziness and sloth, their abhorrence of hard work, their thieving ways. Dammit! I'll rather die than live in a country like this."

He threatened Mother with another move, this time he wanted to try Germany, of all preposterous ideas. Mother, meanwhile, had been dreaming of at last owning a house, after waiting for so many decades. She wanted to settle down somewhere, stop camping out like a gypsy, stop moving from one country to another. Her dream was slipping away again. Instead of her usual whimpering and whining, she tried to put up a fight, which only enraged Father more and made him more violent. He reached the breaking point and started punching her. I tried to stop him, and he turned on me and slapped me several times. He didn't really hurt me, he didn't slap me hard. But it was then I decided that the right time to end my life would be that very night. I could see no other way out, I felt this was the right decision.

I locked myself in the bathroom, swallowed one fistful after another of the pills I had collected, until they were all gone. Then I lay down to sleep on my folding couch in the living room. I woke up in a hospital some time later and overheard a nurse saying something about having my stomach pumped. I was released from the hospital six days after I woke up. My parents never once said anything about what had occurred, not then and not later.

But a few days after I returned home from the hospital, Father wordlessly handed me an envelope. Inside was an airline ticket to San Francisco.

I didn't sleep well on the eve of my departure. I kept waking up every few minutes. The couch was narrow and the mattress lumpy. I heard a shuffle and looked at the window. My father stood there, looking out at the street. I got out of bed, wrapped a blanket around myself, and stood next to him. After a few minutes he said "Rats, abandoning a sinking ship." I didn't know what to say. Then, very softly, he whispered, "It's too late, isn't it?"

One week later, I was back in California, in time to start my sophomore year. As soon as I turned eighteen, I married Ricardo. The ceremony was at the Alameda County Court House. Ricardo and I, the judge and his clerk, who doubled as witness, were the only people present in the judge's chambers. The whole event took less than ten minutes. Even though I had written to my parents, telling them I was getting married, they didn't come to the wedding. Mother called long-distance from Uruguay to make sure I bought a nice new dress. I didn't bother. Father was too busy to call or write, or perhaps he was unaware of my impending marriage. My sister was busy with her new baby and couldn't make it. I invited my best friend, Greta, but she had just flunked out of the university and broken up with her boyfriend and felt too dejected to come.

I had asked Ricardo several times to write or call his parents and tell them about our marriage, but he kept postponing it.

"I really don't want to hurt my parents, they will be devastated when they find out," he said.

"They will feel even more hurt if you don't tell them now. You will have to tell them eventually," I objected.

"You don't understand, getting married is a bit like betraying their trust. They sent me to the States to study, to forge a career, not to get married."

"I think keeping it from them is a betrayal of trust," I said.

After several months, when Ricardo finally confessed that he was married, his parents were extremely upset, as he had predicted. The next summer, when we visited, they had still not forgiven Ricardo. As for me, I think they never forgave me, not until after we divorced.

Susanna

These last pages I'd written are burning a hole in my desk drawer, but I can't send them to my sister. That would be crazy. I've never talked to anybody about what happened after I got married. Much less, to anybody from my family. For the time being, I'll keep on jotting down a few things, just for myself. I'll decide what to do with these pages later. I'll probably throw them in the fireplace as soon as I finished.

Just remembering all the things that happened makes my skin crawl. I could just hear my baby sister calling the whole awful mess a "learning experience." That's her euphemism for what happens whenever she screws up her life. As for me, I call it a life in hell. I hate to relive painful episodes. Heck, life is lousy enough. There is no need to make it any worse. So why am I writing down all this? you may ask. I don't have the answer yet. Perhaps I will when I finished. Perhaps, after I examine my past, I will be able to make sense of the present.

My little sister has really no idea what she's asked me to do. She said it was easier to write when we could blame the parents for all the terrible things that happened. It was much harder now that we had ourselves to blame. Our own choices, our own mistakes. What a depressing thought. One thing for sure, even if I hate to admit it, little miss know-it-all might be right, it is much harder to write about my life now. What really rankles me is when my little sister talks about choices. Choices, my ass! What choices is she talking about? I had no choices. None that I could see. She didn't have the slightest idea what my life was like.

Life has been a breeze for you, baby sister. Your never-ending years in college. Your fancy-shmancy ski trips. Your extravagant tour of Europe. Your artsy-fartsy friends. Your snobbish counter-culture ideas. Life was a bowl of cherries. No responsibilities. No obstacles in your path. For heavens' sake! What you needed was a big dose of reality. To have your nose rubbed in it, like I did. My life was pure hell. You couldn't even imagine that kind of hell. One thing I did learn, if you are desperate to escape one appalling situation you should be careful what you get into instead. I jumped from the frying pan into the fire.

I thought it was enough that Jimmy never raised his voice. He never argued. He never hollered, cursed or yelled at me like Father. Stupid me, I thought I had found heaven at last. I couldn't have been more deluded. I found out there are other ways to control people. Without raging, without shouting. Ways that instill just as much fear. Or even more. Ways that cause even more emotional damage. Wouldn't you know it, my husband proved to be a master at that. I knew how to defend myself from Father's rages. I knew how to deal with that kind of anger. I was an expert. But Jimmy's acquiescence baffled me. I fell for his sweet demeanor. I failed to recognize it for what it was. I failed to recognize the resentment, the hostility, his insidious need to control me. That was a lesson I had to learn bit by bit, slowly and painfully.

This lesson took years to sink in. I didn't see the signs. I must have been blind. Or stupid. I was looking for the wrong clues. The ones I learned to recognize when I lived at home. The things I feared most at home. My sister said that whenever she started dating a new man, she watched very carefully to avoid getting involved with somebody who has the same faults that made her leave her last boyfriend. That blinded her to the faults of her new date, because she was watching out for the wrong things. That's exactly what happened to me, but magnified a hundred times.

I knew damn well how to deal with hollering and screaming. I was inured to that. I had built layer upon layer upon layer of defenses against such behavior. I could stand up to anybody. I could out-shriek, out-scream, out-curse anybody. Defiance was the one thing I learned at home, and learned it well. Far better than my baby sister. Day in and day out I honed that skill. But I soon found out I was powerless when I had to confront my husband. I hadn't the slightest idea about how to deal with Jimmy's mild-mannered, feigned compliance. His strategy was to procrastinate, delay and conquer. That's how I lost every single battle. And then, later, I also lost the war. What's even worse is that I didn't know there was a battle going on, much less a war.

After my wedding, I couldn't wait for my family to leave. My real life was about to begin, at last. The wedding was an awful ordeal, but heck, at least it didn't last forever. Thank God, my parents could not communicate with Jimmy's family. They didn't speak enough English to manage to spoil everything, even though they tried pretty hard, believe me. They were truly offensive, pretentious. As usual, Father was utterly obnoxious. No surprise there. He tried to pay for every meal, loudly insisting with grandiose gestures that everybody should order the most expensive things on the menu because it was all on him. He tried to appear congenial and expansive, engaging everybody in impossible conversations with lots of slaps, hand gestures and sound effects, to make up for his lack of English. You could hear his loud guffaws a mile away. I was embarrassed to death. Fortunately, he got tired of this role after a couple of days and sulked the rest of the time. Mother was even worse. She tried to outdo everybody with her ostentatious clothes and insincere smiles. She wore a shiny black suit, much too short and tight, and wore so much makeup and dark red lipstick that she looked like a cheap south-of-the-border hooker. And Rebecca, following me all the time, asking questions I didn't feel like answering. What a pest. I couldn't wait to get rid of all of them.

The wedding was a disaster. Everybody tried to appear jolly and pleased, but I could tell they just wanted to be done with it and go home. What a farce. I hated every minute of it. The parents were more annoying than ever, even more dreadful than I remembered. I was so relieved when they finally left. My little sister doesn't know how lucky she was that she was spared this particular ordeal. She got married in front of a judge with only one witness, somebody she didn't even know. In fact, if I am not mistaken, her husband Ricardo didn't even notify his own parents about his marriage plans. I've always wondered whether he was trying to avoid an encounter between his family and the rather unsuitable parents of the bride. I wouldn't blame him. Given half a chance I would have done the same.

Here I was, ready to start my new life in America, as I had always dreamed. Jimmy was all I ever wanted in a man. First and foremost, he was a real American boy, a southerner. His ancestors had arrived many generation ago and settled in Florida. He represented everything I had always wanted and never had. Safety, security, stability, a place to call home. Finally I would stop wandering like a gypsy, a despised foreigner wherever I went. At long last I was going to belong somewhere.

Luckily, Jimmy was not a curious person. He wasn't interested in finding out more about me. He was satisfied with what I told him about myself and my family. He never asked any questions. That suited me just fine. Now all I had to do was to become part of his life, to adopt his heritage, to make it my own. I had decided to do that a long time ago, right after I met him. I knew I could fit in, I could adapt. I was ready to do whatever it took to have a normal, conventional life. I was pregnant with Jimmy's child, and I was delighted. I felt so full of hope, I could hardly wait to start the rest of my life.

Before I got married, I had decided to quit the university. I wasn't learning anything—nothing worthwhile, anyway. Nothing that could do me any good in my new life. I had everything I needed right here. I wanted us to start looking for our own house immediately. I wanted Jimmy to find a job. I wanted us to start our ordinary, average American existence. But Jimmy didn't seem to be in a hurry.

We were staying with his parents. They had a small, two bedroom cottage on the outskirts of Tampa. They were older people, reserved and quiet. They hardly ever said a word, at least not to me. Or to their son. A greeting in the morning, a comment about the heat. That was all.

Jimmy's father was tall and awfully thin. You could see every bone through his yellowish skin. Jimmy told me before we married that his father was dying of a heart ailment. He had been dying for more than twenty years. He stayed in bed most of the time. In the late morning, he would shuffle into the kitchen, get a cup of coffee, a piece of toast, the newspaper, and retire to the bedroom. Sometimes, in the afternoon, he would sit in a rocker on the porch and watch the street. There was really nothing to see. This was a very quiet street. Nothing ever happened here. Once in a while a kid on a bicycle would ride by, or a tired-looking dog would saunter down the road.

Jimmy's mother was much younger than her husband, but you couldn't tell by her looks. She was a slight woman, drab permed hair framed her prematurely wrinkled face, thick glasses hid her pale blue eyes. She attended to her husband's needs without fuss, quietly and efficiently, and went to church on Sundays. She had been doing this for twenty years, since he became ill. She was to do it for twenty more, until he died of a heart attack at the age of eighty six. What kind of a life did she have? What if I had been in her shoes? I used to shudder at the thought. Little did I know that in a few years, her life would seem a cinch compared to mine.

I felt we had imposed on Jimmy's parents long enough and I wanted to move out. Now, don't get me wrong, they never gave me an inkling that we were not welcome. They were much too polite. But I knew they must have felt crowded, all four of us in that itty-bitty house. But that wasn't the main reason I wanted to move out. I wanted us to be by ourselves, to start our new life as newlyweds, to live among our own things. I wanted to have my own kitchen to fuss in. My own pots and pans. I wanted to arrange my own furniture according to my own taste. To have a little privacy. Is that asking for too much? That place was so tiny I felt uncomfortable even whispering, or breathing. I felt I had to tiptoe around everybody, literally and figuratively. We could hear them, too, both of them, snoring up a storm. You wouldn't believe such a diminutive woman could make such big noise. I hated to imagine what they thought of us, whenever they heard us.

I started looking for a small cottage. Even an apartment would do. I called several real estate agents. When they heard what I wanted, they seemed to lose interest. A couple of them didn't even bother returning my calls. Jimmy wasn't much help, either. He hated coming along with me to check out houses. I had to go alone. Whenever I found something half-decent, he would make up some dumb excuse to delay seeing the place. We lost a couple of houses I liked because of him. When he did come, always at my insistence, he would find fault with it. It was either too old or too small. Or too far from the beach. Or it needed paint. Soon the two realtors I had been working with were calling me less and less often. I couldn't blame them.

Mornings I would sit in the kitchen, sipping coffee and reading the paper until past noon. Jimmy never got up before noon if he could help it. He always complained about insomnia. He said he couldn't sleep if he heard the slightest noise or felt the slightest movement. I liked to get up really early and get going. At first, I stayed in bed with him. I tried to be very quiet. I wouldn't even read a magazine, I was afraid I'd wake him up when I turned a page. I would just lie in bed, completely still, my eyes wide open, looking at the ceiling. After a while, my whole body wanted to twitch. A few more minutes and I felt like I had to scream. I was like a prisoner in that bed. I had to get out or I would explode. Very slowly, I crept out of bed, trying not to disturb the top sheet. Step by step I approached the door, making sure the floor didn't creak. I felt like a burglar. My heart was pounding. Then, I got to the last obstacle, the door. Softly, I pressed the handle and pushed, holding my breath. Hallelujah! I was out, and Jimmy was still asleep like a baby. I tiptoed to the bathroom. Good. The door was open, that meant I could go in. But there, I was faced with my daily nemesis. The toilet. Should I flush, and risk waking up the whole household with a king-of-the-jungle roar, or should I leave my bodily waste, to be found by the next person who got up? I could never decide. I looked at my watch. Six thirty. I decided to put the cover down and go into the kitchen. Later, in an hour or two, before anybody had time to get up, I would go back and flush.

The kitchen was already hot. Not yet seven o'clock, ninety degrees already. Damn hot. No matter. I couldn't start my morning without a cup of strong black coffee. Didn't taste as good as Venezuelan coffee. Darn. I missed Venezuelan coffee. The best in the world. No wonder they never export it—they hoard it for themselves. The first sip is the best. The aroma in your nostrils, the hot, bitter taste. I picked up the paper from the driveway, sat down with my steaming mug. Too hot to really enjoy the coffee. I started reading the ads. Looking for houses and apartments, or possibly a duplex. With a red pen I circled the ones that looked good. I was hampered in my search because I didn't know the area. I didn't know which neighborhoods were okay and which were slums. I felt irritated. I felt Jimmy should be here helping me. Instead he was in bed, sleeping like a log. I would call the ads I had circled later, after nine, to get more information.

When Jimmy woke up I would make breakfast. Bacon and eggs, toast, the whole works. But he told me he was never hungry in the mornings. Coffee would be plenty enough. I stopped making breakfast, it wasn't worth the trouble just for myself. I would make him a fresh pot of coffee and sit down to read the ads aloud.

"What do you think of this one? Sunny small cottage, one bedroom, wall-to-wall carpets, all appliances, large yard, garage, near shopping. Utilities included $65.00. I called earlier and we can see it today after three."

Jimmy would look up from the sports section. "Where is it?"

"I really don't know. The woman said it was somewhere in the vicinity of Plant City. Is that too far?"

"Too far inland. It's too far from the bay. It gets too darn hot."

"How about this one: duplex, recently painted, one bedroom, large living room, carport, near school. Water only, $50.00."

"Recently painted means it's old, or the last tenant trashed it. I bet it's a slum. No mention of appliances, no yard. Just a carport. No, thanks. Sounds pretty bad to me."

After I read him a few more ads, Jimmy would get tired and mumble monosyllabic replies. I could see he didn't want to be bothered. I became annoyed. How did he expect me to find a house? Goodness gracious, I am not a wizard.

"Hey, I can't do this all by myself. I don't know where these darn places are. I don't even have a car to go see them."

"There is a county map somewhere, in one of the kitchen drawers. Why don't you look for it? And you can take my car, I don't need it today. Chuck is picking me up in a while. We can drive around in his old convertible."

Jimmy's cousin Charlie and his old high school buddies came by every afternoon, around three or four. They would just stay long enough to have a cup of coffee and say their 'thank-you's' politely. Then they would all pile into one car and take off with a squealing of tires. Jimmy told me they had a lot of catching up to do. He hadn't been in touch with them for the longest time, since he went away to college. Most of the time he would also tell me not to wait with dinner. He would just grab a bite somewhere with his buddies. He would save me the bother of cooking in all this summer heat. I was bursting to say I didn't mind the bother. I wanted to cook for him. I wanted us to have dinner together. Like a real married couple. But I kept my mouth shut. I sensed this would be the wrong thing to say. I just kept on reading the paper.

I looked through the employment ads. Jimmy had completed three years of engineering in college. I was hoping he could find a good job somewhere in the vicinity of Tampa–St. Petersburg. This was even more frustrating than looking at the housing ads. I would circle an ad for a company hiring in Orlando, or West Palm Beach, just to find out that this was all the way across the State. But the worst thing was that I didn't understand the lingo. I discarded all the ads that contained the word senior. All the ones that required some experience. But what the hell was HVAC, or pneumatic systems, or a Q.A. position? The more I read the angrier I became. Why should I be the one doing this? Jimmy should be sitting here, reading these ads. It was his responsibility, not mine.

Weeks passed and nothing changed. I started to get really impatient. I hated our situation. I didn't know what the hell he was waiting for. Whenever I mentioned the subject to Jimmy, he would say "What's the hurry?" or "You deal with it." It got so that I couldn't say anything without sounding like I was nagging. And I hated nagging. Mother was a nag, and I wasn't about to become like her. No way. That would be the last thing I wanted to be. I really wanted to be a good wife. To please my husband. To do things exactly as he wanted. Something was wrong but I didn't have an inkling of what it was.

I baked Jimmy's favorite cookies. I made fresh coffee for him twice a day. Or more, if he had some of his buddies over. I did his laundry, ironed his shirts, folded his underwear, rolled his socks, put everything away. I looked for a house for us. A job. I was at his beck and call, all the time. If he wanted to go out to grab a hamburger or catch a movie with me instead of going with his buddies, I was always ready and eager. What else could I do to please him?

Finally, after Jimmy's mother asked me whether we had found a place I summoned the gumption to confront my husband.

"Jimmy, we really need to do something about moving out. We can't keep mooching off your parents."

"Oh, I am sure they don't mind," he told me.

"Perhaps not, but it wouldn't hurt if you helped me look for a house, that way we could be sure you like it, too."

"I've already said I'll go see whatever you want me to see. I just don't want to bother with places that are out of the question."

"I know that. But when I do find a really nice cottage, by the time you get your ass over there, it's taken. We've lost too many nice houses because we didn't act fast enough. You know perfectly well that good houses go real fast. You have to make up your mind right on the spot, or the next person will get it."

"Well, you know I hate being pushed into something. What's the big hurry? We are fine where we are. We have time to look for a place that feels just right. Nobody is kicking us out. It's not like we have to take the very first place that comes along. I don't understand why you are having a fit over this," he replied.

"A fit? Who is having a fit? I am just telling you a few things you need to hear. What the hell are you waiting for? Are you waiting for hell to freeze over?" Suddenly, all the anxiety, all the frustration, all the uncertainty of the last few months welled up in me. I could no longer restrain myself. I felt like a volcano about to explode. I heard myself screaming. I felt hot angry tears on my cheeks. I don't know exactly what I said, but I know it must have been pretty awful.

Jimmy stared at me hard. He got up, walked to the front door, opened the door and walked out, without saying a word. I heard the car door slam, the engine come to life, and the roar of the old muffler as the car pulled away.

My face felt burning hot. I went into the bathroom and splashed water on my face. The water felt warm and sticky. It smelled faintly of sulfur. I've always hated Florida water. I looked at myself in the mirror. Swollen eyes, puffy red cheeks, a face only a mother could love. Not my mother, of course. Somehow that thought seemed funny. I started laughing. I couldn't stop. I barely managed to suppress the guffaws, while I ran into the bedroom. I threw myself on the bed and laughed until I felt tears streaming down my face. I realized I was sobbing.

I sat on the bed, a book in my hands, reading the same page over and over, trying to keep my mind busy. Whenever I heard a car, I went to the window, lifted the corner of the curtain and stared at the street. The street light was about sixty feet from the house. I couldn't distinguish the make or color of the car until it went by. It was past midnight before I understood that Jimmy wasn't coming back that night.

Before we got married, when we had just met and were still courting and talking for hours on end, Jimmy told me he tried to kill himself several times. The first time he was only thirteen. The last time was right after he started college. He felt despondent, like life wasn't worth the effort. As I was listening to him, I felt a huge lump in my throat. My heart turned over in my chest. I felt a intense need to comfort him, to hold him in my arms. To make up with my love for all the things he missed in life. I wanted to tell him things would be different now, that I would always be there for him, no matter what happened.

Now, with Jimmy gone, a bunch of scary thoughts were flitting through my mind. I didn't want to give them shape or form. I was afraid if I put them into words they would become real. I couldn't endure this torture. I got up and went to the kitchen for a glass of water. I went back into the bedroom. It was so terribly hot. I felt like taking a shower, washing my hair. I didn't dare. It would wake Jimmy's parents. I couldn't sleep. I tried to read some more. I couldn't to that, either. I started crying again. I hardly slept that night.

I had so many conflicting feelings. Mostly, I felt angry. Angry enough to hit him, when I saw him coming through that door. But I also felt anxious. No, not anxious, scared. Terrified. Terrified enough to forgive him. And through it all, I felt shamed. Shamed in front of Jimmy's parents. Good God, they had to be aware of their son's absence. But they were tactful enough to pretend that everything was normal. I could just imagine my parents in the same situation. A true vision of hell. They would have been all over me, asking questions. "What happened? Where is your husband? Did you have a fight? What did you say to him? Did he leave? When is he coming back? He is not back yet? Perhaps he was in a car accident. Perhaps he is in the hospital, bleeding to death, as we speak."

Jimmy didn't come back until the next afternoon. When I heard his car in the driveway, I finally admitted to myself how choked up with fear I'd been. I felt an enormous tidal wave of relief. I ran to the window and watched him get out of the car. His clothes were rumpled, but otherwise he seemed his usual self. He sauntered in as if nothing had happened. As if he had only gone to the grocery store to get sodas. I threw myself at him, kissing his face, his neck, his shoulders. Chattering like a magpie, a mile a minute.

"Did you have lunch already? Are you hungry? Where have you been? I was so worried. Would you like some coffee? I'll make a fresh pot. How about some lemon cake? I just baked it this morning." I knew I was acting dumb. I just couldn't stop myself.

We walked toward the kitchen, I was still holding on to him. I made some fresh coffee. I served him a slice of lemon cake, his favorite. I had baked it just that morning to keep my hands busy. Hoping time would go by faster.

Jimmy said the cake was really good. He asked for a second helping. I felt pleased. I had started to relax. That's when he told me.

"Susie, me and my buddy Chuck joined the army this morning. We went down to the recruiting center on Main Street, you know, the one kitty corner from the laundromat."

"You joined the army? I don't understand," I looked at him. "What do you mean?"

"Well, you know, it gives us guys a chance to get out of here for a while, to go somewhere else. Chuck thought it sounded like a swell idea, and I felt, well, what the heck, it's something to do."

I was speechless. I felt dizzy with shock. My world was falling apart, disintegrating right in front of my eyes. For a few seconds, I was stunned. Then I felt a huge wave of outrage, like never before.

"What the hell is wrong with you? Are you nuts?" I yelled. "How could you make a decision like that without asking me, without taking me into account? How could you do this to me, and to your baby? Don't you care what happens to us?" I was in a frenzy. I couldn't stop shrieking.

"You have to go back there. Tell them it's all a frigging mistake. You didn't mean to do it. It's only been a few hours. Tell them to rip up the papers. They'll have to do it! Tell them I am pregnant. Hell, I'll go with you. We'll show them how pregnant I am. For god's sake, it's so obvious. I am due in a couple of months! They'll have to let you go." I was sobbing and yelling at the same time.

Jimmy walked out on me in mid-sentence. He left me alone again that night, the second night in a row. I was in such a rage, I wanted to kill him. Hell, I'd be better off with him dead. Who needs such a moron? Not me, not in a million years! Again that night, I cried myself to sleep.

He didn't come back for two days. I was terrified. I thought of calling Chuck, but I didn't know his phone number. I didn't even know his last name. I didn't dare to ask Jimmy's parents. I felt embarrassed enough by all these scenes, all the screaming and yelling, all these comings and goings. I didn't want to admit to them that something was really wrong. Although they must have known. They would have had to be blind and deaf not to realize that things were rotten between us. I pretended everything was hunky-dory. But inside I felt I was dying.

When Jimmy finally came back, I couldn't bring myself to talk to him. I couldn't forgive him. We didn't talk to each other for several days. When we finally did, he told me he felt he wasn't ready yet to start married life. As if I couldn't see that for myself! He needed time to get used to the idea, he said. This separation would give him a chance to do precisely that. He felt it would be for the best.

I felt so terribly hurt. But I kept my mouth shut. I felt I couldn't say all the things I wanted. I was still seething with rage. But I knew by now that I had to hold my tongue. I didn't dare respond. I was afraid he would just leave and not come back at all. Or do something much worse. But I didn't want to even think about that.

I was in turmoil. I was outraged. How could he have done this? Dammit! And without ever consulting me. Without even asking how I felt. I couldn't believe I had married this spineless man. He was shirking all his responsibilities, just like that, without a second thought. Leaving me with all the mess.

I've never felt so abandoned, so alone, as I did during the next weeks. Jimmy was making preparations to leave. We were hardly talking to each other. There was nothing to say. He was going to Korea. Wives could not accompany their husbands. I was going to stay in Florida. Awaiting the baby. Awaiting Jimmy's return.

My life was shattered. I though I had hit bottom. But I was wrong.

Rebecca

The day after we got married, we rented an apartment in an old Victorian house and started our life together. Ricardo found a job as an engineer, I continued studying at the University. I chose Slavic Studies as my major. I am not sure why, perhaps because I liked languages and loved Russian literature and culture. I didn't think much about how I would make a living. I was enjoying university life and studying was what I did best; or more accurately, it was the only thing I knew how to do.

I was eighteen now and married, but I had trouble thinking of myself as a married woman. I felt as if I was only playing house. Was I expected to get up early and make breakfast for Ricardo? I wasn't sure. Luckily, the problem never arose because Ricardo hated to get up early, so he would give himself only ten minutes from the time the alarm rang, just enough time to shower and get dressed. My only wifely duty, it turned out, was to hand him his wallet and keys as he raced out the door. From the kitchen window, I watched him pull out the car much too fast, with a screech of tires turn toward the street, and wave to me one last time. As I made myself a pot of coffee, I realized with a pang of sadness I would never get the opportunity to wear a gorgeous long white gown. I had missed one chance when I was eight and didn't get to have a first communion, and when I had a second chance, at my wedding, I got married in my street clothes.

A couple of weeks after I got married, Greta, my best friend from my freshman year at Cal, phoned and asked me to meet her in a coffee house in Berkeley. As soon as I saw her, I knew something was wrong. Her face, always made up to the hilt, was free of make-up, her kinky hair seemed unwashed, pulled back into a short pony tail, short wisps fanning out around her face like a halo. The zipper of her skirt was broken and she held the back closed with a large pin.

Before I had time to utter a greeting, she told me she had missed her period for the second month in a row and was afraid she was pregnant. Her timing was terrible, she confided crying, she had just broken up with her boyfriend, an Iranian student, and had been expelled from the University because of bad grades. She was planning to start her freshman year again at San Francisco City College, but hadn't had the courage to tell her parents, who were still writing to her at her dorm in Berkeley.

As I sat there, sipping my coffee and listening to the litany of misfortunes that had befallen Greta, a strange idea popped into my mind. "Did you have sex with your boyfriend?" I asked.

"Of course not! What do you think I am, a slut?" she replied, quite offended.

"In that case you have nothing to worry about. You can't get pregnant if you don't have sex." I felt I was an experienced married woman imparting my newly acquired knowledge to my best friend. We were both eighteen and products of a Latin American education who knew almost nothing about sex and reproduction.

"Well, we didn't actually have sex, at least, I don't think we did. Well, I am really not sure. We just necked and petted heavily." Greta started crying.

"Did you take off your clothes?"

"Of course not, I wouldn't let anybody see me undressed! What do you take me for? He only lifted my skirt and lowered my panties. And he didn't even take his pants off, he only unzipped them," she told me between sobs.

I was stymied. I didn't know what to say. The situation seemed quite inconclusive to me. I told Greta we should ask someone else, who was better informed about all these minutiae. Or better yet, she could have a pregnancy test.

Greta was horrified, but after a few more minutes of sobbing, she agreed. When I volunteered to go with her to the clinic she accepted gratefully. She gave a false name and my phone number. Three days later I got a call. The test results were positive. Greta fell to pieces when she heard the news. She didn't know what to do. She was an observant Catholic and all alternatives seemed equally horrible. I promised I would support her no matter what she decided, but I couldn't help her reach a decision. I had grown up with Catholicism but was not a believer. I felt she should have an abortion, but I didn't want to exert any influence on her.

A couple of weeks went by. Greta would call me several times a day. "I've made up my mind, I am having an abortion. God will have to forgive me," she would tell me sobbing.

"All right, let's make an appointment. I'll go with you."

A few hours later she'd call again. "I can't do it. I am going to have the baby and bring it up as a fatherless bastard, to my eternal shame and punishment. This baby will always remind me of my sins." I couldn't listen when she said such stupid things; I almost felt like hanging up. But I knew this was the time when she needed a friend, so I would grind my teeth and say nothing.

I started getting worried. I knew that by failing to make a decision, Greta was deciding to keep the baby. I reminded her that time was of the essence. She would have to have the abortion soon, if that was what she wanted to do. I really wanted to discuss the situation with Ricardo, but I did not feel I could reveal Greta's secret.

Then, as if this were a fairy tale, Greta met a young man from Germany and within a month they were married. They moved to a small town in southern California, and every year since I've gotten a Christmas card showing an increasing number of children seated under a Christmas tree. I never saw her again.

Ricardo and I were happy those first few years. We were both very busy. He working overtime as an engineer in a San Francisco company, and I, studying at the university, and later, in graduate school, teaching Russian and Polish. The only note of discord occurred on our trip to Venezuela the first summer, when I met Ricardo's parents.

The fact that they lived in Venezuela, the country where I had grown up, was a coincidence. They were Spanish Republicans who left their country after Franco won the civil war and established his dictatorship. They went to Mexico, where the legitimate Spanish government in exile had taken refuge, then moved to Cuba, and finally to Caracas, just a short time before Ricardo and I met. Ricardo's father, who worked for a large pharmaceutical company, had had to travel for months at a time when Ricardo was a child and his mother, who suffered from severe agoraphobia, could not bring herself to leave the house alone. Ricardo, who at the time was barely six years old, became the head of the household in his father's absence. He was in charge, and his wishes were always obeyed. When he took up sailing as a young boy, the family bought a sailboat and everybody started sailing. When he took up water skiing, he made the family buy a motorboat and a vacation home on the coast, and that became their favorite form of recreation. He was like a benevolent dictator who did what he felt was best for everybody and, of course, what was best for everybody was what he liked most.

Ricardo did not tell his parents about our marriage until a few weeks before our arrival. I did not understand why he thought they would be so unhappy about the news. But he was so distraught about his parents' feelings, that he asked me to participate in a small subterfuge. He wanted me to take the blame for his continued stay in the United States. He felt his parents would feel less affronted if they believed that if it were his choice, we would have long ago returned to Caracas to live near them. He wanted me to convince them that the reason he stayed in Berkeley, even after he finished his studies, was because I was still at the University. Eager to please Ricardo, I consented.

As became obvious soon after we arrived, this falsehood poisoned the relationship between Ricardo's parents and myself. His father, who professed to be a socialist even though now he was president of one of the largest pharmaceutical companies in the world and owned lots of property, would taunt me constantly. I fell into this trap time and again, because I tried to focus on the issues and didn't see the emotional undercurrent of his discourse.

"Rebecca," he would say, showing his perfect teeth in a fake smile, "you can't be so blind and naîve as to believe that there is democracy or freedom in the United States. The American system favors the rich and powerful, the corporations, the business sector, the upper and middle classes. It never works for the working masses, the poor and the blacks."

"The working masses are middle class in the States," I would reply, earnestly. "They work hard, they can afford cars and in a few years they can afford houses in the suburbs, furniture, appliances, and other conveniences. I don't think there is any other country where this is true."

"Well, has it occurred to you that they can afford all this because they exploit all the neighboring countries? They have imperialistic designs for the whole American continent, and beyond. They install puppet governments in third world countries so they can reap huge profits and support dictators who rob the country blind and allow the destitute masses to perish of hunger," Ricardo's Father would intone with glee, his bald head shiny with sweat, as he swatted one of the many flies that hovered around the dinner table.

I didn't know what to say. I felt I had been cornered into defending and justifying positions that I didn't really believe in. How did I get there? There was nothing Ricardo's father liked better than a good debate, especially when he saw the chance to move in for the kill. My mother-in-law, a meek, large woman who only contradicted her husband when he was not around, nodded approvingly. Even Ricardo's younger brother, who idolized me, did not dare to disagree with his father.

These discussions would go on for hours after every dinner. Nothing I said made any difference, it was all four of them always siding against me.

We were seated at the table, waiting for the maid to bring the food. Every two or three minutes Ricardo's Father would yell, "Carmen, hurry up and bring the main course."

"Just a minute, Don Miguel," came the reply from the kitchen.

Half an hour went by and there was no food on the table. Finally, Ricardo's father would order his wife into the kitchen to see what was holding things up. More often than not there was some minor disaster, the butcher had delivered only four filets instead of six, the gas burners wouldn't come on because the tank was empty, or the steaks were burned. A whole new menu had to be devised and put on the table forthwith, a chore my mother-in-law hated. She was an unaccomplished cook, preferring almost anything to kitchen chores.

While we waited, Ricardo's father started a diatribe on the character of the American people.

"Americans are shallow, they don't know the meaning of friendship, loyalty, or any other honorable trait. At first they fool you," he would press on, "they seem so easygoing and friendly. But the more you know them, the sooner you realize that it is all a farce. They only seem friendly because they are so informal. They call you by your first name from the very moment they meet you. Just imagine, they have the effrontery of calling their own president 'Ike'! In any other normal country they would get a month in jail for doing that. Even their damned language doesn't make a distinction between the formal and the informal form of address. But that friendliness is deceptive, it means nothing, it's just a habit, and a very disrespectful one at that." He stopped long enough to yell for food once more. When there was no answer from the kitchen, he went on. I was hoping against hope that my mother-in-law would appear with the food before I started crying.

"All Americans care about is the mighty dollar, how to line their own pockets. They are so greedy and acquisitive." Another pause to roar at his wife "What is going on in that kitchen of yours?" She would hiss back, "Just a couple of minutes more." Then, reassured, he continued with his train of thought, "Their ethics leave a lot to be desired, they are wobbly at best. And how about their bias against people of other races? They discriminate against anybody who isn't whiter than a sheet. It's a well known fact that everybody is a member of the Ku Klux Klan, if not openly, then secretly."

I felt that this whole harangue was directed at me. I was guilty of wanting to live in the United States. I knew some sort of answer was expected.

"But these are characteristics of the human race," I countered inadequately, "not just of Americans. Most people are racists, they fear and dislike people who look differently, speak differently, behave differently. You can find all kinds of people in the States, and like everywhere else, some are greedy and some are caring and dedicated to helping others. Isn't that right, Ricardo?"

"Well, maybe, I wouldn't know," my husband said.

My mother-in-law sailed into the dining room, followed by the maid who carried a large platter piled high with huge chunks of fried steak floating in a sea of oil. I couldn't look at the meat, much less eat it. I nibbled on a piece of bread.

"I don't eat meat very often, and I am not hungry tonight," I explained feebly. Ricardo's parents exchanged looks of displeasure. By the end of most evenings I was close to tears. I could hardly wait for the summer to be over.

I was disappointed that I couldn't get closer to my mother-in-law. Ricardo had talked about her a lot. He was upset about the way his father treated her, always ordering her about, as if she were a slave. But I also saw that she had her little ways of getting revenge. While we were vacationing in Caracas, Ricardo's father bought a fancy new Mercedes Benz, which was his pride and joy. He warned his wife she would never be allowed to drive it, although everyone in the family knew she was the better driver. One day, as they were coming back from the beach, late in the afternoon, a gargantuan traffic jam stopped them dead in their tracks. Drivers got out of their cars, talking to each other and walking ahead to find the cause of the problem. Ricardo's father walked away, while his wife sat in the passenger seat, knitting a sweater for her younger son. An hour went by. Slowly, cars started inching forward, then moving faster and faster. Soon a highway patrol car with flashing lights pulled up behind the Mercedes. My mother-in-law didn't look up from her knitting.

"What's going on? You can't park in the middle of the fast lane" the officer barked at her as he was exiting his vehicle.

"I am waiting for my husband," said my mother-in law, primly, as she continued knitting.

"You have to move the car to the shoulder. You can't stay where you are, you are blocking traffic and somebody will run into you."

"But, officer, I don't know how to drive," lied my mother-in law.

The officer called for another unit with an extra policeman to drive the car away. The new Mercedes, with my mother-in-law still knitting, ended up in the parking lot of an inner-city police station. Meanwhile, my father-in-law got back to where he left his car but didn't find it. He walked up and down the freeway for more than an hour. Finally, he figured his wife must have driven the car home. He took a taxi home, but there was nobody there. He started calling various police stations, and after the initial ridicule he endured whenever he explained his wife was missing with his new Mercedes, he finally managed to locate her. By midnight, he reached the police station and, after paying a hefty fine and various other charges, both the car and his wife were released to him. The next morning, when I heard the whole story, I didn't know whether to cheer or to cry for my mother-in-law.

Ricardo and I visited Susanna for a few days on our way back to California. We stayed in her new house. She had moved to Alabama and now had a second child, a girl. We went to see some large caves, learned a lot about stalactites and stalagmites, and spent the rest of the time playing with the children. I never got the chance to talk with my sister as we had when we were young. She seemed strangely subdued in the presence of her husband. I had never seen her so quiet. She answered most questions with monosyllables and in a flat tone.

That night, in bed, I had trouble falling asleep. In a whisper, I mentioned my concerns to Ricardo, "You know, I've never seen Susanna like this. She seems so listless, so discouraged." He tried to put my mind at ease. "Don't worry. She is probably worn out, what with two small kids and having guests on top of that. That would tire even the hardiest soul." I wasn't convinced. He didn't know my sister as I did. When things got tough, she fought harder.

We left that same weekend because my classes were about to start at the university, but I was troubled.

Back in Berkeley, Ricardo and I were getting to know each other and enjoying the process, isolated from what was going on in the world. But these were the sixties, when great changes were shaking the very foundation of society. There was a political and social revolution on campus. The free speech movement, the radicals, the free love advocates, the sexual revolution, the druggies, the flower children, the hippies, all converged on Berkeley.

I kept going to school, studying, working, feeling quite happy and uninvolved in the political turmoil. While I was a teaching assistant in the Slavic Department, the campus was rocked by student and faculty strikes protesting restrictions on free speech. Most of my students were in the graduate program and didn't want to waste class time on political issues but didn't want to cross the picket lines, so we took a vote and decided to hold classes off campus. We had trouble finding an adequate place to meet. We tried a nearby coffee house, but it was too noisy and distracting. We tried a park, but soon the rain chased us away. We finally settled on having the class in my living room, which was just barely large enough. Nobody seemed to mind sitting on the floor, and my cat had a great time jumping from lap to lap.

When our next-door neighbors were arrested during a sit-in at the University, Ricardo and I were recruited to move into their house and take care of their two small children. Their closest friends had been arrested with them, two couples who also had children. Before we knew it, three more toddlers were delivered to the house. Suddenly, what had started as an interesting experience became a nightmare. I had no experience with babies, I had never babysat, and had no younger siblings. All I could do was to try to keep everybody safe, fed and clean, which meant dispensing lots of bottles, cookies and hot dogs and constantly changing diapers and taking toddlers to the bathroom. I was so relieved when Ricardo came home from work I almost cried. Between the two of us we managed to get everybody bathed and ready for bed. Then the one-more-story, one-more-glass-of-water routine started. The second night was even harder. The children were cranky because their parents weren't there and their routine had been disrupted. I was upset because I couldn't tell them when their parents would be back and my routine had been disrupted. On the third day, everybody was released from jail, and we moved back into our own apartment.

My friends were all falling prey to different movements, quitting school, dropping out, becoming drug addicts, losing their scholarships, their jobs, getting divorced, pairing up with multiple partners, going to live in communes, joining different religious cults. Everybody was breaking with tradition, breaking new ground, doing things differently, making sure nothing resembled the way things were done before.

My only contact with drugs was at a potluck wedding party. Among the desserts, I saw some delicious-looking brownies with a sign on a toothpick that said Alice B. Toklas. I assumed this was the person who had baked the brownies. I brought a chicken casserole, but it never occurred to me to affix my name to it. I suppose I wasn't that proud of my cooking. I ate a couple of these brownies. The next thing I knew, I was standing naked in the garden, talking to the parents of the bride. It wasn't as bad as you may think, a lot of people were undressing to get in the sauna in the backyard. But the next two days were really strange. I lost all sense of time and distance. I didn't dare drive the car, so I took a bus and walked the rest of the way to class. Each block seemed to stretch on and on. I thought I would never make it on time. I was in such a fog I don't remember how I taught my class. I knew I didn't want to try drugs again.

Shortly after my marriage, my father had separated from my mother and went to live in Germany. Mother, for the first time in her life, had taken a stand. She refused to go with him and stayed in Uruguay, in the house they bought in Punta del Este.

Since his arrival in Germany, Father had been writing me long letters. At first, they were full of enthusiasm. "I am a European. I have finally returned to my roots. I see myself living the rest of my life here, with all the respect and recognition that I've earned and deserve. I always felt uncomfortable with every American handyman and janitor calling me by my first name. I studied and worked my fingers to the bone to earn my degrees. I am the first one in my whole family to receive a title from a university, and not just any university, but the Jagellonian University, a world renowned institution. Here in Germany, everyone calls me *'Herr Doktor'* and I feel this is how it should be."

Germany, indeed! I thought he had gone berserk. But little by little, his letters started losing some of the superlatives. Perhaps, after all, Germany wasn't all that wonderful. Then something happened that changed my father's plans.

Father had moved to Germany to join his former business partner, Leshek, and his wife Marysia, who had sold their store in Caracas and moved to Munich to start a new life. Leshek and Marysia had been my parents' best friends in Venezuela. They were Jews from Warsaw, who had survived the war. Tragically, they had lost their two young children. The oldest, a boy who was almost nine, was sent to England on a train with thousand of other Jewish children, to be adopted for the duration of the war. The second one, a three-year old girl, was too young to go on the train and was entrusted to a Polish peasant family, with the hope that food would be available in the countryside much more readily than in the city. The Polish family was generously compensated with all the jewels that Leshek and Marysia possessed, which were many, since Leshek had been a diamond dealer before the war. After the war, neither of the children could be found. The Red Cross and other international agencies searched fruitlessly for several years, but all leads proved to be dead-ends. Leshek and Marysia were devastated. They moved to Venezuela to forget and start a new life. Marysia suffered from paralyzing depression. Most days she was unable to get out of bed. Leshek dedicated himself to his work and did well, but inside he was as broken up as his wife. After several unhappy years in Caracas they decided to move back to Europe. They felt this was their last chance.

When my father joined them in Munich, they had been there for eight months. The man and his wife had made a secret pact with each other. If in one year from their arrival the quality of their life had not improved markedly, they would commit suicide. One Sunday evening, they invited my father to dinner. They seemed relaxed, almost serene. The next morning they were both dead. They left a note of apology and explanation to my father, their only friend in Munich.

In less than a week Father returned to Uruguay, where my mother had been expecting him, hoping that he would change his mind and abandon Germany. She mourned the death of her two friends, but couldn't help feeling blessed for Father's return. They tried once more to rebuild their life in Uruguay, but failed. Father felt frustrated and unhappy with his life. He couldn't find work he wanted to do in Montevideo and wasn't ready to retire. They remained another year, knowing that they were not going to stay. In 1965, when their number in the immigrant quota finally came up, my parents were allowed to reside legally in the United States. Father came to California to make arrangements for their new beginning. Mother remained in Uruguay to sell the house, the very first and last one she had ever owned.

Father stayed in our apartment while looking for a more permanent home. The second day he asked me to buy the paper. He wanted to read the housing ads. I brought the paper on my way home from campus. He sat on the couch and read the ads while I busied myself with dinner. A few minutes went by in complete silence. Suddenly he started cursing, hollering, and shouting at me. "What's the point of you giving me this stupid, fucking paper? I have no idea where anything is! You lazy slut, you fucking princess, you should be sitting here with me, helping me, instead of making that damn racket in the kitchen. You think you are too busy to help? You are an ungrateful, slovenly bitch, no better than the whore who brought you into this world!

I was completely taken by surprise. I had been with Ricardo for more than three years. I had lost the habit of being bullied and yelled at. My father's insults, which I had tried to tune out as a child, reverberated with a surge of recognition in my mind. I couldn't believe that for years I had accepted this kind of behavior from him. This time I didn't hesitate. I knew what to do.

I grabbed Father by the arm, yanked him off the sofa, dragged him to the front door, opened the door, and shoved him out without a word of explanation.

An hour later I found him sitting quietly on the steps by the front door. I told him he could come back in if he never again yelled and cursed at me. He came in, and that was the last time he ever screamed at me.

I also found a way to deal with the commotion my father created when we would go to a restaurant. When I was young, Father behaved atrociously every time the family went out to dine. Father screamed at the waiters, tossed his food on the plate, Mother cried and apologized for his behavior, while my sister and I whimpered in fear and shame. On Sundays, after the beach, we frequently ate at a garden restaurant under the shade of sea grape trees. Father always ordered fried chicken for all of us. Invariably, he would complain and send back the pieces he was served, they were either too dry, undercooked, greasy, or too spicy. He raised hell so often that Mother would boil some chicken the day before to take along to the restaurant and, saying that Father couldn't eat fried foods, we would order only for the rest of us. Then Father would find something else to fuss about. He didn't like the canned peaches that came with the meal. The waiter told Father that he could bring him fruit cocktail, but Father wasn't appeased. He wanted compote. Finally we stopped going there, to the relief of everybody involved, and Mother started bringing along a cold picnic of boiled chicken pieces for the whole family. Although my sister and I missed the delicious fried chicken, we were happy to avoid the humiliating tantrums that were part of the experience.

After Mother arrived in the United States, Father took us to a Chinese restaurant. Once we were all seated, he declared loudly that all he wanted for dinner was a soft-boiled egg, a piece of toast and a boiled potato. The waiter was thoroughly confused and tried to steer my father to other choices, perhaps egg foo yung would do?

"What kind of an accursed establishment is this, where a man cannot have something as simple as a soft-boiled egg and toast, if that is what he wants?" Father hollered.

Then he bellowed that he wanted to see the owner immediately, and berated and humiliated as many of the staff as he could find. Mother tried to placate Father and apologize to the staff, explaining that he had a delicate stomach. But Father raged and cussed louder and louder, until finally he stormed out of the restaurant and sat fuming in the car. We stayed seated at the table, but none of us could swallow a thing. We were all embarrassed to the point of tears, the whole dining experience was a nightmare. We asked for the check and left as soon as we could.

Variations of this scene had been repeated over and over whenever we dined out. Now I decided it would never again happen in my presence.

The next time Father pulled this stunt, I simply said that if he didn't stop shouting and berating the waiter that very instant I would stand up and leave, and never again set foot in any restaurant with him.

"But Rebecca," Mother chimed in, "you can't do that, we already ordered. It would be much too embarrassing to us if you did something like that."

Father stopped his tirade for a minute, fixed his gaze on me, then started cussing all over again. I stood up, picked up my purse, and left. I rode the bus back home. The trip took over two hours, but it was worth it. From that time on, I never again went to dine out with Father, even though Mother kept begging me to go with them, especially when other family members visited from abroad.

After I received my bachelor's degree, I was offered a teaching assistant's position in the Slavic Department while I worked for my master's. I enjoyed my graduate years much more than my four years as an undergraduate. I also loved teaching, which was, I discovered, the best way to learn a subject. I had access to the library stacks, even obtained a cubicle of my own in the stacks to do my research. Things started falling into place. I could continue studying and earn money at the same time. I didn't need to look for an outside job, a prospect I dreaded.

A year later, I was awarded a much coveted scholarship to Russia. Ricardo wouldn't hear of quitting his job and going to Russia with me even though the money would be enough for two. I considered going alone, but I discarded the idea. Reluctantly, I turned down the scholarship.

Ricardo had became chief engineer in his company. Nevertheless, he started planning a long trip around the world. The obstacles that seemed insurmountable when I wanted to go to Russia turned out to be negligible when he wanted to travel. I had finished my master's degree and was taking post graduate courses, when we left for South America. From there, we headed for Europe.

Before leaving, I had to do something about my passport. My family and I had become Venezuelan citizens in the early fifties. But between the ages of eighteen and twenty five, I had to declare my wish to remain a citizen. When I had tried to do this at the Venezuelan consulate in San Francisco, the young secretary had been too busy doing her nails and gossiping on the phone to help me. I was told to try when I was in the country on one of my occasional visits. In Caracas, after waiting in countless lines in several different government offices, I was told I could file the papers only in my place of residence, California.

My passport was due to expire in less than a year, and I was anxious about embarking on a trip with this complication hanging over my head, but decided to take a risk. My plan was to find some out-of-the-way consulate where rules weren't followed too closely and get a temporary extension. In Glasgow, the Venezuelan Consul told me snappily, "You weren't born in Venezuela, you don't reside in Venezuela, so explain to me again why you think you ought to get a Venezuelan passport." I just mumbled something about needing a provisional passport, until I could get back to Venezuela to do the necessary paper work. No dice. On my second try in Belgium, I had the same result. Finally, on my third try, when I was starting to become disheartened, the Consul in Marseilles, after a lot of hemming and hawing, gave me a two year extension. After we returned from Europe, I did lose my Venezuelan citizenship and remained stateless for several years, until I became an American citizen.

Susanna

J immy left for Korea at the beginning of December. I was sick with pain. But I made sure his family didn't suspect anything was wrong. I didn't feel like giving any explanations. I don't know what they thought. I have no idea what he told them. I never asked. I didn't want to know. I didn't care. For my part, I told everyone who asked, that Jimmy had been drafted.

A week later, I left Jimmy's parents' house. I rented a room in an old wooden house on the road to Clearwater, just a few miles away. The room suited me, it was medium sized, with bare floors, a single bed, a small dresser, and twin windows overlooking the backyard. I liked the shade trees and forlorn look of that backyard. It suited my mood. There was a decaying set of swings, a reminder of children long gone, and a rusty, old barbecue. I shared the dilapidated kitchen and tiny bathroom with the owner of the house, a widowed lady in her sixties. It wasn't a perfect arrangement, but I had to be careful with money. I was getting only ninety dollars a month. I was glad to get this place, since by now it was more than obvious that I was pregnant and soon there would be a new-born baby in my room. My landlady didn't seem too concerned. All she said was that she could hardly remember how it felt to have little babies in the house and if she couldn't get used to it, I would have to make other arrangements. That was good enough for me.

I also had Jimmy's old car, the one with the rotting muffler. The next Sunday, I drove all over town looking for garage sales. I came back with a small woven rug, an old rickety brass lamp, and a baby crib. Now all I could do was wait for the baby to be born. I hoped it would be a girl. I didn't want a boy. Boys grow up to become men, and men, I was starting to realize, are a lot of trouble. More trouble than they are worth. I didn't know one could be so unhappy so soon after getting married.

My son Ricky was born at the end of January. I had a very difficult labor and delivery. I felt weak and depressed for days. I hated being alone through the whole thing. Jimmy's mother visited me in the hospital. But seeing her didn't help much. My landlady also came. She brought an old camera and took a couple of pictures. Those are the only newborn pictures I have of Ricky. When I got home I wrote to Jimmy and sent him the pictures of the baby and an old picture of myself. I didn't want to send a new one because I hated the way I looked then. He wrote back, sounding pleased. I reread his letter many times, trying to read between the lines. Was he just being polite? Or was he pleased because he had avoided going through this ordeal? My letters were always long and full of details. About the baby. About all the things I did. About my visits with his family and whatever else was happening in town. I would always finish my letters by telling Jimmy how much I missed him, how much I loved him. His letters were short and curiously childish. I don't know whether it was because of the large even handwriting or the phrasing, but they always made me think of a boy writing home from camp.

Ricky kept me very busy during the day. At night, when I couldn't sleep, I would get into bed and read one book after another. This wasn't how I had imagined married life to be. I was a military wife now, waiting for my husband to come back from the front. I told my parents Jimmy had been drafted. I didn't want anybody's pity, especially my family's. They could never offer consolation without attaching blame. I didn't want to hear any more variations on the theme "You made your bed, and now you have to sleep in it." I didn't need anybody to remind me of something that I already knew. I felt awful enough as it was, more awful than I had ever felt in my life. I didn't tell my little sister either. She was always a blabbermouth. And besides, I didn't think she could do or say anything that would help. I had to get through this alone.

Many days I thought I would go crazy. Just taking care of Ricky and being alone all day long was hard enough. But not knowing what would happen later, not knowing whether Jimmy would want to come back and live with us, was killing me. I willed myself to stop thinking about it. I would just have to take life a day at a time. But at night, when I was trying to fall asleep I couldn't stop myself from thinking. I couldn't imagine the future. I couldn't picture what my life was going to be in a few years. My dream was shattered. My dream of the perfect American life, the dream I had nurtured for so long, the dream that had sustained me through thick and thin, was no more. There was nothing left in its place, nothing to fill that empty space. Somehow I had to learn to live for the present. But dammit, I couldn't do it, I didn't know how. I had always lived for the future. A much better future. I was always preparing myself for the wonderful life I would make for myself. But not this, never this. I felt helpless, no longer in charge of my own destiny. Waiting. God, how I hated waiting. I had to try to fill my time to make this waiting more bearable. Every night, I cried myself to sleep.

One day at the laundromat, when I was doing several loads of diapers and trying to get Ricky to stop bawling, a woman started a conversation with me. She was unsuccessfully trying to control two small children. We started talking about taking care of children, doing laundry, shopping and babysitting. Her name was Barbara. She told me I should call her Babs, everybody did. She was a large, clumsy looking woman, in matching pink shorts, halter, and hair curlers. She smoked like a chimney and cursed like a sailor, both traits I find loathsome. On the other hand, she was friendly, laughed loudly and often, and was eager to talk to me. I had been feeling isolated and lonely the last few months, so I welcomed the chance to have a chat with someone who seemed to be in the same boat.

"Hey, Sooze, how about if you come over to my place for lunch when you finish with all your crappy diapers?" she boomed. "Don't expect any fancy shit, just peanut butter sandwiches. That's all I am good for right now."

I went to her place, a dilapidated two-room cottage off Main street, none too clean. She lived there with her two bratty children, a dog and a cat. She told me she had divorced her no-good drunkard of a husband two years ago, after he beat her one too many times. Now she had slapped a restraining order on him, but it didn't do much good. Whenever he got plastered, he would pound at her door until she or the neighbors called the police to take him away.

Babs and I spent most of that afternoon together. She worked part time at the local drive-in at the edge of town. This was her day off. She told me she was sure they would be glad to hire me, since

I was so cute. I would look good in the little short skirts they all had to wear.

"I don't see how I could, really," I told her. "What about Ricky? He's just a few months old."

"Hey, Sooze, no problem, I'll babysit. Or better yet, we could ask the boss to give us the same work schedule, and share the babysitter. Wouldn't that be a blast?"

Soon I was working at the drive-in. I didn't mind the work, but I didn't like being ogled by all the men, especially the boisterous college crowd. Some of the guys thought it was really funny to try to cop a feel when I was carrying a tray and couldn't get out of the way fast enough. Low-life slime buckets! Babs taught me to 'accidentally' drop a milk shake on their crotch. I found it worked even better with a cup of hot coffee.

Babs and I became friends. My landlady told me she couldn't believe I would run around with such a low-life. So what? It's a free country. But I have to admit, even I was surprised. It really was an odd friendship. We were totally different from each other, but got along great. I couldn't stand Babs' constant smoking, drinking, and swearing. I thought it was disgusting and low-class. I could just imagine what Jimmy would think of her! But Jimmy wasn't here and I could do as I pleased. I was drawn to her warmth and to her outgoing personality. She had a heart of gold. She was always dying to do things for me, to share everything she had. And she never expected anything in return. Nobody had ever been this good to me before. She would invite me over for dinner almost every night, throwing a couple of TV dinners in the oven, or just making sandwiches and iced tea if it was hot. Then we would watch TV together while her kids played and Ricky slept. She gave me lots of baby clothes and furniture, things her kids had outgrown. That saved me plenty of money. She babysat for me whenever I wanted to go out by myself, which wasn't often. A couple of times we got a teenage girl to take care of the kids and we went out for a burger and a movie. We even went dancing once, but I felt uncomfortable with all the attention I was getting from men. It was different for Babs. She welcomed the attention. She was divorced and looking for a boyfriend. I was married and waiting for my husband to come back from Korea.

We never talked about Jimmy. I told her only that he was in the army, in Korea. I didn't want her to know the truth. Hell, I didn't even want to know the truth myself. I was better off pretending. I knew that as soon as Jimmy came back, I would have to drop Babs like a hot potato. He would never approve of our friendship. He hated people who smoked and drank and peppered their speech with obscenities. He would consider her too coarse and vulgar to be my friend. I couldn't blame him, I often felt the same.

But for now, Barbara was a life saver. She kept me grounded. She saved me from going crazy. She was totally without conceit, unselfconscious, unaware of her failings. Hell, I suppose she wouldn't even consider them as failings. She never read a book, just women's magazines, and only the articles about hair, make-up, and fashion. She watched all the stupid soap operas and game shows on TV. She couldn't resist any candy bar, cup-cake, donut, or bag of potato chips at the supermarket checkstand. She had to buy it, and eat it right away, while still waiting in line. No wonder she was so fat. She openly admired what she called my willpower and "classy, refined taste." Actually, there was no willpower involved. I really didn't like any of the stuff she found so irresistible, the junk food, the trashy TV shows, or the scandal sheets she read.

Except that we were both bringing up children alone, we had nothing in common. She always admired and praised how I looked, how I dressed, how I spoke. I felt accepted, even admired. With her, I could be myself. It would never have occurred to her to criticize anything I did or didn't do. I have never felt this free with anybody else. I always felt I had to bite my tongue, watch my back, be vigilant. No wonder I feel most comfortable when I'm by myself. Or in the company of my beloved cats.

Days I spent with Ricky, busy with my daily chores. Nights I thought of Jimmy and pictured the rest of my life. But I never pictured what happened later.

Rebecca

In the spring of 1967, we went south. We drove my father's old Chevy down the Pan-American Highway to Panama on the Pacific Coast, stopping along the way to visit friends. In Mexico City, we stayed with Ricardo's uncle and aunt, who showed us the sights, took us to the best restaurants, and insisted we stay longer. In Guatemala we lingered in the old capital of Antigua with one of my classmates' parents. I marveled at the beautiful landscape, high peaks, volcanoes, lakes, the emerald-green jungle, and masses of brightly colored flowers. We stayed for the Easter procession and watched the virgin slowly moving down the street carpeted with flowers, surrounded by thousands of children all dressed in white. In El Salvador we were stopped every few miles and at one checkpoint our suitcases where taken out of the car and the back seat was dismantled. Ricardo suspected that the military police were looking for smuggled guns. I did have a gun and ammunition hidden in my purse, but it was never checked. Knowing quite well that it was against the law in every country we would cross we still had decided to carry a gun. Ricardo felt we needed it for self-defense, since we would be traveling through deserted and remote areas. Honduras and Nicaragua were engaged in a war that started over a soccer match. The situation was deteriorating quickly, and we were afraid the border would close. Martial law had already been instituted in Honduras and our movements were limited. We were not allowed to visit some places and we were not supposed to be outside after six in the evening. We stayed only one night in Tegucigalpa, with Greta's family. We left the next day, in spite of the very heartfelt objection of Greta's parents, who wanted us to stay until the weekend so they could show us around. We crossed into Nicaragua and found the same situation.

We were incredibly relieved to reach Costa Rica and spent three weeks in San Jose, the capital, enjoying the feeling of freedom. One day, as we were sitting on a bench in a tree-lined plaza in the city center, somebody pointed out to us a man crossing the street, carrying a briefcase. He was the president of the Republic. No entourage, no retinue, no bodyguards, a total lack of fanfare. This was hard to believe in a Latin American country.

Before leaving, we visited the volcano, which had recently spewed ash all over the city, and walked for several hours in a crater that resembled a lunar landscape.

Panama was the last stop in our itinerary by land, it was terribly hot and humid. We would go to the cinema in the early afternoon and stay well into the evening because our hotel didn't have air-conditioning. As soon as we could, we sold the car and left for the Panamanian islands. They were much cooler than the city. The beaches were pleasant and not at all crowded. We just sat around and relaxed. We had been three months on the road and needed some respite.

Finally, we took a ship across the canal to Venezuela, where we visited Ricardo's parents and spent some time by ourselves in their house at the beach. We had access to a sailboat and Ricardo bought a water skiing boat while we were there. We would have been in seventh heaven, except that I had not had my period for almost two months, and I was concerned I might be pregnant. I told Ricardo about my fears. This was the last thing he wanted to hear. A pregnancy would only throw a monkey wrench into our plans. Ricardo decided I had to get an abortion. Of course, abortions were against the law in Venezuela, and we didn't have the necessary contacts to get an illegal procedure. Ricardo was totally against informing his family, which made things even more difficult, since we were staying with them.

I went for a pregnancy test by myself. I kept on remembering Greta's experience, and I felt very apprehensive.

"Even if you get a positive result, there is no reason to worry," Ricardo tried to be reassuring. "You can always go to Sweden to get an abortion, and then we'll meet up in London. Or you can even return here for a little bit, after you recover. We'll make up some story for my parents, so they don't find out what happened."

I was scared to death. "Go to Sweden, all by myself, to get an abortion? I can't. I just can't." I felt betrayed and couldn't believe it.

"You want me to go to a country where I have never been, where I don't know anybody and don't speak the language, find a hospital, have the abortion, and then stay all alone in a hotel until I am well enough to travel? I can't do all that alone, I'd be terrified."

"There's nothing to be scared of. I'm sure women do it every day in Sweden. It's legal, you see. I am sure it'll be quite easy."

"You don't want to come with me because you don't want to miss any days of sailing and water skiing. I know it, and it really hurts." I could feel tears welling up in my eyes.

"Well, I can't see how my presence there would be helpful. It won't make things less painful or time go by faster. We'll only spend more money on airplane tickets, hotels, meals. I'll stay here and wait for you to come back, it's the most practical plan," Ricardo reasoned.

We debated this issue for a week. When I finally got the results of my pregnancy test they were negative.

"You see, there was nothing to worry about, everything turned out fine," Ricardo told me. "Let's celebrate. Let's go to dinner to a fancy restaurant." Ricardo felt that nothing had changed. But I felt let down. His lack of emotional support when I really needed it still rankled.

For several months we lingered on the Venezuelan coast and sailed the warm Caribbean waters, returning to the capital only long enough to visit Ricardo's parents and make sure they were not offended by our prolonged absences.

At the beginning of the summer, we flew to London and bought a British camper van that was small enough to maneuver through the narrow European inner cities but large enough to stand up in without having to bend over. We named the van Chubby and it became our car and home for the next year and a half.

The time we spent in Europe was glorious. We stayed wherever we wanted, as long as we felt like it. We had no schedule to follow, we just followed our own desires and whims. We toured England and Scotland, saw a few plays in London, visited all the tourist sights and explored the countryside. We toured France, slowly, leisurely, village by village. I was surprised at how well I remembered Paris from my visit with my family, I even remembered the Metro routes and how to get from one monument to another. We stayed in campgrounds in the Bois de Bologne and in Versailles. Contrary to what we had heard from other tourists, the French were friendly and gracious. When our camper got stuck in the sand on the banks of the Loire, a whole crowd rallied around to help. One man produced a shovel, another wedged a wooden plank under the spinning wheels and before we knew it, the van was free. The crowd clapped and congratulated us as if we had done something extraordinary. We were invited to dinner by our rescuers and by the time darkness fell, the most fabulous aromas had spread all over the campground. Our newfound friends had prepared a feast. There was a delicate mushroom soup, a sausage cassoulet, fresh ripe tomatoes with mozzarella and Parmesan cheese, bread and a bottomless carafe of red wine. We had little trouble communicating, we used a little French, some Spanish, many gestures, laughter, and a lot of wine. Next morning, when we opened the door of our camper, there were two freshly baked loaves of bread and a basket of peaches.

At the end of the summer we visited Switzerland and Austria, hiked in the Alps, went to several music festivals and fairs. Everywhere we went there were concerts, traditional plays, good food and drink.

When we left Vienna, we went off the beaten path and headed for Eastern Europe. We drove into Prague one rainy evening in October. Cities like this, I mused, existed only in fairy tales. The river Vltava, the castle, the old square studded with amazing rooftops, emerged from the fog. The city seemed unreal, dreamlike. We were directed to the only campground in the city, the stadium at the edge of town. Our camper stood alone in the middle of the arena, not too far from a couple of bedraggled tents, surrounded by high tiers of empty seats on all sides. All the lights were turned on, illuminating the arena to a blinding brightness. We felt like we were in a fish bowl. We drew the curtains of the camper, but inside it was still brighter than the noon sun. After a few minutes, we couldn't stand it in the camper and went to the old town to grab some dinner. That was the beginning of one of the most surreal evenings we had in our entire stay in Europe.

We walked toward the city center and jumped on a passing tram. There was no collector, no turnstile, no obvious way to pay the fare. After a long tortuous ride on cobblestone streets, we made it to the old town square. It was still drizzling when the clock on the square struck nine. We found a tavern in a narrow street leading away from the clock tower. We went down several steps and pushed open the ancient door. The stench of stale cigarettes and beer encircled us.

The room was crowded and smoky. We stood in the middle of the room, not knowing what to do, since there were no tables available, when an older couple beckoned to us and squeezed together to make room at their table. They were both in their late fifties, with round weather-beaten peasant faces and gray hair. The woman was fat, the man small and wizened. Somehow they managed to attract the waiter's attention in spite of the noise and din in the room. They ordered a bottle of red wine for us and brought out a package with pickles and sausage and placed it on the table. I could only catch half of what they said, because we didn't have a common language. The warm room and the wine started to have an effect on us, we both felt a little light-headed. Our new friends seemed to be getting jollier and more expansive by the minute. They called the waiter back and ordered another bottle of wine and bread. They plied us with questions. They were interested in our travel plans, where we had stopped, where we were going next and for how long. After a while, our new Czech friends told us to watch the table against the wall, where a foreign couple sat staring intently at us. Those were British agents, we were told in a whisper, and we should be very careful. Ricardo and I were sure this was the fanciful imagination of old people trying to appear interesting.

When I went to the bathroom the British woman surreptitiously handed me a note. *Be careful! You are talking to government agents. Destroy this note immediately!* Some time after midnight our Czech friends gathered their belongings and left. As soon as the door closed behind them, the British couple approached and took the empty seats. Speaking English was quite a relief. They introduced themselves and started asking lots of questions. They warned us that we had fallen in with a bad lot. The old couple were government spies. After another round of drinks, they invited us for a night cap in their apartment, a couple of blocks away.

We all left the tavern together. As soon as we stepped outside we were enveloped by a dense fog. It had stopped drizzling, and it had become very cold. We followed our hosts to a block of old, dilapidated buildings. We went through a cobblestone courtyard and reached an old iron gate. Down a few steps and our new friends opened a creaky basement door. When they turned the lights on, we stared in amazement. We were in a large modern flat, luxuriously furnished.

We sat in their elegant living room, drinking expensive liqueurs and eating bonbons, admiring their fancy stereo and short-wave radio equipment. Then, they tried to recruit us into the British Service, but we declined politely. Could we at least take a couple of packages out of the country? We declined again, citing the fact that our next destination was Poland. They offered to pay us to go meet a man in Germany and deliver these packages. Again we refused. By now, I was starting to get scared. We tried to take our leave a couple of times, but they insisted we stay for another round of drinks. They wanted to phone some friends and have them come over for a little party. Finally, at around three in the morning, we managed to disentangle ourselves and we were back on the street.

The fog had gotten denser, we couldn't see farther than five feet. As we walked back toward the town square, we heard steps ringing on the cobblestones behind us, but we couldn't see anybody. Trams had stopped running long ago. It took us a good hour to reach the campground. When we reached the stadium, we couldn't find an entrance. We circled half the building before we found a door, but it was locked. A second door was also locked. After several more tries, we found one that led us to a long narrow hallway carpeted in red. At the end of the hallway there were more doors. We tried the closest one, hoping to find the entrance to the arena, but instead we found ourselves in a large, noisy room full of African men, drinking, smoking, and singing very loudly. They tried to entice us to join their party, but we pleaded fatigue. By now, it was after four in the morning. We backed out and tried another door. Finally we were in the center of the stadium, the lights were still on, ours was the only camper in the whole place. We unfolded our bed and fell onto it, exhausted, but couldn't sleep. This was a night we wouldn't forget soon.

In Poland, we stayed with my Berkeley friends from graduate school, who were on a year-long exchange program. Warsaw was the most bizarre city I have ever visited, a reproduction of the city that existed before the Germans blew it up and left a high pile of rubble. A tall wedding cake-style skyscraper, a gift from Russia, towers over the city. A cavernous elevator takes visitors to the highest floor, from where all of Warsaw and the surrounding countryside are visible. After we bought our tickets, we waited in a long line for three hours before we got to the elevator doors. When the doors opened, the crowd pushed from behind crushing the people who were trying to get out, letting only a few lucky ones exit. When we came down, we pressed against the door and shoved hard, but didn't succeed on our first try and had to ride to the top once more. Now we understood the cause of the long line. But in spite of annoyances such as these, we had a fabulous time in Warsaw. We visited different parts of the country, drove on miles and miles of cobblestone roads, and slept in our van in the middle of the forest.

We camped in the Tatra mountains, in the southernmost part of Poland. One morning, when I got out of the van to heed the call of nature, I crossed a small creek looking for the perfect spot. Suddenly, I was rudely interrupted by a dozen soldiers, all pointing their machine guns at me. They looked serious and menacing when they informed me that I had crossed the border into Czechoslovakia when I forded the creek. I hastily pulled up my pants, apologized profusely in several languages, and hurried back to the camper before they could make an international incident out of my innocent blunder. My fantasy was that later that night the soldiers sat around a campfire, drinking vodka, and laughed until their sides split and tears came into their eyes.

In Krakow, we found the house where my mother was born and raised until, at twenty six, she left to marry my father. Before the war, my grandfather's pharmacy occupied the ground floor. If you looked carefully at the dark dilapidated plank of wood over the front door, you could still distinguish the word APTEKA. We took a few pictures of the house. When we showed these pictures to my parents upon our return to California, my father cried out "Basia, that's your house!" My mother looked and looked, then finally said, "Oh no, no. My house, my parents' house where I grew up, was much larger and prettier than this one. I remember it quite well."

In winter we took a four month break from touring, and went skiing. We spent two months in a tiny village in Austria. The first day I skied down the mountain it took me two hours, that's not counting the three or four times I sat down on the snow to cry in frustration. At the end of the two months, I could make it down in ten minutes. I learned to ski and enjoyed the difficult terrain. We befriended the villagers and were invited to their birthdays and family celebrations. When the snow melted we went to higher ground, to Italy and Switzerland. The end of the winter season found us in St. Moritz.

In spring, we went south to Italy. Again, as in France, we visited this country slowly, savoring every little village and town. A few months later, we made our way into Yugoslavia, Bulgaria, Greece, and finally Turkey. We were in Bulgaria when the Russians invaded Czechoslovakia. We knew something extraordinary had happened because all the roads were closed and we had to remain in our campground, cut off from the world. On the second day of our enforced stay, we heard a low rumble that seemed to come from everywhere. The rumble kept getting louder and louder. A few hours later we saw thousands of tanks moving toward the border. I turned on the radio in our camper. Only one station was broadcasting, repeating the same message over and over, sometimes in Russian, sometimes in another language I assumed to be Bulgarian. Bulgarians and all Slavic Peoples had been mobilized to fight with their Czech brothers against the German invasion. We were horrified. Was this the beginning of another world war? Had the Germans again invaded a defenseless European neighbor? We hadn't followed the news for a few weeks. What had happened in the world? On the third day, as I listened to the radio, one new adjective was inserted. Now, the German invasion was referred to as the German economic invasion. Two days later, the roads reopened and we left for Greece and Turkey. It wasn't until we reached Thessalonika, when some British campers lent us English newspapers, that we found out what had happened.

In December we sold our camper and flew back to the United States. We had been traveling for two years, and although we were sorry when the trip ended, we knew it was time to resume the life we had left behind.

Susanna

W hen the two years in Korea were up, Jimmy returned. He greeted us very tentatively, and I had to restrain myself not to jump into his arms and hang from his neck. We kissed very lightly, on the cheek only. I lifted Ricky so that Jimmy could look at him. I was hoping he would take him into his arms. But Ricky started shrieking and hanging on to me, hiding his face in my shoulder. My husband mumbled something about being surprised how grown Ricky seemed, and how much work it must be taking care of him.

I was surprised at how different Jimmy looked. I couldn't put my finger on what exactly had changed. Physically he was the same, perhaps a bit older, a bit thinner. But he projected a much different image, more subdued, quiet. I don't know how to describe it, but he seemed dimmer, as if he had been washed too many times and faded in the sunlight.

I wanted him to be ready to settle down. I certainly was more than ready. My dream of a settled life in America with my husband and child had only been deferred. Now it was about to start.

When we got to the parking lot, Jimmy went to the driver's side. I handed him the keys, and sat in the back seat holding Ricky, who was still whimpering. I told Jimmy where to go, but he knew the road quite well, I didn't have to give him directions. I had told my landlady that my husband was arriving soon, and she had taken pains to make the house more welcoming. She had washed all the lace curtains, waxed the old wooden floor, polished the furniture, dusted the overstuffed couch and the faded lamp shades. She even bought several flowering plants for the living room, and asked me to help her choose the best spots to place them. The day before Jimmy's arrival, she had surprised me by giving me her double bed and her quilted bedspread. I helped her move it into my bedroom. Then we took my bed and dragged it into her room. The house was pleasant and cozy. But Jimmy took one look, and I could see he hated it. I could tell by the way he wouldn't look at me when I showed him around. Later, when Ricky had finally fallen asleep in his crib and we were in bed with all the lights off, Jimmy asked me how could I stand to live in such an old dump. I wanted to tell him that it was not a dump. It had character, it felt right to me. But I was afraid of starting our life together on the wrong foot. I said I was sorry he didn't like it. We could start looking for a new place the very next day. I remembered then that he liked contemporary houses, wall to wall carpeting, modern kitchen and bathroom fixtures and Scandinavian furniture.

The biggest problem was that Ricky slept in our room. He was a normal, noisy, curious and active baby, and it was almost impossible not to like him. At least that's what I thought. But Jimmy seemed uncomfortable with the baby. All the noise and the fuss seemed jarring to him. He told me he wanted some quiet in the evenings, to relax, read, or watch television. So I took to feeding Ricky early and putting him to bed before dark. Of course, that meant Ricky would wake up before five in the morning and start fussing and crying. Jimmy liked to sleep late. He hated to get up early, especially if he didn't have to. I could see that my husband and my son were on a collision course from the very beginning, and I was caught in the middle.

I wasn't too surprised when Jimmy said we needed to find a decent house to live in. But first he would look for a job. It made more sense to do it that way. I was relieved. I hadn't forgotten the problems we had had two years ago, right after we got married.

I knew things wouldn't be easy. I was prepared for that, I am not dumb. Reentry is always difficult, even after a short absence. And Jimmy had been away for two years. A lot had changed. So it didn't seem unnatural to me that Jimmy was troubled and distant. God only knew what he had gone through in Korea. He certainly didn't want to talk about it. A couple of times I tried to bring up the subject. But he told me all that was better forgotten.

Getting used to a baby isn't easy either. At least, that's what I told myself. Especially a baby like Ricky, so active and lively. I had had almost two years to get used to him. I couldn't expect my husband to do it in one week. After a few weeks, everything would be all right.

Jimmy found a job in the space program and we moved to Alabama. At first, I hated the idea of moving. I wanted to stay put where Jimmy had his roots. I had made up my mind that I wanted to be part of this community, where Jimmy had grown up. But Jimmy seemed keen on the idea of moving, and I had rarely, if ever, seen him excited about anything. So I decided to give in without a fuss. I would follow my husband wherever he wanted to go, even if it meant leaving the place I had chosen as my home.

Moving away had one advantage. It made it easy for me to drop Barbara, without having to resort to excuses and lies. That was a bonus. Distance is always a useful pretext for not seeing or keeping in touch with somebody. I said my good-byes to Babs and my landlady. Both of them shed some tears. I felt an unexpected pang of regret at leaving. I guess I had grown more attached to them than I realized. Both had been good to me for no reason at all, just because they felt like it.

When we arrived in Huntsville, there were a million things to do. First, we had to find a house. Because of the growth of the space program, housing was at a premium. We rented a tacky duplex for a short while, and finally managed to find a house that would do, at least, for the time being. Jimmy was busy at his job, working overtime every day, just like the other engineers in the space program. I was put in charge of furnishing our place and did it in record time. Everything came from Sears, the only department store in town. The house had royal blue, wall-to-wall carpeting and I bought Danish-style furniture. All tan and beige, nothing dark or heavy, nothing that looked overwhelming. I thought Jimmy would like it, and I was right. He liked it so much that he insisted we buy plastic covers for the couch and chairs. He wanted it Ricky-proof. Practical? I guess so, but not pretty. I said okay, anyway. The kitchen was large and sunny, and had all the modern conveniences. I also bought a washer and dryer. Finally, I could stop going to the laundromat, a chore I hated.

Huntsville was a boom town. There were lots of young couples with small children. Everybody was an outsider, resettling here to work on the space program. We were just like thousands of other couples who arrived daily. Nobody asked any questions. That suited me just fine. I found myself liking this place very much indeed, more than I expected. I made friends with all the neighbors.

Before long I was pregnant again, and feeling very stressed.

This pregnancy was much more difficult than the first. I was sick to my stomach the first three months. I felt lethargic. I had a devil of a time taking care of Ricky. He was a holy terror. He didn't like having to share me with his father, and he had also entered "the terrible twos." I was glad to have neighbors who were willing to take him off my hands once in a while.

I had a difficult time during labor and delivery. I gave birth to a little girl, Jennifer. Jimmy adored her from the very first time he set eyes on her. Thank God. I gave a great sigh of relief. Now I could admit to myself that I had been worried sick, afraid that Jimmy wouldn't like the baby. I was worried Jimmy didn't like children. Now I could rest easy. He liked kids after all. I didn't want to reach the next logical conclusion. I just couldn't admit that he didn't like his own son.

Rebecca

Ricardo and I came back from Europe ready to settle down. After looking for a couple of months, my husband found a job as an engineer in Berkeley. We were happy about that because jobs were scarce. During the two years we had been abroad, the economy had changed drastically in the United States and the job situation was bleak. I went back to the University to work on my doctorate, but I soon discovered that my heart wasn't in it. All my friends in the department had finished their degrees and had scattered to the four corners of the world in search of jobs. I felt isolated and I had lost my sense of purpose. When I found out I was pregnant I was delighted and I quit without a second thought. We bought a house. Before long, we had a little girl, Carin.

I never knew that one little baby could bring so much joy and engender so much love. My husband and I were ecstatic. We thought she was perfect in every way. It was as if my baby, as she was growing inside me, was carefully tiptoeing through a garden of genes, selecting for herself all the best qualities we each had to offer and sidestepping to avoid our worst traits.

I no longer cared to go to lectures, theaters, concerts, avant-garde movies, art exhibits. I started frequenting parent groups, talking about the benefits of breast feeding, when to start solid foods, play groups, early child development, educational toys, baby books. When I was pregnant, my husband and I had talked to friends about leaving the baby with them while we went hiking, skiing, or to Hawaii for a few days. After she was born, we found we wouldn't dream of doing such a thing. We wanted her with us all the time and brought her along everywhere we went. We took her with us to museums, parks, beaches, to the ski slopes. She loved Hawaii. Leaving her behind became unthinkable.

I don't want to give the impression that I was never tired of being a full-time mother, sitting at home taking care of my baby. Some days were hard. No one to talk to, too tired to do anything or to go anywhere. As much as I adored Carin, at times I thought I would go crazy if I didn't get a break. I found work I could do at home. I started translating Polish and Russian for the State Department, but I still wanted work that would get me out of the house for a few hours every so often. I finally got a job teaching Spanish in a language school. The pay was low, but I liked teaching. I met an elderly insurance broker, a student at the school, who asked me to interpret at a legal proceeding for one of his clients. I discovered I loved interpreting even more than teaching.

I became a court interpreter, and soon also a conference interpreter. I found it exciting and challenging, at least most of the time. I enjoyed the variety of subjects, people, and places. Once I was finished for the day, the evenings were all mine to spend with my family, friends, or by myself doing other things that interested me. What I liked best about interpreting was a feeling I got when I performed perfectly, when the exact words came effortlessly, at top speed. Then I felt as if I were a pianist playing a piece, hitting every note right, with perfect timing.

Time started racing by. Before I knew it, years had passed and Carin was about to start school. Ricardo and I were no longer getting along. I don't know at what point love vanished, but without that our relationship started falling apart. We were both busy with our differing activities and long ago had stopped being each other's priority. Ricardo was working late every night, and on weekends he wanted to do the things he liked, working on his boat, sailing, or water skiing. I didn't enjoy sailing, and although I went water skiing with him every Saturday during the season, I didn't like the rough and noisy ride in the boat or the whole motor-boat culture. Many a time I wished I could be somewhere else.

One evening, when I came back early from teaching one of my Spanish classes, I found Carin playing alone on the front porch with a new teddy bear.

"Carin, where is your daddy?" I asked, surprised.

"He is in the bedroom. Linda came over and brought me this teddy bear, but then she and Daddy went into the bedroom and locked the door. They didn't want to play with me." Carin had never before seen a locked door in our house. Even our bathroom door was always wide open.

That's how I found out Ricardo was having an affair with one of my girlfriends. Whenever I went out to teach she would come over, ostensibly to help him babysit. When I confronted him, he demanded a post factum open marriage.

Open marriages were the rage in the early seventies. The book *Open Marriage* had just come out, and every couple I knew was talking about it. People were having affairs and bragging about how it didn't damage their marital relationship at all — quite the contrary, it served to strengthen it. At first I balked at the idea. "If I start sleeping around, I'll soon want to spend the whole night with my lover, then have breakfast with him, then spend weekends with him. Finally I'll want to move in with him."

"We are talking about sex, for God's sake, not falling in love," replied my husband impatiently.

Ricardo said there was no risk of one of us falling in love outside of our marriage. Those things didn't happen, not to people who were conscious of what they were doing. Before long, we each had extramarital relationships.

But of course, it didn't work out like in the book. Ricardo did mind my having an affair. He said it was okay as long as I didn't like the guy. But why would I want to have an affair with a guy I didn't like? Of course I liked my lover. I was excited about seeing him and I wanted to spend time with him. We had met at an encounter group at the university; we found we had a lot of things to talk about. One thing led to another and before long we had become lovers. Ricardo had trouble holding back his rage. "Why do you have to go out with the same guy all the time? The deal was that we were supposed to have casual lovers. I am not going to allow you to go out with this good-for-nothing bum. He can see you are stupid and inexperienced and he is taking advantage of you."

Ricardo would question me, check my clothing for clues, listen in on my phone calls. He called me names, threatened me. He picked rows with me. Home was no longer a happy place. In fact, it started resembling the home of my childhood, something I dreaded more than anything in the world.

Soon we talked about separating. What had been inconceivable a few years before, became the nightly subject of our conversation. I remember seeing Bergman's film about the deterioration and eventual break up of a couple, *Scenes from a Marriage,* and thinking it was a great movie, but didn't have anything to do with us. Well, we had become like the main characters of that film. We bickered and fought about everything. We went into counseling, but all that did was to define our differences even more clearly.

I had always yielded to Ricardo's wishes, whatever he wanted and whatever he said, we did. His wishes were always obeyed. This had been the pattern at his home when he was growing up and this was the pattern we had established early on in our relationship. I learned to do all the things he did. I learned to ski, to water-ski, to hike, to camp, to sail, and to enjoy some of this, at least, some of the time. I learned to travel the way he liked to travel, and I enjoyed that, too. As long as I did everything he wanted me to do we got along well.

Now I was thirty, and I started having my own ideas about what I wanted for myself. Ricardo had allowed me my hobbies as long as they were inexpensive and didn't interfere with whatever he was doing. But he was not interested, he never wanted to participate. I loved to listen to music, go to art exhibits, lectures about books and language, poetry readings, plays, but I went alone or with friends. I dreamt of doing all this with my soul mate, who would be as enthusiastic as I about these pleasures. I didn't want my wishes discarded before they were heard and acknowledged. I wanted to have input into what happened in my life and in our life together. Ricardo couldn't see why things should be different. He wanted his sweet little wife back, the one who always said yes and clapped with enthusiasm whenever he proposed something. The one who never questioned him and agreed to everything.

Now, after fourteen years of marriage, he did not understand this new Rebecca who had ideas and desires of her own and who dared to doubt and challenge him. He no longer found her attractive; he no longer loved her.

"I hardly know you now, Rebecca, you used to love to water ski with me. What's all this stuff about wanting to do something different? You know quite well that if we don't go water skiing now, soon it will be too cold. We can always go see a play later, in winter, when the rains come. If we don't get to see this play tonight, it's no big deal, there will always be other plays."

Even though Ricardo no longer wanted me as his life partner, he had trouble letting me go. I belonged to him and he didn't want anybody else to take his place. I could see we were headed for divorce.

I didn't know what to do. I didn't even know whether I wanted to stop it from happening. I didn't know how I would go on with my life and I was afraid I wouldn't be able to cope, emotionally or financially. Ricardo had warned me that he would not give me a cent. I knew he meant every word. If I wanted child support, he would battle me in court for custody. The fight would be fierce and hurt us all, especially our daughter.

I was so engrossed in my own problems that I hardly paid any attention to what was going on with my sister. I knew that she was unhappy. Ever since her baby died, her husband had shown signs of deep depression. Susanna had mentioned to me, in an unguarded moment, that Jimmy had attempted suicide a few times, before she knew him. I knew that she had a penchant for picking up strays, abandoned cats and sick puppies. She had been doing this since she was a kid. Now she had expanded her ministrations to include human beings afflicted by misfortune. Lonely, sad cases, on the verge of despair. She tried to fix those who were broken, to nurse them back to health. She surrounded herself with weak, ineffectual people who needed help desperately. She was at her best with those who were almost beyond help. But I was afraid that now she was in over her head, that she had found someone who couldn't or did not want to be saved.

I didn't know how much the situation had deteriorated in the last year. Had I known, I would have tried to help. Instead, I remained uninvolved until it was too late, in spite of all the clear indications of disaster that were thrown in my path.

$\mathcal{S}$usanna

Ricky was becoming an uncontrollable brat. There is no other way to put it. Sharing me with both his father and a new baby proved to be too much for him. He was acting out something awful. He was unbearably jealous of his new baby sister and I had to watch him every second so he wouldn't hurt her. Not one day went by when I didn't have to punish him. And I hated doing it. But if I didn't discipline him, Jimmy would do it, and that would be much worse. My husband believed we had to break the kid's will, so that he would become an obedient little boy. I was terrified that we would break the child first. I should have disabused my husband of his foolish ideas. I should have intervened. But I found myself having to control and thwart my son in order to placate my husband. I was still trying to fulfill the role of a good wife.

I knew I wasn't handling things right. But I didn't know where to seek help. I kept hoping that Ricky would outgrow this phase before we really lost patience with him. Before something awful happened. Now, thirty years later, I could see the error of my ways. And as much as I hated to admit it to myself, I was bothered by the thought that I was following exactly in my mother's footsteps, when she failed to protect us from Father's rages. Good God, I was failing Ricky. My poor baby felt he could do nothing right. Whatever he did was wrong. He was always in trouble, and most of the time he didn't even understand why. I writhe in agony when I think about my poor little boy. But that didn't occur to me then. I was sheepishly following the accepted child-rearing practices of that time.

A year later, I was pregnant a third time. I was barely twenty-two. I was exhausted and in tears all the time. I didn't want to go

187

through with it. Things were getting to be too much for me. I was afraid I was going to go crazy. Jimmy was gone all day at the plant. On weekends, he wanted peace and quiet. I had to take the kids and tire them out at the playground or the mall, so they would sleep when they came home and not bother Jimmy. My life was a constant round of diaper changing, bottle feedings, cooking, washing and folding baby clothes, cleaning, shopping for food, going to the pediatrician. There was no end in sight.

I had no time for myself. To read a book, enjoy a cup of coffee with a friend, write a letter, or just simply relax couldn't be further from my reality. Those luxuries were long forgotten. I had no friends of my own. Just other mothers as harried as I was. All we talked about was scheduling. Whose turn was it to drive the kids. Whose turn was it to babysit while some of us did the marketing. We never went out to dinner or a movie, or got together just to chat. I didn't even have time to watch TV or read a magazine.

Now I would have one more baby to take care of. I didn't think I could handle it. Abortion crossed my mind. No, that would be terrible. I couldn't. Not me. It was a crime, against the law and against morality. I had to rid myself of those awful thoughts. Besides, it would be nearly impossible. I would have to go somewhere. To Europe. But I couldn't leave, not now. Who'd take care of my children? It was out of the question. I didn't have anybody to talk to. I didn't know anybody who'd done it. I bet Babs would know. She would know somebody who could give me a name. What would she do in my shoes? Could I write to her? No, I couldn't. Not on paper, not in black and white. But I could call her. But no, I hadn't talked to her for a couple of years. I just couldn't. I'd have to do a lot of explaining. A lot of catching up and stuff like that. I just couldn't. And how would Jimmy react? We had never talked about that before. I bet he'd be against it. I am darn sure he'd be horrified. No, I wasn't going to do it. I was going to have this baby. The last one. No more. Then I would have my tubes tied. I had to make myself believe I could handle three children. Convince myself of it. After all, other women did, right? I could too. It wouldn't be easy, but nothing had been easy in my life. Of course I could do it. No more thinking. No more agonizing. I would have this baby.

A few weeks later, the doctor told me I was carrying twins. I panicked. That couldn't be true! There were no twins in my family. Nor in Jimmy's. This had to be a mistake, a horrible mistake. This was not happening. I had become resigned to the idea of three children. Three children, okay, but that was it. Three children were in the realm of the possible. But good God, four? No. It couldn't be true. But true it was. The doctor said he clearly heard two distinct heartbeats. He had no doubts about it. I was carrying twins.

I remembered a silly game my little sister used to play. Rebecca must have been around eight at the time, and someone had given her an old magic set. Many items were missing from the box, but there was a crystal ball. My little sister adored that crystal ball, and would spend hours pretending she was a magician and could see into the future. She would make up the most horrible cruel fates for everyone, and then she would throw a fancy cloth over the ball, uncover it, and yell "presto!" and giggling say it was all a mistake, she could see this person actually living happily in the lap of luxury. One afternoon, when she was pestering me to play with her while I was trying to read a book, she said that she saw me in her crystal ball dressed in old rags like Cinderella, having to clean house and cook and take care of lots of screaming brats all day long. I guess she thought of that as the worst possible fate. But right before she did her trick of uncovering the ball, she dropped it, and it shattered into a thousand little pieces. She burst into tears and told me, sobbing, that I had to try to help her find another crystal ball. She assured me that she was about to foretell that a handsome prince was coming to save me from my horrible destiny. We never managed to find another crystal ball, no matter how hard we tried. We looked in used toy stores, garage sales, we even went to a store that sold theater props. Nobody had a crystal ball or knew where we could find one. Rebecca was heartbroken.

I left the doctor's office in a daze. I couldn't think. I felt like crying. Like lying down on my bed and crying for a whole year. Not getting up. A whole year in bed, doing nothing. Absolutely nothing. A nervous breakdown, they would call it. Poor thing, she had a nervous breakdown. She couldn't handle it, poor thing, they would say. I had to pull myself together. Stop fantasizing. This wouldn't do. I had to compose myself. Tonight, after dinner, I would tell Jimmy. I would make roast beef with baked potatoes. His favorite. Then I would tell him. I would be calm and reassuring. God has seen fit to bless us with twins, I would say, smiling bravely. Four children? Well, a little more work than three. A little harder. But we might as well do it all at once, you know. It's better this way.

When I came back from the hospital with the twins, there was complete chaos in the house. My neighbors cared for my two older children, while I was away. But now I had them back. Ricky had just turned four, Jenny was almost two, and the twins, Keith and Karen, were barely a few days old. I felt exhausted, sick, miserable, unable to cope. I wanted to hire help. But I felt too guilty to admit that I couldn't handle this. Too guilty and afraid to ask my husband for help. I thought I should be able to manage by myself. After all, there were lots of other women who had four children. Right? And they managed quite well. What I really wanted to do was to just lie down. Close my eyes. Sleep. And wake up with the house cleaned. The shopping and the laundry done. Dinner ready. The kids fed, bathed and ready for bed. A vision of Paradise.

My little sister offered to come and help. But she would have to wait until after finals, two months later. My neighbors brought us casseroles for dinner and took Ricky and Jenny whenever they had a chance. But still, I had loads of things to do. I felt too tired to even think about them. Whenever I sat down for a few minutes, instead of resting, I would start worrying about all the things left undone.

At first, Jimmy tried to help out a little. But soon it became too much for him, too. He was the kind of person who didn't like noise. He hated a mess. And that is exactly what he found at home. I knew him well by now. His response didn't surprise me. He started coming home later and later. Avoiding the whole commotion. He converted the basement into a workshop, a den for his own use. He hid there in the evenings and on the weekends to putter, to read, to listen to music, to unwind. Unless there was a real emergency I wasn't supposed to bother him. This was really unfair. I couldn't be expected to do everything. Whenever I reached my limit, which was happening often now, I would try to get him to help out.

We had the same fight over and over. We used the same stale words.

"Jimmy, I never get any help from you. For Christ's sake, it wouldn't kill you to do something once in a while. I spend my whole day running around, doing things for everybody, from morning until I fall dead in bed at midnight. Nothing ever gets done unless I do it. Chores are still piling up like crazy. I can't go on like this."

"I help as much as I can. What do you want from me? You know perfectly well I work ten- and twelve-hour days. For God's sake, sometimes I even go in on Saturdays. I need time to unwind, to be by myself. Okay, I'll take the kids to the park this Saturday, just stop griping about it all the time."

But Saturday would come and go, and if the kids went to the park it was because I took them. Once in a while, Jimmy was willing to take Jenny to the hardware store or into his shop. All he accomplished was to enrage Ricky, who would spend the whole time screaming and banging on the basement door. When Jimmy could stand it no longer, he would spring out of the basement in a frenzy and yell at Ricky until I begged him to stop. There was nothing I detested more than these scenes. I never knew whose side to take.

All this hollering and fighting was exactly what Jimmy hated. So I wasn't too surprised when he started withdrawing from family life. Spending the little time he had by himself in his own quarters.

Whether I wanted it or not, I was in charge of child-rearing and everything that had to do with home life. Jimmy was too busy at work, and remained uninvolved with the children. Once in a while he would put Jenny to bed, but most of the time he got home too late. He didn't even want to look at the twins, much less help out with them. All he wanted was his dinner, and more often than not he would take it down to his workshop, where he had installed a TV and a recliner chair, and wouldn't reappear until bedtime. He wanted me to go to bed at the same time he did, so I wouldn't keep him awake, waiting. Most nights I would collapse into bed and fall asleep, but sometimes I was so tense and wired up that I couldn't fall asleep. Jimmy was bothered if I shifted positions.

"For heaven's sake, stop squirming. You know I can't fall asleep if you keep on turning like a windmill. Besides, you are twisting and pulling the blankets, every time you move. It's almost midnight and I haven't slept a wink. I'll be a zombie tomorrow at work."

"But you are the one hogging the blankets." After a few times I stopped arguing. It wasn't worth it. Besides, I had to get up several times a night, whenever one of the kids cried. I just took to falling asleep on the sofa with a book. Later, around three in the morning, after the last feeding, I would creep into bed very quietly. By then, Jimmy was into such deep sleep he rarely heard me.

Ricky was about ready to start nursery school. I could hardly wait to be free of him for a few hours. At home he was like a tornado run amok. Both my girls were easy babies. But Keith was colicky and fussy from the start and required lots of attention. I had my work cut out for me.

So where were those choices you were talking about, little sister? Have you ever tried to take care of four children under the age of four, a husband, a large house, all by yourself? Did it ever occur to you that most people don't spend seven years in college, playing at being a student, going to lectures, concerts, plays, traveling, enjoying a life of privilege? For Christ's sake, you have no duties, no responsibilities. You don't know what it means to get up five times a night when you are dead tired. Drive to the supermarket with four babies in tow. Try shopping like that once, and then talk to me about choices! Make dinner while three of your kids are crying. What do you know about real life?

Things would have been a lot easier if I didn't have that little worm of doubt about Jimmy. I had trouble admitting it even to myself. I couldn't understand why he had not warmed up to his kids. Was it too much to expect from him? Sure, it's not easy to care for four children, two of them just a few weeks old. But other fathers did it. Sometimes, when I got my act together and managed to take everybody to the park on a Saturday morning, I would see lots of fathers playing with their children. So what was so difficult? The more I needed Jimmy, the more distant and unavailable he became. I felt angry and depressed. I didn't know what to do. And then something happened that made these few months seem a happy time in comparison.

I had just taken the twins for their three month check up. The doctor was concerned that Keith was failing to gain weight at the same rate as his twin sister. He recommended I try a new formula. I was to feed him a little less so he wouldn't spit it all up. But more often, approximately every couple of hours. The next day, a Saturday, I put the babies down for a nap. I asked Jimmy to watch them while I ran to the drugstore to get the new formula. Thank God, Ricky was at the neighbors' house playing. I was back before half an hour had elapsed. Jimmy stayed home, reading a car magazine. When I returned, he hadn't moved from his chair. He said he hadn't heard a peep from the children's room. They were all asleep. I poured some of the new formula into a small bottle, warmed it a little, and went into the babies' room to wake up Keith and feed him. When I turned him around, he felt cold and stiff. I looked at his face. It was gray. Bluish-gray. I started screaming. Jimmy ran into the room. He couldn't wake him up. We rushed him to the hospital, I carrying both Karen and Jenny. But it was too late. Keith was dead. The doctors called it a crib death. They told us there was no known cause for this. It could not be predicted or prevented. It just happened.

After Keith's death, Jimmy became even more withdrawn and unwilling to take care of the children. He must have been scared to death. And feeling terribly guilty. I know I was. Even though the doctors told us again and again that it wasn't anybody's fault, I kept blaming myself. I couldn't help it. Secretly, I was afraid that somehow I had willed this to happen. It was all my fault. Although I swear by God that never, not even in the darkest and most hectic of times, had I wished for this. It's true, I had complained that four kids were too many. But when we lost Keith I was devastated. My life lost its meaning. There are no words to describe the pain of losing a child. Those who have not experienced it, cannot understand. I couldn't stop obsessing. What could I have done differently to avoid this tragedy? There were a million things I could have done differently. But none that would do any good now. And that I couldn't accept. Not yet.

After I lost the baby the only thing that kept me going was that the kids needed me more than ever. I was afraid to leave them alone, even for a minute. I would get up to check on them several times a night. Poor Jimmy, now he didn't dare to complain about my getting up every five minutes, about my keeping him up all night, about losing his precious sleep. It got so bad that I suggested he move a bed into the basement to get a good night's sleep.

Had I been able to predict the future, I would have acted differently. Had I known where we were headed, had I seen what was coming, I would have insisted Jimmy get professional help. I would have begged him to get professional help, on my knees. Beseeched him. Threatened him. Coerced him. My husband was following step by step his own *danse macabre* toward his destiny. I watched Jimmy deteriorate. I was unable to stop his rapid slide into despondency. Once, eons ago, I had promised I would be there for him forever, no matter what. But I was older now, no longer a romantic teenager. I didn't do enough to help. I couldn't. I didn't know how. I was preoccupied with a million other things. I was too busy. I had the kids to take care off. And I still had a tough lesson to learn. You can't help a person who doesn't want help. No matter what the experts say. Don't let them fool you. You can't. I know, I tried. Not hard enough, but I did try.

Every time I suggested some sort of therapy or counseling Jimmy would scoff.

"I don't believe in psychiatrists and all their mumbo jumbo. That's for New Yorkers and Californians, with more money than common sense. I can deal with my own problems, in my own way. I just need time."

So I just let things slide, hoping that they would get better. They had to get better. God knows they couldn't get any worse. But I was wrong.

Rebecca

A couple of times we invited my nephew and nieces to California for a week or two. I always enjoyed having them, even Ricky, who was such a terror at home, seemed delighted to come and visit with us, and he behaved faultlessly. He was marvelous with Carin, who was ten years his junior. He would carry her piggyback everywhere, explain things and talk tirelessly to her, push her swing in the playground, get on the seesaw with her, hold her in his lap while they sped down slides. Ricardo and I took the kids water skiing, and they all learned quickly and enjoyed it enormously. Ricky even came up on a single slalom ski, quite an achievement for a first-timer, and bragged about it endlessly. The kids loved going to the lake and riding in the boat. The only discordant note happened at dinner, when Ricky complained bitterly about his father.

"Every evening and weekend he hides downstairs in his den and nobody is supposed to bother him. And if he stays upstairs, in the living room, it's even worse. He just sits in his chair, reading magazines or watching TV, and we have to be quiet and tiptoe around him. He never talks to us anymore. All we hear is 'sshh, be quiet, shut your mouth, don't bother me now, I am busy' and we never get to watch what we want on TV."

Ricardo and I took this as just complaints from a disgruntled teenager. We didn't think about it, until a few months later, when my sister called to tell us that her husband had just committed suicide.

My heart bled for Susanna. I felt as if someone had punched me in the stomach with an iron fist. I had a lump in my throat. And I was angry at Jimmy. How could he inflict this much pain on the people he loved most? Didn't he know how much he hurt his children, his wife? I couldn't muster any sympathy for him. I didn't want to remember that once, eons ago, I had tried to do the same. I didn't want to recall the obsessive thoughts that made me believe that there was no other way out, that death was the only solution. I held on to my anger, unmitigated by compassion or understanding.

I called my sister and wanted to come out immediately, but she asked me not to come right then, to wait until things were less hectic. She asked me to make sure that our parents didn't come to the funeral.

"Please, please Rebecca, I've never asked you for anything before. Just this once, you must make sure the parents don't appear on my doorstep. I couldn't stand to see them now. If you see them going toward the airport, shoot them."

"Okay, Susie, just calm down. I'll talk to them. Don't worry about a thing. But are you sure you don't want me to come out and help with the details? Or take care of the kids?"

"What I really want is for all of you to just stay away. How many times do I have to say it before you get it?"

Nobody from our side of the family attended the funeral. That's how my sister wanted it. None of us dared to go against her wishes.

My sister's husband committed suicide at the age of forty, leaving behind a fifteen-year-old son and two daughters, aged eleven and twelve. There are so many different versions of the circumstances surrounding his death that I don't know which one to believe. My sister has rarely spoken about what happened. The few times she broached the subject, it turned out to be a fabrication.

My parents told everybody that Jimmy had died of a heart attack. They resented all their nosy friends who wanted to know whether their son-in-law had prior heart problems, or whether he was overweight, or whether he smoked. They felt people were perversely curious and refused to answer any questions. They avoided their relatives and friends and went into seclusion for several weeks.

My cousin Andrea told me recently that she and my uncle Stasik and aunt Eva believed Jimmy had died in a car accident. My parents had confided to them that although they had been telling everybody that their son-in-law had died of a heart attack, they wanted the family to know the truth. "He died in a car wreck," they said, "but don't tell anybody. We are only telling you because we hate to lie to family." And they swore them to secrecy. My uncle and aunt wondered whether he had been drinking before he got in the car, or whether it happened after a fight with my sister, or whether he had found her in bed with some other man, then driven away in a fit of anger or jealousy and crashed. But they didn't dare to ask my parents about the details because they didn't want to add to my parents suffering over this tragic event.

My sister once told me that her husband locked himself in the garage while the car was running and was found dead the next morning. She said he had made sure that none of the cats were in the garage, so that he wouldn't kill one by accident. The car smelled of exhaust fumes for months until the day she sold it. She also confided that this was not the first time Jimmy had tried to commit suicide. He had attempted it several times before, when he was a teenager. The only difference was that this time he succeeded.

A few days later, she confessed that what she had revealed to me had actually happened a few months before Jimmy killed himself, and that he had spent several days in the hospital after that suicide attempt. But she hadn't called me to talk more about this, all she wanted was my promise that I would make sure the parents didn't come to visit. She didn't want to see them now, or ever again, for that matter. She couldn't deal with them on top of everything else. She needed to be alone to deal with things the best way she could and get on with her life. She would call them later, when things had quieted down.

Ricky told me his father didn't come home one night and my sister called the sheriff to start a search. The sheriff found the car three days later, parked by the side of a country lane. Jimmy had rigged the car so the exhaust fumes would be funneled into the vehicle, and had locked all windows and doors. When the sheriff's call came, my sister went to identify the body, but that was a mere formality. There wasn't much doubt in anybody's mind, the car had already been identified by the police as his.

Ricky mentioned that several months before his father killed himself, my sister had asked Ricky to dismantle Jimmy's gun and give her the essential parts to hide in a bank safe box. In the middle of a fight, Jimmy had pointed the gun at Susanna several times, and then pressed it against his own temple, threatening to shoot himself if she didn't stop seeing a certain neighbor. My nephew was convinced that his father had discovered that his mother was having an affair. In fact, he told me, he believed his father had once come upon his mother and this despicable man in bed. Ricky was sure he knew who the man was, and he loathed him with all his heart. He could never forgive his mother for what she did. Or his father either, for taking the easy way out and abandoning them all.

My sister denies ever having an affair. I met the man Ricky suspected. He is a low-life, a redneck, a drunk, and on top of that, he is married and has several children. He embodies everything my sister despises in a man: he smokes, gets drunk, curses. I don't believe for a minute that Susanna was having an affair with him. My finicky sister could never feel attracted to a man like that. Not in a million years. I think Ricky must have imagined something that simply wasn't there, or misconstrued something he saw or heard. The only thing I did find puzzling is that many years later, when my sister finally got her hands on the money from my parents' estate, she gave a large chunk of it to this loathsome man so that he could open a car repair shop. She called it a business decision, but as far as I know, she hasn't made a cent from the investment.

Several years later, when I was walking on a beach in Maui with my two nieces, they told me how they had found their father that morning. They had gone to the supermarket with their mom, and when they returned with their arms loaded with grocery bags and they opened the front door, a pair of shoes were swinging right in front of their faces. They looked up to see their father's body hanging from a beam in the hallway. They were frozen, unable to comprehend what they were seeing. The groceries spilled down the entrance steps, some of the cans rolled onto the driveway. Then they started shrieking. My sister, who was still unloading the car, ran to the front door, took one look, and herded them back outside.

I don't really know which is the real story. I only know that soon after, my sister went into her bedroom and stayed there for three years. She never got out of her nightgown and never left her bed for more than a few minutes. She read hundreds of novels, watched TV, and played with her cats. She let herself go completely. She let the cats take over the house, tearing the place to shreds. It looked like a dump and it stank. My two little nieces bought groceries, always remembering to get a new book for their mom. They cooked, washed the dishes, did the cleaning, the laundry, took care of the garden, and went to the library to get more books for Susanna. They couldn't count on their brother, who was behaving atrociously. They finally asked him to move out of the house because he couldn't control the seething rage he carried inside him.

The insurance company wouldn't pay death benefits because

Jimmy had committed suicide. The family had to survive on Social Security payments. My father also contributed to their support. Susanna was going through hell. But when I visited, some weeks after her husband died, she pretended everything was under perfect control. All she wanted was to be left alone in her room reading her books.

Susanna

Perhaps it was Charlie's jumping off a bridge in the middle of the evening commute that precipitated the beginning of the end. What happens after all your worst fears come true? What happens after what you have been dreading for so many years finally takes place? My husband was dead at forty. We buried him next to our little baby, Keith. I don't remember how I got through all the things that needed to be done. Jimmy's family came to the funeral. Thank God, they were too polite to say anything besides expressing their most heartfelt condolences. They didn't ask any questions. The only good thing was that my family never came. My baby sister managed to keep them away.

I don't think I'll ever get over the guilt feelings that Jimmy's suicide brought about. Or the grief, either. I kept blaming myself. I saw it all coming and didn't do anything to stop it. When Rebecca came to see me she wanted me to talk about it. She thought it would help. For God's sake! She should have known that some things are best forgotten. My pain is private. I hate to parade it in front of other people.

Every evening, after dinner, when we were alone in the kitchen, my little sister would try to get me to talk to her as she finished cleaning up the dishes.

"Susie, sweetheart, I know you must feel awful about all this. There is no way you can go through it without talking to somebody. A professional would be best, but you've told me a million times you don't believe in all that. Talk to me then, I'll just listen, I won't interrupt."

"Rebecca, you know perfectly well I can't stand all that trashy cheap psychology. All the psycho-babble doesn't do anybody any good. I despise it, it's all crap! Stop spouting nonsense. How can it help to talk about it? The best way to get on with your life is to put one foot in front of the other," I told her.

"Come on Susanna, don't pretend to be so tough, I know you better. I know you are hurting like crazy. Don't keep it all inside," pleaded my ever silly little sister.

"Subject closed, okay? Now that the kitchen is squeaky clean, let's go to bed. It's late. You know we have to get up early in the morning."

My little sister had no idea what I went through, what hell I lived in. She didn't have an inkling of how it felt to watch my husband fall apart. First he lost his job at the plant. President Johnson was moving the whole space program to his own state, Texas. The government started laying people off, little by little. Morale was at its lowest point. At first, Jimmy saw other people losing their jobs, in other departments. The cafeteria closed. The food truck stopped coming. Then, some of his co-workers went. There were doors that stayed closed all day. The phones stopped ringing. They even turned off the heat. Jimmy had to wear a woolen sweater to work every day. Poor thing, he was always cold. Then it was Jimmy's turn. He was among the last to leave. Before long, nobody was left. They closed down the whole plant. Jimmy was invited to go down to Houston. But he would have none of it. He hated the idea of moving. He was not the kind of person who could tolerate change.

Looking for another job in our own area was impossible. A pipe dream. Thousands of people had been laid off. They were all looking desperately. They were ready to do anything to get a job. Even kill, if that's what it took. My poor, defenseless husband had no chance competing in a world of sharks. In a short time, Jimmy had gone from a person who worked ten and twelve hours a day, sixty hours a week, to a wreck of a man sitting in front of the TV staring vacantly at the screen. I couldn't stand watching him. Sometimes it made me feel so bad I had to take the kids and leave the house, just to get away from him.

The whole town became a ghost town. People were moving away in droves. Apartments buildings were deserted. Some houses were sold for a pittance. Other houses, the ones that didn't sell even at ridiculously low prices, were simply abandoned. I knew quite well what a disaster this was. I had just managed to get a real estate sales license. Talking about lousy timing! There was no way anybody, not even God, could sell anything in this kind of market.

Stores, coffee shops, small businesses started closing down. Even some of the larger department stores moved out of the two shopping malls at the edge of town.

Father had given us some money when I got married. Following the old-fashioned Polish custom that every woman came with a dowry, even if it was only a cow. He always insisted that you could never lose money in real estate, and I, who should have known better than to believe anything Father said, followed his advice. We invested this money in a down payment on a couple of small fourplexes. At first, the rent we collected had been sufficient to pay the mortgage, the taxes and the insurance premiums. But soon the apartments stood empty. We were unable to make the mortgage payments. We went into bankruptcy. The buildings were repossessed by the bank, even though it didn't want them, either. The bank didn't know what to do with so many abandoned homes and apartment buildings.

I looked for a job. No easy task in a ghost town. There wasn't much I was trained to do. At last, I got a job in a restaurant-bar as a hostess. Not because of my prior experience. Just because I was still cute, even after having the children. I had to wear a short skirt that didn't hide anything. And very high heels. Every time Jimmy saw me leave home in that hostess outfit he would wince. He wouldn't say anything, not out loud. But his eyes said it all. "Slut, slut, slut!" At night, when I came home he would give me the silent treatment. He no longer wanted to sleep with me. We stopped having sex. We stopped talking to each other. We never did anything together. It got so bad that I hated coming home. Talking about life in hell! I hated being at work and I hated being home. I got harassed in both places. I hardly knew which was worse.

Now that Jimmy was home all day long he suspected me of doing stuff I would never even dream of doing.

"Where did you go? Why are you so late?" he would grill me.

"To the supermarket to pick up some milk and bread. We were out of almost everything. I also picked up the dry cleaning."

"Well, I expected you home a couple of hours ago. What took you so long?"

I remembered my father and all his ridiculous excuses whenever he had a rendezvous with his latest lover, how he would babble on about traffic jams, construction work on the freeways, a long line in the hardware store. I wasn't about to fall into that trap. I knew I hadn't done anything wrong.

"Just the usual stuff. Besides, I don't need to give you any explanations. If you really wanted me to get home earlier you could have gone to the supermarket yourself. It wouldn't hurt you to do something around here, you know," I would snap at him.

He started shadowing me. Monitoring my comings and goings. Lifting the extension phone whenever I got a call. He thought I was having an affair with one of the neighbors. A man whose only sin was that he was trying to be helpful and supportive. A man who really cared about me and the kids. Every time I worked overtime, Jimmy imagined I was shacked up with this guy. Having sex in some god-forsaken dingy motel. Well, I wasn't. Even though I wasn't getting any at home. I quit my job after just a few months. I figured my family was more important than this miserable job. But it didn't really help, things only got worse.

One day, I had trouble starting the car. I took it to Dick's garage down the road. Dick, the owner, was the neighbor Jimmy suspected of being my lover. When he saw my car he got upset because it was in such lousy condition. The tires were bald. The brakes were worn out. The muffler was about to fall off. He called Jimmy and told him that I shouldn't be driving that car, especially when I was carrying the kids around. He felt it was not safe. He tried to talk Jimmy into letting me have his new Ford, instead of this clunker. Jimmy got enraged. He told Dick that this was none of his damn business. He knew the car better than anybody and it was plenty safe. When I got back home, Jimmy was seething with rage. He hated it when someone tried to stick his nose in our lives or dared to criticize him. On top of that, he couldn't stand Dick. This incident only added fuel to the fire. All Dick had done was to show some concern for me and the kids, which made me feel that at least somebody cared. It made me feel less lonely, like I was not the only one struggling to keep things afloat. But now I had to account for everywhere I went. Everything I did was suspect. Even the most innocent activities took on sinister meaning. I couldn't stand it any more. For the first time in my life, I seriously considered leaving Jimmy. I was ready to explode.

A few days later, Jimmy decided I should drive his car after all, since now that he was not going to work I drove more miles than he did. I still had to cart the kids around, do the shopping, go to the post office, pick up things at the laundry. It made more sense for me to have the better car. It was as if he had sensed that he needed to give in a little so I wouldn't leave him. But I hadn't said anything about leaving him. I knew I couldn't do that. I was going to stick it out no matter what happened.

The final blow came a few months later. When Jimmy was one of the last engineers still working, he would exchange a few polite words with the guard at the gate. He was one of the only other employees still working at the plant. Soon they were on first name basis. Leroy, the guard, was a large black man with a mile-wide smile and large teeth. He was friendly and well-mannered. When the plant finally closed, Leroy went to work at a gas station his brother-in-law owned. One day, with the whole family in the car, we stopped to buy gas at that station. Leroy was at the pumps. He greeted Jimmy like a long lost friend. When he found out that Jimmy had not been able to find work yet, of his own accord and out of the goodness of his heart, he went to talk to his brother-in-law to see whether he would hire Jimmy to work evenings and weekends. He came back all smiles. He told my chagrined husband that the job was his, but Jimmy politely declined. That was the last straw; we left the gas station so fast that the tires squealed on the pavement.

When we got home, Jimmy locked himself in the basement and wouldn't stop sulking. He felt mortified. Humiliated. Insulted. A black man had felt so sorry for him that he tried to offer him a job. Poor Leroy had mistaken a few polite pleasantries for friendship. Jimmy couldn't put the incident out of his mind.

I don't mean to make light of my husband's problems. He was not the only prejudiced man in the world. After all, he had grown up in the South. His family had lived there for eight generations. He didn't get his beliefs and attitudes from thin air. He had learned them from the time he was at his mother's breast. No one likes to get a job offer he considers beneath him. And from a person who used to work in a much lower position. Even if his would-be benefactor weren't black, it would still be hard to take. But coming from a black man? It was unbearable. Jimmy was utterly crushed. He couldn't let go of it, he kept mulling it over in his mind.

Jimmy must have felt completely cornered. He didn't want to move out of state to Houston, where the space program had relocated. And I agreed with him, I didn't want to move either. This was our home and uprooting the family seemed unthinkable. A few weeks before we had put the house on the market at a ridiculously low price, but there had been no takers. Moving would have meant losing everything we had, not just our savings, but our home, too, which was the only thing we had left. Jimmy didn't want me to go to work, either. At least, not at the only job I was able to get. And he didn't want to take a job he considered much beneath him. Not even temporarily. There were no other jobs around. He must have felt there was no way out.

A few months earlier Charlie, Jimmy's favorite cousin and best man at our wedding, had killed himself by jumping off a bridge. He parked the car in the middle of the bridge, climbed over the edge, and jumped. Right in the middle of the evening commute. Jimmy really took this hard. Charlie was a couple of years older than my husband. They had grown up together and been inseparable as kids, they went to the same school, and to summer camp together. Charlie had recently gone through a bitter divorce. His ex-wife remarried and moved away with the kids. Jimmy complained bitterly that life had not been fair to his cousin. All I could do was agree, Charlie had a really rough time. Jimmy kept obsessing about what a rotten deal Charlie got. He felt that their lives were following a parallel course.

I wish to God I could have saved Jimmy. To stop him from doing what he had been preparing for all his life, even before we married, even before we had ever met. But I was too involved in my own pain. Too resentful of Jimmy for not helping me deal with all our problems. I felt I had to take care of everybody and everything. I got no help at all from my husband. I started getting angry more often. I could hardly look at Jimmy without feeling annoyed. There he was, sitting in front of the TV, with a can of soda pop, moping. Feeling sorry for himself, for the rough deal the world had handed him.

"Now that you are home all day long you could at least help me with the children, or do the shopping," I would tell him. "There is a lot of stuff that needs doing around here."

"Not right now. In a few minutes, when I finish watching this program," he would reply.

A couple of hours later he was still watching TV. I would get angry. I just couldn't help it.

I felt I was a monster. A fiend. Maybe not in the eyes of society.

In my own eyes, which is much worse. That's the one opinion that really counts, my own. The one I will never be able to escape. I'll never stop blaming myself. Thinking that somehow I could have prevented this horror from happening. After all, I knew what was going on. I knew what was coming. It wasn't Jimmy's first try. He had a history of trying to kill himself. Everybody who knew him knew that. It was just a matter of time. Everybody expected it. Nobody was really surprised. I could see everything unfolding, like in a movie in slow motion. And like in a bad dream, I couldn't stop it, I couldn't wake up.

I could see it coming in everything Jimmy did. The way he looked at me and the children. As if we weren't there. The way he moved. Like an old man protecting himself from the cold. The way he smiled. Slowly. Painfully. With his lips only. Opening one side of his mouth. He looked like he was about to cry whenever he smiled. His tone of voice. Dull. Inert. Without any inflection. Like he knew nobody would listen. He wasn't worth listening to. His eyes, devoid of hope. Eyes that reminded me of an old blind cat I had to put to sleep before we came to Alabama. I should have done something to break out of this nightmare. To help him break out of it. Because I knew, without a shadow of a doubt, he wouldn't break out on his own. He couldn't.

I should have loved him more. Showed my love for him more often. Made him feel good about himself. Bolstered his self-confidence. Convinced him that he was wonderful. That we all needed him. That we couldn't live without him. But, God knows, I wasn't perfect either. I, too, needed some respite from this constant gloom and despondency. To find solace and comfort, wherever I could get it. I, too, needed to feel appreciated. Loved. Protected. Taken care of. I was so terribly alone. I couldn't be blamed for needing this, for trying to find it, even if I had to go looking outside our home.

In an effort to make things more bearable for Jimmy, to lighten his load, I took over most of his responsibilities. I did everything he didn't have the strength or the will to do for himself. I took care of the kids, their school, their activities. I took care of the house, the shopping, the gardening, even the repairs. I took care of all of our business decisions, the bills, the taxes. I took care of all our medical and dental appointments. I even took care of the car. He didn't have to do anything, just sit in front of the TV if that's what he wanted. Much later I understood that in the end, I was the one who made him feel superfluous. Not the loss of his job. Nor the loss of the houses we owned. Nor the bankruptcy. I was the one who put the nails in his coffin.

I felt so awful that I couldn't protect my children from this horrible tragedy. My worst nightmare was that they would never forget what they saw. What they heard. What they felt. That the scars they sustained would stay with them until the day they died. This is what I find truly unbearable to behold. This is my most awful fear, my most awful nightmare, my greatest sorrow.

After Jimmy died my life changed completely. Some of the time, at least during the day, I was able to keep a semblance of normality. But more often than not, I felt such pent-up rage. Such awful dread. It was all so hideous, so atrocious. My thoughts scared me. If it weren't for the children, I also would have chosen to die.

Rebecca

W hen I returned to Berkeley after visiting my sister, I felt an overwhelming sadness. Her husband was dead, I was separating from mine. Why had our lives gone so terribly wrong? My husband had moved out, and I was glad. I had become afraid of him, I didn't feel safe. He had become violent and abusive when angered. Once, during a particularly nasty argument, he started to choke me. If Carin hadn't heard our raised voices and walked into the bedroom, I don't know what would have happened. We thought of the separation as temporary. We were both sure we would get back together. That never happened.

For months after we separated I lied to my parents whenever they called asking to talk to Ricardo. I would make up excuses, he wasn't home yet, he was in the shower, he couldn't come to the phone. Then I would call him and ask him to return the call. I dreaded telling them, but I was tired of pretending. Finally, one Sunday morning we went to my parents' to tell them we were no longer living under the same roof. They took Ricardo's side.

"Are you out of your gourd? At thirty-one, with a six-year-old child, you are no bargain," my father told me, sententiously.

"Don't worry, Ricardito," piped in my mother, "she'll come back with her tail between her legs, begging you to take her back."

"Are you crazy?" she said later when we were alone, "He doesn't drink, doesn't beat you, and he earns good money. What else in the world do you expect from a husband?"

I wasn't surprised. I could never count on Mother to take my side. Granted, she loved Ricardo, but didn't she care whether I was happy? Her self-respect had been destroyed by Father long ago. She had watched him destroy Susanna's and mine. Susanna ran away as soon as she could, cutting off the parents, and me too, in her anger.

I stayed behind, but in my heart, I left too. I looked at Mother and tried to understand why she let this happen, why she never fought for us. In her eyes, I no longer saw the fear that poisoned our childhood. Now, her reaction had become a reflex, part of her personality. All I could think of as justification was that she grew up valuing security over happiness.

Now I had to rebuild my life. I wasn't getting alimony or child support. Ricardo had already warned me if I wanted money he would fight for child custody. I didn't want to fight, even though I had a good chance of winning. I feared the damage a court fight would inflict on our daughter if it got ugly. And it would. Ricardo was angry, not because I instigated the separation, he wanted it as much as I did, but because he had lost his wife, who had been his property for so many years.

Luckily, time intervened and as always cured most of the problems. At first Ricardo had a few turbulent short-term affairs. I remember once he took a girlfriend to Hawaii and gave her a beautiful turquoise-and-gold bracelet, which he showed me as if he needed my approval. I recognized the bracelet and felt a pang of envy. I had seen it in the window of a Berkeley jewelry store and every time we walked by, I would gaze at it and comment how exquisite it was and how much I loved it. Some time later, Ricardo started dating a woman who had a son Carin's age, but the boy was a holy terror and Carin hated spending time with them. I felt miserable knowing that Carin was unhappy the whole weekend. When Ricardo finally found a steady girlfriend, he became more mellow and life was easier. Carin got along well with Mei-Mei and enjoyed spending time with them. I felt relieved.

Even then, Ricardo didn't find it in his heart to provide child support for his daughter. He simply told me if she needed a pair of new shoes or a rain jacket, I could ask him for the money. But I never did. He could keep his money and eat it, as far as I was concerned. He bought a large sailboat and took a couple of six-month sailing trips to the Caribbean. I felt resentful, but I hid my feelings, at times even from myself. I felt ashamed that the man I had once loved was behaving like this. My parents had taught me well. I could almost hear them saying 'you make your bed, and you better be ready to lie in it'.

Once Carin told me that she and her daddy had spent the weekend car shopping. Ricardo really liked expensive Italian cars, but he felt he ought to buy a cheaper, more practical Japanese model. "Poor Daddy," she said "He has so little money he can't buy the car he really wants. Tomorrow I'll get all my money out from my savings account and give it to him." Instead of being touched by her generous impulse, I felt indignant. He didn't contribute to her support even though he owned a fifty-foot sailboat and a house on prestigious Grizzly Peak Boulevard, and now he made her feel sorry for him because he couldn't afford to buy the car he liked. This wasn't fair.

Being a single mother was not easy. I felt lonely, although Carin was wonderful company. She had a very outgoing personality. Once, when she was only three, Ricardo and I got to our favorite picnic site and were annoyed to find that the place was crowded and all the tables had already been taken. My little baby took one look and yelled "Mommy, Mommy, look at all these friends I don't know yet." She made friends easily and kept them forever. Through her I met my best friends, who are my family by choice and with whom I spend every Thanksgiving and Christmas. But even though I had good friends, in my day-to-day life I felt isolated. I needed somebody to talk to, to share my concerns with, especially when I was alone during the long evenings of winter. Going to bed had always been difficult for me, and now it became almost impossible. I had to keep a number of books by my bedside, and I would fall asleep at dawn with a book in my hands. I missed Ricardo. I had met him when I was sixteen, and we spent fourteen years together. It was almost as if I had grown up with him. He had been my mentor, my best friend, my traveling companion, the center of my life. Now, I had to get a life of my own, and I was scared.

Money was another big problem after we separated. I wasn't earning enough teaching Spanish and I wasn't getting enough assignments as an interpreter to make a living. Around the middle of the month, I would start worrying that I wouldn't have money to pay the mortgage and the utilities. I needed some source of steady income to cover basic expenses. I decided to advertise for a housemate. Soon Ingrid, a nurse with a six-year-old daughter, moved in. We each occupied a small bedroom, and the two girls shared the larger one. This arrangement worked out well. I not only got rent, but I also earned a few extra dollars taking care of Ingrid's daughter when Ingrid worked evenings.

Ingrid, a tall blue-eyed blond from Finland, drank like a fish. But

I never saw her drunk, at least not drunk enough to fall on her face. Every Friday and Saturday night, she went to singles' bars to meet guys. She would make their acquaintance over drinks, get them to buy her a steak dinner, then bring them home to spend the night. Every Saturday and Sunday at dawn, I would see another business executive tiptoe out of my house carrying his shoes in his hand.

One night, on one of the rare occasions when Ingrid and I were having dinner together, we started talking about men and sex.

"I can't imagine living without regular sex. I started having it at the age of twelve, in the barn behind the farm, and by now I've had sex with at least a thousand different men," she exulted. I had to admit, lamely, that I only had sex with three men in my whole life and I had been in love with every one of them.

Ingrid revealed that the week before she had met an Italian businessman, Marcelo. "He is such a great lover, that on a scale from one to ten, he would be an eleven," she gushed.

"An eleven!" I said breathlessly. I couldn't imagine what an eleven would be like. "Ingrid, how is he different from the others?"

"You certainly need to try him out if you need to ask such a question," she said, emitting a great whoop of laughter. "You know, all the usual stuff," she mumbled, enigmatically.

"What usual stuff? What do you mean?" I couldn't stop myself from asking. "Come on, just give me an example."

"Well, you know, size, endurance. That kind of stuff. He just keeps on going."

"Oh, I see. So that's what makes an eleven?"

"No, not just that. There are also a lot of other things. Technique, experience, you know. I can't describe it in words. You'll know when you experience it."

She must have felt pity for me because of what she saw as years of deprivation. "I want you to meet Marcelo. You can date him this summer, while I am away in Finland," she said.

I was taken aback by Ingrid's generosity and awed by the long years of experience and practice she had in these matters. I had been regretting that the sexual revolution, that wondrous season of free love, had passed me by. I felt that I had missed out, that everybody was having a ball except me. I was anxious to really live, to experience life before it was too late. I had been a goody-two-shoes all my life and it had gotten me nowhere. There was no reward for being a good girl, I realized.

A few weeks later, Ingrid left for Finland. When her friend Marcelo called and learned she was already gone for the summer, he asked me out to dinner. I was about to refuse, when I remembered what Ingrid said about him as a lover. I saw my chance to start out with the best. Curiosity got the better of me, I couldn't pass up such an opportunity. I accepted his invitation. Finally, at thirty, I was about to join the ranks of the bad girls, the ones that had fun without regard to consequences.

Marcelo picked me up in a new white Cadillac, wearing fashionable Italian clothes, and took me to an out-of-the-way French restaurant. My menu didn't have prices, only his did. I soon realized I had never before been in such an elegant restaurant. I felt out of place. After a very long and sumptuous dinner, he drove me to his home. His wife, he explained, was away for a month, visiting her mother in Italy. It was a beautiful, warm night, stars covered the whole firmament. Marcelo dragged a mattress out by the pool and we had sex. No cuddling, no kissing, no loving looks, no hugs—just plain sex. The in-out, in-out, thump-thump-thump kind of sex. So this was it. This was who my roommate had pronounced the best lover ever. I kept on looking at my watch and at the stars, wondering when I could ask to be taken home, without appearing rude. I wondered what Ingrid was talking about when she billed him as an eleven. As far as I was concerned, Marcelo could get a couple of points for his excellent manners, his impeccable Italian clothes, and his great choice of restaurant.

I stopped looking at Ingrid with awe tinged with envy. Her way of life was not right for me, I had discovered. I had to find my own path.

Meanwhile, my work had been growing exponentially. As I became better known, I acquired a good reputation and kept very busy. Quite often, I had more work than I could handle by myself. Increasingly, I started thinking of finding a business partner. After my sister became a widow, I fantasized that she would come and join me and we would launch an interpreting agency together. We would live next to each other, help each other in every way, and things would be just like when were kids. But I found out Susanna didn't want any part of this dream.

We were on the phone when I happened to mention this fantasy of mine.

"You know, Susanna, sometimes I dream of you moving out

here. We could both work as interpreters. There is enough work for both of us, and the pay is decent. We could have a great time working together."

"Rebecca, don't be silly. I don't want to move. I've told you a million times I don't like California. I won't live near the parents. I want to stay where I am. I like it here. Thanks, but no thanks. I am doing just fine. I don't need you, or anybody else for that matter, to try to fix my life."

"Susie, I am not trying to fix your life, just trying to fix mine. Besides, you wouldn't really be that close to our parents. They are at least an hour away by car. Mother doesn't drive, so she wouldn't come to visit. Father always makes sure he is too busy to drive her all the way over here. I only see them once every six weeks, and even then, I spend most of the time swimming or playing with Carin in their pool. It isn't like they live next door, you know."

"You are not listening to me, baby sister. That's one of the most annoying things about you. You get an idea into you head and you never let go. Geez! I don't know what's happened to you. You were never this obstinate as a kid. You were really sweet and docile."

"Come on, Susie, say you'll think about it. It would make me so happy to live close to you."

"Now, little dunce, listen to me carefully. I truly don't like California. In fact, I hate it. I am not going to leave Alabama. Not for you, not for anybody. Got it?"

"But, Susie, you'd have a job that is interesting and pays well. Doesn't that figure in your decision?"

"I don't want to work as an interpreter. Interpreter, my foot! You are like a flunky, running from one courthouse to another. Always at the beck and call of sleazy attorneys or stuffy judges, who think they are God's gift to the planet. That kind of work doesn't interest me. Not one bit. It sounds totally boring and demeaning. So, lay off."

"But it isn't! It is terribly interesting. I think it's great to go to different places, meet different people. The courtroom is like the stage in a play, the judge and lawyers are the actors. Each case is different, I am always learning new things. I never get bored. I am sure you would enjoy it too. It's a lot of fun. Come on, Susie, just say you'll think about it."

"Fun, my ass! That's what you have never understood about real life, baby sister. Work is not an unending party, as you seem to think. Work is not fun, it's hell! What you do is play-acting, you yourself admit that much. You pretend you are working."

Now I was starting to get upset. "What do you mean I pretend to work?"

"You never had a real job, like most people. The kind where you have to go in every day. From morning till night. Rain or shine. Makes no difference whether your kids are sick or healthy. You go there, day-in, day-out. You do what they tell you to do, or else you get fired. You, baby sister, have no clue what life is all about."

"Well, you don't need to get all huffy about it. And there is no need to raise your voice, either. I can hear you perfectly, there is nothing wrong with my hearing. But, you know, you are wrong, Susie. I do work, and I always have."

"How can you say that? How can you fool yourself like this? You've always 'enjoyed' yourself. It's so much fun, you say. In fact, these are exactly your own words. Fun, my ass! That's what you've always done, not just in the work place, but in college too. Just look at what you chose in college! Slavic Languages, linguistics, literature. A cop out. You knew you could excel without ever having to lift a finger. Big deal! How come you didn't study engineering or medicine? Too much of a challenge? Too afraid you would have to work hard for once in your life? Too afraid you wouldn't succeed? You just don't live in the real world. Always choosing the easy way out. You never do anything that is really hard, anything that you hate to do. Anything you are afraid to do. Anything where you might fail. For once, get a taste of failure in your unsullied mouth. See how that feels! Then come back and we can talk. That's what you need to learn. That's what life is all about!"

"Hey, wait a minute. Stop!" I could hear my sister sobbing in the background. "What are you talking about? Of course I worked hard in college. I just didn't complain about it all day long. And all I did was to chose something I liked. Is that a crime? So what if I did enjoy it? Does that make it less worthwhile? And what if I enjoy what I do? There is no law against it. I don't see why I should choose something I am not interested in."

Once I got going I didn't want to stop, even though my sister was crying. Was I too hard on her? "There is nothing that says you have to hate your work so that it can be considered work. Quite the contrary. If you hate your work, you better do something about it, because otherwise you'll be hating a great chunk of your life. And that is a sure recipe for unhappiness, if I ever heard of one."

"Don't lecture me about hating my life! Don't you think I know all about it, more so than you?"

"Wait a minute. I do a lot of things I hate to do."

"Oh, yeah? Like what, for instance," my sister said, starting to raise her voice again. "Pray do enlighten me, your majesty!"

"You don't need to get sarcastic. I hated to do term papers in college, but I did them anyway to get good grades. I hate to do my taxes, who doesn't? I hate to drive to the central valley to work; I leave at dawn and come back after ten at night. But I do it, because I get paid well and I need the money. I also hate to clean house, but I do it because I like having a clean house. I hate going to the supermarket, but somebody has to go buy food. So there, you see, like anybody else I do a lot of things I hate."

"I am underwhelmed by your list of hardships. Dammit, Rebecca, just listen to yourself! You sound like a princess trying to justify her lifestyle! I don't want to argue with you. You are being frigging dense just to annoy me. The truth is that you don't know what you are talking about. It's obvious. You have never experienced what it feels like to go every single day to a job you hate. Just because you have to, just because you need to earn the money. And then, to lose that job when you are laid off, and nobody helps you. You still think life is a bowl of cherries, but I know better. It's quite the opposite. Subject closed. Lets stop wasting time and talk about something else."

"I just don't understand why you get so irritated. All I was trying to do was to invite you to come and live near me and work with me. I don't see where it became a contest of who suffered the most and who had the hardest life."

"I said, subject closed. I don't want to talk about this any more. Got it?"

"Okay, okay. I'll call you later, when you are in a better mood. Sorry I annoyed you. I really didn't mean to."

Sometimes my sister gets really touchy about the most unexpected subjects. But this time, I must admit reluctantly, she hit the target. Was I fooling myself? I had often wondered about my choices. I am overly cautious and afraid of the unknown. I am always preparing for the future, for all kinds of contingencies, trying to predict how things will turn out. Did I choose the line of least resistance? Did I choose what I already knew, what I could do easily? Am I really afraid of failing? I have noticed I am more afraid than most of my friends, less willing to take risks. I don't believe there is a safety net, and I am not willing to test my belief. I always think I am just one step away from disaster. I am not willing to let myself slide back that one step and find out. I am fighting to stay afloat, threading water. I am afraid if I relax, if I let go, if I become less vigilant, I will become like my sister. And I can't let that happen.

Susanna

Whenever it seems that things cannot get any worse they do. This is something I had to learn. There were other things I had to learn, too. Like how to live with a heart full of hatred, unable to forgive, wracked by guilt. What's the use of reviling a man who was unhappy, who tried, but didn't know how to love his wife and his children? I curse him silently every night before I fall asleep, and I pray for strength to forgive him. And then, I wake up in the middle of the night, drowning in guilt. What did I do wrong, what was my sin? Blindness? Ignorance? Why couldn't I save my family from this disaster? Why couldn't I protect those I loved?

There, in the darkness of night, alone in my bed I know why. Those who always judge others will say I could have left. I could have abandoned Jimmy to his life of despair, cut him out of my life and that of my children. I could have packed up, taken my children and gone to live elsewhere, far away from him. I could have started anew, perhaps in California, the place my sister touts as the cure to every malady. But I didn't expect things to turn out like this, not at the beginning. I had hoped for a normal, happy life with a family of my own. I was willing to take the bad times in the hope that good times would follow. I was married to Jimmy and as his wife, it was incumbent upon me to make things work. When I realized that I couldn't make things work, I couldn't save my family, by then I couldn't leave either. It was too late. Had I abandoned Jimmy then, had I divorced him, he would have committed suicide, just like his cousin Charlie did when his wife left. I would have been his murderer, just as surely as if I had thrust a knife in his heart. My children would have hated me, blamed me, looked at me with loathing in their eyes. I couldn't expose myself to their accusing stares. Even if I knew in my heart that everything I did was to save them, they would never understand. So what was my sin? Cowardice? I stayed to the bitter end. I allowed myself to be swallowed up by Jimmy's despair. I tried to live my life as I thought he wanted it, to view the world through his eyes. But his were the eyes of death. In the end, staying didn't help.

Once, when I was on the phone with Rebecca, who after I became a widow would call several times a week, she dared to compare how I felt after I lost my husband with how she felt after her divorce.

"Are you out of your mind? It's not the same thing at all. How can you compare divorce with suicide? You don't know what you are saying. It's totally preposterous! How can you be so stupid! I thought you had more common sense than that. Don't you see the difference?" I yelled. "This is final. There is nothing I can do, no second chances. I can't make amends. Not to my husband. Not to my kids. I can't undo what happened." I really let her have it. I hardly ever remember being so angry at her. Hell, I felt I could have killed her at that moment., but all I did was weep with rage.

"Your ex-husband is still there. Polluting this world, as you say. He takes your daughter out on weekends. You don't even begin to know how much that's worth. It's not fair. I don't have that luxury. You don't know how lucky you are!" I really lost it. I was yelling at the top of my voice, and crying at the same time.

"Don't you understand the difference?" I screamed. "It's like when you tell me how you get really enraged when you hear talk about the extermination of the Jews. And some stupid American Jew nods his head and tells you he understands very well because he also suffered discrimination when he was growing up. Remember how you told me you feel? Well, that's how I feel right now. Remember what you always say? Discrimination and extermination are not the same thing, you stupid ass! Well, divorce and death are not the same thing! How can you be so dumb? You can have a second chance, if you want to take it. You can fix things. I can't! And I have to live the rest of my life like that. Knowing I can't undo any of the things I did!"

I wasn't about to shut up. I kept on going, until my sister was completely silenced. Reduced to tears. How could she be so insensitive? How could she compare her fate to mine? For God's sake, her divorce had been mutually agreed on. They talked about it endlessly. My husband Jimmy made his decision to die all by himself, just like his decision to go to Korea. I was never consulted. I felt so powerless, as if my hands had been tied. All I could do was deal with the consequences of his actions. Had I known what was going through his mind right that minute, I would have tried to stop him. I would have told him that his suspicions were unfounded. That we could still patch things up, have a marriage. And if not that, then at least a future. A life. That he didn't need to destroy himself and his family.

My sister's daughter keeps seeing her father. She has a father. He is part of her life. Even after he moved out of the house. Even after the divorce. My children will be forever fatherless. They have to live with the knowledge that their father bailed out on them. They will never forget the last time they saw him. Hanging from a beam in the entranceway. The scene of their father's suicide will remain engraved in their minds. Forever. Rebecca didn't know what I was going through. She didn't know about the dreadful, unbearable guilt. The feeling that if I had done things just a little differently, none of this would have happened.

Rebecca sounded extremely contrite when she apologized. She was still crying. Most of the time I avoided talking about the whole mess. But this time my sister had really got to me, and she deserved what she got. She made me raging mad. Usually, she is quite perceptive. But this time she really put her foot in her mouth. She really blew it. It just made it crystal clear to me, that if you haven't lived through this, you can't really understand all the guilt. The despair. What I wanted was to turn the clock back. To get a second chance. To do things differently. To do things right. And I couldn't do it. Or tell anybody about it.

I don't know how I managed to keep on going. I felt part of me was dead. My two daughters were an enormous help. Thank God for those two little angels. Even though they were only eleven and twelve, they not only took care of their own needs, they took care of mine, too! They took care of the whole house. Of everything. Ricky was no help. He had a hell of a time accepting what happened. He was in a frenzy. He started throwing violent tantrums. He raged at everybody like an exploding volcano, spewing angry obscenities, insults, vicious accusations that had no bases in fact. He yelled at me the most, accusing me of things that were untrue, hating me for vile acts that I never committed. He scared his sisters to death with the force of his rage. He was angry at the whole world, and at God. I hoped that this was just his reaction to unbearable grief. A passing phase. But instead of getting better, he got worse. Soon Jenny and Karen became afraid of him. At times, even I was.

When Ricky dropped out of high school, I started getting seriously worried. I couldn't talk to him. He didn't want to listen to anything I had to say. As soon as I said something, he would start screaming at me or turn around and leave.

"Ricky, we need to have a talk. We can't go on like this," I would begin. "We need to discuss some things."

"I have nothing to say to you, Mom. Nothing! You hear me? And I don't want to hear anything you have to say. Dammit! Save your breath. Save your lies for the birds. Just shut up! You should have thought of all these things before. Not now. Hell, now it's too late." He would march out of the room. I would hear the front door slam. The stained glass panel rattled so hard I was afraid it would break.

He would often spend nights out. I never knew were he went. I supposed he was with friends, sleeping at their house. I couldn't bear the thought that he might be sleeping somewhere on the street. I worried constantly.

I worried about how all these painful events affected his attitude toward life. Too often I saw in him some of the same characteristics Jimmy had. The same things that made my husband's life hell. The same negativity. The same displaced anger. The same pitiful inability to deal with the world. The same helplessness. The same accursed suspicious and jealous nature. And I couldn't stop worrying. I wish I could have kissed his pain away, like I used to when he was a toddler and he fell and hurt himself. Instead, I had to leave him alone. Let him deal with his pain, the best way he could. I had to harden myself against him, not because I didn't feel his pain, but because I felt it too strongly, on my own flesh. Finally, his rages became so disruptive that my daughters asked him to move out. We had some peace for the first time in months.

After Ricky left, I was blessed with another daughter. No, not the way you think. I didn't give birth to her. Perhaps I was always meant to have four children. My youngest daughter, Karen, found this skinny little girl sitting on our doorstep. She found out where she lived and walked her home. The next day, the little girl was back on our doorstep. Karen gave her a snack and walked her back to her house again. Before long, this sweet little girl, Susie, started spending more and more time in my house. Before I knew it, she was living with us. She would call her mother to say that she was spending the night at our place, then she would have dinner with us, and go to sleep in one of my daughter's bedrooms.

After a while, Karen simply put another plate out on the table without asking any questions. Susie wore my daughters' discarded dresses, the ones they had already outgrown, which were still much too long for her. She wore their shorts, which she secured with a belt that went around her waist twice. She wore their shoes, which would fall off her feet when she ran, and socks that rolled down at every step. She rummaged in some boxes we put away in one of the closets and found some of my daughters' old dolls. She played house, sometimes pretending she was the mommy, sometimes that she was the baby. She was quite a few years younger than my daughter Karen, and liked to play quietly by herself or watch TV. She was so unobtrusive, sometimes I hardly even noticed she was there.

Once in a while, her mother, Betty Sue, would drop in to pick Susie up. I would make some strong black coffee, just the way she liked it, and we would sit at the kitchen table and chat for a while. When it was time to go, Betty Sue would ask her daughter whether she wanted to go home with her, but more often than not, she would end up leaving her at my house anyway. Susie was always in the middle of a TV show, or doing homework, and would say she couldn't leave just right then.

Betty Sue told me she had broken up with her fourth husband a while ago, when she found out that he had another wife in Birmingham. She also told me she was a white witch, the good kind. But still, she had a lot of special powers. She could put spells on people to make them do what she wanted, especially men. When she wanted a man, she would put a spell on him and he would fall in love with her and not rest until he married her. That's how she ended up having four husbands, she explained. I had been wondering why men found her attractive. She was drab looking, hair tinted and permed until it looked like dry straw, sallow skin, and overly ample hips. I felt like asking her whether she could put a spell on all her men so they wouldn't leave her, but I decided to hold my tongue. She must have put some sort of spell on us, because little Susie lived with us from the time she was six until she eloped and married at the age of fifteen. Betty Sue didn't seem to mind her daughter's defection. She seemed relieved that Susie had found a good home.

One day, I got a call from the school's social worker. She wanted to know whether Susie lived with me permanently. If not, they would have to find her a foster home. That's when I learned that Betty Sue's house had been repossessed by the bank a couple of months before. Betty Sue had remarried and moved to Florida with her new husband. Nobody had told me. But, when I started thinking, I realized I had not seen Betty Sue for a while. That afternoon, when Susie came home from school I confronted her. She admitted that sometime ago her mother had asked her where she wanted to live. She could choose between going to Florida with her or stay with me. Susie chose to stay in my house. She just forgot to tell me about it.

Susie's mother rarely wrote. Just birthday and Christmas cards now and then. Sometimes there was a five dollar bill tucked away in them. She visited us only once, on her way to North Carolina with her sixth husband. The last time I heard from her she was divorced again, and was undergoing treatment for cancer in a hospital in Louisiana.

Once my two girls started going to college and working part-time, and little Susie eloped and got married, I decided to try to do something with my life. I took a few nursing courses in the local college. I liked the subject and learned a lot. Soon I was working nights as a geriatric caretaker. I did this for a time but found it too depressing. Dealing constantly with illness and death was something I didn't have the stomach to endure. Heck, I already had enough of that in my own life, I didn't need daily reminders. I quit after several of the old people I had grown fond of passed away. I decided I would rather work in something inconsequential, where feelings were not served up as part of the daily menu. I didn't want to deal with sickness and death all day long. I couldn't stand it.

I found work as a saleslady in a department store, where middle-aged, middle-class Southern ladies bought home furnishings, linens, and drapes. That suited me just fine. All I had to do was to help people match sheets, bedspreads, and drapes with whatever they had at home. The store had a licensed interior decorator, but most of these polite Southern ladies would say that her taste was too sophisticated. They liked my choices better. To my surprise, I had a talent for this sort of thing.

I knew Rebecca wanted me to do something more with my life. She kept on bugging me with her telephone calls, her constant "Susanna, why don't you study this, Susanna why don't you do that." No matter how often I told her I am happy the way I am and don't need anybody to tell me what to do. "You are so talented and smart," she would tell me, "you could do so many different things. You could do anything you wanted," she would repeat.

"That's precisely it, little sister. I am doing exactly what I want. I accept myself the way I am. I don't need to apologize to anybody. Too bad you don't. And, by the way, don't you always preach tolerance? Is that tolerance only for people you don't know, or can you be tolerant with members of your own family too?"

"I didn't mean to offend you. I just don't like to see you wasting your talents on that kind of mindless work. It's not challenging. You are not using all your skills and your brain," she persisted. "All I want is for you to be happy and fulfilled."

"I am happy and fulfilled. Haven't you learned anything from your California new age gurus? Don't you know that what is important is accepting who you've become? Don't try to make me fit your role models, because what I see is women who are overachieving, overextended, always-on-the-run nervous wrecks. That's not for me. Just accept that and stop pestering me. Okay? Subject closed."

The neighborhood we had been living in had gotten shabby in the last few years. Give it a couple more years and you could have called it a slum. My house had been slowly torn to pieces by my cats. The carpets, the upholstery, the drapes, were full of rips and hanging threads, and smelled of cat urine no matter how many times I cleaned them. I even had a professional cleaning service come to do the entire house. It didn't help. The whole place looked like a pigsty. Even worse, it smelled like one, too. I was going to do whatever it took to move to a nicer house in a better neighborhood. I felt like a couldn't stay there one day longer.

Rebecca

Ingrid moved out to live in her own apartment and I started looking for a new housemate. I advertised at the co-op market in North Berkeley. That was when I met Alan. He called even though I had wanted a woman. He said that he was neat and would enjoy living in a household with a child. I liked him immediately, from the moment I opened the door. He moved in and before three weeks had elapsed, we were lovers. We stayed together eleven years.

Alan was twenty-nine when we met. He worked a couple of days a week as a computer programmer, enough to make a living, and spent the rest of the time learning to play the guitar, learning to speak Spanish, cooking, and riding his bicycle. This lifestyle I admired and treasured. There was something tender and childlike about Alan. Before I knew it, I was deeply in love.

This turned out to be my most difficult relationship. I loved Alan with all my heart, more than I can ever express. But he told me he could not reciprocate my love, he couldn't open up. He was afraid to make a commitment, he said. He was afraid he would become dependent on me. Intimacy, he felt, would rob him of his integrity, make him weak. I didn't know how to deal with his fears and tried to tiptoe around them.

Once, about five years into our relationship, he met another woman and started spending nights out. He told me all about it as he didn't want to lie or sneak around. I couldn't sleep nights, waiting for him to come back, knowing where he was and what he was doing. I felt devastated. We decided the best thing was for him to leave.

He moved out while I was at work. I didn't want to be there and see it. I came home, fed Carin her dinner, put her to bed, and then wandered from room to room. I looked in the empty closet, where his clothes had been. My bedroom was dark, cold. I got into the icy bed and just lay there until dawn. Then I got up and made some coffee. I knew I had to put one foot in front of the other and keep on going.

As I was making breakfast for Carin, Alan called. He needed to talk to me, as soon as possible. He said he would come over after dinner. All day long I couldn't think of anything else. I worked like a robot, unaware of what I was doing or saying. When he finally arrived that evening, he told me he wanted to come back. He had known that even as he was moving out, but was afraid that if he didn't, he would always suspect his own motives, he would always believe that he stayed because it was the way of least resistance. I asked him to wait three months, and then, if he wanted to live with me, he could move back. He rented a room in another house in the Berkeley hills, not too far from mine, and for the next three months spent every night at my house. Only his belongings lived elsewhere.

In the many years Alan and I were together we traveled, visited friends, went on hikes, picnics, holiday dinners with his family, and finally, bought a house together. Alan taught me to love bicycle riding, I taught him to speak Spanish. But I always knew that something was missing. Alan rarely, if ever, told me he loved me. It was not enough that he stayed in my life so long. I wanted to hear the magic words "I love you." I had grown up in a home where love was dispensed sparingly, but now I craved it with my whole being.

I could see where Alan got his inability to express feelings. His parents would drive for two days to visit us and talk only about the road conditions and the weather or read the newspaper all day long. I felt that what mattered was that they came several times a year and made a special effort to do it. Once, when his father was about to have surgery, Alan was trying to decide whether he should hop on a plane and visit him in the hospital.

"I wouldn't be any help to him, I wouldn't know what is the right thing to say," he fretted.

"What you say doesn't matter. Your presence will be enough. If you go to spend some time with your father he will know you care for him," I said.

Alan did go. During his stay he visited his father in the hospital and in the evenings, cooked dinner for his mother. Both his parents were delighted with his visit and so was he. He felt he had finally managed to communicate his affection to them.

Alan's father taught me everything I know about wine. He knew a lot about California wineries and every time they visited we would go for a hike in the wine country and then to one of the wineries. He chose them carefully, reading about the terrain, the soil, the grapes, the methods the vintners used to process their grapes and even the personal life of the owners. I enjoyed every moment of those sunny, unhurried long days. Alan's brother, his wife and two children, who lived in Napa, would often accompany us on these outings. Alan's mother tried to teach me how to recognize plants and mushrooms, but I proved to be a slow student. Even the children were better at this than I, which delighted them no end.

My parents never accepted Alan. They acted as if he didn't exist, as if he were a momentary lapse in my life. Ricardo was still my husband in their eyes, even after he remarried and started bringing his wife Mei-Mei and their baby to their house. Mother even thought of Ricardo's son as her grandchild, but what Father thought I never found out.

A few years later, Alan and a handful of his computer buddies started a new software company. Gone were the days when he only worked a couple of days a week. Now eighteen-hour days were the norm. We converted the garage into a computer station and soon an array of nerdy looking guys started coming in and out at all hours. In less than a year, Alan's company took off like a rocket, moved into much larger quarters, went public and everybody who owned shares became instantly wealthy. One year before all this happened, around Christmas, Alan asked me whether I wanted a pair of peridot earrings. Knowing he had very little money, and not wanting him to spend all of it on me, I chose stock certificates from his company instead. At that time, I thought this was just paper worth nothing. A year later, I had good reasons to change my mind. The stock I owned appreciated in value rapidly and I no longer worried where Carin's college money would come from.

Suddenly, Alan had a lot of money. All these years, he had been riding his bicycle for city errands, and borrowing my old Honda when he needed to travel further. Now he bought a new car for himself. We had outgrown my house, a small older house with only one bathroom and no space for an office. Alan suggested we start looking for a new, larger house. We found one on a ridge overlooking the San Francisco bay, with a view of the three bridges. To my surprise, Alan, who until then had never shown any interest in how our home looked and how it was furnished, started getting involved in remodeling and furnishing the new house. He selected the wood, tile and marble. He befriended the architect who had built the house and together they redesigned the computer room and added a workshop and a guest cottage. He learned about native plants and supervised the landscaping. The house became his favorite project.

When Carin was in her last year of high school, she met a foreign-exchange student in one of her classes. Celine was unhappy in her present home. She had been placed with a family with no children her age, where she was expected to baby-sit two toddlers in the evenings and teach the parents French. We asked the Rotary Club, the institution that sponsored Celine's trip to the States, to allow us be her hosts. A committee of Rotarians convened to decide whether we were suitable for this task and scheduled us to appear at a formal interview. We tried to impress the committee with our traditional family values and respectable lifestyle because we knew how much Carin and Celine wanted to live together in this last year of high school. Alan wore a coat and tie, something he had not done since his brother got married fifteen years before.

"If they ask me whether we are married, I'll tell them the truth," Alan warned me, as we were getting dressed for this occasion. "You don't expect me to lie, do you?"

"Okay, okay, just don't feel you have to blurt out this information if you are not asked."

Luckily, nobody asked. They must have assumed we were married. We passed inspection and Celine was allowed to come live in our home.

Having Celine at home was a marvelous experience for all of us. Before long, we all loved her. My daughter, who hadn't shared her bedroom since she was a little girl, gained an experience that would prepare her for college life. And I gained a daughter. Celine liked to come into the kitchen while I was preparing dinner. She would sit on the tile countertop, sip from a can of diet coke, and talk to me about her life in France, her hopes and dreams. I was in seventh heaven. I felt I had a real family now.

Soon that year was over and both girls graduated from high school. I was so proud, watching Carin and Celine pick up their diplomas. Ricardo missed the graduation because he was out of town, but Alan and I and Ricardo's wife clapped and cheered like crazy. Afterward, we all went to dinner to celebrate this milestone. The day of the senior prom, the two girls looked like fairy tale princesses. Celine went to the prom with one of her best friends, another French exchange student. Carin had also chosen a friend more than a date, one of her classmates, who was from Zimbabwe.

When we got the pictures from the prom, I made the mistake of showing them to my mother.

"What, you allowed you daughter go to the prom with a Negro?" Mother lamented. "What if she marries him? What are you going to do then?"

"Mother, for goodness sake, it's a prom, not a wedding. He is a classmate and a friend. Don't make a mountain out of a molehill."

"But think of what will happen if you encourage that kind of relationship."

"Like what? Do enlighten me."

"She'll end up moving in with him and they will have lots of coffee-colored babies. That's what! And what will you do then?"

"Love them like crazy, spoil them to death, babysit every chance I get." I had to start laughing. "Mother, please, keep a sense of proportion."

But she wasn't mollified. "You never worry about the consequences of what you do. You think you know everything. Remember what I am telling you now, and don't come crying to me later, when things turn out wrong."

"Don't worry, I won't. When have I come crying to you with anything? I never have before, and I am not planning to do it now." Now I was starting to lose my cool. "Stop worrying and lets go down to the swimming pool."

"You never take anything I say seriously. You must think I am stupid." Mother started to cry.

"Mom, for God's sake. It's just a prom," I repeated, exasperated. "Next fall everybody will start college and scatter all over the United States. Carin is going to UC San Diego and her friend is going to Harvard. So there's nothing for you to worry about. See? Come on, lets get into our bathing suits and take a swim. Carin and Celine are waiting for us downstairs, by the pool. It's a really warm day."

We all wished Celine could have stayed forever. For me, she was like a second daughter. I had always wanted to have more children. I had always wanted to be part of a large happy family, a loving family, who did things together. And finally my wishes had come true.

Alan and I, with Carin and Celine in tow, would pile into the car and go out for ice cream. Or we would take an afternoon off and go for a walk on the wharf. Or take the train to San Francisco to play tourist and show Celine the sights. We went skiing, we went on hikes, we went on picnics, we went to the movies. It was a wonderful year. I stayed in touch with Celine, writing to each other several times a year and I visiting her in Paris. She knows that there is always room for her in my house.

Alan got along well with Carin and lavished love and attention on my two cats. He enjoyed the family life he found with us. I believed that in time and with patience and good will we would develop an intimate, trusting relationship. I was in love with him and wanted to live with him for the rest of my life. I waited ten years for things to get better. I thought we were getting there, albeit slowly. But I guess I must have been wrong. We broke up in the late eighties, and I moved out of the house we had bought together. I felt my life had come to an abrupt halt.

Those of my friends who know me well always joke about how I keep my exes around. I have a very good relationship with my ex-husband and I like his wife. I took care of my ex-husband's baby son Daniel, when his mother was in the hospital. Now that he is eleven, I often pick him up from school. I am in touch with several of my old boyfriends. We go on hikes, bicycle rides, to dinner, to concerts, lectures and parties. One of my former lovers always leaves his musical instruments at my house when he goes on a trip. He says he is afraid that they will be stolen if his place is burglarized, but I think he loves them so much that he can't bear to leave them alone in an empty house. But with Alan, the break was complete. After we separated, his parents wanted to stay in touch with me. They wanted to keep visiting and maintain our friendship. Although I had always enjoyed their visits and felt great affection for them, seeing them was too painful for me. I had to let them know that. I think they understood, they complied with my wishes. During the years that Alan and I were together I learned to think of them as my family. I really miss them.

Although my parents lived only an hour away, they never came to visit me while I lived with Alan. They didn't approve of him, never mentioned his name or asked about him. It was as if he didn't exist. They had been very friendly with Ricardo, even after we divorced. He spent more time with them than I did. But just like when I was a child, when my parents never came to school and never met my

friends, I didn't mind. In fact, I was relieved. I knew it would be difficult for me to bridge the gap between my family and Alan. I would
be caught in the middle, trying to explain two different world views,
one foot in the old world and one in the new. I was afraid that I
would look at Alan through my parents eyes and find him wanting,
or even worse, look at my parents through his eyes and clearly see
all their failings. And that would be hard to endure.

Once in a while, on Sundays, I would visit my parents, with
Carin in tow. We would arrive before lunch and swim in the pool for
an hour or two. Mother and I would chat about this and that, clothes,
recipes, her health concerns. We would have a picnic lunch on the
lawn, or if it was cold and cloudy we'd have a light meal in her
kitchen. Sometimes Father would come down to the pool area and
sit on a lawn chair and watch us, but after a few minutes, he became
bored and read the paper or tried to find a partner to play chess.
Around mid-afternoon, I would kiss my parents good-bye. Mother
would run into the kitchen and hand me a bag of leftovers from
lunch, a few slices of ham, half a basket of strawberries, a couple of
muffins, saying, as usual, that she couldn't have me leave empty
handed. And then she would ask me whether I would be there next
Sunday, knowing perfectly well that I would make up some excuse
to not come. This ritual would be repeated six weeks later. I never
left my daughter alone with them. She never spent one night with
her grandparents. Had they asked, I would have said no, but they
never did.

Once, when I was sitting by the pool Father sat next to me. He
just sat there, staring at the pool and didn't say anything for the
longest time. I was wearing a purple sweatshirt Susanna had sent
me, which had University of Alabama written in large gold letters
on the front.

"I talked to your sister last night. I invited her to come visit us
with the children for my birthday. It's coming up soon."

"Did she say she would?" I asked, surprised.

"No. She said she couldn't afford it. So I told her I would pay the
airfare."

"Is she coming then?"

"No. She couldn't leave the cats alone." He sighed. "Why does
she hate us so much? What did we ever do to her?"

"It's nothing like that, Daddy."

"Then what is it? I just don't understand."

"We remind her of the past, of her origins she worked so hard to forget. When she is with us, she can't deny she is a Pole and a Jew."

"But there is nothing we can do about that. She surely knows that."

"She knows, Daddy, but it doesn't help." In the bright afternoon light the skin around his cheeks and forehead appeared sallow and loose, his neck wrinkled. He had become an old man.

On several occasions, family members arrived from Venezuela or Israel to visit my parents in Palo Alto. When my cousin Adam came I showed him around with pleasure. I hadn't seen him since we were in our teens, playing all our silly adventure games, and I remembered him fondly. Adam was now a thrice-divorced doctor, with two lovely little daughters. While he was visiting my parents he watched some children's programs on color TV, and decided to surprise his daughters by bringing back a large color TV. He asked me to take him around to several stores, which I did gladly. A month later, I got a letter from him telling me that the TV was defective. It never worked right, from the very first day he turned it on it only transmitted in black and white, he wrote. He asked me to go back to the store to complain. This was the kind of errand I hated, but I felt I owed it to my cousin. I had never owned a TV and knew nothing about them, but I went all the way to Palo Alto to comply with Adam's wishes. When I explained the problem to the manager he was baffled. Then he asked why my cousin didn't come in person. I told him my cousin lived in Venezuela. Suddenly, the manager got a look of comprehension on his face, and asked me whether they broadcast in color in Venezuela. I phoned my cousin that evening and posed the question to him. After some research, we found out that there was no color broadcasting in Venezuela yet. Since then, we both have had occasion to laugh at our ignorance, and this has become a family joke.

I became very close to my two nieces, Susanna's daughters, Jenny and Karen. I love them as if they were my own. They visit me quite often, and we've traveled together to Hawaii and Mexico and to the mountains to ski. Sometimes, when I am with them, suddenly, a gesture, a laugh, the way they smile or push off the hair from their face, reminds me of my sister, thirty years ago. And then I feel sad. When did all that energy, that strength, that intensity disappear? My sister had more life, more fire, more passion, than any other person I knew. To me, she was larger than life, invincible. I always thought that if there was anyone who could accomplish whatever she set her mind to, it was she. Hadn't she changed her name, her past, before she was sixteen? What happened? Was she like a fire that burned too hot and now there were just ashes left? Did life defeat her, sap her strength, destroy her will? Did she believe that this limited, reclusive existence she has chosen was all that life has to offer? Is she really content, or is she lying to herself, a master of denial to the very end?

Susanna

I was mighty relieved when I finally moved away from that old house. After my father died, I used my inheritance to build the house of my dreams. I bought some land in the country, half an hour from town. The boondocks, as my little sister calls it. I hired a contractor to build me a large Victorian house, exactly the way I wanted it. I love my house. I furnished it carefully, piece by piece. I got a turquoise brocade Queen Anne Settee, a coral Windsor chair, and both complement my rug beautifully. I've chosen every object and every ornament with the utmost care. I have created rooms where I feel an instant rush of pleasure whenever I enter. These rooms are my sanctuary. When I was younger, I allowed my husband to have the furniture that made him happy. There was so little happiness in his life. Poor soul, he did not have a talent for happiness. My husband liked Danish modern furniture and I didn't give him any grief about it. But I have always detested modern furniture, perhaps because my parents liked it so much.

After Jimmy died, I started to give away all the hideous stuff he had accumulated. Little by little, piece by piece. My cats, God bless them, helped with great enthusiasm in this endeavor by clawing the ugly stuffing out of the old sofa and chairs. Now I only have things I like. Things that make me feel good.

I like to collect things, too. I am finally making up for not having any dolls to speak of during my entire childhood. I have the most marvelous doll collection from all over the world. Whenever I see a doll I like, I buy it. I order dolls from catalogs and go to local doll shows. I don't care what the price is. I also collect tiny fine porcelain cups and saucers. Thimbles. Civil war memorabilia. All kinds of things. I enjoy displaying and looking at my collections, and adding to them. It gives me a feeling of permanence. Of continuity. Of putting down roots. My attic is full of stuff I've bought these last few years.

My little sister scoffs at my collection of keepsakes from the civil war. She says I am trying to borrow, or worse yet, buy somebody else's past. She says I buy wholesale all the bagatelles that other people have accumulated in their attics. She believes I am trying to build a fake past. To create a heritage that isn't mine. To that I can only say, mind your own business! This is a free country. I couldn't care less what she chooses to think. My favorite collection, the one I display with the most pride, the one I show most often to friends and visitors, the one that arouses the most interest among my neighbors and acquaintances, is my civil war souvenir collection. So there, baby sister, you can stuff your comments you know where! I won't apologize for anything.

I love staying home. Tending to all the beautiful things I have collected. Caring for my cats. I don't like going out. My idea of a perfect evening is sitting at home, rearranging my favorite collections. Reading. With only my cats to keep me company.

If this is what Rebecca calls the life of a recluse, well, too bad. It is certainly better, in my humble opinion, than all the pain and heartache she went through. She exhorts me to spill my guts about the painful episodes in my life, but she keeps quiet about the anguish she felt in the long years she lived with Alan. She was always insecure, always afraid that he would pack up and leave for no reason at all, that she would come home from work and find a goodbye note on the kitchen table. My gullible little sister doesn't believe he was running around with other women while they lived together. But I know better, I know all the signs. I am no fool.

She had been thinking things were going really well, the little dunce. They had just bought a house together. My baby sister was in seventh heaven. She naively took this to mean that finally they were a couple, together forever. She believed they had a quasi-marriage. Talking about being naive! And a few months later, after they moved into their new house, that's it. Good-bye. The end.

Then came the agony of the breakup. That's what she called it, so demurely, a "breakup." He dumped her unceremoniously, if you want to know the truth. There is no other way to put it. One day, he came home and said, "That's it, I want you out. Out of my life. Out of my house." No warning, no nothing.

Now, little sister, who is it that lives in denial? Me? Wishful thinking. That's what I call it. I could see the breakup coming for miles, like a speeding train about to derail. Mind you, he never told her that buying the house meant they would be like a married couple. No way. He never told her he loved her, either. In fact, he banned that particular 'four letter' word. He told her not to say that she loved him. It made him too uncomfortable. She used to make a joke of it, to hide her pain, as if she could fool me. She would tell friends that Alan had told her he loved her three times during their eleven year relationship. Once when it slipped out involuntarily, just as they had finished making love, so he added 'I guess' right after. Once he said it to her in German, *Ich liebe dich*, so that he could deny responsibility. The third time just a few days before he dumped her. He said it so softly that she hardly heard him, and when she said "what?" he refused to repeat it.

Can you believe that she took this kind of crap for over ten years? That she was heartbroken when he threw her out on her ass? Shucks, I guess she did learn something from Mother. How to be a doormat. How to let a man walk all over you. How to be satisfied with scraps and crumbs. And then, after ten years of unhappiness, she fell to pieces after the whole sorry affair ended. I watched her became a total wreck when he dumped her. And I am not sure she has ever recovered completely, no matter what she says. She fills her days with too much activity. She sleeps too little. She dresses too garishly. She talks too fast. She laughs too hard. And she dates too many men.

Heck, that's what happens when you let a man into your heart. I know that quite well, you don't need to ask me how come. Alan destroyed her self-confidence, her self-esteem, her faith in herself. And it's her own damned fault. She let him do it. What kind of a man would live with you for ten years and refuse to marry you? Didn't she see the writing on the wall? A gullible fool, that's what she was. Just thinking about it makes me wince.

What's even more awful is that as soon as he dumped her, he took up with one of her friends. The one who had been her best friend since college, for over twenty years. The one she had loved so much, confided in, trusted. The one who knew her most intimate thoughts and feelings. The one she thought of as a sister. Sister, my foot! The three of them had done all kinds of things together. They were inseparable. Just because her friend was so lonely, Rebecca said, so starved for company. My little sister can be really dumb. Before long he married this so-called best friend, leaving no doubt about how he felt about my half-witted baby sister all those years.

Rebecca tells me that all her friends say that those two had been having an affair for the longest time. That this so-called "best friend" was just after my sister's boyfriend. Right in front of my dumb little sister's eyes. But, even now, my baby sister still maintains she didn't see a thing. She is sure her friends must be wrong. More likely, she didn't want to see what was happening right in front of her own eyes. Just imagine. To this day she insists that her boyfriend and her best friend were not capable of such deception, they wouldn't sneak around behind her back. They cared too much for her to do something like that. It must have happened later, after the break-up, accidentally, not intentionally, she tells me. Fat chance! As if it mattered how much you love your partner when you start an affair. As if there were people who are incapable of sneaking around and having affairs behind your back. Open your eyes and look around, little sister! There are no such people. They don't exist! Believe me, I know what I am talking about. Everyone is capable of it, when circumstances are ripe. Even saints. I don't understand how such a bright girl could be so blind. Now, who is the one in denial? Who is deluding herself?

And then she is surprised that I don't want to go through all that. Watching her die inside was painful enough for me. It broke my heart to see her suffering. All those tears, all that pain, for what? No way. Sure as hell, I am not going to expose myself to that, a real life soap opera. Not again, not in this life. Hell, you won't see me waste my life loving a man who is making it behind my back with my best friend. You won't see me squander my affection on a woman who pretends to be my best friend and behind my back is scheming and plotting to take away my man. Good God, I'd have to be crazy! I'll take my cats anytime.

I am on the phone again with Rebecca. We are talking about our lifestyles. Our choices. It's become one of our favorite subjects of conversation. It's as if we had to defend the path we chose when we came to a fork in the road. As if each of us wanted to justify the choices we made.

"Now that you have experienced all this heartache on your own flesh, baby sister, you surely must see why I would much rather live the life of a recluse. Why I prefer to let my life go by 'unlived' as you so frequently like to tell me. It makes more sense than plunging in with both feet and ending up with a broken heart, like you did," I tell her.

"I much prefer to love, to get involved, even if at the end I get hurt. Avoiding the pain of loss isn't my main goal in life. At least I get some of what I want some of the time," she replies.

"Those are just empty words and you know it. I guess you haven't learned life's lessons yet. How many times does it take for you to learn? You don't know how to protect yourself. How to become less vulnerable. Heck, I learned real early, in the school of hard knocks. I am surprised you never learned. You are just as gullible as you were when you were two."

"Come on, Susanna. You exaggerate, as usual. Besides, every two-year-old is gullible. That's their perogative."

"But not as gullible as you were. And I can prove it to you. Remember how you wouldn't eat chocolate until you were almost five?"

"Sure. So what of it? I've certainly made up for it later, with a vengeance, you could say."

"Did you ever stop to wonder, little gullible sister, why you wouldn't eat chocolate?"

"Nope, kids get aversions to lots of ordinary things for the weirdest reasons. Are you trying to tell me something? I don't get it."

"Well, perhaps I better not tell you, after all. You'll get all riled up."

"Come on, Susanna. That's not fair. I am already riled up by this childish game. You start telling me something, and when you get my attention you shut up. Let's drop the games, we are too old for that."

"Okay, okay. But don't go blaming me, you wanted to know. When you were just two, Mother would give us a small chocolate bar to share. I wanted it all to myself, so I convinced you that chocolate is made from poo, just like the yucky stuff you had in your diapers. Wasn't it clever of me?"

"You didn't!"

"Sure did. And it worked beyond my wildest dreams. You wouldn't touch the stuff for years."

Rebecca starts laughing. "I'll be damned! You were an ingenious little brat. Now if you could only come up with something so I won't eat any now, I'd be really grateful."

"But seriously, Rebecca, you need to learn once and for all how to protect yourself from the heartache of failed relationships. And they all fail. Look around you. Can you name one person who has a relationship that works? Surely you know now that this is so, even if you didn't before. And the best way, no, the only way of not getting hurt is not allowing men into your life. I aim to make damn sure that this never happens to me." Silence from my sister. My words seem to fall on deaf ears. "Do you really think that I want to allow this kind of thing in my life again? Forget it! I'd have to be nuts."

"Well, I think you already are," says my baby sister.

"There is no need to get insulting. You know, I just want the best for you, I am just trying to protect you the best way I can. I hate to see you suffer, I hate to see you in pain."

I can hear Rebecca laughing like crazy. "What's so funny?" I ask.

"You may not believe it, but I, too, want to protect you. I, too, hate to see you suffer."

"Protect me? Who told you I need to be protected? I can protect myself quite well, thank you. I don't need anybody's protection."

"Likewise," she says.

"Well, I beg to differ. That's a matter of opinion."

"Likewise," she says again. Sometimes she can be really infuriating.

I'll bet my little sister never mentioned that after her boyfriend dumped her, for the longest time, she felt a huge painful lump in her throat and couldn't swallow. Well, the doctors found she had cancer of the thyroid and she had to have surgery to have it removed. Now, you tell me, where did that come from, if not from grief? Or even worse, from denial, from being afraid to face her situation and admit to herself how she had failed miserably, how she had wasted so many years and so much love to end up being dumped with hardly a good-bye. And she thinks she doesn't need protection. She thinks I am the crazy one.

Watching her collapse, watching her shatter into a million little pieces, was enough of a painful reminder for me. Or should I say it was a very timely warning? I certainly don't need to repeat my mistakes. I've learned my lesson. Once in a lifetime is enough.

But let us go on with the story of my life. Bear with me, there is very little left to tell. My two daughters became nuclear engineers, I am so incredibly proud of them! There are some things I did get right. Both got married and moved away, one lives in France, the other one in the Pacific Northwest.

My son is a different kettle of fish. He's had his problems, I must admit. He had a lot of false starts, a lot of different jobs. He can't keep a job and can't stand other people telling him what to do. Perhaps he gets this trait from me, I wasn't too good at it either. Recently, he started in business for himself, as a handyman, and he is doing much better. He lives nearby with his girlfriend, and I see him once in a while. He takes me out for lunch on my birthday, and invites me over for Thanksgiving, if he is making dinner at his place. None of my children want to have children of their own, except for my foster daughter Susie, who has three already. So I am not going to become a grandma, at least, not in the foreseeable future.

Before long, I quit the job at the department store. I really wasn't getting much satisfaction, or money, for that matter, from doing that kind of menial work. I was being taken advantage of. The store decided to give me a split shift. What crock. I would work four hours in the morning, from nine to one, and four hours in the evening, from five to nine. I wouldn't put up with a schedule like that, and I am sure that management was well aware of that. For God's sake, it was a forty five minute drive just to get to the mall, and that's at top speed. It was sheer torture. The other alternative, waiting at the mall 'til the five o'clock shift began, was even worse. So I quit, and I am sure glad I did. I don't miss it a bit.

Now I only work as a volunteer, a few hours a week. I help out at the humane society one day a month, and I teach foreign students catechism and English as a second language, in an adult school. I enjoy doing what I do. I love working with animals. They always show their gratitude and affection without holding back. They are always glad to see me. I feel appreciated. Animals couldn't care less whether I am a Polish Jew or a South American Catholic. Isn't that wonderful? I am sure I couldn't wish for a better relationship.

I also get a charge from teaching catechism and English to foreign students. They are very eager to learn. They understand well that knowing English is essential, that it will open doors that otherwise would remain closed. They are thankful that I have chosen to spend my free time and my energy helping them. That's much more rewarding than any other work I've ever done, be it for free or for money. I finally feel appreciated and respected. And at last, I feel at peace with myself.

It was here, at this school, that I met the rabbi who inspired my little sister to start writing our life story, who fueled her delusions that I might change my life once more. No matter how many times I've told her the contrary, she still hopes there is a chink in my armor. That instead of hiding in the boondocks, as she puts it so eloquently, I am going to start living the life I was meant to have all along. I had seen the rabbi before, at several meetings of various environmental groups and other community affairs. But we had never done more than exchange greetings and a few pleasantries. Until a short time ago, when we met in the hallway of the school. We started chatting and he asked me out to dinner. I couldn't refuse. It wouldn't have been friendly or polite to do so.

I even went to the mall and bought a new dress for the occasion. But then, I needed a dress, and it was on sale. Heavens, I hadn't gotten a new dress for ages. Since Jimmy's funeral—twenty years ago, now that I think of it. And I also got a pair of shoes. Not high heels, mind you, I wouldn't dream of wearing those instruments of torture. Just regular flats. They looked good with the dress. I couldn't wear my usual white sneakers with a dress, could I? I looked in the mirror and I didn't look half-bad, if I say so myself. Not that it matters to me how I look. I really couldn't care less.

Surprisingly, I enjoyed myself. Even though it felt weird to be in a restaurant sitting at a table across from a man I hardly knew, a stranger. I hadn't done that kind of thing since before Jimmy got back from Korea, thirty-some years ago. We chatted about the school, the students, the various save-the-environment groups we belong to, the city and county services and facilities. Nothing about ourselves, nothing personal.

Wouldn't you know it? It turned out we think alike about most matters in life. We have a lot of things in common. He really is an open-minded person. Well read in all kinds of subjects. He also has a wonderfully caustic sense of humor, which I greatly appreciate. I must admit I was pleasantly surprised.

We wrangled a bit about who was going to pay for dinner. I

wanted to contribute my share. But in the end he won. He insisted he had invited me and chosen the place, so he wanted to pay.

"Next time, if that makes you feel more comfortable, you can invite me for dinner. Choose your favorite place, and I'll let you pay," he told me with a chuckle. "But the wine, or even better, the champagne will be my treat."

It was charitable of him to assume I have a favorite place. I hadn't eaten out in a decent restaurant for years and years. But I didn't want to argue him out of his false image of me. That is one door I am not planning to open.

It was almost midnight before we said good-bye to each other. I could hardly believe how fast time had flown. We both remarked at the same time that we should do this again really soon. And I believe we both meant it. In fact, I almost think I am looking forward to it. I guess I might even buy another dress, just so he doesn't think I only have one. That would be too embarrassing. But I can wear the same shoes, they go with everything.

One thing that makes me a little uneasy is this matter of my roots. I wonder if he suspects something. I tell myself he has no reason to doubt the image I have chosen to present to him and to the world. He has no reason to disbelieve that I was born in South America and that I am an observant Catholic. I don't intend to disabuse him of this notion. I wouldn't dream of telling him the real circumstances of my origins. Although, when the idea crosses my mind, I can see how it would be funny. Just to watch his face when he found out. But I am not going to tell him. Contrary to what my blabbermouth of a sister thinks, some secrets are better kept secret.

Rebecca called last Sunday. As usual she tries to stick her nose in what doesn't concern her.

"So how did it go with the rabbi. Did you enjoy yourself?"

"Okay, not too bad. He is pleasant enough. Not at all stuffy, which was my fear."

"What did you talk about? Are you going to see him again?"

"None of your business, little sister."

"Well, did he ask you?"

"As a matter of fact, he did. But don't go about buying a new dress for my wedding. It's not going to happen. I could never marry a Jew."

"Ha," she says crisply.

"What do you mean by ha? You know how I feel about all that.

And I don't see you marrying one either, in spite of all your high-falutin ideas about our heritage. Tell me, really, would you do that?"

"Of course I would!" she replies. But I detect some hesitation in her voice.

"My turn to say 'ha.' The proof is in the pudding. I haven't seen you dating any Jews."

"Of course I date Jewish men. It's just that none of them proposed marriage."

"Excuses, excuses. Well, the rabbi hasn't asked me either. There is nothing like that going on," I tell her.

"But what if he did? What would you say?"

"Would you stop beating a dead horse? First of all, he won't. Second, if he did, I told you already, I wouldn't. So quit pestering me about it. Subject closed."

"You know, Susanna, the lady doth protest too much."

Gosh, what an exasperating creature. And to think she used to be so sweet and docile at five. Now she always needs to have the last word.

Before anybody misguidedly starts imagining that this whole episode presages a return to my Jewish roots, I must state unequivocally that in the last few years I have become a very devout Catholic. I enjoy going to Mass and I find pleasure and comfort in prayer. My baby sister believes this is bizarre. That I am still rebelling against my family and my birth. But I couldn't care less what she chooses to think. It's a free country, as I've said many times. She loves to bait me, and all her Jewish and Catholic friends, by saying she can't see anything but superficial differences between all these religions. She says she can't put much credence in a God who would care about such trifling details. This, of course, upsets both groups of people equally, which is probably what she is trying to accomplish. As for me, I don't argue that point and I don't get upset. I really like being a Catholic. It's the religion I have chosen to embrace of my own free will, not the one I was assigned by life's lottery. I've always loved going to church. As I child, it was the one place I felt safe from my parents' bitching and hollering, and I still love it to this day. It is the place I go to find peace and solace.

As for the rabbi, I have no expectations for the future. It's much too early to tell. Besides, I don't think he would want to get into a relationship with a woman outside his faith. As soon as I wrote this down, the irony of the situation hit me like a ton of bricks. Wouldn't it be odd if we ended up together, and once again, like in my marriage, I kept my origins a secret? Isn't there something really absurd about this situation?

Yet, I guess I have surprised my little sister. And myself, too, I must admit. Recently I started corresponding with my first cousin Zygmunt, who lives in Tel Aviv. He wrote asking for information about myself, my husband and children. Birthdates and marriages, that sort of thing. He is putting together a family tree. He says that as the oldest child of my mother's oldest sister Roza, he can remember a hundred and sixty relatives in my mother's family who lived in Poland before the beginning of the war. Names, where they lived, who they married, how many children they had. That was before he managed to pull off his escape to Palestine in 1940. Only seven of those were still alive after the war. I am one of the seven. Can you beat that?

Rebecca

Time kept moving on, inexorably, faster and faster, as we got older. Good things came to an end, but luckily, bad things did too. The Berlin Wall was dismantled. The Communist system collapsed, crushed by the weight of its own inefficiency. I feel sorry that Father didn't get to see all this. He, more than anybody else I know, would have relished it, though it happened fifty years too late to do him any good. I wish he had been here to see it with his own eyes.

Father died in the late eighties in Palo Alto, after a short illness. He was totally unprepared. He had counted on having Mother die first, that's how they planned it. But sometimes, the best-laid plans have a way of falling apart.

Most of the family gathered at Father's deathbed. Even my sister, who hates to travel, came to see him. My two nieces, my daughter and I, my ex-husband, and Mother, we all took turns sitting in the darkened room around his bed, listening to him talk about his various business deals. My sister pleaded with Father to call her son Ricky, who couldn't come because someone had to stay home to feed the cats. Father said he didn't have the strength to go to the phone. We managed to find him a cordless one. He wouldn't know what to say to Ricky, he told my sister, he would call a little later. But he never did call his only grandson. A few minutes later, the phone rang. I answered. It was my father's real estate manager, calling about a problem in one of Father's apartment houses. I tried to get rid of him. I told him to do whatever he felt was best. But before I knew it, Father leapt from his deathbed, grabbed the phone away from me, and we heard him barking instructions to his manager.

"Goldfarb, I want you to check the whole apartment carefully, room by room. Make sure all the appliances and all the fixtures work, especially in the kitchen and bathroom. Don't forget to flush the toilet a couple of times, you hear me? And then and only then, you can start thinking about returning the deposit. Remember, there's no hurry. There is always plenty of time to do that later." I guess Father was true to himself to the very end. He died just a few hours later.

Reluctantly, I took charge of Father's estate. I devoted long hours to disentangle the huge muddle he had created. Father, who had been a lawyer in Poland and was convinced he knew better than anybody how to write wills and establish trusts, relied on a book on estate planning he had picked up at a garage sale for fifty cents. The book was published before the war, and the law had drastically changed. I soon found myself learning more than I ever wanted to know about wills, trusts, taxes, real estate purchases and sales. It took four years and a few different lawyers before everything was straightened out. I was threatened with litigation and had to settle with tenants, who, knowing Father had died, swooped in like vultures wanting to get a piece of the action. Business affairs had always bored me, but now I learned to hate them.

I was also under a lot of pressure because my sister needed a quick distribution of the estate. She had already spent whatever money she was going to get to build her large Victorian house, complete with guest cottage and all. They stand one in front of the other, connected by a cage-like structure inhabited by her cats. That is, most of the cats. A few of them, because of their advanced age, or because they can't get along with the rest of Susanna's cat population, are allowed to stay inside the main house. My sister took out a hundred thousand dollar loan, due in one year, to pay the builder. But at the end of the year she still didn't have the money from Father's estate. She called on Mother for help, but Mother was only willing to advance her a thousand dollars. She called me in despair, telling me she was about to lose everything. I bailed her out. When she finally got the estate money, it turned out not to be enough, so the money I had loaned her became a gift.

Before his death, Father had taken me aside because he wanted to talk to me about something that was preying on his mind.

"Rebecca, I am very worried about Susanna. I feel she is incapable of taking care of her own finances in a responsible manner. She doesn't show good judgement when it comes to money, she spends it as if it grew on trees. I have always taken care of her." Then, his voice breaking, he begged me, "please promise me that when I am gone, you will always look out for your sister. You will always make sure she has a roof over her head and enough to get by." I was touched by Father's words. I had no problem promising I would do that. I would have done it anyway, whether Father had asked me or not.

A couple of weeks later, Mother took me aside and made me promise something very different.

"Rebecca, you have to promise me that you won't let Susanna squander your part of the inheritance. I want to make sure you will protect your share. Your Father worked hard and economized all his life so that both of you would have something after he goes to his final resting place. Your sister will waste her money in a few months, and then she'll come to you begging for more. If you give in, you'll both end up in the pauper house."

I promised Mother that I wouldn't let that happen. But I am not sure I have the strength to say no if she asks me. Many a time I've heard Susanna complain bitterly that if the parents had given her enough money early on, instead of hoarding it all until the very end, she wouldn't have had to wait until she was in her fifties to live in the house of her dreams. I must confess, though, I can't help feeling upset when she goes on one of her spending binges. One evening, she called to tell me she had ordered parquet floors for her house for an additional twenty-two thousand dollars. I cringed as I realized the money would have to come from my pocket, but I refrained from saying anything to her. I didn't want to follow in my parents' footsteps and give her a lecture on thrift and financial responsibility with every check. But I have not forgotten my mother's words and, at night, I lie awake worrying about what I'll do if the situation grows worse.

Mother survived Father by four long years. Physically, she stayed fit. She was strong and sprightly. But mentally she deteriorated quickly. I thought that once free of the crushing weight of Father's constant anger, Mother would open up like a flower that had been watered. I was wrong.

I remembered the times Father had been away, how relaxed Mother had been, how a happier person shone through. One evening long ago, when Mother came to spend the night with Ricardo and me in Berkeley, we took her out to dinner to a Polish restaurant. Mother was enjoying the evening immensely. She was radiant. Her blue eyes sparkled, her skin glowed. Suddenly, a man who was seated at a nearby table leaned over and said, "Madam, permit me to be so bold as to tell you that you look wonderful. Your beautiful soul shines through your eyes. I would feel blessed if you allowed me to kiss your hand."

Ricardo jumped up to protect her from this kind of harassment, but before he could intervene, Mother put her hand out to be kissed and then, unexpectedly, stood up and kissed the stranger on the cheek. She sat down and kept on recounting some gossip she had been telling us earlier, as if such incidents happened to her all the time.

But that time was long gone. Now, instead of opening like a bud in spring, Mother withered. She gave away most of her clothes, keeping only those that were black. She wore black to show the whole world her grief. She covered all the geraniums and fuschias on her balcony with black cloth, murmuring that she didn't want anything that would remind her that beauty still existed while Father no longer did. None of my objections made a shred of difference. I told her I believed Jews didn't wear mourning, only Catholics did. She didn't care. Once, when I was visiting her, soon after my father passed on, she told me what was going through her mind.

"You know, Rebecca, I am so glad that I was there for your father, so that he could vent his rage on me. Otherwise, I am sure he would have died much sooner, he would have had to hold his rage inside and that would have killed him. I believe that every life has a purpose and I, finally, understood what the purpose of mine was. What was God's design for me." Big tears were slowly streaming down her face. "I was put in this world to ease your father's suffering, to provide an outlet for his wrath."

"If that had been God's intention he would have made you a doormat instead of a woman," I told her. But my words meant nothing to her.

"God hid the sun behind a huge black cloud," she told me, sobbing. I didn't know what to say.

A few months after Father's death, while we were having lunch, Mother started to talk about her will. Father had written both of their wills, and as long as he was alive she didn't dare to go against his wishes.

"I am wondering," she told me, "whether I can do whatever I want with my estate." I told her that, indeed, she could. She wanted to draw up a new will leaving all the property under her control to my ex-husband Ricardo. "He has always been good to me and I am very fond of him" she told me. "He visits me every week, at times even more often than you do. And when he can't make it because he is out of town or too busy, his wife Mei-Mei comes over and brings their little boy. I want them to have all I own."

I called the lawyer who had prepared our parents' testament. He was a large Russian man who looked like a bear. He had arrived in the States as a teenager, had studied law at night while he worked, and dealt mainly with Poles and Russians who lived in the area. Speaking in a mixture of English and Polish, he tried to dissuade Mother from changing her will. He even invoked Father's name, "Your husband, God rest his soul, would have been livid with rage," he told her, in his booming baritone. But Mother was adamant.

Susanna and I quarreled over the new will. She felt I should have done whatever it took to stop Mother.

"Rebecca, don't let Mother squander the fortune Father worked so hard to accumulate. All his life he worked like a dog, he scrimped and saved, he denied himself and the family even the smallest luxuries. He did it because he wanted us to have the money, the product of his hard work."

"But this is Mother's. It belongs to her."

"It's not Mother's to give away. Darn! Just look at his will and the will he wrote for Mother. He wanted to leave everything to us. He owed it to us," she insisted.

"Susie, I am afraid Mother has a right to do whatever she pleases with her property."

"Mother is not in her right mind anymore. Can't you see that? Tell her to leave things alone. Tell her blood is thicker than water."

"She has deteriorated a lot, but she knows what she's doing," I said, trying to soothe my sister. "She always wanted to leave her money to Ricardo, but you know Father, he wouldn't hear of it. She is so obsessed with this whole issue, she won't be able to relax until it's done."

"But why? I don't see why, unless it is to prove to us once more that she never really cared for us," Susanna objected, bursting into tears. "I've always known it, but she kept it hidden from the rest of the world. Now she wants to rub our noses in it, before she dies. Don't let her, Rebecca."

Once Mother changed her will, she didn't want anything to do with business affairs or other details. She asked me to take care of everything for her, the rent, the utilities, the bills, her doctor appointments. She stopped driving and gave the car to Ricardo's brother. Each day she did less and less. She lost interest in her daily life, her family and her friends. She stopped asking about her grandchildren and when I tried to tell her about their studies, their boyfriends, their travels, she would close her eyes and wave her hand dismissively. She stopped tending to the plants on the balcony, the fuchsias and the geraniums she had been so proud of. Little by little, she stopped taking care of the apartment, shopping for food and eating. She also stopped taking care of herself. Stopped bathing, combing her hair. One day, when she called me on the phone twelve times and left messages for me, I realized things could not go on like this. I had known for a long time that I would have to make some difficult decisions about Mother, but I kept postponing the moment, hoping that I would see clearly what was the best thing to do. I couldn't have her live with me, I reasoned, because I lived alone and she would need somebody to care for her during the day, when I was away at work; and, of course, also at night, whenever I went out of town on assignments. But when I looked inside my heart I knew that the real reason was that I didn't have the love and the patience required for such a selfless act. Instead, I found a nearby nursing facility with beautiful gardens that offered constant care. It had a vacancy. That same weekend I moved Mother into her new residence.

I visited her often after that. For me, these visits became my own private hell. My mother lost her mental faculties, but she knew she was unbearably unhappy. Time and again, in a tiny, tremulous voice, she would beg me to kill her.

"Rebecca, little daughter, please kill me, I can't go on. I want to die."

"Mommy, I can't do that. I would end up in prison if I did. You wouldn't want me there, would you?"

And she would say tearfully, "Oh no, no, no, of course not."

Two minutes later she would forget and the whole conversation would be repeated again, sometimes twenty or thirty times during each visit. I dreaded these visits. I felt so distraught after each one that the thought of helping her die actually did cross my mind. I considered all kinds of alternatives and options. What if I took her home for a weekend, and gave her a batch of my thyroid pills to swallow? And what if, instead of killing her, this caused her a lot of pain and injury? I couldn't bring myself to do that. Besides, I had never taken her home before. There would be a lot of questions if the very first weekend at my home she died of an overdose of pills. When I talked it over with my sister, she was very definitely against the idea.

"Rebecca, don't be silly. You can't do it, no matter how many millions of times she asks you. First of all, it's against the law. If you are found out, you'll be guilty of murder. Second, it's against all moral and ethical principles. It's matricide. Third, even if you didn't take into account the law and the morality of it, you just don't know how. You'd botch the whole thing. The consequences would be unendurable. Besides, I know you can't do it. And I am sure that in your heart of hearts you know that too. Now, if Father were here, he would do it without a second thought. I suspect he would even enjoy it," she chuckled at her own cleverness. "So just put the thought out of your mind. Keep on visiting Mother."

"It's easy for you to say. You aren't the one listening to Mother when she begs me to kill her. Or looking at the tears in her eyes."

"It won't be forever, you know. It will end sometime."

But my sister was right. There was nothing I could do. After a year my mother's condition had deteriorated to the point the nursing home asked me to find a different facility for her. They had come up with a litany of complaints about her behavior. A couple of times, she fled from the home and was brought back by a police officer, who found her stretched on her back looking at the cloud formations in the sky in the police parking lot across the street. This caused enormous consternation among the nursing home staff. The supervisor reminded me that this facility had an open door policy and they could not control my mother's comings and goings. At night, Mother would wander into other rooms and get into bed with other residents, who would wake up terrified and screaming. The night orderly had to escort Mother back to her room time and again. She developed the habit of standing by the entrance door of the home, mooning and flashing every visitor. The last straw came when she took an aversion to the toilet in her own bathroom and started defecating under the magnolia tree in the gardens that were the pride and joy of the home. After a few days, the staff locked the doors and all residents who wanted to take a stroll were required to ask for a key.

I started looking for a new home for Mother, but my choices were limited. The only nursing home that was willing to take her had myriads of restrictions. Most of the day, Mother remained confined to a chair. The nursing home staff placed her in restraints. I hated seeing her sitting there, tied to a chair. She had always loved to walk. Even now, she could easily walk several miles. But her mind was wandering through a different place and time. She had gone back to the war years in Krakow. Every morning, before the orderly came into her room to get her bathed and dressed, she would hide in the closet, in the laundry hamper or in a kitchen cabinet, and scream when she was found, terrified that the Nazis had finally caught up with her. She would would hit, scratch, bite, and scream murder when somebody from the staff tried to pull her out. She would hurl whatever she could lay her hands on at the nurses, and when she had nothing else to throw, she took her dentures out and threw them.

The next time I visited, the staff had taken away her dentures. I looked at her and realized that, overnight, she had turned into an old woman, wretched and frightened. As I looked at her, lying on the bed, so shrunken, so frail, so defenseless, it dawned upon me, suddenly, that I never truly understood the tragedy of her life, that I couldn't fathom how much she had suffered during the war, hiding from the Nazis, expecting to be discovered any minute, watching the extermination of her family, her friends, her community. My heart felt heavy. I did everything I could to calm and reassure her, to convince her that she had nothing to fear now. But it was not enough.

When I transferred her to the new nursing home, all her belongings fit into one brown paper bag. She had a light pink sweat suit, a bra, two pairs of underwear, a nightie, a pair of slippers and a photograph of Father. It was as if her whole life had been reduced to these few paltry possessions and could fit in this one paper bag. I couldn't look at it without remembering the summer we had spent in Europe, in the fifties, when Mother brought three large suitcases filled to the brim, a hat box and two small toiletry bags, just for her own belongings.

Mother died at the beginning of 1991, all alone in the nursing home. I would have liked to have been there to hold her hand at the end, but I was too late. She died barely ten minutes before I arrived. The sadness I felt took me by surprise. The relief I expected.

After Alan and I broke up, I found myself alone again. This time I was truly alone. My daughter had gone off to college. Celine, who had lived with us for a year, had gone back to France. My two old cats had died, one right after the other. Just a few months ago we had been a noisy, rambunctious household of four, a real family. Suddenly there was only me left. My fantasy of a happy family had come true, but it didn't last long. It was as if I had been allowed to live in paradise just so I would know how good it could be, and then I had fallen from grace and was back in hell. I felt my life was over.

Just like in my childhood, I reacted to the pain of loss by flinging myself frantically into all kinds of activities, as if there was no tomorrow. I knew this was only a palliative to take the edge of the pain, but it kept me alive and going. It kept me from dwelling on my grief every minute of the day. I would face the grief and sorrow later, when I felt stronger. I guess my sister was right after all. Some things are too painful to talk about.

I must have sleepwalked through the next few years. I bought a house, furnished it and got two new kittens to keep me company. I threw myself into my work and soon rose to the top of my profession. I started accepting out-of-town assignments, several times I even went abroad. Just last year I had a case that took me all the way to Poland. I took a part time teaching position at San Francisco State University, which filled most of my evenings. During the day, I worked as an interpreter in court. I was busy, busy, busy, day and night.

I made a effort to explore interests that I had neglected before. I bought a cheap camera and I took pictures of everything that crossed my path. Those that turned out well I used as ideas for paintings. I went through a period of taking pictures and painting scenes of small villages in the south of France. That had one advantage. I kept going back to France to take more pictures. When I paint in my studio and things go well, time flies. Before I know it it's nighttime and another day is gone. I feel serene and renewed.

I started studying hypnosis, which had fascinated me from the time I was a child, when my sister had gotten me a magic set. I took several courses, read books and practiced on friends. I even went as far as hypnotizing myself to forget what had happened in the last ten years. Friends mention trips, events, conversations of that time and I have only the fuzziest recollection of what they are talking about.

I joined a ski club and a hiking club, which keep me busy on weekends. It's also a good way to meet men who like to do some of the same things I like. I've dated some of them. I even had a few short relationships. But I don't think I feel ready for anything permanent at this stage of my life.

My sister disapproves of my going out with men I hardly know. "Dating strangers is dangerous," she warns me. "Every day there is something in the papers about another woman getting raped or killed by her date. You could get hurt, you could get raped, you could catch some awful disease and die."

"So far, the worst thing that has happened on my dates is that I've died of boredom," I reply.

"Don't be a smart-ass. You should listen to me, instead of making fun of everything I say. I am only saying this because I worry about you. I don't want you to get hurt. I care about you."

"I know, I am sorry. I'll be careful, I promise."

"I bet you answer those disgusting single's ads in the paper where men look for women with big boobs who are twenty years younger. You think I don't know about those ads just because I live in a backwater? I am not dim-witted, you know!"

"Who said anything about you being dim-witted? But don't worry. I promise I'll never answer an ad worded that way and never date a man I didn't meet in church, even though I never go to church. But don't forget that not everybody can date a rabbi."

"Here you go again, making light of whatever I say. It's impossible to have a serious conversation with you."

"Sorry. You really have nothing to worry about. I am prudent by nature." But I haven't changed my habits.

I took up traveling. I've always loved visiting and learning about far away places. I finally made it to some of the countries I always wanted to visit. I went to Russia and at last I got the chance to speak the language and experience the culture I had studied for so many years. I visited all the sights I had read about and pictured in my imagination. The trip was sponsored by a local college. Our group met with delegations of university professors in Moscow and Leningrad. Our Russian hosts drove us around in a large, dilapidated bus to museums, palaces, parks, the ballet, concerts, restaurants, and nightclubs. We even took a short cruise down the Volga. Before the end of our stay, we separated into small groups and were invited by our new friends to dinner in their homes. These highly educated professionals were dying to abandon their country and come to live in the States. I've never had so many marriage proposals in such a short time. I came away with the feeling that the whole country and its people were for sale. Every Russian I met wanted to live in a capitalist country and become an entrepreneur, running his own business and only working when he felt like it. They refused to believe me when I explained that owning and running a business, even a small one, meant many additional hours of work in the evenings and weekends. This concept seemed totally foreign to them. They just didn't get it. After a very interesting visit, I returned to California, worried about the fate of my new friends.

Last year I went to Krakow, and wandered about in the town where I was born. I visited the Jagellonian University, which my father had attended and where he obtained his law degree. For the first time since his death, I truly missed him. I could see him sitting in these old wooden benches, always on the left side of the class-room were Jews were supposed to sit. I wanted to take a walk on these ancient brick courtyards and have him tell me about his life in those bygone times. I wanted to see the old classrooms through his eyes, to hear him reminisce about his teachers, his friends, his long forgotten dreams.

From Krakow, I went to Budapest. I had always dreamt of visit-ing Hungary, slowly sailing down the Danube, walking in the forests of Transylvania. I was not disappointed. The last stop of my trip was Prague. I had been there with Ricardo, twenty five years ago and remembered it as a stunning city. My memory didn't deceive me. The old parts of the city are as captivating as ever, in spite of the new freeway that divides the city into two halves. The newer sections have succumbed to Western-style business types with gray suits and briefcases. Nevertheless, I still revel in the old fascination I always felt for Eastern Europe. For me, it's still a place of mystery and enchantment, of magic and fairy tales. I shall return.

My sister called again last night. Once again we touched upon our favorite subject, our lifestyle, fraught with emotional significance for both of us.

"You know, the problem with you, Rebecca, is that you don't know how to be a good American. I chose America to start anew, to never look back. My family's history will start from here. To be American is to be free to choose your past, to choose what to remember and what to forget."

"I think for me it is quite the opposite. I chose to live here to have the freedom to openly acknowledge and embrace my heritage, my past. To pass it on to my children," I tell her. But I know I am not being completely honest. Not too long ago, my Salvadoran house-keeper complained that she was owed some money and treated poorly by a Jewish woman she worked for. "What can you expect from Jewish pigs? They are all Christ-killers" she grumbled. And sud-denly, my throat closed up and I couldn't get one word out. I couldn't tell her I am one of them. Those words, spoken in Spanish, took me back forty years, to my childhood in Venezuela. Later, I regretted my silence and thought of letting her know at the first opportunity that I was also Jewish, and that I was terribly upset about her words. But I haven't yet.

"What a dreamer you are, baby sister," Susanna went on. "Children should be free from all that useless baggage. There are plenty of other difficulties they will have to overcome in this life. Why add to their problems? Why burden them with all the ghastly and tragic history of the Jews during the war? Why remind them of all their relatives who were sent to the ovens? Those who survived the Holocaust will never again believe that being Jewish is not danger-ous. I feel it is my duty to free my kids from all that. I take full respon-sibility for making this decision for them, so that they will have a chance at happiness. I only wish somebody had done that for me."

"How about letting your children make this decision on their own? What's wrong with that? I think you are depriving them from their history and taking away their choice."

"I am protecting them the best way I can. As I see it, that's the true role of a good parent. Didn't you protect your daughter from dis-ease by giving her all her shots? Well, this is just as important. You are like our parents, Rebecca. Too faint of heart to make the decision for your child. That's what's wrong with you! Do you want your daughter to grow up like you and me?"

"What's wrong with that? We didn't turn out so badly, did we?" But I was not being truthful. Susanna had put her finger on some-thing that had been bothering me for a long time. Something I think about every night before I fall asleep. Did we fight hard enough to get what we wanted? Or did we allow circumstances to dictate how our lives would turn out?

"As usual, you are deluding yourself, baby sister. You ought to know better. We are marked people. We can never forget, no matter how hard we try to fool ourselves, and God knows that I have tried harder than anybody. For us, it was all over before it started, we never had a chance. But it doesn't have to be like that for our kids."

"What are you talking about, Susanna? We did the best we could, under the circumstances. I can't believe you are saying this, you who fought so hard to escape and managed to wrench yourself away from our family and our Jewish roots and create a new life for yourself here in the States."

"And much good it did me! I escaped a place, but I couldn't escape our dreadful legacy. Don't play dumb, you know that as well as I do. I stopped myself from looking and listening to the horrors of the Holocaust, but that doesn't mean I didn't know. I always knew. For me, it was always too late, from the very beginning. But, thank God, my children are free to live away from all those ghastly events. For me, it was always about saving the next generation, not about us. That's the one thing I accomplished. And I am proud of it. Hell, what's the use talking about this old stuff! Let's talk about something else, this is getting too tedious."

"Are you suggesting that your life is not worth bothering about? That you didn't have any hopes and dreams for yourself?" I said, astounded.

"Quite the contrary, I am saying I accomplished what I set out to do. And believe me, that's enough for me."

"But it wasn't at all like that when we were growing up. I remember quite well. You wanted so many things!" I remonstrate. "You are reinterpreting your life's plan, you are rewriting history."

"And I have a perfect right to do it if it pleases me. It's my life. Who appointed you judge of what I choose to do and think?"

That night I had the eeriest dream. I dreamt that I was a little girl playing alone in a dark Victorian house, a house that is terribly familiar to me, although as far as I know, I've never lived in such a house. Suddenly, I hear faint steps upstairs and a door closing. I call out "Susanna? Susanna? Is that you?" No answer. I start walking through the house, opening doors, still saying softly "Susanna? Susie?" Nothing. By now I am beginning to feel scared. I run up the stairs, now yelling "Susanna! Susie!" I open door after door, the bedrooms are all empty. Finally I get to the last bedroom, I open the door, and there is my sister, sitting on the bed, smiling at me. I burst into tears, and yell at her "Why didn't you answer? Didn't you hear me calling?"

"Of course I heard you, you were making such a racket even the dead could hear you. But don't you remember, you silly, my name isn't Susanna. It's Stela. That's what it has always been."

My sister believes I am not a good American. She lists a whole litany of things I do wrong. She says I don't show enough interest in my community, I don't participate in neighborhood groups, in block meetings, committees and such. She accuses me of not donating my time and effort to take part in the activities around me. She complains that I remain detached, doing my own thing, living in a world of books, music, art. A rarefied world I have created for myself, a world that has nothing to do with the realities that surround me. But I always thought she was the one who lived in a world of her own making, pretending to be somebody she is not, having fabricated her own past, unable to come to terms with her heritage.

I tell her that the beauty of being here, in our adopted country, is that no one has to fit one mold. There are lots of different ways to be a decent human being, to make a contribution. There is room for different lifestyles, different customs. I try to remind her that we left Venezuela because we knew that we would never be accepted, we would never fit in. We were born elsewhere, we looked different and no matter how hard we tried to blend in, we were always outsiders. Here, at last, I can be who I am, I can show my stripes and spots, and it is finally all right.

I walk alone on the long beach. My boyfriend sits on a blanket, reading technical magazines. I walk several miles, alone with my thoughts, the waves gently wash my footsteps away as soon as they appear on the sand. I love the smell of the ocean, the sound of the waves, the birds flying above, the sand in between my toes. I walk back, tired but at peace. My boyfriend looks up from his reading and smiles. I sit down on the blanket next to him.

IRENE PASTOR was born to a Jewish family in Poland during World War II. She attended UC Berkeley and now lives in the Bay Area in California.